THE GLADIATOR

THE GLADIATOR

SIMON SCARROW

headline

First published in 2009
by HEADLINE PUBLISHING GROUP

1

Cataloguing in Publication Data is available from the British Library

ISBN 978 0 7553 2778 2 (Hardback)
ISBN 978 0 7553 3916 7 (Trade paperback)

Typeset in Bembo by Avon DataSet Ltd,
Bidford-on-Avon, Warwickshire

Printed and bound in Great Britain by
Clays Ltd, St Ives plc

Headline's policy is to use papers that are natural, renewable and recyclable
products and made from wood grown in sustainable forests. The logging and
manufacturing processes are expected to conform to the environmental
regulations of the country of origin.

HEADLINE PUBLISHING GROUP
An Hachette UK Company
338 Euston Road
London NW1 3BH

www.headline.co.uk
www.hachette.co.uk

This book is for Mick Webb and the staff of
Stoke Holy Cross Primary School.
Thank you for everything you have done for my sons,
Joe and Nick.

Once again, my heartfelt thanks to my wife, Carolyn, for road-testing each chapter as it came off the word-processor. Also to my agent, Meg, and surely one of the best editors in the business, Marion, who always manages to rein in my excesses and point me towards a leaner, cleaner tale. Finally, huge thanks to my son Joe, who now has an encyclopaedic knowledge of the series and thus saved me from making a very embarrassing error. Joe, you're a star.

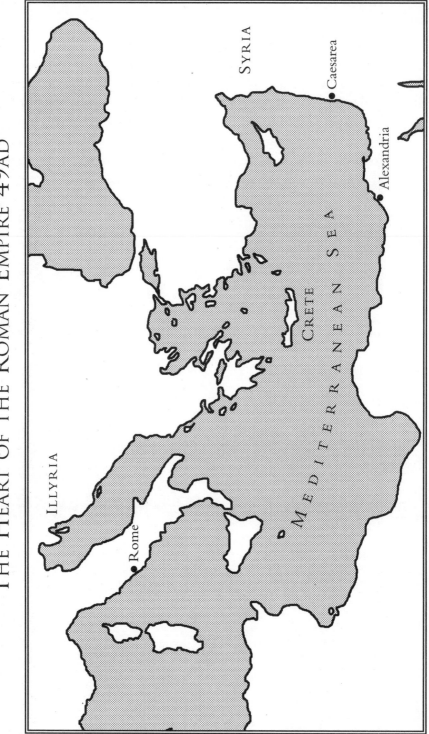

The Heart of the Roman Empire 49AD

ILLYRIA

Rome

SYRIA

Caesarea

Alexandria

MEDITERRANEAN SEA

CRETE

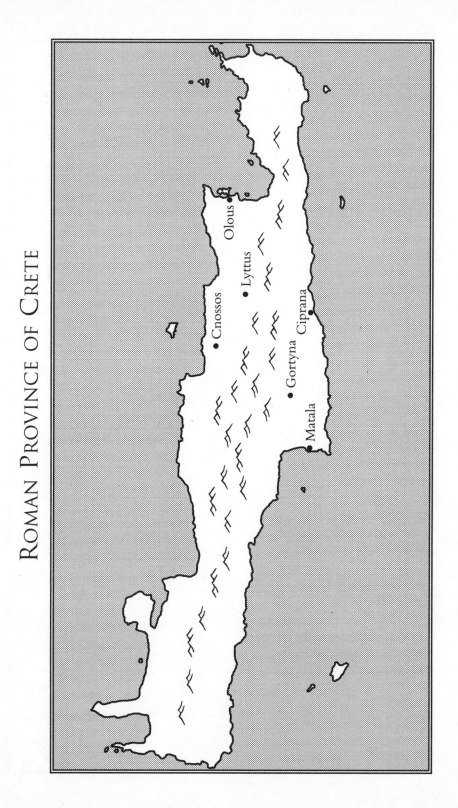

CHAPTER ONE

'We should reach Matala on the next tack,' announced the captain as he shaded his eyes and gazed at the coastline of Crete off the starboard beam, burnished by the late afternoon sun. Beside him on the deck stood some of his passengers, a Roman senator, his daughter and two centurions, bound for Rome. The four had boarded at Caesarea together with the daughter's maidservant, a young Judaean girl. The captain was proud of his vessel. The *Horus* was an old ship from Alexandria, retired from the fleet that shipped grain across the Mediterranean to Rome. Despite her years she was still a tough, seaworthy vessel and the captain was confident and experienced enough to take her out of the sight of land when necessary. Accordingly, the *Horus* had headed directly out to sea when she left the port of Caesarea, and had made landfall off the coast of Crete three days later.

'Will we arrive at Matala before night?' asked the senator.

'I'm afraid not, sir.' The captain smiled faintly. 'And I'm not going to attempt an approach in the dark. The *Horus* has a full hold and rides low in the water. Can't risk running her up on any rocks.'

'So what happens tonight then?'

The captain pursed his lips briefly. 'We'll have to stand off the coast, hove to until dawn. Means I'll lose a day, but that can't be helped. Best offer a quick prayer to Poseidon that we make up the time after we leave Matala.'

The older centurion let out a frustrated sigh. 'Bloody sea travel. Never straightforward. Should have taken the land route.'

The other officer, a tall, slender man with a curly mop of dark hair, laughed and slapped his stout comrade on the shoulder. 'I thought I was the impatient one! Easy there, Macro, we'll still reach Rome long before we ever could if we had gone by land.'

'You've changed your tune. Thought you were the one who hated the sea.'

'I'm not fond of it, but I have my reasons for wanting to reach Rome as soon as I can.'

'No doubt.' Centurion Macro winked, with a faint nod towards the senator's daughter. 'I'll just be glad to get a new posting. Back with the legions, permanently. The gods know we've done enough to earn it, Cato, my friend. Two years on the eastern frontier. I've had my fill of heat, sand and thirst. Next time I want a nice cushy post somewhere in Gaul. Somewhere I can rest a while.'

'That's what you say now.' Cato laughed. 'But I know you, Macro. You'd be bored witless before the month was out.'

'I don't know. I'd like to get back to some proper soldiering. No more doing the dirty work of the imperial palace for me.'

Cato nodded with feeling. Ever since they had carried out their first mission for Narcissus, the emperor's private secretary and head of the imperial spy network, Macro and Cato had faced perils from every quarter, besides the usual dangers of being soldiers. Cato's expression hardened. 'I fear that's rather out of our control. The more problems we solve, the greater the chance that we'll be called on again.'

'Ain't that the truth,' Macro muttered. 'Shit . . .'

Then, remembering that the senator and his daughter were present, he glanced at them apologetically and cleared his throat. 'Sorry, miss. Pardon my Gallic.'

The senator smiled. 'We've heard worse in recent months, Centurion Macro. In fact I think we have become rather used to the rough ways of soldiers. Otherwise I'd hardly countenance the attention Cato has been showing my daughter, eh?'

She grinned. 'Don't worry, Father, I'll tame him sure enough.'

Cato smiled as she took his arm and gave it an affectionate squeeze. The captain looked at them and scratched his chin.

'Getting married then, Miss Julia?'

She nodded. 'As soon as we return to Rome.'

'Damn, had hoped to ask for your hand myself,' the captain joked. He examined Cato briefly. The centurion's features were unmarked by the scars one tended to see on the faces of experienced soldiers.

He was also, by far, the youngest centurion the Greek sea captain had ever met, barely in his twenties, and he could not help wondering if such a man could only have been promoted to the rank through the patronage of a powerful friend. But the medallions fixed to the centurion's harness spoke of real achievements, hard won. Clearly there was far more to Centurion Cato than the captain had first thought. By contrast, Centurion Macro looked every inch the hard fighting man. Shorter by a head, but built like a bull, with well-muscled limbs on which numerous scars clearly showed. Some fifteen years older than his comrade, he had cropped dark hair and piercing brown eyes, yet the creases in his face hinted at a humorous side, should a suitable occasion arise.

The captain turned his attention back to the younger officer, with a touch of envy. If he married into a senatorial family, then Centurion Cato was set up for the rest of his life. Money, social position and career preferment would be his for the taking. That said, it was clear to the captain that the affection between the young centurion and the senator's daughter was real enough. At the end of each day the two of them were on deck to watch the sun set, arms around each other as they gazed across the sparkling waves.

As evening approached the *Horus* steered parallel to the coast, passing one of the bays that the captain had become familiar with in the long years that he served aboard merchant vessels sailing the length and breadth of the Mediterranean. While the sun slipped below the horizon, brilliantly gilding the edges of the island's mountains and hills, those on deck stared towards the shore. A large agricultural estate lay close to the sea, and in the gathering dusk, long lines of slaves returned from their labours in the fields, groves and vineyards. Shuffling wearily, they were herded back into their compound by overseers with whips and clubs.

Cato felt Julia tremble at his side and turned to her. 'Cold?'

'No. It's just that.' She indicated the last of the slaves entering the compound, and then the gates were shut and barred. 'A terrible existence for any man or woman.'

'But you have slaves at home.'

'Of course, but they are well cared for and have a degree of liberty in Rome. Not like those poor souls. Worked hard from first light to last. Treated no better than farm animals.'

Cato thought a moment before responding. 'That is the common lot of slaves. Whether they work on estates like that one, or in mines, or construction sites. It is only a small portion of them that are lucky enough to live in households like yours, or even to have the chance to train in the gladiator camps.'

'Gladiators?' Julia looked at him with raised eyebrows. 'Lucky? How could you consider anyone lucky who suffered such a fate?'

Cato shrugged. 'The training is hard, but once that's done they don't have it so bad. Their owners take good care of them and the best fighters make small fortunes and enjoy the high life.'

'As long as they survive in the arena.'

'True, but they risk no more than any man in the legions, and have a far more comfortable life than most. If they live long enough, gladiators can win their freedom and retire wealthy men. Only a handful of soldiers ever achieve that.'

'Too bloody true,' Macro grumbled. 'I wonder if it's too late to retrain as a gladiator.'

Julia stared at him. 'I am sure you don't mean that.'

'Why not? If I am going to kill people then I might as well be nicely paid for it.'

Senator Sempronius chuckled at the disgusted expression on his daughter's face. 'Ignore him, my child. Centurion Macro is joking. He fights for the glory of Rome, not a slave's purse, no matter how loaded with gold.'

Macro cocked an eyebrow. 'Now who's joking?'

Cato smiled and then looked back towards the shore. The slave compound was an ugly blot on the side of the hill overlooking the bay. All was still, save for a single flickering torch above the gate, and the dim form of a sentry standing close by as he kept watch over the slaves inside. This was the industrial side of slavery, which was largely invisible to most Romans, especially those well born, like Senator Sempronius and his daughter. The perfumed, uniformed slaves of a rich household were a far cry from the ragged masses who laboured in work camps, always tired and hungry and carefully watched for any sign of rebellion, which would be punished with brutal swiftness and severity.

It was a harsh regime, but the empire, and indeed every civilised nation that Cato knew of, depended on slavery to create wealth and feed its urban multitudes. For Cato it was a harsh reminder of the terrible differences in destiny that fate dealt out to people. The worst excesses of slavery were a blight on the world, he reflected, even if the institution was, for the present, a necessity.

He suddenly felt a faint tremor in the deck beneath his boots and glanced down.

'What the fuck?' Macro growled. 'Do you feel that?'

Julia grabbed Cato's arm. 'What is it? What's happening?'

There were cries of surprise and alarm across the deck as the crew and other passengers of the *Horus* glanced down at the deck.

'We've run aground,' said Sempronius, as he gripped the side rail.

The captain shook his head. 'Impossible! We're too far off the shore. I know these waters. There's no shallows for fifty miles. I swear it. In any case . . . Look there! At the sea.'

The captain thrust out his arm and the others followed the direction and saw that the surface of the water was shimmering faintly. For a brief time that seemed far longer than it was, the dull shudder of the deck and the quivering surface of the sea continued. Several of those on board fell to their knees and began to pray fervently to the gods. Cato held Julia in his arms and stared over her head at his friend. Macro gritted his teeth and glared back, hands clenched into fists at his sides. For the first time, Cato thought he saw a glimmer of fear in the other man's eyes, even as he wondered what was happening.

'A sea monster,' Macro said quietly.

'Sea monster?'

'Has to be. Oh, shit, why the hell did I agree to travel by sea?'

Then, as suddenly as it had begun, the faint shuddering stopped, and a moment later the surface of the sea returned to its steady chop as the *Horus* gently rose and dipped on the easy swell. For a moment no one on the ship moved or spoke, as if they were waiting for the strange phenomenon to begin again. Julia cleared her throat. 'Do you think it's over, whatever it was?'

'No idea,' Cato replied softly.

The brief exchange had broken the spell. Macro puffed his cheeks as he let out a deep breath and the ship's captain turned away from his passengers and scowled at the steersman. The latter had released his grip on the tiller of the great paddle at the stern of the *Horus* and was cowering beneath the fantail decoration overhanging the stern post. Already the ship was slowly swinging round into the wind.

'What in Hades do you think you're doing?' the captain blazed at the steersman. 'Return to your bloody post and get us back on course.'

As the steersman hurriedly took up the tiller, the captain turned round to glare at the other sailors. 'Back to work! Move yourselves.'

His men reluctantly returned to their duties as they adjusted the sail that had begun to flutter at the edges as the *Horus* luffed up for a moment, before the steersman leaned into the tiller and the ship settled back on to her original course.

Macro licked his lips nervously. 'Is it really over?'

Cato sensed the deck under his feet, and glanced at the sea, which looked just as it had before the tremor had begun. 'Seems to be.'

'Thank the gods.'

Julia nodded, then her eyes widened as she recalled her maid, who had been resting on her mat in the small cabin she shared with her mistress and the senator. 'I'd better check on Jesmiah. Poor girl will be terrified.'

Cato released her from his arms and Julia hurried across the deck towards the narrow gangway leading down to the passengers' quarters, where those who could afford it had paid for a cabin. The rest of the passengers simply lived and slept on the deck of the *Horus*.

As Julia disappeared from sight, a faint cry reached them from the shore and Cato, Macro and Sempronius turned towards the land. Though the light was dim, they could clearly see figures stumbling away from the estate's slave compound. Or what was left of it. The walls had been flattened, exposing the barrack blocks inside. Only two were still standing; the rest were in ruins.

'Bloody hell.' Macro stared at the ruins. 'What could have done that?'

'An earthquake,' said Sempronius. 'Has to be. I've experienced something like it before while I was serving as a tribune in Bythinia. The earth shook, and there was a dull roar. It went on for some moments, and shook some buildings to pieces. Those inside were crushed and buried under the rubble.' He shuddered at the memory. 'Hundreds died . . .'

'But if it's an earthquake, then why were we affected, out here at sea?'

'I don't know, Macro. The work of the gods is beyond the understanding of men.'

'Perhaps,' Cato remarked. 'But surely, if the tremor on land is severe enough, it would communicate itself through the water to us?'

'That may be so,' Sempronius admitted. 'In any case, we're the lucky ones. It is those on land who will have felt the full power of the gods' wrath.'

For a moment the three men stared towards the ruined slave compound, slowly slipping into the distance as the *Horus* sailed steadily away from the coast. A fire had broken out in the ruins, most likely from the kitchens preparing the evening meal, Cato decided. Flames licked up into the dusk, illuminating the shocked figures of the survivors. A handful were desperately picking away at the rubble to free those trapped beneath. Cato shook his head in pity.

'Be thankful we are at sea. I would not want to be ashore now. You should be grateful for that at least, Macro.'

'Really?' Macro replied quietly. 'What makes you think the gods have finished with us yet?'

'Deck there!' a voice suddenly cried from aloft. 'Captain, look!'

The sailor sitting astride the spar close to the top of the mast had thrust his spare arm out, along the coast to the west.

'Make your report properly!' the captain bellowed up to him. 'What do you see?'

There was a pause before the sailor replied anxiously. 'I don't know, sir. Never seen its like. A line, like a wall, right across the sea.'

'Nonsense, man! That's impossible.'

'Sir, I swear, that's what it looks like.'

'Fool!' The captain crossed to the side of the ship, swung himself

7

up on to the ratlines and began to clamber aloft to join the lookout. 'Now then, you bloody fool, where is this wall of yours?'

The lookout thrust his hand towards the horizon, into the fading light of the setting sun. At first the captain could see little as he squinted. Then, as his eyes adjusted to the distant gleam, he saw it. A faint glitter of reflected light rippling along the horizon, above a dark band that stretched from out to sea right up to the coast of Crete. Where it touched the land there was a churning foam of water.

'Mother of Zeus,' the captain muttered as his guts instantly turned to ice. The lookout was right. There was a wall ahead of the *Horus*, a wall of water. A vast tidal wave was sweeping along the coast directly towards the ship, no more than two or three miles away and racing towards them faster than the swiftest of horses.

CHAPTER TWO

'A tidal wave?' Cato's eyes widened. 'How big?'

'Big as a bloody cliff,' the captain replied. 'And heading this way, straight along the coast.'

'Then we must alter course,' said Sempronius. 'Get out of its way.'

'There's no time for that. In any case, the wave stretched as far as I could see. We can't avoid it.'

The senator and the two centurions stared at the captain for a moment before Sempronius spoke again. 'So, what now?'

'Now?' The captain gave a brittle laugh. 'We say our prayers and make our final farewells and wait until the wave hits us.'

Cato shook his head. 'No. There has to be something you can do to save the ship.'

'There's nothing, I'm telling you,' the captain said bleakly. 'You haven't seen the size of that thing yet. But you will, any moment.'

All eyes turned towards the horizon, and then Cato noticed what looked like a dark shadow on the rim of the world, at the moment only a fine line and one that looked wholly unthreatening as yet. He stared at it briefly before turning back towards the captain. 'You've been in storms before, haven't you?'

'Oh, yes. Storms are one thing. A tidal wave is something else. There's no hope for us.'

'Bollocks!' Macro growled, and then grabbed the captain's tunic in both hands and drew the Greek close to his face. 'There's always hope. I haven't survived fuck knows how many fights and injuries just to die on this tub. Now then, I ain't a sailor. That's your job. You've got a dangerous situation on your hands. So you deal with it. Do what you can to give us the best chance to live through this. You understand me?' He gave the captain a shake. 'Well?'

9

The Greek wilted before the intense gaze of the centurion and nodded. 'I'll do what I can.'

'That's better.' Macro smiled and released his grip. 'Now then, is there anything we can do to help?'

The captain swallowed nervously. 'If you don't mind, it would be best if you stayed out of the way.'

Macro's eyes narrowed. 'Is that all?'

'You could tie yourself to the mast, or one of the cleats, to save yourselves from being swept over the side when the wave hits us.'

'All right then.'

The captain turned away to shout orders to his crew and the sailors hurried aloft to shake out the reefs in the huge mainsail. At the stern, the steersman strained at the tiller, turning the *Horus* towards the sunset.

'What is he doing?' asked Sempronius. 'The fool is heading straight for the wave.'

Cato nodded. 'Makes sense. The bows are the strongest part of the ship. If we meet the wave head on, we might break through it, if we can't ride over it.'

Sempronius stared at him. 'I hope you are right, young man. For your sake, my sake and all our sakes.'

As soon as the senator had spoken, Cato's mind focused at once on Julia and he called to Macro as he hurried towards the gangway leading to the cabins. 'Get yourself tied to the mast, and take the senator with you.'

'Where are you going?'

'To get Julia and Jesmiah. They'll be safer on deck.'

Macro nodded, then glanced towards the horizon, and now he could see the wave more clearly, rising up in a great bar that extended far out to sea, while the other end foamed and crashed along the coast. 'Be quick, Cato!'

Cato ran across the deck and jumped down the short flight of steps into the passengers' quarters, where thin stalls accommodated those who had paid the most for their passage to Rome. Thrusting aside the canvas curtain that formed the makeshift entrance to Julia's quarters, he ducked his head inside. Julia sat on the deck, cradling Jesmiah in her arms.

'Cato! What's the matter?'

'No time to explain.' He stepped towards her, stooped and drew her up on to her feet. Jesmiah scrambled up at her side, wide-eyed with terror.

'Master Cato,' her lips trembled, 'I heard someone say there's a monster.'

'There's no monster,' he snapped, thrusting them both out of the stall and up towards the gangway. 'We have to get on deck, as quick as possible.'

Julia stumbled up the steps towards the deck. 'Why? What's happening?'

With a quick glance at Jesmiah Cato replied, 'Trust me and do as I say.'

They emerged on to the deck in a scene of terror and chaos. Macro had tied the senator to the foot of the mast and was hurriedly doing the same for himself. All around the other passengers and crew were doing the best they could to secure themselves to the vessel. The captain had joined the steersman on the small steering deck and both men braced their arms on the tiller and stared grimly ahead.

Jesmiah stared round in horror and drew up.

Cato grabbed her arm and dragged her roughly towards the mast. 'Come on, girl! There's not much time.'

As soon as they reached Macro and Sempronius, Cato thrust Julia and her maid down on to the deck and took up the tail end of the rope Macro had used to secure himself to the mast. Glancing up, he saw that the wave was much closer now, travelling at an extraordinary speed as it swept along the coast. He snapped round to the two women.

'Raise your arms!'

Running the rope round their stomachs, Cato circled the mast and tied the end into the loop round Macro's waist.

'What about you, lad?' Macro looked up anxiously.

'I need more rope.' Cato stood up and glanced round. Every spare length seemed to have been taken. Then his eyes caught sight of something over the side of the *Horus*, no more than fifty paces away in the sea. The glistening tip of a rock was exposed above the surface, and as Cato looked, more rocks emerged. Closer to the shore it seemed that some tidal current had drawn the water away, laying bare reefs and even the stunted upper works of an old wreck. The sight astonished him for an instant before a terrified shout from one of the crew snatched his attention back towards the wave. It was visible to everyone on the deck now. A great dark monster, crested with a haze of white spray as it came on in a rippling, glassy mass, straight towards the *Horus*. Ahead of it, the tiny wings of a seagull glimmered in the fading glow of the sunset, then the bird was lost in the shadow of the wave.

'Cato!'

He turned and saw Julia staring at him, struggling to reach out and grasp his hand. Cato knew there was no time to tie himself down. It was too late for him. He slumped down on the deck and squeezed himself between Macro and Julia as best he could, grasping them both round the shoulders. The light breeze that had been blowing along behind the ship abruptly died and the sail sagged like old skin from the spar, before suddenly being taken aback as the wave thrust the air ahead of it. The great mass of water rose up ahead of the ship, high, higher than the mast, and Cato felt his stomach knot as he gritted his teeth and squinted at the oncoming monster.

The deck suddenly lurched as the bows swept up, and the air was filled with cries and wails of terror and the sound of the sea surging past the sides of the *Horus*. Those clustered about the base of the mast clung to each other as the deck canted at a crazy angle and a mountain of sea swelled up above the ship, dwarfing it. For an instant Cato was lost in abject awe before the mighty apparition hanging over the ship, and he saw the spume and spray fringing the top of the wave. With a scream, one of the crewmen came tumbling down the deck, silenced as his head cracked against the deck hatch.

At that moment the *Horus* lost the brief struggle with the wave and slid back. A torrent of water crashed down over the vessel, snapping the mast off ten feet above the heads of the Romans tied to its base. Just before the black deluge of tons of water smashed down on the ship, Macro shouted up at the wave, 'Fuck you!'

Then the sea crashed over them. Cato's head was snapped back against the mast and for an instant he saw white. He opened his mouth to cry out and at once it was filled with salt water. A great force tore at him, dragging him out of the grasp of his comrades. He tightened his grip on the rope around Julia's waist while he clamped his fingers into Macro's shoulder for all he was worth. All sense of direction was lost as the ship rolled over, and his ears were filled with the roar and rumble of water boiling around him. Something struck him, and then thrashed around, tearing at him, and he realised it must be another of the crewmen. Fingers groped at his face and tore at his cheek. Fearing for his eyes, Cato had to release his grip on Macro and fight back, desperately thrusting the other man away. Then a fresh surge of water swept up both him and the other man, swirling them away from the stump of the mast in the darkness. For a moment the other man struggled like a wild animal, fighting for its life. Then he was gone and Cato felt himself rolling and twisting, over and over, as he clamped his mouth tightly shut and held his breath as best he could. Then, at last, he could bear it no longer and opened his mouth, desperate for air to ease the fire in his chest. Salt water surged down his throat and into his lungs, suffocating him, and he knew he would die.

The wave swept on, leaving a swirling maelstrom in its wake. The hull of the merchant vessel came to the surface in a froth of bubbles and spray and lay glistening in the failing light for a moment before it slowly rolled upright. As the side rail and then the deck struggled to break the surface of the sea, there was little of the original super-structure that could be recognised. The figurehead of the Egyptian god had sheared off, leaving a splintered stump. The mast, sail and rigging had been swept away and the steering paddles were gone, taking the captain and the steersman with them. As the waters parted across the deck and gushed out of the scuppers, the *Horus* continued to roll, and for an instant it seemed that she might overturn again. Then, at the last moment, she paused and rolled back to settle low in the water, a floating wreck where once there had been a proudly kept vessel. Around the *Horus* swirled the flotsam of the shattered mast and spar, together with tendrils of the rigging. A few bodies bobbed to the surface and then settled on the water like old rags.

Macro's head swayed to one side, and he blinked his eyes open and coughed, spraying salt water as he struggled to clear his lungs. He shook his head and looked around the deck. A handful of other figures were stirring, battered and dazed but alive, thanks to the ropes that secured them to the ship. Macro vomited up some water from the pit of his stomach, and spat on the deck to clear his mouth.

'Charming . . .'

He turned his head to see Sempronius smiling weakly at him, before he too began to cough and splutter. Sensing movement on his other side, Macro turned and saw Julia's face tightened into a painful grimace as she retched.

'All right, miss?'

'Oh, perfectly fine, thank you,' she muttered, and then froze. 'Cato! Where's Cato?'

Macro's gaze swept the deck, but there was no sign of his friend. He tried to think back, through the terrible darkness of the sea that had engulfed him. 'He was holding on to me when the wave struck. Then . . . then I can't remember.'

'Cato!' Julia cried out into the gloom, struggling to free herself from the rope that still bound her to the stump of the mast. Once she had loosened it enough she wriggled out and stood up. 'Cato! Where are you?'

Macro eased himself out of the cords looped round him and rose up beside her. He took a good look around the deck, but it was clear that there was no sign of Cato.

'Cato's gone, miss.'

'Gone?' She turned to him. 'No. He can't be.'

Macro stared at her helplessly, then gestured around the deck. 'He's gone.'

Julia shook her head and stepped away from the centurion, raising her voice to cry out hoarsely, 'Cato! Cato! Where are you?'

Macro watched her for a moment and then turned to help the senator to his feet.

'Thanks,' Sempronius muttered. 'Better see to the girl, Jesmiah.'

Macro nodded and looked down at the maidservant. She sat slumped against the foot of the mast, her head flopping loosely as the ship wallowed heavily on the swell. He knelt down and raised her chin tenderly. The girl's eyes stared blankly into the mid-distance. Then he saw the dark bruising that had begun to appear on the nape of her neck, visible even in the failing light. He lowered her chin and stood up with a heavy heart. 'She's had it. Broken neck.'

Sempronius whispered, 'Poor devil.'

'Dead?' Julia looked round. 'She can't be. She was tied down beside me.'

'She's gone, miss,' Macro said gently. 'Something must have hit her when the wave struck. A loose block, part of the mast. Could have been anything.'

Julia crouched down in front of her maid and grasped her shoulders. 'Jesmiah! Wake up. Wake up I tell you! I order you to wake up.' She shook the shoulders violently and the dead girl's head wobbled obscenely. Macro knelt down at her side and took her hands in his. 'Miss, she's gone. She can't hear you any more. There's nothing you can do for her.' He paused and took a breath to calm his own emotions. 'And nothing for Cato, neither.'

Julia looked at him angrily, and then her features crumpled and she was racked by a deep sob as she clasped her hands to her face. Macro hesitantly put an arm round her and tried to think of some words to comfort her. But none came and they sat there as the dusk thickened about the ship. Now that the wave had passed on down the coast, the sea gradually settled into a calm, gentle swell. At length Macro rose to his feet and tugged the sleeve of Sempronius's tunic.

'You'd better take care of her, sir.'

'What?' The senator frowned for a moment, still dazed by the wave, and the fact that he was still alive. Then he looked down at his daughter and nodded. 'Yes, you're right. I'll look after her. What now, Macro?'

'Sir?'

'What are we going to do now?'

Macro scratched his chin. 'Try to keep the ship afloat for the night, I guess. Have to see where things lie in the morning.'

'Is that it?'

Macro took a deep breath. 'I'm no bloody sailor, sir. I'm a soldier. But I'll do what I can. All right?'

As the senator sat down and put his arm round his daughter, Macro straightened his back and called out across the deck. 'On your

15

feet, your dozy bastards! Over here, on me, sharpish. We've got a bloody ship to save!'

As the figures shambled towards him out of the gloom, Macro glanced over them, still hoping to see Cato emerge from the shadows, alive and well. But he was nowhere to be seen amongst the scared and stunned expressions of the survivors who clustered around the stump of the mast.

CHAPTER THREE

'Your captain's gone,' Macro announced. 'And the man on the tiller. So who is next in the chain of command?'

The crew looked at each other for a moment before an older man shuffled forward. 'That'd be me, sir. The first mate.'

'Can you work the ship?'

'I suppose so, sir. I share watch duties with the captain. Well at least I did, until . . .'

The man gestured towards the stern and shrugged his shoulders. Macro could see that he was still in a state of shock and could not yet be counted on to meet the challenge.

'Right then, I'll take charge for now. Once the ship is seaworthy again you will take over as captain. Agreed?'

The mate gave a resigned shrug. Macro looked round the deck as a small wave sent spray bursting over the low side of the waterlogged ship. 'First thing we do is lighten the ship. I want all the passengers and crew to start jettisoning the cargo. Once we're riding higher in the water we can begin to bail out.'

'Sir, what cargo should we begin with?' asked the mate.

'Whatever's closest to hand. Now open the deck hatch and get on with it.'

The timbers of the hatch had splintered as the cargo tumbled around when the ship had rolled over. Once the ties had been undone, Macro and the others wrenched the battered planks away and threw them over the side of the *Horus*. The last light of the day was fading fast as Macro leaned over the coaming and stared down into the hold. Whatever order there might have been in the loading of the cargo, there was no sign of it in the jumbled heap of broken amphorae, sacks of grain and bales of material that filled the hold. Sea water sloshed about below.

'Right then, let's get to work,' Macro ordered. 'Take what comes to hand and get it over the side.' He pointed at the nearest of the crew. 'You four, into the hold. The rest of you take what they pass up and throw it overboard.'

The crewmen swung their legs over the side of the hatch coaming and warily eased themselves down into the hold, bracing their feet carefully on the jumbled cargo. Macro spotted some small wooden chests near the top of the pile. 'We'll have those first.'

As the first chest came up on deck the mate stared at it and swallowed nervously. 'Sir, you can't throw that over the side.'

'Oh? Why not?'

'These chests are the property of a Roman lord. They contain rare spices. They're valuable, sir.'

'That's too bad,' Macro replied. 'Now pick the chest up and get rid of it.'

The mate shook his head. 'No, sir. I will not be held responsible for that.'

With a sigh Macro bent down and lifted the chest up, strode over to the side and threw it into the sea. Turning back to the mate, he could not help being amused by the man's horrified expression.

'There you go. See? Not so difficult when you try. To work, the rest of you. I don't give a shit what anything's worth. It all goes over the side. Got that?'

The crewmen in the hold began to work in earnest, heaving the loose items of cargo up on to the deck, where their comrades stood ready to dispose of it all. Macro returned to the mate and muttered in a low voice, 'Now then, if you don't mind, I think you should lend a hand saving your bloody ship.'

The mate saw the serious expression on the centurion's face and nodded quickly before jumping down into the hold to help the others.

'That's better,' Macro nodded.

As more chests, and bales of sodden material were heaved up on deck, Sempronius and his daughter approached Macro.

The senator cleared his throat. 'Can we help?'

'Of course, sir. The more hands the better. If these sailors look like slacking, kick 'em in the arse. We have to lighten the ship as quickly as we can.'

'I'll see to it.'

'Thank you, sir.' Macro turned to Julia. 'You might as well take shelter in the stern, miss.'

Julia raised her chin defiantly. 'No. Not while I can do anything to help.'

Macro cocked an eyebrow. 'I know what Cato meant to you, miss. Best that I let you deal with your loss. Besides, it's man's work. No offence, but you'd just get in the way.'

'Oh really?' Julia's eyes narrowed. She slipped the drenched cloak from her shoulders and let it flop on to the deck. Bending down, she lowered herself into the cargo hold, picked up one of the chests with a grunt and heaved it up towards the deck. Macro looked at her and shrugged.

'As you will, miss. Now then,' his expression hardened, 'I'd better see to the dead.'

'Dead?' Sempronius looked at him. 'It's a bit late to do anything for them, don't you think?'

'We must lighten the ship. They have to go over the side as well, sir,' Macro explained gently. 'I'm no stranger to death, so let me do it.'

'Over the side?' Sempronius glanced towards the stump of the mast where Jesmiah's body lay slumped. 'Even her?'

'Yes, sir.' Macro nodded sadly. 'Even her.'

'Such a shame,' Sempronius mused as he stared at the body. 'She's not had much of a life.'

'More than some get, sir. And her death wasn't as bad as it could have been.' Macro briefly recalled the siege of the citadel at Palmyra where he had first met Jesmiah. If the citadel had fallen then, she and all the other defenders would have been put to the sword, after being tortured, or raped. But the senator was right: Jesmiah's life had been cut short, just when she might have had some happiness. Macro sighed as he crossed the deck and bent down. She was still fastened to the mast by a rope around her middle, and Macro drew out his dagger and quickly sawed through the coarse rope and tossed the ends aside. Sheathing his blade, he slid his hands beneath the body and picked her up. Jesmiah's head lolled against his shoulder, as if she was dozing, and Macro paced steadily to the side of the ship and lifted her over the rail.

He took a last look at her young face, and then lowered her to the sea, letting her drop with a splash. Her hair and clothes billowed in the water before a slight swell bumped the body against the side of the hull and carried her out of reach. Macro sighed and turned away to find the next corpse. There were only three more; the rest of those who had been lost had been swept over the side, like Cato, when the titanic wave struck the *Horus*. Macro paused as he thought of his friend once more. Cato was the closest thing to family that Macro had in the world. In the years they had served together he had come to regard him as a brother. Now he was dead. Macro felt a weary numbness in his heart, but he knew that the grief would come later on, when he had time to think.

'Poor Cato, he never did like the water . . .'

With a sad shake of his head, Macro turned to pick up the last body, a short, thin merchant who had boarded the ship at Caesarea. With a grunt he raised the body and tossed it as far from the ship as he could before making his way back to the deck hatch to help the others lighten the vessel.

The burning agony in Cato's lungs seemed to last an eternity and then, as his vision began to fade, he was aware of a lighter patch in the dark water that surrounded him. He kicked out with the last of his failing strength and his heart strained with hope as the light grew and he knew he must be heading for the surface. Then, just as the pain was becoming so unbearable that Cato feared he might black out, there was an explosion of noise in his ears and he burst from the surface of the sea. At once he coughed up the water in his lungs in agonising gasps as he kicked feebly in an effort to stay on the surface.

For a while his breath came in ragged gasps. Water slapped against his face and into his mouth, causing fresh bouts of spluttering and retching. His eyes stung so badly that he was forced to keep them shut as he struggled to stay afloat. The tunic and heavy military boots weighed him down and encumbered his efforts to stay on the surface. He realised that if he had been wearing anything more than this, he would certainly have drowned. Slowly he recovered his breath, and then, as his heart ceased pounding in his ears, he blinked his eyes open and glimpsed around the choppy surface of the sea that surrounded him.

At first he saw nothing but water, then he turned his head and caught a glimpse of the coastline of Crete. It seemed to be miles away, and Cato doubted he had the strength to swim that far. Then something nudged his side and he swirled round in a panic. A length of the ship's spar, complete with a ragged strip of the sail and tendrils of rigging, bobbed on the surface beside him. He let out an explosive gasp of relief as he grabbed hold of the spar and rested his arms over it. While he rose and dipped on the swell, he took in the scene around him. The sea was dotted with debris from the *Horus*, as well as a handful of bodies.

For a moment Cato was struck by the horrific thought that he was the only survivor from the ship. All the others must have gone down with the vessel when the wave struck and swamped the merchantman. Macro . . . Julia, her father and Jesmiah, all gone, he thought in a blind panic as a deep groan welled up in his chest.

A fresh swell lifted Cato up, and then he saw the ship, or rather what was left of her. Some distance from him the hull floated very low in the water. The mast and stern post had been carried away, and in the gloom of the gathering dusk Cato could just make out a handful of dazed figures stumbling about on deck. He tried to call out, but all he could manage was a painful croak, and then a small wavelet splashed into his face and filled his mouth. Cato spluttered for a moment, tried to call out again, and then trod water, fighting off a surge of despair as the last of the day's light began to fail. Those on the ship could not see him. In any case, they would be too pre-occupied with their own problems to look for survivors in the sea. Cato trembled. The water was already cold enough, and he doubted that he had the strength to last through the night.

Clutching the wooden spar, Cato struck out towards the ship. It was hard going, but the prospect of being saved lent him desperate strength, enough to keep kicking out, working his way across the swell towards the *Horus*. His progress felt painstakingly slow, and he was fearful that darkness would soon be upon him and he would lose sight of the ship.

The distance gradually closed, and even though the night had settled across the sea, there was just enough starlight in the heavens to illuminate the darker outline of the ship against the black swell of the water. As he drew closer, Cato tried to call out again, but his feeble cry was drowned by the surge and hiss of the waves and the splashes coming from the side of the ship. Not far from the *Horus* he bumped into a wooden case floating low in the water. He steered it aside and continued to close up on the ship. Two figures appeared above him, grunting as they struggled with a large amphora.

'On the count of three,' a voice growled, and they began to swing the heavy jar to and fro. Cato recognised the voice well enough, but before he could try to shout a greeting, the sound died in his throat as he realised that the large jar would land right on top of him.

'Wait!' The shout ripped from his throat as he raised a hand and waved frantically to attract attention. 'Lower that bloody jar!'

'What the fuck?' Macro's voice carried down to the water. 'Cato? That you?'

'Yes . . . yes. Now put the bloody thing down, before you drop it on my head!'

'What? Oh yes.' Macro turned back to the other man on deck. 'Easy there. Put the amphora down, careful like. Cato, wait there. I'll get a rope.'

'Where else would I go?' Cato grumbled.

A moment later Macro's dark form appeared above the rail and a rope splashed into the water.

Cato's cold fingers struggled to find the end of the rope. When he had it he held on as tightly as he could before muttering through clenched teeth, 'Ready.'

With a grunt Macro hauled his friend out of the sea, and as the young centurion surged up he leaned down with one hand and grasped his tunic to haul him aboard. Cato thudded down on the deck and slumped against the side, chest heaving with the effort of the swim back to the *Horus* and shivering violently as a cool breeze blew across the deck. Macro could not help smiling grimly.

'Well, you're in a right state. Proper drowned rat, you are.'

Cato frowned. 'I fail to see the humour of our situation.'

'Then you're not trying hard enough.'

Cato shook his head, then his heart stilled as he glanced round the deck and took in the damage that had been done to the ship, and the handful of figures working around the cargo hatch.

'Julia . . . Where's Julia?'

'She's safe, lad. And so is her father.' Macro paused and cleared his throat. 'But Jesmiah's gone.'

'Gone?'

'Dead. Her neck snapped when the ship went over. We lost quite a few of the crew and passengers. Mostly swept away. The rest were killed or injured by the ship's kit when it broke loose.'

'Julia's safe then,' Cato muttered to himself as a surge of relief flowed through him. He took a deep breath to calm his pounding heart and looked up at Macro. 'She thinks I was lost?'

Macro nodded. 'Putting a brave face on it, of course, what with her being the daughter of a senator. But you might want to put her mind at rest sooner rather than later. Then we need to get this tub seaworthy again, otherwise we'll all be for the chop.'

Cato struggled to his feet. 'Where is she?'

'In the hold. Helping get rid of the cargo. Her idea, not mine, before you ask. Now then,' Macro turned to a nearby sailor, 'give a hand with this.'

Leaving Macro and the other man to ditch the unwieldy amphora, Cato crossed the deck towards the open cargo hold. As he approached, he saw Sempronius looking up. The senator broke into a broad smile.

'Well now! I'd given you up for dead, Centurion.'

Cato grasped the hand that was offered to him, and clasped the senator's arm. The older man stared at him for a moment and then spoke softly. 'It's good to see you, my boy. I feared the worst.'

'So did I,' Cato replied ruefully. 'Seems the gods aren't quite finished with me.'

'Indeed. I will make a sacrifice to Fortuna the moment we reach dry land.'

'Thank you, sir.' Cato nodded, and then looked past the senator down into the ship's hold. Even in the gloom he could make Julia out at once. She was bent over a waterlogged bale of finely woven cloth, struggling to lift it on to her shoulder.

'Excuse me, sir.' Cato released the senator's hand and hopped over the side of the hatch, dropping slightly behind Julia. He leaned forward to help her, brushing her arm as he took hold of the cloth. She flinched and snapped.

'I can manage!'

'Let me help, Julia.'

She froze for an instant and then responded in a whisper, without turning her head. 'Cato?'

'Of course.'

Dropping the bale, Julia rose up and spun round, throwing her arms around him. 'Cato! Oh, Cato . . . I thought . . .' She stared up into his eyes, her lips trembling. Then she buried her face in his sodden chest and clenched her fists into the back of his tunic. He felt her shudder and then he heard a sob. He prised himself back so that he could look down at her face.

'It's all right, Julia. Shhh, my love. There's no need for tears, I'm alive and well.'

'I know, I know, but I thought I might have lost you.'

'Really?' Cato raised his eyebrows. It was a lucky thing indeed that he had survived the wave. He forced a smile. 'Takes more than a bloody wave to finish me off.'

Julia released her grip and thumped him on the chest. 'Don't ever do that to me again.'

'I promise. Unless we run into another wave, that is.'

'Cato!' she growled. 'Don't!'

They were interrupted by a loud cough and turned to see Macro, hands on hips, looking down into the hold with a bemused expression. 'If you two have quite finished, can we get back to work?'

The first hours of the night were spent getting rid of as much cargo as possible. The work became progressively harder as the survivors began to get deeper into the hold, where the heaviest items had been loaded. Much of the cargo had been thrown out of position and smashed against the hull or the underside of the cargo hatch. But slowly the *Horus* began to ride higher in the water, to the relief of all aboard. However, as they delved further into the hold, it was clear that the vessel had shipped a great deal of water.

'We can start bailing that out once we've shifted a bit more of the cargo,' Macro decided. 'That'll keep us afloat.'

The mate scratched his chin. 'Yes, I hope so.'

Macro turned to him with an irritable expression. 'Problem?'

'Of course.' The mate sounded surprised. 'The cargo's shifted all over the place, and the *Horus* has been capsized. We were lucky she righted herself. Very lucky. Shows how well she was built that she's still afloat. But there's bound to be plenty of damage. Some of the seams will have been badly strained, and are probably leaking already.'

Macro shrugged. 'Then we'll just have to bail the water out faster than it gets in.'

'We can try.'

'Bugger try; we will,' Macro said firmly.

The mate nodded slightly. 'If you say so. But once it's safe enough I'll have to go into the hold and examine the hull for leaks. Then try to stop them up if I can.'

'What's the danger of going in there now?'

'There's still loose cargo in there, Centurion. The swell's getting up and I don't fancy being crushed or buried alive if the *Horus* heaves too far to one side. We have to get as much of the cargo out as we can first.'

'Fair point. When it's safe to go in. I'll give you a hand.' Macro glanced round the deck and his gaze fixed on the shattered stump of the broken mast. 'Something else occurs to me.'

'Sir?'

'Keeping afloat is one problem, but how are we going to get this ship under way again?'

The mate indicated a spar lashed along one of the sides of the vessel. 'We'll have to jury-rig a new mast. There's some spare cable and an old sail for'ard. Then we'll need to rig a new rudder and tiller from what's left of the cargo hatch. Should give us steerage way, but she'll be slow, and I doubt if we can weather any storm.' He shivered. 'Or any wave half the size of the one that hit us.'

'That'll have to do then. Soon as we get going we'll make for the nearest harbour on Crete.'

The mate thought a moment and nodded. 'Matala's the best bet.'

'Matala it is then. Now back to work.'

As soon as he felt that the hold was safe enough, the mate climbed carefully across the remaining cargo and waded towards the side of the hull. Macro lowered himself down and followed the mate, carrying a sack of tarry strips of old sailcloth. Hardly any of the light from the stars filtered into the hold, and the steady creak of the timbers and rushing swirl of water on both sides of the hull was unnerving.

'This way,' the mate called. 'Stay close to me.'

'I will, don't worry about that.'

The mate headed forward, picking his way over the timber ribs of the *Horus*. Then he steadily worked his way aft, feeling for any leaks and holes. Every so often he paused to check and then asked Macro for a piece of cloth, and the two of them squatted in the cold water and did their best to stuff the thick material into the small gaps that had opened in the seams. When they had worked their way round the stern and back to the bows and groped their way to the cargo hatch, Macro climbed the ladder on to the deck and slumped down, cold and exhausted.

'Will that keep the water out?' he asked the mate.

'It'll help. It's the best we can do for now. Once we have the jury mast rigged, we'll have to organise two watches to take turns at bailing the water out.'

'Fine. I'll lead one. Cato can take the other. I want you to concentrate on keeping the ship afloat and getting us to port.'

The mate sighed. 'I'll do the best I can, Centurion.'

'Of course you will. If the ship sinks and we all drown, then I'll have your bloody guts for garters.' He slapped the mate on the back. 'Let's get this mast up.'

With the Roman officers' help, the crewmen untied the spar and positioned the butt up against the stump of the mast. Then, with four ropes tied to the far end, Macro and five men heaved the spar up. The mate, with two strong men, kept the butt in position as Cato oversaw two teams of men heaving on the ropes. Slowly the spar rose up, carefully guided into a vertical position against the mast's stump as

Macro and his men took the other two ropes to steady it. At once, the mate and his men hurriedly lashed the spar to the stump, and then tied more ropes around it, as tightly as possible, until satisfied that the makeshift mast was as firm as it could be. There was no rest for the crew as they improvised the necessary shrouds, sheets and a cross spar from the ship's sweep oars, lashed together. Lastly they fetched out the old sail from a locker and fastened it to the spar. The makeshift rudder was lowered over the stern and a man assigned to the tiller before the sail was carefully hoisted up the mast.

A light breeze filled the sail with a rippling series of thuds, as the mate looked on apprehensively. Then he gave the order to sheet home, and the *Horus* began to make way through the gentle swell, just as the first glimmer of light appeared on the horizon. On deck, those who were not helping to crew the ship lay down to rest, exhausted. Senator Sempronius cradled his daughter's head and shoulders in his lap and covered her with his cloak. Once the mate was satisfied that the ship was performing as well as it could under the rough repairs that had been carried out through the night, he came to report to Macro and Cato.

'We're holding a course along the coast, sir. Should make Matala before the end of the day. We can put in for repairs there.'

'Good job.' Macro smiled. 'You've done well.'

The mate was too tired for any modesty, and just nodded before he made his way aft to give his orders to the man at the tiller, and then leaned on the side rail. Macro rubbed his hands together and gazed towards the coming dawn. 'You hear that? Safe and sound on dry land by the end of the day.'

Cato did not reply. He was staring at the distant coastline of Crete. After a moment he stretched his shoulders and rubbed his neck. 'Safe and sound? I hope so.'

Macro frowned. 'What now? The prospect of being saved from a watery grave not good enough for you?'

'Oh, I'm pleased enough about that.' Cato forced a brief smile. 'The thing is, if that wave almost destroyed the ship, then the gods only know what it has done to the island of Crete . . .'

CHAPTER FOUR

As the *Horus* crept round the point, those on board got their first glimpse of the devastation that had been visited on the port of Matala by the giant wave. The warehouses and wharves had been smashed to pieces and the debris swept up the slope beyond where the densely packed houses had collapsed under the weight of the sea water surging ashore. Fishing boats and ships lay shattered across the rocks and cliffs either side of the bay. Further inland, above the high-water mark where the wave had come ashore, the destruction continued. Buildings large and small had been flattened, as if crushed under the foot of some titan. Further inland fires burned out of control and columns of smoke swirled into the afternoon sky. Only a handful of people were visible amongst the ruins, some desperately plucking away at the debris to find their loved ones and valuables. Others simply sat and stared at their surroundings in shock.

Macro swallowed. 'What in Hades happened here?'

'The wave,' said Julia. 'It must have destroyed the port before it reached us.'

'Not just the wave.' Cato shook his head. 'The wave swept in over the land for some way, but beyond that, there's still plenty of damage.' He turned to the senator. 'Seems like that earthquake in Bythinia you told us about.'

Sempronius stared at the scene opening out before them for a moment before he replied. 'This is worse, far worse. I've never seen anything like it.'

They continued to stare at the devastation as the *Horus* crept into the bay. Despite the repairs of the previous night, the ship was still steadily taking on water, and regular shifts of the surviving crew and passengers had taken turns on a human chain to bail the water out of the hull. The water level in the hold had been slowly rising all day, making the vessel steadily settle in the swell and reducing its already slow speed to a crawl.

The mate stared down into the water, noting a dark patch of submerged rocks projecting beyond the point. He straightened up and pointed towards a strip of shingle below the cliffs on the opposite side of the bay. 'I'm going to beach the ship over there. She's not going to stay afloat for much longer, sir,' he explained. 'If she's beached, then at least she can be salvaged, along with what little is left of the cargo.'

'Fair enough,' Cato conceded. 'However, I doubt there's any chance of having the ship repaired in this port for a while. Or come to that, any port on this side of the island. What happened here is going to be the same everywhere else.'

'Do you really think so?' Julia said with a surprised expression.

'You saw the wave. What was to stop it carrying on all the way along the coast, and then out to sea? Why, I wouldn't be surprised if it had continued all the way to Syria before it died away completely.' Cato gestured towards the shore. 'That wave and the earthquake will have destroyed almost everything.' His mind went back to the slave camp they had seen crumble the previous day. 'There will be hundreds dead. Maybe thousands. And it looks like hardly a building has been left standing. Who knows what we'll find when we get ashore. It'll be chaos. Complete chaos.'

'But we have to get the ship repaired,' Julia insisted. 'So we can return to Rome. If all the other ships are smashed, we have to repair this one.'

'And who will repair it?' Cato asked. 'The docks are gone. The shipmakers' workshops have gone, and most of the carpenters will have been caught by the wave and are probably dead.'

Julia thought a moment. 'Then what are we going to do?'

Cato wearily ran his fingers through his salt-encrusted hair. 'We'll go ashore, and try to find out who is left in authority. Perhaps when they hear that your father is with us they might provide some help, and shelter.'

'Shelter?' Macro gave a dry laugh. 'That's a good one. What shelter? As far as I can see, there's only a handful of structures still standing, and most of those are just shacks.'

29

'True,' said Cato. 'But I was thinking of shelter in a somewhat wider sense.'

'Eh?'

'Think about it, Macro. The island's been turned upside down. You saw what happened to the slave compound yesterday. Those slaves are loose now. I imagine the same thing has happened on every estate. Everyone will be looking for food and a safe place to ride out the disaster. Soon they'll be fighting for it. We'll need to find some protection somewhere, or make our own. At least until help arrives, and order is restored.'

Macro looked at him sourly. 'By the gods, you're a cheerful soul, Cato. We've barely escaped from drowning, and already you're looking for the downside.'

'Sorry.'

Macro glanced at Julia. 'Are you sure you want to marry him, miss? Mister the amphora's-always-half-empty.'

She did not reply, but moved in closer to Cato and grasped his arm.

Under the mate's command the *Horus* edged across the bay towards the strip of beach, and as they drew closer to shore they could see a thin layer of flotsam strewn across the shingle. A handful of bodies sprawled amongst splintered lengths of wood and tangles of vegetation. The ship steered steadily towards the shore, with the mate constantly looking over the side to gauge the depth as they approached. As the cliffs loomed over them, Cato felt a gentle lurch beneath his feet, then the deck was motionless.

'Let fly the sheets!' the mate shouted to his crew. Then, as the sail billowed in the gentle breeze, he drew a sharp breath and gave another order. 'Lower the sail!'

The men untied the ropes fastening the makeshift spar and carefully lowered the spar and sail to the deck. Then, overcome by the exhaustion and strain of the desperate hours of the previous night, and the following day's shifts bailing the water from the hold, the crew slumped down and rested.

'What do we do now?' asked Julia.

'We?' Macro turned to her. 'I want you to stay here, miss. You and the rest of the crew and passengers. Meanwhile, Cato, your father and I are going into Matala to check on the lie of the land.'

'I'm coming with you.'

'With respect, miss, you aren't. Not until we are sure that it's safe.'

Julia frowned and then looked up at Cato. 'Take me with you.'

'I can't,' Cato replied. 'Macro is the ranking officer. If he says you stay, then you stay.'

'But Cato—'

'He's right, my dear,' Sempronius intervened. 'You have to stay here. Just for now. We'll be back soon. I promise.'

Julia met her father's gaze and after a moment, nodded. 'All right. But don't take any risks.'

'We won't, miss,' said Macro. 'Come on, Cato. Let's get our kit from the cabin.'

'Kit?'

'Most of it survived, I checked,' Macro explained. 'If what you said earlier is anything to go by, I'd be happier if we went armed.'

A short time later, the two centurions and the senator splashed down into the shallows from the end of the boarding plank that had been lowered from the bows. The mate of the *Horus* had ordered two men to take the main anchor and carry it a short distance up the shingle before wedging its flukes into the beach. He was testing that the anchor was securely fixed as the Romans came ashore and made their way up the shingle to firmer ground.

'All done?' Macro asked.

The mate nodded. 'The ship's as safe and secure as she can be. At least she can't sink.'

'Good. You've done well. Your captain would have been proud of you.'

The mate bowed his head. 'I hope so. He was a good man, sir. Best captain I have sailed with.'

'A sad loss,' Macro responded flatly. 'Now then, we're heading into the port, or what's left of it, to see what the situation is. Meanwhile, you're to remain here. Make sure the crew stays close to the ship and don't let anyone come aboard.'

'Why?'

'Just do as I say, all right? Hopefully someone has restored some kind of order to Matala. But if they haven't . . . then I'd rather you made sure that you looked after your people, and the senator's daughter. Understand?'

'Yes, sir.' The mate nodded solemnly. 'We have a few weapons in the stern locker. In case of pirates.'

'Let's hope you don't need to use them.' Cato smiled thinly. 'But use your judgement. If there's any sign of trouble, then get everyone back on board and pull up the boarding plank.'

'Yes, sir. Good luck.'

'Luck?' Macro patted the sword hanging at his side. 'I make my own luck.'

The two centurions and the senator set off along the shingle towards the port. Cato glanced back over his shoulder and saw Julia following their progress from the foredeck. She waved her hand hesitantly as she saw him looking back and he resisted the urge to wave back. He was thinking like a soldier again and was already closely watching the cliffs to their left for any sign of danger as they trudged along the top of the shingle. It was only a quarter of a mile to the port, and as they approached, the debris that had been carried on the backwash of the wave increased in intensity. Then they came across the first bodies. Twisted figures in sodden clothing mingled with the remains of houses, boats and goods from the warehouses. The wave had struck its victims down indiscriminately and the three Romans stepped over the corpses of old and young alike. Cato felt a stab of pity as he saw a young woman on her side, an infant still strapped to her chest by a sling, both of them quite dead. He stopped a moment to stare down at the bodies.

Macro paused at his side. 'Poor devils. Didn't stand a chance.'

Cato nodded silently.

His companion looked up and surveyed the beach and the ruins of the port. 'By tomorrow this place is going to start smelling a bit ripe. The bodies will have to be dealt with.'

'Dealt with?' Sempronius cocked an eyebrow.

'Yes, sir. It ain't the smell that worries me. It's the sickness that follows death on this scale. I've seen it at work after a siege. Small town in southern Germany, many years back, soon after I joined the Eagles. The defenders had just left the dead where they had fallen and the weather was hot. Baking hot. Anyway, by the time the survivors surrendered, the air inside was higher than a kite. The place was a den of pestilence.'

'What did you do?' asked Sempronius.

'Nothing we could do. The legate ordered the survivors to stay inside the walls and then had the gate closed up. Couldn't afford the sickness spreading to our troops. After a month there was only a handful of the townspeople still alive, and most of them were too sick to be worth anything as slaves. If they'd only disposed of the bodies properly, then many more would have lived.'

'I see. Let's hope that whoever is still in charge of the port knows what to do then.'

Macro clicked his tongue. 'It'll be a bastard of a job, sir.'

'Not our problem.' Sempronius shrugged. 'Come on.'

They continued along the shoreline until they reached the remains of a watchtower that had guarded the entrance to the port. The blocks of stone still stood, as high as a man, but above that the timber posts and platform had gone. So had the gate, and the walls had given way under the pressure of the sea water bursting over Matala. Beyond the barely discernible line of the wall, the port was a mass of rubble, timber and tiles, with no sense of the lines of the neat grid of streets that had once thronged with the inhabitants of the town. Now a handful of figures stumbled about the ruins, or sat and stared abjectly into the distance.

The three Romans paused at the edge of Matala, shocked by the scene in front of them. Macro took a deep breath.

'No easy way through that lot. Better to work around the edge and see what the situation is further inland.' He gestured up the slope. The cliffs on either side of the bay gave way to steep-sided hills that flanked the town, narrowing into a defile that bent round, out of sight, as it led away from the coast.

They set off again, a short distance from the shattered remains of the wall. The slopes had been stripped of much of the shrubs and trees that had grown there and now they were covered by the same dismal tide of debris and dead people and animals that the three men had witnessed on the beach. They passed the remains of a small cargo ship that had been carried up on the wave, before it struck a large boulder and smashed to pieces, leaving only the ribs and some timbers still caught around the rock. Cato could not help being awed by the sight. The power of the wave was as terrible and mighty as the wrath of any of the gods.

As they reached the defile, Cato and the others found that the easiest path was to cross the remains of the wall and pick their way warily across the ruins. A small gang of young men was busy pulling valuables out of a ruined house that must have belonged to one of the port's wealthier families. A handful of busts had been extracted and discarded, and the looters were busy removing silver plates and small chests of personal effects. They stopped their work and looked up warily as the three Romans passed by. Macro's hand went casually to his sword hilt.

'Ignore them,' Cato muttered. 'We can't deal with that now.'

'Pity.' Macro sniffed, and let his hand drop back to his side.

They passed on by without exchanging a word. On the far side of the defile, the ground opened out into a wide plain, and here the damage caused by the wave gave way to the effects of the earthquake that had shaken the island to its roots. There was no debris washed up from the port. Instead most of the houses had just collapsed, on top of those inside. Others were partially damaged and a few seemed to have suffered no damage at all. It was the same for the larger buildings. Some of the temples were little more than piles of rubble surrounded by broken columns that now looked like bad teeth. Others were intact, standing defiantly above the ruins. There were far more people visible here than down in the port. Hundreds were picking over the rubble, rescuing what they could from their homes, or liberating the possessions of the houses of the dead. Little clumps of humanity lay scattered across the slopes of the hill, and on the plain, a short distance from the city. Thin tendrils of smoke drifted up from small fires that some of the survivors had lit to warm themselves through the night.

On a large mass of rock stood the town's acropolis, relatively untouched by the disaster. The walls still stood, although one of the squat towers had collapsed down the small cliff on to the town below, flattening several houses. A squad of soldiers stood guard at the end of the ramp leading to the gates of the acropolis, and beyond the walls they could see that the main administration building was still standing.

'That looks like our best bet,' said Cato. 'We should head up there.'

Sempronius nodded and led the way down the main thoroughfare that stretched through the town towards the acropolis. Once, the street had been fifteen paces across, but now the sides had been buried and only a thin path through the rubble remained. They reached the ramp and started up the incline towards the gates. The sentries immediately stirred and moved to bar their path. Macro eyed them coolly. The men carried the oval shields of auxiliary troops, but they looked nervous and out of condition. Their leader, an optio, stepped forward and raised his hand.

'That's close enough. Who are you, and what's your business?'

Sempronius cleared his throat and stiffened his posture. 'I am Caius Sempronius, senator of Rome. These are my companions, Centurions Macro and Cato. We must see the senior official in the town. At once.'

The optio cast his eye over the three men before him. Certainly the man who claimed to be an aristocrat had the right bearing for such a rank, and the shorter of the other two men was scarred and burly enough to be a soldier. But the other was thin and young, and did not exude any obvious authority. Besides their army pattern swords, there was no other proof of the first man's claims. The three wore simple tunics and their skin was grimy and their chins stubbled.

'Senator, you say?' The optio licked his lips nervously. 'Forgive me for saying so, sir, but can you prove it?'

'Prove it?' Sempronius frowned and thrust out his hand to show the gold senatorial ring that had been passed down to him from his father. 'There! Good enough?'

'Well, I suppose . . .' the optio answered cautiously. 'Is there anything else?'

'What do you want?' Sempronius answered irritably. 'The ring is enough. Now, let us in and have someone take me to whoever is in command here. Before I have you placed on a charge for insubordination.'

The optio stood to attention and saluted. 'Yes, sir. Open the gate!'

Two of his men sprang towards the heavy wooden timbers and

thrust them back. With a groan the door swung open. The optio detailed four of his men to stay on guard and then ushered the senator and the two centurions inside the acropolis. Beyond the gate there was a small courtyard, on either side of which stretched store-houses, and ahead of them lay a basilica. Some of the tiles had fallen off and the roof had collapsed at one end. Otherwise the building was intact. More auxiliary troops squatted in the shade of the walls of the acropolis and some watched curiously as the optio and four of his men escorted the Romans across to the entrance of the basilica.

'Seems you've been lucky,' said Macro. 'Not too much damage up here.'

'Yes, sir.' The optio glanced round. 'But many of the lads were down in the town when the tremor struck. And after that, the wave. Still can't account for over half of the cohort.'

'Cohort? Which cohort is that?'

'Twelfth Hispania, sir.'

'Garrison troops?'

'For the last fifteen years,' the optio conceded. 'Before that the unit was on the Danuvius frontier. Before my time, though.'

'I see.' Macro nodded. 'And who is the commander here?'

'Prefect Lucius Calpurnius, but he's up at Gortyna, the province's capital, along with the rest of the quality. He left Centurion Portillus in charge while he was gone.'

They entered the basilica, passing empty offices, and crossed the main hall to the suite of rooms on the far side. The optio paused outside an open door and rapped on the frame.

'Come!' a voice called out wearily.

The optio indicated to his men to remain outside and led Sempronius and his companions into the prefect's office. It was a large room with shuttered windows that looked out over the town towards the sea. Normally it would have been a fine view indeed, Cato reflected, but today the windows provided a panorama of destruction and suffering. In front of the windows, seated at a desk, was a thickset man in a red military tunic. He was completely bald and his features were heavily wrinkled. He squinted towards his visitors.

'Yes? Oh, it's you, Optio. Who are these men?'

'They approached the main gate, sir.' The optio indicated Sempronius. 'This gentleman claims to be a Roman senator, Caius Sempronius. He says the others are centurions.'

'I see.' Portillus squinted again, then rose from the chair and strode up to his guests, where he could examine them more closely. 'So then, sir, might I ask what you are doing here in Matala?'

'Certainly,' Sempronius replied patiently. 'We were on a ship bound for Rome. Yesterday evening we were struck by a giant wave, just off the coast of Crete.'

'Where did the ship sail from?' Portillus interrupted. 'What port?'

'Caesarea, on the Syrian coast,' Sempronius said at once.

'Can the ship's captain verify this?'

'The ship's captain was swept away by the wave. But you can ask the first mate, if you feel you need to.'

'I may do that. Later.' Portillus eyed them suspiciously for a moment. 'I take it you have seen what the wave did to us here in Matala. Which rather begs the question, if it was powerful enough to destroy a town, then how did a simple ship manage to survive?'

'We bloody well nearly didn't!' Macro interrupted and then glared at Portillus. 'Still, *you* seem to have come out of it untouched. Care to explain that, eh? Sitting pretty up here while everything goes to shit down there in what's left of the town.'

Sempronius laid his hand on Macro's shoulder. 'That's enough. Centurion Portillus is right to be careful. There are bound to be plenty of people roaming the island in the days to come. They could claim to be anybody. All I have on my person to identify me is my senatorial ring. See here.' He raised his hand for Portillus to examine closely.

Portillus scratched his chin for a moment. 'All right then, let's agree for the moment that you are who you say you are. What are you doing here?'

'It was the nearest port we could make for after we had repaired the damage as best we could,' Sempronius explained. 'We had hoped to have the ship made seaworthy again, or at least take passage in another and continue our voyage. But now, having seen what's left of Matala, well, it's clear that we will be stuck here until another ship arrives. In which case we will need accommodation while we wait.

37

I had hoped to ask your commander for help, but it seems that he is away at the moment.'

'That's right. He went to the governor's palace at Gortyna for the annual banquet. The prefect and all the local worthies. As soon as the earthquake and the wave hit us, I sent him a report. He should be back to take charge at any time.'

'How far away is Gortyna?' Cato asked.

'Fifteen miles or so.'

'And the prefect has not returned yet, nor sent a reply?'

'No. Not yet.'

Macro took a deep breath to calm his growing sense of frustration. 'And what have you done in the meantime?'

'Done?'

'To help the people down there.' Macro jerked his thumb in the direction of the window. 'To help rescue those trapped in the ruins, to treat the injured and organise food and water for the survivors, and to restore order. Well?'

Portillus's brow creased into a frown. 'I have done all that is necessary to make sure the men of my cohort were seen to first, and to make them ready to carry out whatever orders the prefect gives them the moment he returns from Gortyna. That's what I've done.'

'Bullshit!' Macro growled. 'Bloody jobsworth. You and your men are sitting on your arses while the people down there need you. It is your duty to keep the peace. There's bugger all else for you to do on a garrison posting.'

Sempronius coughed. 'Macro. I'm sure that Centurion Portillus and his men will do what's needed the moment his prefect returns.'

'Assuming he does return,' Cato added.

The others turned to look at him.

Portillus raised his eyebrows. 'Why wouldn't he return?'

'When exactly did you send the message to him?'

'Last night.'

'Then he has had time to respond or return. So why haven't you heard from him?'

'I don't know!' Portillus flapped an open hand. 'Could be any reason. Perhaps he is needed in Gortyna.'

'Perhaps,' Cato conceded. 'Then again, if what has happened here in Matala is anything to go by, surely Gortyna will have been hit hard as well.'

As Portillus struggled to come to terms with the implications of Cato's words, the sound of a horse's hooves clattering across the courtyard echoed faintly through the basilica. Macro turned towards the sound and went to the door. A cloaked figure came running through the entrance and across the hall, making straight for the prefect's office.

'Seems that we may be about to find out what's happened at Gortyna,' Macro said quietly.

A moment later the new arrival was standing in front of the three officers and the senator, struggling for breath. His cloak and face were grimy with dust from a hard ride. He made an effort to stand up straight and salute before making his report.

'Is this the man you sent to Gortyna?' asked Sempronius.

Portillus nodded as he faced the man. 'Did you find the prefect?'

'Yes, sir. That is, I saw him.'

'Saw him? What do you mean? Speak sense, man!'

'I saw his body, sir. The prefect's dead. So is nearly every other official in the province, sir.'

'Dead?' Portillus shook his head. 'How?'

'They were all in the banquet hall at the governor's palace when the earthquake struck. The roof collapsed on top of them. The survivors on the governor's staff have been pulling the bodies out all day, sir. There's only a handful left alive. Some of them won't live long.'

'I don't believe it,' Portillus mumbled. 'It's not possible.'

Cato edged closer to the messenger. 'What about the governor? Is he dead?'

'No. At least not when I left Gortyna, sir. He was hurt bad, like. His legs have been crushed. He sent me back here to report to Centurion Portillus.'

'Me?'

'Yes, sir. You are the senior Roman official in Matala. He's ordered you to take charge here.'

'Me?' Portillus's eyes widened with shock, and not a little anxiety. 'There has to be someone else.'

'No, sir.'

'I . . . I need to think.' Portillus backed away and then turned to gaze out of the window. 'I need time to make a plan. Time to restore order. I . . .'

He fell silent and his shoulders slumped. Macro leaned towards Cato and Sempronius as he muttered, 'Now that is not what I would call a safe pair of hands.'

'You're right,' Sempronius replied. 'We have to do something. Right now.'

CHAPTER FIVE

Senator Sempronius cleared his throat and took a step towards the prefect's desk. 'Centurion Portillus!'

The officer turned quickly at the tone of command in the senator's voice.

'Centurion Portillus, I am assuming the authority of the governor for the present emergency. I will also take command of all military and naval forces present in Crete, starting with this cohort. Do you understand?'

Portillus looked shocked, as did the others in the room. After a moment he swallowed and clasped his hands. 'But sir, the governor has appointed me, as you just heard.'

'The governor was acting on the basis that you were the senior surviving official. He could not have known that I, or these other officers, were present on the island. Since they are legionary centurions they outrank you, and as a senator I carry the authority of the senate with my rank. I would be the most suitable replacement for Governor Hirtius and I intend to take command. Is that clear?'

Portillus nodded and then bit his lip.

'Do you have a problem with my decision?'

'Well, yes, sir. There's the question of protocol.'

'Protocol?' Macro grumbled. 'What are you talking about?'

'Strictly speaking, the senator needs the permission of the emperor to enter a province,' Portillus continued nervously.

'What?' Macro raised his voice. 'What the hell are you talking about? Our bloody ship is leaking like a sieve. Where else could we go? Or do you think we should have nipped back to Rome first to get the emperor's nod that it's all right for us to set foot on this bloody island?'

'That's the regulations, sir.'

'Bollocks!' Macro spat back. 'Bollocks to regulations, you fool.'

Sempronius intervened. 'Centurion Portillus is right to raise the issue. However, given the circumstances – the extraordinary circumstances – I think the normal rules have to be ignored. Besides,' he turned back to Portillus, 'I am sure that you would be content to pass the responsibility for the cohort on to a more senior official. Is that not so?'

Portillus bowed his head. 'Of course, sir. As you wish.' He glanced towards the messenger still standing near the door, and then continued in a very deliberate tone. 'Naturally, I will want it on record that you insist on taking command, and that you assume full responsibility for your actions, sir.'

'As you wish, you'll have that in writing,' Sempronius replied, struggling to keep the contempt from his voice. 'So then, I am now in charge. Agreed?'

'Yes, sir.'

'Then the first priority is to restore order here in Matala and help the survivors.' The senator looked towards Cato and Macro and thought for a moment before he made a decision. 'Centurion Macro, you are to assume control here in Matala. I authorise you to do whatever is necessary to help the local people. You are to commandeer any remaining food stocks and existing shelter. Priority is to be given to rescuing those still trapped in the rubble and the injured. There is to be no looting, such as we saw on the way here. Use whatever force is necessary to prevent such lawlessness. Is that understood?'

'Yes, sir.'

'Good. Now then, Centurion Cato, you and I must head for Gortyna at once. We have to see what's left of the province's administration. That's where we need to be in order to regain control of Crete and deal with this chaos.'

Cato nodded. 'Yes, sir. What about the ship, and those still on board?'

Sempronius smiled. 'Julia is safe where she is for now.'

'But she would be safer if she was brought here, sir.'

'Of course. Centurion Macro will take care of it.'

Macro patted his friend on the shoulder. 'Trust me.'

'And you might as well take charge of the crew and passengers,'

Sempronius continued. 'Add them to the cohort. They may not be soldiers, but they're good men. They've more than proved that they can be useful in a crisis.'

'I'll see to it.'

'Sailors?' Centurion Portillus shook his head. 'In the Twelfth Hispania? The lads'll not stand for it, sir.'

'They'll stand for whatever I tell them to,' Macro said firmly. 'And from what I've seen so far, they'll be a welcome addition to the slackers lounging around the acropolis. Now then, Portillus, I want all the men and officers assembled for parade. Time for them to meet their new commander.'

As Portillus hurried off to carry out his orders, Sempronius clasped Macro's hand. 'Good luck, Centurion. Do what you can. If you need to report anything, send word to me at Gortyna.'

'Yes, sir. How long do you intend staying there?'

Sempronius thought for a moment and then shrugged. 'As long as it takes, I suppose. The gods only know what we will find there, and what the situation is across the rest of the province. Once I've assessed the situation I will send word to you here in Matala.'

The senator and Cato took some cloaks from the prefect's quarters to keep them warm during the night's ride to Gortyna, then chose two of the best horses from the prefect's stable in the corner of the acropolis's courtyard and mounted up. As they clopped out of the gate, the men of the cohort were already shambling into formation, under Macro's disapproving glare as he stood in the shade of the basilica's colonnade. Cato twisted in the saddle as they rode past.

'See you soon, Macro.'

'Take care, Cato. I've a feeling we're in for a bastard time of it.'

Sempronius clicked his tongue and urged his horse into a trot as they approached the gate and then rode down the ramp towards the main street of the town, lined with ruins. As they passed through the remains of the gate, Cato took a last look towards the sea. Although he could not see the side of the bay where the *Horus* was beached, he felt his heart stir with anxiety for Julia's safety.

Sempronius noticed the expression on the young officer's face and smiled. 'Rest easy, Cato. No harm will come to her while she's in Macro's care.'

Cato forced himself to smile back. 'I know. I pity any man who would try and cross him.'

They rode away from the city following the Gortyna road over rolling hills, where they passed further scenes of destruction caused by the earthquake. Many more villas, farms and roadside shrines had been toppled and were now no more than heaps of bricks, tiles and timber. The survivors had dragged out the injured and some of the bodies, which lay in makeshift shrouds waiting for burial or cremation. The living stared at the passing horsemen with gaunt expressions of horror and numbed shock, and Cato felt guilty as he followed Sempronius and tried to ignore the suffering that stretched out mile after mile along the road to Gortyna.

As dusk settled, Sempronius gave the order to stop and rest the horses at the edge of a small village. Not one house had survived and there was a dreadful stillness in the gathering gloom as figures huddled in whatever shelter they could find for the night. There were no cries of grief, and no moans from the wounded. The only sound was a light sobbing from the remains of a small farm close by. Cato tethered his horse to the stump of a tree and made his way over towards the source of the crying.

'Cato,' Sempronius called softly. 'Don't go far.'

Cato nodded and continued forward cautiously. In the gloom he could make out the line of a fallen wall and tiles scattered across the ground. The sound came more clearly. Crouching down close to the blocks of stone that made up the wall, he saw a flicker of movement beneath some of the tiles close by. He leaned forward and carefully removed the nearest tile. There was a startled cry, and Cato saw the top half of a small child, no more than two years old, lying on its back. The child was naked and the puffy pale flesh was smeared with grime and blood. The tile had struck its head, gouging a patch of scalp away, and a tacky black mass of dried blood and matted hair covered one side. The child's eyes were open, and wide blue eyes gazed intently at Cato as the whimpering continued.

'You're all right,' Cato said gently. 'Shhh, you're all right.'

He cleared the debris away from the exposed half of the child's body and then saw that a large slab of stone lay just below the waist, covering the legs. He took hold of the edges of the stone and eased it up, now able to see that the child was male. As the pressure came off the boy's pelvis and legs he screamed, a shrill, piercing cry of agony. Cato flung the stone aside and took the boy's hand.

'There, it's gone. Hush now. Shhh.' He glanced down, and at once a wave of nausea threatened to overwhelm him. The stone had crushed the boy from the waist down, shattering bones and laying open the delicate flesh. The thin shafts of the shin bones spiked out from the skin where the legs had been violently broken.

The boy let out a scream and suddenly started shuddering violently. Cato hurriedly undid the clasp of his cloak and covered the child, tucking one end under his head to act as a pillow. All the time the boy's tiny hand clasped Cato's fingers with surprising strength, until the screaming died away and he lay, staring at Cato, shuddering as he drew breaths in ragged gasps. There was a crunch of boots on the rubble close by and Cato glanced up to see Sempronius, who had come to investigate the screaming.

'What's that you have there?'

'A boy.' Cato shuffled aside so that the senator could see. 'He was caught by this wall when it fell.'

'How is he?'

Cato swallowed the bitter taste in his mouth and felt his throat contract. He cleared it harshly before he could reply. 'His legs are broken.'

'I see . . . Will he live?'

For a moment Cato was silent. He wanted to say that the boy would live and could be saved. But it was a lie. Even if, by some miracle, he survived, he would spend the rest of his days as a cripple. No one had come to rescue him and Cato glanced at the ruins of the house beyond the fallen wall, where no doubt the rest of his family lay buried under the rubble. He looked down at the child, and forced himself to smile as he quietly replied to the senator.

'I doubt he will survive another night if we leave him here, sir. It's a miracle he's still alive. He might live, if we can find someone to take care of him. The surgeon of the Twelfth Hispania might save him, but only at the cost of his legs.'

Sempronius glanced at Cato with narrowed eyes and then said deliberately, 'Too bad we can't take him back to Matala.'

'Why not? It's only two hours down the road.'

'Two hours there, two hours back, more like three once we start riding in the dark. I'm sorry, Cato, but we can't afford to return to Matala. We have to press on.'

'Why?' Cato stared up at Sempronius. 'We should do what we can for him first.'

'There isn't time. Now leave him and let's go.'

'Leave him?' Cato shook his head. 'Like this? He wouldn't have a chance.'

'He doesn't have much of a chance as it is. You said so yourself.'

Cato was still holding the boy's hand. He bit his lip. 'No. I can't leave him, sir. It's not right.'

Sempronius took a deep breath. 'Centurion Cato, it's not a question of right or wrong. I'm giving you an order.'

There was a tense silence as the two men stared at each other. Then the child groaned slightly and Cato looked down and stroked the boy's fine hair with his spare hand. 'Easy now, lad. Easy.'

'Cato,' Sempronius continued in a gentle tone, 'we have to go on. We have to get to Gortyna as soon as possible. We have to do what we can to restore order, to help people and to save lives. There's not much we can do for this one. And if we lost the best part of a day by taking him back to Matala, then other lives might be put at risk as a result.'

'They might be,' Cato replied. 'Who can say for certain? But if we abandon this boy now, then we can be sure he will die, cold and alone.'

'Perhaps, perhaps not. He might be saved by someone.'

'Do you really believe that?'

'Do you really believe that a delay would not put lives at risk in Gortyna?' Sempronius countered.

Cato frowned, torn by the truth of the senator's words, and his own moral compulsion to do what he could to save the boy. He decided to try another tack. 'What if this was Julia? Would you still say we should go on?'

'But it isn't Julia, fortunately. Now, Cato, my boy, please see reason. You're an officer, with wider obligations to your duty, to your empire. I'm sure you have had to leave badly wounded men behind you on campaign. This boy is a casualty, and one you can do nothing for. Why, I dare say that the slightest movement would be the most terrible agony. Would you really put him through the torment of a ride back to Matala? Only for him to die there? It is kindest to leave him.' Sempronius laid his hand on Cato's shoulder and squeezed gently. 'Believe me . . . Now we have to go. Come.'

Cato felt a bitter pain in his throat as he fought to accept Sempronius's argument. Whatever his heart said, he had responsibilities to others, many others. He tore his eyes away from the boy's face and released his tender hold on the small hand. At once the fingers scrabbled and grasped at Cato's as the boy's eyes stared in terror. Cato hurriedly stood up and backed away, pulling his hand free.

'Come.' Sempronius drew him away, towards the tethered horses. 'No time to waste.'

As Cato turned and followed the senator, a shrill, keening cry of panic and terror split the dusk and pierced his young heart like a javelin. He felt that he wanted to be sick, that he was a cold, inhuman creature who had forsaken any claim to those qualities that defined a good man.

'We have to go.' Sempronius raised his voice, grasping Cato's arm and pulling him firmly away from the intensifying cries of the small boy. 'Get on your horse and let's be away. Don't forget what I said. Others need you.'

He steered Cato to the side of his mount and helped heave him up on to its back. Then he hurriedly untethered the horse and thrust the reins into Cato's hand before slapping the animal's flank to send it on its way with a shrill whinny. Sempronius mounted his own beast and spurred it on, after the other horse. When he drew alongside the centurion, he glanced at him quickly and saw the grim set of Cato's expression in the twilight. Sempronius felt a heavy weight of guilt settle on his heart. It had been a hard but necessary duty to leave the stricken child, and it had clearly affected Cato far more than himself. The young man had a good soul. He felt deeply, and was not afraid to show it. As Sempronius urged his horse ahead, there was one small grain of comfort he could glean from the situation. That was the realisation that his daughter had chosen her man well.

As night closed in over Crete they rode on, following the main route across the rich agricultural plain to Gortyna. On either side the groves of olive trees, fruit orchards and vineyards stretched out towards the distant hills. Much of the land had been bought up and concentrated in estates, owned by some of the wealthiest men of the empire. While they lived lives of luxury in the cities, the estates were managed for them by stewards. Beneath the stewards were the overseers who commanded the gangs of slaves that toiled from before dawn to dusk. For most of the slaves life was brutal and short and death was a release. Now, though, the situation had changed, Cato reflected. The earthquake had flattened many of the estates, and the slaves would snatch the opportunity to escape, or turn on their former masters.

It was a clear night, and even though a crescent moon and the star-speckled heavens provided dim illumination, Sempronius slowed the pace to a walk.

'No point in having the horses stumble,' he explained. 'Besides, they could use a rest.'

'So could I.' Cato shifted his buttocks and rubbed a hand on the small of his back. The night air was cool, and now he wondered at the wisdom of leaving his cloak with the dying boy. At once he dismissed the unworthy thought and glanced round at the surrounding landscape. The road climbed up on to a low ridge, and as they reached the crest Cato saw a fire blazing across the fields to his right, no more than quarter of a mile away.

'What in the name of the gods is going on over there?' Sempronius muttered.

Both riders reined in as they gazed towards the lurid red flames licking up into the night. A pyre had been built close to the ruins of a collection of farm buildings. Around it were four stout timbers with crosspieces, from which hung the naked bodies of three men and a woman, close enough to the fire to be scorched by the heat. They writhed in agony and their cries, thin and distant though they were, chilled Cato's blood.

In the glow of the flames, and the stark shadows of those slowly roasting on the crosses, Cato could make out a ring of figures watching the spectacle. Some of them carried jars and drank freely from them as they looked on. Others were dancing, while a few lobbed stones at their victims.

Cato swallowed. 'Looks like the slaves are taking their revenge.'

The two of them stared at the grim scene for a moment before the senator muttered, 'The poor bastards.'

'I fear this won't be the last time we witness this kind of thing,' said Cato. 'It will be breaking out across the island, I imagine.'

As they watched, a burly man emerged from the crowd with a mallet and went over to the cross bearing the woman. He knocked out the wedges, keeping the crosses in place, and then, bracing himself against the stake, pushed it towards the fire. The cross lurched over, hung still for a second as the woman thrashed uselessly against her bonds, and then toppled into the blaze in a burst of sparks and a sudden flare of flames that licked up into the night, along with a last scream of pain and terror.

'I've seen enough,' said Cato. 'We'd best go, sir.'

'Yes . . . yes, of course.'

Cato tugged his reins to turn the horse back in the direction of Gortyna, and was about to dig his heels in when he saw a figure stroll out on to the road, ten paces ahead.

'And where do you think you're going?' the man called out cheerily in roughly accented Latin. 'Two riders out on the road in the middle of night can't be up to any good.'

Senator Sempronius breathed a sigh of relief at the man's amiable tone, while Cato's sword hand slipped casually down to his thigh.

'You'd better get out of here,' said Sempronius. 'There's a slave gang on the loose nearby. You should escape while you can.'

'Oho!' the man called back and took a few paces towards the riders. 'From the sound of your voice, you must be part of the quality, a very proper Roman and no mistake.'

'I am a Roman official,' Sempronius acknowledged. 'I have to get to Gortyna as swiftly as I can, so I'd ask you to step aside, my good man, then we can all be on our way.'

The stranger was close enough now for Cato to make out some detail. He was tall and broad with unkempt hair and a beard, and dressed in a ragged tunic. A long club swung from his hand. He laughed as he lifted the club and let it rest on his shoulder.

'The thing is, this here road belongs to me now, and I've decided to charge a toll for road users.' His tone hardened. 'Beginning with you two. Now, get off those horses and hand them over. The horses and anything else of value you have on you.'

'What?' Sempronius stiffened in his saddle. 'How dare you?'

As the man had been speaking, Cato was aware of movement either side of the road, and now he could see several figures closing in around them. His fingers tightened around the handle of his sword as he spoke quietly. 'Sir, we're in trouble. Draw your sword.'

'Trouble?' Sempronius looked round and froze as he saw men emerging from the shadows, each one holding a club, or pitchfork, and all as ragged as the first man. There was a swift clatter as the two Romans snatched out their swords and held them ready.

'Now then, don't push your luck, gentlemen,' the man said evenly. 'No sense in anyone getting hurt. There's far more of us than you. You put up any fight and I swear I'll gut you both. So, nice and easy like, throw your swords away and get off those horses.'

Cato's heart was pounding and there was the familiar icy tingle on the back of his neck that came before a fight. He gritted his teeth and growled, 'Since you've been good enough to play fair by us, I'll give you one warning. Get out of our way.'

There was a moment of stillness as the two Romans stared intently at the men surrounding them, then someone roared:

'Get 'em, lads!'

The shadows raced towards the horsemen. Cato kicked his heels in. 'Ride, sir!'

Sempronius urged his mount forwards, but he was an instant slower to react than Cato, and before his horse had gone ten feet the man had snatched at the reins, while others rushed in from the side.

'Cato! Help!'

Cato twisted round in his saddle and saw the senator slashing wildly with his short sword at the figures flitting around him.

'Shit!' Cato hissed, and savagely wrenched the reins as he swerved his mount round. With his sword arm tensed he charged back into the loose melee about Sempronius. The horse let out a snort as it barged into the man holding the reins, and Cato slashed out with his sword in a wide arc, forcing the other men back. Then he gripped tight with his thighs as he swung across to the other side and hacked down at the hands still grasping the reins of Sempronius's horse. The blade thudded down, cutting flesh and shattering bone, and a shrill scream tore out of the man's lungs as he fell back staring in horror at his nearly severed hand. Cato leaned forward and snatched up the reins before pressing them towards the senator. 'Here!'

'Roman bastard!' a voice cried out, and Cato looked round just in time to see a man charging him with a pitchfork clutched in both hands. He snatched his sword blade back and chopped at the oncoming prongs. There was a sharp ring as metal met metal and Cato's blow knocked the prongs down, away from his chest. An instant later he felt a blow, like a punch, in his thigh, and there was a whinny from the horse as the other prong stuck into its side. Cato gasped, then snarled as he drew his arm back and slammed the tip of the blade deep into the man's chest, just below his neck. The attacker collapsed with a grunt, releasing his grip on the shaft of the pitchfork as he slumped to the ground. For a moment the shaft sagged, tearing at the flesh of man and horse, before Cato knocked it free with his sword. Then he glanced round, and saw that the two men he had put down had shaken the rest of the attackers.

'Go, sir!' he shouted at Sempronius.

This time he waited until the senator's mount had cleared the loose ring of men before he slapped the side of his blade into his own horse's rump and galloped after Sempronius. He heard a grunt, and another pitchfork narrowly flicked past his left side before dropping out of view. He ducked low, clenching his fist around the sword handle to ensure he did not drop it as they rode down the road to Gortyna. Behind them the attackers howled with rage and ran after them for a short distance, before giving up and hurling insults that gradually faded behind Cato as he followed Sempronius along the road.

CHAPTER SIX

Macro let out a weary sigh as he looked over the reports he had demanded from the officers and clerks of the auxiliary cohort. Outside night had fallen, and from the window of the office he could see the flickering glow of torches along the walls of the acropolis. He blinked and rubbed his eyes as his mouth opened in a long, wide yawn, before returning his attention to his work. Several wax note-books were stacked on his desk detailing the strength of each century in the cohort, with the names of the best men in each unit underscored by their centurions. Those dead or missing were marked with a cross. There was also a detailed inventory of the cohort's stores compiled by the quartermaster and a report from the only assistant assigned to the cohort's surgeon. The surgeon who had been in the port when the earthquake struck and was still missing. The barracks room that served as sick quarters was overflowing with injured, and the surgeon's assistant requested more men to help him deal with the casualties.

In addition to his other concerns, Macro had sent out a patrol to the bay to find the crew and passengers of the *Horus* and have them escorted back to the acropolis. They would be given shelter, and Macro would need the fittest of them to fill out the ranks of the cohort until the emergency was over.

As soon as he took command of the cohort, he had carried out a close inspection of the men formed up in their centuries in the courtyard of the acropolis. It was as Portillus had said: only half his men had survived when the earthquake struck Matala. Those that remained were badly shaken by the loss of their comrades, and the mortal terror they felt towards whichever god it was who had decided to wreak his fury upon the port. As Macro slowly paced along the ranks of the Twelfth Hispania, his experienced eye quickly saw that the cohort was typical of most of the garrison units stationed in the safer provinces of the empire. There was a mixture of worn-out veterans, impatiently awaiting their discharge, and those whose health had been broken on campaign and who had been transferred to Crete where they could manage to carry out gentle policing duties. Finally there was a handful of simpletons and scrawny youths who could just about be trusted to hold a weapon and not do themselves, or their comrades, any harm.

Macro shook his head. As things stood, the cohort was going to be little use in restoring order and helping the civilian survivors. He would need better men, and more of them, in the days to come. Meanwhile, he resolved to do what he could with the resources at hand. Not that there were many resources, he sighed. The quarter-master's inventory revealed that the cohort had been run down in recent years. A string of governors had done their best to cut the costs of running the province right down to the bone in order to curry favour with the emperor and senate back in Rome. Worn-out equipment had not been replaced and the soldiers had had to make up the shortfall in the local markets. They wore an odd assortment of standard-issue kit and a range of old Gallic and Greek helmets and swords. There were very few slings, almost no lead shot for them, and very few reserves of essential rations and drinking water. Two of the cisterns of the acropolis were bone dry and the third only half full, and what was left was barely potable, as Macro had discovered when he accompanied the quartermaster down the steps into the cool interior of the cistern, cut from living rock.

'That is fucking disgusting!' He spat out the rank-tasting liquid and wiped his mouth dry on the back of his hand before climbing back out. 'When was the last time this was drained and cleaned out?'

The quartermaster shrugged. 'Don't know, sir. Must have been before my time.'

'How long have you been here?'

'Seven years, sir.'

'Seven years,' Macro repeated flatly. 'And you just chose to ignore it?'

'No, sir,' the quartermaster replied indignantly He was a thin old stick, with dark, wizened features, but he carried the scars that spoke

53

of some active service, Macro conceded. The quartermaster continued. 'The prefect told me not to bother. Said that how as we were a garrison unit, and the province was at peace, there was no point in preparing for a siege, sir.'

'I see. Right, well, that's going to change. At first light I want you and your clerks down here. The cistern is to be drained, thoroughly cleaned, repaired and made ready to store any rain that falls.'

'Yes, sir.'

Macro stared at the quartermaster. 'Look here . . . what was the name again?'

'Corvinus, sir. Lucius Junillus Corvinus.'

'Corvinus, eh?' Macro smiled. 'Crow – it suits you. Now then, we have people out there who need our help. For now we are just going to help the survivors. Dig out any of those trapped in the ruins, then we have to feed them, see that they have fresh water and shelter. In the longer term we will need to make sure that there is order. If the food runs short then we're going to be hard pressed to keep things peaceable. In that event, I need every man of the Twelfth Hispania properly equipped and ready to fight. So that means you will need to pull your thumb out of your arse and make sure the men have what they need. Got that?'

'Yes, sir. I'll do my best.'

Macro shook his head. 'Best isn't good enough. You will do what I need you to do. If you can't do the job then I'll send you back to the ranks and find someone who can.'

'B-but you can't do that,' Corvinus stammered. 'I will protest to the prefect, sir. You have no authority to remove me.'

'You can protest all you like. The prefect is dead.'

'Dead?'

'He was killed when the earthquake hit Gortyna. Him and most of the senior officials running the province. That's why Senator Sempronius is taking charge of things. That's why I am in charge of the cohort, and why you are going to have to start earning your pay for the first time in years.' Macro paused and then gently punched the man on the chest. 'It's all down to us, Corvinus. We're all that stands between those people out there, and starvation and chaos. Now, I'll ask you one time only. Can you do your job?'

Corvinus took a deep breath and nodded.

'Good man! Now then, I want a full inventory of the cohort's kit in my hands before the first change of watch tonight. You'd best start now.'

'Yes, sir.' Corvinus saluted and turned away, hurrying across the courtyard to the supply office and storerooms. Macro watched him for a moment and then sighed. He hoped that this was going to be the briefest command he would ever hold. Just long enough to set the cohort back on its feet and deal with the crisis in Matala before a new prefect arrived. Then he, Cato and the others could continue their voyage back to Rome. The sooner the better, he mused as he made his way back to the prefect's office.

Once he had finished reading through the waxed note tablets, Macro sent for Portillus. While he waited, he helped himself to one of the small jars of wine that the prefect had kept in a small rack in the corner of the office. Several tiles had fallen in and smashed the jars in the upper section of the rack, but some at the bottom had survived. He tugged the cork stopper out and sniffed. A fine aroma wafted up into his nostrils and he smiled. Clearly the prefect had been a man who knew how to indulge himself. Shutting one eye, he peered into the jar.

'And half full.' He smiled to himself as he took the jar and a silvered cup back to the desk and filled the cup almost to the brim. 'Not a total disaster then.'

There was a knock at the door, and without waiting for a response, Portillus opened it and entered the office. A quick frown flitted across his face as he saw the wine, and then glanced to the surviving jars in the corner of the room. Macro realised that he had hoped to have them for himself now that the previous commander had no earthly use for such luxuries.

'Ahem, you sent for me, sir.'

'Yes. Shut the door.'

Once the door was closed and Portillus was standing at ease in front of the desk, Macro cleared his throat and began. 'This is not a good cohort, Centurion, as I am sure you know. The organisation is slack, the men are generally second-rate and the officers are worse.

However,' he paused, 'that is about to change. And since you are my second in command, you are going to help make that change. Is that clear?'

Portillus nodded doubtfully.

'I can't hear you, Centurion.'

'Yes, sir. It is clear.'

'Good.' Macro tapped the wax tablets. 'I want the best eighty men in the cohort to form a fighting century. They are to have the best of the kit, and they are to be commanded by the best officer. Who would you recommend?'

Portillus pursed his lips a moment before he replied. 'Centurion Milo, sir. He was promoted from the legions a year ago.'

'Then he shouldn't have gone soft yet. Fine, Milo it is. He is to choose his standard bearer, optio and clerk as he sees fit.'

'Yes, sir.'

'As for the rest of the men, they are going to work in the town at first light. They are to leave their kit here in barracks, but keep their swords, and divide into two teams. Half can deal with rescuing people from the ruins and carrying the injured up here to be treated. The others are to forage through the ruins for any supplies of food and wine. You can detail some of them to start carrying water from the nearest streams to start filling the cisterns.'

'But that'll take ages, sir.'

'Well, we're not going anywhere for the moment, are we, Portillus?'

'No, sir.'

'Fine, then those are the orders for tomorrow. Make sure the men are told that there is to be no pilfering, mind. If they encounter any civilian looters they are to put a stop to it. Knock heads together if you must, but don't go straight in with the blade. The people out there have suffered enough already. One final thing. According to Corvinus we have some tents in stores. They're old and probably haven't been used for years, but they might be serviceable for the local people. Have some of the men set them up on the slope facing the acropolis, outside of the town.'

Portillus nodded, and then chewed his lip. 'Sir?'

'What?'

'Something just occurred to me. Most of the food in Matala was stored down in the warehouses. Near the main market.'

'So?'

'The wave destroyed the area, and carried away most of the debris when it receded. What's left will have been ruined. The only other food will be what was in the houses when the earthquake struck. That won't amount to much, sir.'

'Hmm, you have a point.' Macro sat back and stroked his jaw. 'So we'll find what we can and then look for other sources of food. Any estates near to the port?'

Portillus thought for a moment. 'The nearest one is further along the coast, owned by Senator Canlius. It produces olive oil and grain.'

'That's good for a start then. I'll send some men with wagons. They can take what we need and let the landowner bill us when word gets back to him in Rome.'

'Senator Canlius won't like that, sir.'

'Probably not.' Macro sniffed. 'But it won't be my problem by then, so I don't care. We have to ensure a good supply of food so our men and the people don't starve while we sort things out.'

'Let's hope we can, sir.'

'Oh, we will.' Macro smiled. 'I won't stand for anything else. Now then, that's all for now, Portillus. I'll have the clerks draw up the assignments for each unit. They'll be with you and the other officers once they are ready. As soon as the sun rises I want the Twelfth Hispania to get to work.'

There was another knock at the door.

'Come!'

The door opened and an auxiliary entered the room and saluted. 'Patrol's returning from the bay, sir.'

'Have they got the crew and passengers with them?'

'Yes, sir.'

'Good. Soon as they are through the gates, have the men sent to the barracks. Spread them around. Once they're there, you can tell 'em they have just been inducted into the cohort and normal military discipline applies. Better explain what that means to them, eh?'

The auxiliary grinned. 'Yes, sir.'

'Have the women and children brought to the basilica. They can kip down in the admin hall. Then ask the senator's daughter if she would be kind enough to join me.'

'Yes, sir.' The auxiliary saluted and left the room.

Centurion Portillus raised an eyebrow. 'Sempronius's daughter? She's landed herself right in the middle of it. I doubt that the kid of a purple-striper is going to like the accommodation.'

Macro thought back to the desperate time when he had first encountered Julia during the siege of the citadel in Palmyra. She had taken her chances along with the rest of the defenders and had required no more than the meagre rations provided to the others, while devoting herself to the care of the wounded and the dying. Julia was no whining member of the pampered aristocracy. She had proved her worth.

'She'll cope,' Macro replied. 'She's no kid. Julia Sempronia is tough enough. Besides, she has no choice.'

Portillus puffed out his cheeks. 'I'd sooner you tell her that than me, sir. Perhaps I'd better be off then. Duties to attend to and all that.'

'Yes, get on with it,' Macro responded gruffly. 'Bear in mind what I said. There'll be no slacking in this cohort from now on, and that applies to officers as much as the men.'

'I understand, sir.' Portillus bowed his head and hurried from the room. For a moment Macro was alone, and he looked at his cup of wine for an instant before greedily raising it to his lips and draining it.

'Ahhh! Needed that.' He wiped a dribble of wine from his chin and eased himself back in the chair with a gratified smile. His entire body ached with the exertions of the previous day and night, and his eyes were sore. He closed them for a moment, relishing the soothing comfort of a brief instant of relaxation. The wine still tingled in his throat and felt warm in his stomach as he folded his fingers across his belly.

'Just rest a moment,' he told himself drowsily. 'Just a moment . . .'

'Am I disturbing you?'

'W-w-what?' Macro struggled up in the seat and blinked his eyes open. Julia was standing in the threshold of the office grinning at him.

'It's just that you were snoring so loudly.'

'Snoring?' Macro shook his head guiltily. 'Bollocks. I was just mumbling to myself.'

'With your eyes closed.'

Macro frowned at her. 'I can do two things at once, you know, miss.'

'I'm sorry, Macro. I meant no offence. You must be exhausted after all that we've been through. As are we all.'

'Where are my bloody manners?' Macro muttered to himself as he jumped to his feet and hurried to pull a spare chair over towards the table. He patted the seat. 'There you are, Miss Julia. Sit you down.'

'Thank you.' She let out a deep sigh. 'So, then, where is my father, and Cato?'

'Gone, miss.'

'Gone?'

'To Gortyna. Soon as we got here we heard that the governor, his staff and senior officers were caught up in the earthquake. Killed most of 'em outright. Your father said he had to take charge of things at once. He and Cato took two of the horses from the stables and left as soon as they could.'

'Typical,' Julia said with a trace of bitterness. 'No last word for me, then?'

'Er, not as such, no.'

'And Cato?'

'Oh, he said to be sure to send you his love and that I was to take care of you until he got back.'

Julia stared at Macro and shook her head. 'You're a poor liar, Macro. Better leave that sort of thing to people who are trained for it, like my father.'

'If you say so.'

Julia looked round the office and then through the window towards the hillside opposite the acropolis. A handful of fires had already been lit and tiny figures clustered about the glow of the flames. 'I could hardly believe what I saw on the way up here,' she said quietly. 'I thought we had had it bad on the ship. But this?'

'We did have it bad on the ship, miss. We're lucky to be here. But you're right, it must have been terrifying when it struck the port.

Portillus told me there was a bloody great roar and a rumbling sound, and then the buildings started to shake and collapse, the weakest and oldest ones first. Naturally, that was where the poorest people in Matala were packed in. Thousands of them are buried under the ruins. Then, as suddenly as it had started, it stopped. Poor souls who were left alive must have thought it was all over.' Macro shrugged. 'Until the wave hit the port, and swept up through the gorge some distance, destroying everything and everyone in its path. Portillus reckons that as many again were drowned as had died in the earthquake.'

Julia stared at him for a moment, then she shook her head and muttered, 'Dear gods . . . What can they have done to deserve this?'

'Who knows the will of the gods?' Macro yawned. 'But whatever the people of Crete have done to piss them off, they've paid a high price.'

Julia glanced out through the window, her mind still struggling to take in the scale of the destruction she had seen on the way up from the ship. It was impossible to imagine that many more towns and cities had shared the fate of Matala. Suddenly she froze. 'Do you think it's over? Do you think it could happen again?'

'I've no idea, miss. I'm just a soldier, not a soothsayer.' Macro leaned forward and tried to sound reassuring as he continued. 'There's been no more tremors since we arrived. We can only pray to the gods to spare us any more suffering.'

'Yes, there is that. If you really think prayers can help.'

'Well, they can't hurt.'

'I suppose not.' Julia was quiet for a moment before she fixed her gaze on Macro again. 'Do you think they're safe out there? My father, and Cato?'

'Don't see why not. They have their swords, and people have too much on their minds already without causing them any trouble. They'll be fine, miss. Cato's a tough lad. He'll see that your father gets through to Gortyna, and then they can start sorting things out. Trust me, Cato knows what he's doing. They'll be all right.'

CHAPTER SEVEN

'What the hell did we think we were doing?' Cato growled through clenched teeth as the senator tied his neck cloth tightly about the wound. 'We should have waited until light before setting off.'

'Shhh!' Sempronius glanced nervously at the surrounding trees. 'They might have followed us.'

'I doubt it. We must have covered at least two miles before the horse gave out.' Cato paused as another burning spasm shot through his leg. When it had passed he let out a deep breath and continued. 'I'm sure they'd have given up the chase long before then.'

'Let's hope so.' Sempronius tied off the knot and checked the makeshift dressing to ensure it would not slip. 'There. That should do it. It's my fault, Cato. I should have slowed the pace once we were clear. It was madness to keep galloping along the road in the dark like that. It's a miracle your horse didn't fall earlier on, or mine.'

'Well, we've only got the one now.' Cato smiled grimly. 'So no question of galloping anywhere.'

They had abandoned Cato's wounded horse back on the road where it had collapsed, bloody froth in its mouth and nostrils. Sempronius had hauled Cato up behind him and they had continued another mile before taking a narrow track off into a grove of pine trees and then stopping to tend to Cato's wound. The prong had passed through the muscle at the back of his leg without striking bone, or severing any major blood vessels. The wound was bleeding freely, but despite the pain, Cato found that he could still bear weight on his leg. He walked a few paces to the spot where he slumped down and let Sempronius examine and dress the wound as best he could in the dim light cast by a crescent moon and the stars.

Sempronius eased himself back and sat on the ground clasping his hands together in his lap. 'What do you think we should do now?'

'I don't fancy blundering into any more gangs of renegade slaves. Best to wait until first light when we can see the way ahead and avoid any trouble.'

'Yes, you're right.' Sempronius turned his head to look back in the direction of the road. 'Are you sure they were slaves?'

'I think so. They were all in rags, and we were near that estate where we saw . . .' Cato flinched at the memory and cleared his throat noisily. 'They must have gone to the road looking for easy pickings. We were lucky to get away. If those slaves, and what we saw back there, are typical of what is happening elsewhere on the island, then we've got more of a problem than I thought.'

'How so?'

'What if we find ourselves fighting a slave revolt?'

'A revolt? I don't think so. There's bound to be some temporary disorder. It's only natural that they would take advantage of the situation to turn on their overseers. Once they've drunk themselves insensible and woken up with a hangover, I'd be willing to bet they'd have no idea what they want to do next. Some might run off into the hills to try and join the brigands, but the rest will drift around the estate until someone comes along and sorts them out.'

'You think so?' Cato said doubtfully. 'I think you underestimate the danger, sir.'

'They're only slaves, my boy. Chain-gang slaves – the lowest of the low, little better than beasts. Trust me, they have no experience of making their own decisions. Without overseers to lead them, they won't have a clue what to do about the situation.'

'I hope you're right. But what if they did find a leader amongst their ranks? What then?'

'They won't. I've been on enough estates in my time to know how they operate. Anyone showing an ounce of spirit or independence is either sold off to a gladiator school, or broken and punished as an example to the rest. We'll have them back in hand before long. Once the ringleaders responsible for that sickening display we witnessed have been identified and rounded up, they'll be crucified and their bodies left to rot. I think that'll teach the rest a lesson they won't forget for a long time.'

Cato nodded. Yet he still felt uneasy. He had no idea quite how many slaves there were on the island. If they did manage to organise, and find a leader, then they would pose a grave danger to Roman interests in Crete. Nor were slaves the only concern. There were brigands up in the hills, criminals, runaway slaves and outcasts, who would be sure to exploit the chaos. If the slaves and the brigands made common cause, then nothing short of a major campaign would ensure that the island remained part of the empire.

He shifted and shuffled back to prop himself up against the stump of a felled tree. 'I think we should get some rest now, sir. We've been on the go for the best part of two days without sleep. I'll take the first watch. I'll wake you when it's time for your turn.'

'Fair enough, but make sure that you do. I can't afford to have you too tired to offer me help when we reach Gortyna.'

'I'll wake you, sir. On my word.'

'Very well.' Sempronius cast his eyes about the ground and then picked a spot by the next tree, where there was a soft mound of pine needles. He pulled his cloak around him and settled down, resting his head on a root. After a while, his breathing became steady and deep until he began to snore.

Cato leaned his head back and stared up at the heavens. It was a clear night, and stars and moon gleamed against a pitch-black backdrop. The view helped to calm his troubled mind for a moment and he wished that Julia was with him, nestled into the crook of his arm, her hair brushing softly against his chin. For a moment he recalled the aroma of her favourite scent and smiled faintly. Then a distant light caught his attention and he lowered his gaze and stared out across the dark landscape. A fire was flaring up on the plain, some miles away, and as he watched the flames spread quickly until a whole building was engulfed. He watched for a while longer, with a growing sense of foreboding in his heart.

Senator Sempronius took over and woke Cato just before dawn. Cato stirred, and found that he lay under the senator's cloak. He nodded towards it and muttered his thanks.

'You needed it more than me.' Sempronius smiled. 'It was easy enough to walk up and down to stay warm. Actually, it reminded me of my days as a junior tribune in the Ninth Legion on the Rhine. Not much comfort there, I can tell you. But I forget, you were stationed on the same frontier, weren't you?'

'Yes, sir. Once you've spent one winter there you never want to experience another. Cold as Hades.'

'Yes, I remember.' Sempronius shivered, and then offered Cato his hand. 'Come, we have to go.'

Cato groaned as he rose to his feet. His injured leg felt stiff and immediately began to throb as he put weight on it.

Sempronius regarded him anxiously. 'Bad?'

'I've had worse. As long as I get the wound cleaned and rested for a few days I'll be fine.'

'Rest is something that will be in short supply, I fear.'

He clambered up on to the horse's back and then leaned down to help Cato up. The horse staggered a little as it adjusted to the additional weight. Once Cato had tucked an arm around his waist, Sempronius clicked his tongue and walked the horse back down the track towards the road. As they emerged from the pine trees, Cato glanced in the direction of the fire he had seen the previous night, but there was nothing more than a blackened shell remaining. Several other burned-out buildings dotted the surrounding landscape, and a column of distant figures picked its way across a field. Whether they were slaves or civilians, Cato could not tell. The road ahead of them was clear, and Sempronius turned the horse towards Gortyna once again and proceeded at a steady trot.

They sighted several more bands of people as the sun rose and bathed the province in a warm glow. Along the road they also encountered a few more survivors picking over the remains of their property as they looked for valuables. Some just sat and stared vacantly as the horse rode by, while others held out their hands and begged for food. Sempronius did his best to ignore them as he stared ahead and kicked his heels in to move on as swiftly as possible. Now and again they came across bodies bearing sword and knife wounds, adding yet more death to the number of those killed by the earthquake. As the morning wore on, Cato wondered if there was anything that the senator and he could do to help restore order to the province in the face of such destruction and loss of life. The task looked quite hopeless.

At last, shortly before midday, the road curved round a hill and there ahead of them lay the provincial capital of Gortyna. The city spread across the plain with a fortified acropolis on a hill to the north. The wall was pierced by gaps where sections had collapsed. There were still some sentries on the main gate where the road entered the city. Beyond the wall they could see that nearly all the roofs had been damaged and there were gaping holes amid the red tiles of the largest public buildings and temples that remained standing. To one side of the city stood a sprawl of tents and makeshift shelters where smoke from small cooking fires trailed up into the blue sky.

Sempronius had raised a hand to shade his eyes as they approached the city. 'Seems to be less damage than we saw at Matala.'

'There would be. The people here did not have to cope with the wave as well. A small mercy perhaps.'

The sentries at the gate stirred warily as the two men on horseback clopped along the paved road towards the gate. When the horse was no more than fifty feet away their leader raised his arm and called out. 'That's close enough. What is your business here?'

Sempronius held out the hand with his ring. 'I am Senator Lucius Sempronius, come to see the governor of the province.'

The sentry leaned to one side and pointed at Cato. 'Who's that?'

'Centurion Cato. We were travelling to Rome by ship when the wave struck.'

'Wave?' The sentry approached cautiously as Sempronius reined in a short distance from the gate. 'We've heard that a wave had struck the coast, sir, but the stories we've been hearing are, well, a bit wild. Entire ports and coastal villages destroyed.'

'It's true,' Sempronius replied. 'We landed at Matala, what's left of it. That's where we learned that the governor was injured. I've come to see what the situation is.'

'It's bad enough, sir. There's hardly an officer left in the garrison; most of them were at the governor's palace when the earthquake struck. Only a handful of his guests escaped from the banquet hall when the roof fell in and buried the rest.'

'Where is the governor?'

'He's at the palace stables, sir. The stables survived well enough to be used as a hospital. That's where we've been taking the injured.'

Sempronius paused a moment. 'What's his condition?'

The sentry pursed his lips. 'The official word is that he'll recover.'

'But?'

The sentry glanced round and then lowered his voice. 'That's not what my mate in the palace guard says. If you want to speak to the governor, you'd best do it quickly, sir.'

'Very well, let us pass.'

The sentry nodded and turned to call to his men. 'Open the gate!'

There was a deep groan as the men thrust against the timbers of the right-hand door and it began to open. The groan changed into a grating sound and then a shrill squeal before it came to rest and would not budge any further. There was a gap just wide enough for the horse to pass through and the sentry shrugged apologetically.

'Sorry, sir, but the masonry has shifted and that's as far as she'll move.'

Sempronius nodded his thanks and edged the horse through the gap. Inside the city was the familiar panorama of shattered buildings and rubble strewn across the paved main street. There were more people amid the ruins and damaged buildings than there had been at Matala, and for the first time Cato began to feel a small measure of hope. Some settlements had evidently not been as badly affected as he had feared, but then, he mused, Matala had prepared him for the worst. The horse picked its way along the main street towards the heart of the city, past a marketplace where scores of stalls had collapsed and their ruined wares lay strewn about them, picked over by survivors. As they approached the centre of the city, the large civic buildings crowded the street on either side, and where they had collapsed Cato saw that great columns of stone had toppled like skittles, their sections laying scattered across the street and the steps leading up to where the temple doors had stood.

The governor's palace stood at the very centre of Gortyna, on the intersection of the two main streets. There was a tall outer wall, pierced by an impressive double-arched gatehouse, and inside a vast paved courtyard opened up on the other side. The palace, a fine building of white stone, looked as if it had been mauled by siege engines. There were great gaps in the walls and only a few expanses of tiles gave any indication of the original lines of the roof.

Sempronius sucked in his breath. 'It's a wonder anyone survived that.'

'Yes,' Cato muttered. 'That looks like the stables over there.'

He pointed to a narrow walled yard to one side of the main building. A small crowd stood or squatted outside, some holding infants or supporting others as they waited to be seen. Two army medics in black tunics were assessing the patients and admitting only those with the worst injuries. It was clear that the mood of the crowd was sullen, and Cato heard angry grumbling as they approached the stables.

'Make way there!' Sempronius called out. 'Make way, I said!'

The crowd parted in front of the horse and the expressions of those closest hardened as they stared up at the riders.

'The young 'un's wounded,' an old man growled. 'See there, on his leg.'

'Bastard's jumping the queue,' another voice called out, and at once there was an angry murmur sweeping through the crowd, and those still ahead of Sempronius refused to give way.

'Take your turn like the rest of us!'

Sempronius glared in the direction of the last shout. 'I am a Roman senator, damn you! Now do as you are told and move aside.'

'Fuck you!'

'One rule for the rich, another for the poor!' another man shouted.

'That's right!' Sempronius shouted. 'That's how it is. Now clear a path before I clear it for you!' He drew his sword to emphasise his words and dared anyone in the crowd to defy him. The people glared back, but as Sempronius kicked his heels in to move the horse on, they parted before him.

As he reached the arch and passed through into the courtyard, a man raised his fist and cried out, 'Bloody aristocrats! Our people die out here and they look after their own!'

The anger was taken up in other shouts and bitter cries, but Sempronius kept his face fixed in an expression of haughty contempt as he walked the horse up to a rail and slipped from the saddle to tether it. Cato dismounted beside him, wincing as a shaft of pain shot through his leg. He clasped a hand to his thigh as he looked round and saw a man in a dark tunic with red trim on the sleeves emerge from one of the stalls.

The man gestured towards Cato's leg. 'I'll have a look at that.' He wiped some blood off his hands with a soiled rag as he approached the new arrivals.

'Romans?'

Cato nodded.

The surgeon pointed at Cato's bandaged thigh. 'How did that happen?'

'We ran into some escaped slaves. One of them stuck me with a pitchfork.'

'Nasty. I'd better see to it.'

'Later. We need to speak to the governor.' Cato gestured to Sempronius. 'We have urgent business with him.'

'So does everyone.' The surgeon laughed mirthlessly. 'But he's in no condition to see anyone right now, poor devil.'

'That's too bad,' said Sempronius. 'I must insist that he sees us. Immediately.'

The surgeon shook his head. 'I can't let you disturb my patient. You'd better go and see Marcus Glabius if you want to know what's going on.'

'Who?'

'Glabius is in charge now. He persuaded the governor to appoint him as his successor yesterday.'

'What office did this Glabius hold before?' asked Cato. 'Civil administration? Military?'

'Neither. He was one of the province's tax collectors.'

'A tax collector?' Sempronius could not hide his disgust. 'Why on earth did Hirtius hand power over to a bloody tax collector? Surely there must have been an official on his staff he could have turned to?'

'No, they were all at the banquet when it happened. For some reason Glabius was late arriving. Otherwise . . .' The surgeon wearily ran a hand through his hair. 'In any case, they're close friends and business associates. Do I need to spell it out for you?'

Cato could guess the arrangement easily enough. Governor Hirtius sold the tax concession to Glabius for a knock-down price. In exchange, the two of them had a private arrangement whereby Hirtius quietly pocketed a percentage of the tax squeezed out of the islanders and any merchants who paid duties on cargoes leaving or arriving in Crete. A common arrangement throughout the empire, and one of the means by which provincial governors amassed a fortune during their term in office. It was an illegal practice, but since provincial governors accused of malpractice had the comfortable prospect of being tried before their peers, and those who aspired to be governors in turn, there was little prospect of prosecution. That said, governors had to be careful not to exact too much from a province lest their wealth provoke a dangerous degree of interest from the emperor. It was not unknown for an emperor to dispose of a wealthy Roman in order to confiscate his property.

'Just take us to the governor,' Sempronius said firmly. 'Right now.'

'If that is your wish.' The surgeon bowed his head. 'This way, sir.'

With Sempronius offering support to Cato, they followed the surgeon down the line of stables until they reached a large tack room at the end. It had been cleared out and a couch lay against the far wall. A man lay on the mattress. He was still, apart from the steady rise and fall of his chest. His breath came in laboured rasps. They crossed the room and Sempronius indicated a simple bench against one of the other walls and spoke to the surgeon. 'Give me a hand with that.'

As they dragged it over towards the couch, Governor Hirtius turned his head to the side to observe them. By the light of a small window high up on the wall Cato could see that one side of his face was heavily bandaged. A loose sheet lay across his body and covered his legs. Once Sempronius and Cato had settled on the bench, the surgeon stood by the couch and drew the sheet down to the governor's waist. His chest was bare and the pale skin was covered with black and purple bruising down his right side. Beneath the discoloured flesh the bones and muscle appeared to Cato to be misshapen. The arm had been broken and was fixed in a splint.

Sempronius leaned forward and spoke in a comforting tone. 'Greetings, Aulus Hirtius. We've met once or twice before, at the senate back in Rome.'

The governor licked his lips and nodded faintly before whispering hoarsely, 'Lucius Sempronius . . . I remember . . . What are you doing here?'

'I've come to take charge of the province.'

Hirtius's eyes widened and he made to raise his head as he responded sharply, 'Who sent you?'

The slight effort caused a sudden spasm of agony to course through the governor's body and he fell back with a keening groan as he gritted his teeth. The surgeon leaned over his patient anxiously.

'Lie still, sir. You must lie still.'

Sempronius waited until the tension left the governor's body and he was breathing more easily. Then he spoke again.

'No one sent me. My ship was passing the island when the earthquake struck. I learned that you had been injured, my friend, and came to offer my services. Now that I see you, it is clear that you'll need time to recover. As the ranking official in the province I should take charge, until you are ready to resume your duties.'

'No need . . . I have already found someone.'

'So I understand. But Hirtius, I cannot allow a tax collector to take on such a responsibility. They are corrupt dogs at the best of times. We cannot let such a man govern Crete.'

Hirtius struggled to raise a hand in protest. Sempronius took it and patted it gently. 'There's no need to worry now that I'm here. Your province is in safe hands. I swear it, on my honour.'

'No . . .' Hirtius slumped back with a deep groan, face muscles clenched as he fought a wave of agony. At length his body relaxed and beads of sweat trickled from his brow. His breathing was ragged as he stared at the ceiling and muttered, 'My wife, has she been found yet?'

'Wife?' The senator turned to the doctor and whispered, 'What's this?'

'Antonia. Apparently she left the feast shortly before the earthquake. Hasn't been seen since. But we're still finding bodies in the rubble. I fear it's only a matter of time before we find hers.'

'I see.' Sempronius gazed at the stricken governor for a moment and then turned to the surgeon. 'I'll leave him in your hands. Do your best for him.'

'Of course, sir.'

The senator lowered his voice. 'A brief word with you, if I may?'

He rose from the bench, gesturing to the others to follow him. At the door he paused and spoke softly to the surgeon. 'Will Hirtius live?'

'I'm doing what I can for him. With enough time, he might recover—'

'Spare me the bedside manner. Will he live? Yes, or no.'

The surgeon licked his lips and then shook his head. 'Both legs are crushed. He has internal injuries, crushed ribs and organs. I doubt that he will last more than a few days.'

'I see. Well, do what you can to make him comfortable then.'

The surgeon nodded.

Cato looked towards the couch. 'One other thing. Hirtius is to have no more visitors. Isn't that right, sir?'

'Yes,' Sempronius agreed. 'Of course. That is my strict order.'

'Not even Glabius?' asked the surgeon.

'Him especially, understand? He is not to disturb the governor. As far as everyone is concerned, Hirtius is glad that I have arrived to take charge. He has confidence in me and has granted me full powers over the province, until he has recovered or a replacement is sent from Rome. That's our story, and you will stick to it. Is that clear?'

'Yes, sir.'

'Good, then I want you to examine the centurion's wound. Clean it up and put on a fresh dressing. I need him as ready as he can be when I go to relieve Glabius of his temporary appointment.'

CHAPTER EIGHT

Macro mopped his brow and squinted up at the midday sun blazing in the clear sky. From the gatehouse of the acropolis he could see the teams of auxiliaries working amid the ruins, carefully searching for survivors beneath the rubble. Once they had been located, the long process of digging them out began. Some were found easily enough, but many were trapped under several feet of masonry and had suffered terrible injuries. Still, he conceded, Portillus and his men were proceeding in a methodical manner as they worked their way across the city towards the gorge that led to the port. A number of slaves worked alongside the soldiers; those who had chosen to remain after the earthquake. Most of the surviving slaves had taken the chance to run away. They would be recovered in due course, and punished, Macro reflected. Many slaves were branded and would find it hard to blend in amongst those who were free. Their only other choice was to hide in the wilderness, a precarious existence that had few attractions over slavery.

On the slope outside of Matala the goatskin tents from the auxiliary cohort's stores had been set up, and several hundred people were now sheltering from the sun in their shade. There were still another two thousand people who had lost their homes and had to make do with sleeping in the open, or finding what shelter they could in the clumps of trees that grew higher up the slope. There was a stream up there, and a plentiful supply of water flowed from the mountains that formed the spine of the island. Macro could see a number of townspeople carrying full skins and amphorae back to the tents, and at the base of a small waterfall near the top of the hill a handful of children were splashing happily in the glittering silver cascade.

Even though they had a good supply of water, the most pressing problem was food. It had been three days since he had taken command of the cohort, and at once it was clear that the port was desperately short of supplies. A small amount had been gleaned from the estates of Canlius and the ruins of Matala and added to the meagre reserves in the acropolis. Macro had been forced to issue an edict that any private stocks of food must be surrendered to the cohort. From there a daily ration would be issued to the survivors. Those who were caught hoarding food, or dealing food in the black market, would be denied rations and banished from the city and its environs. If they attempted to sneak back in and were caught then they would be locked into one of the cisterns, which Macro had chosen for a temporary prison. The last item on the edict warned that those who were caught attempting to steal food from the cohort's stores would be summarily executed.

There had been protests when the edict had been read out in the camp, and the mob had readily accepted a mouthpiece in the form of the father of the merchants' guild, a stocky individual named Atticus, who could have passed for Macro's brother, if he had had one. Macro held firm in the face of the protests and raised his hands to calm the crowd, and when that had not worked he drew his sword and rapped it sharply on the rim of one of his men's shields. When the last angry murmur had died away, he drew a deep breath and pointed at Atticus.

'I don't care what you think. We must ration what food we have, or people will starve. Once the food supply to the town is restored, then things can return to normal. Until then we must have discipline, and patience.'

Atticus snorted. 'And you would have us believe that you and your men don't take more than your fair share, I suppose?'

'I will see to it that the food is fairly shared,' Macro replied in his parade-ground voice, so that all might hear him. 'Priority will go to those who are helping to find survivors and supplies in the ruins, and those who are responsible for ensuring order.'

'Ha!' Atticus raised his hands and clapped. 'I knew it. The army takes care of its own and damn the rest of us! Well, Centurion, we won't stand for it.' He turned to address the crowd. 'I say we keep whatever food we have for ourselves! Let the soldiers fend for themselves!'

The mob cheered his words and Atticus milked his support for a while, pumping his fists in the air, before crossing his arms and turning back to Macro with a smile.

'Quiet!' Macro bellowed. 'QUIET, I SAID!'

But this time there was no response from the crowd, who continued to jeer and whistle and shake their fists.

At length Macro gave up and turned to the twenty men he had brought with him to lend force to his authority. 'Let 'em hear it, lads!'

The soldiers drew their swords and began to pound the inside of their shields, filling the air with a deafening drumming that drowned out the din of the crowd. Gradually they fell quiet and Macro gave the order for his men to still their weapons.

'That's better. Now then, I have told you how I intend to run things, and it will be so. I will not tolerate any attempts to undermine my authority as acting prefect of the cohort. If anyone wishes to increase their rations then they will have to work for it by helping the cohort's work parties searching the ruins. In addition, I could use more men to replace those lost in the disaster. If there are any men out there with previous military experience then they may apply to enlist at the acropolis.'

'Don't do it!' Atticus called out to the crowd. 'Don't betray the rest of us. If we stand up against this bully, then there's nothing he can do!'

'Right!' Macro clicked his fingers. 'That does it. First section! Arrest that man, at the double!'

Atticus's mouth opened in surprise, but before he could react, the auxiliaries had surrounded him and two of them sheathed their swords and pinned his arms behind his back. He struggled uselessly for a moment while the crowd began to protest angrily. Macro kept his calm and gave the order for his men to march back to the acropolis, pursued by the jeers and insults of the mob. He took up position beside Atticus and the men holding him.

'This wouldn't be necessary if you had been a good boy and kept your mouth shut.'

Atticus sneered. 'That's what all tyrants say.'

'Tyrant?' Macro pursed his lips. 'Me? No, I'm just a soldier trying to do his job, and you, mate, are a loudmouth pain in the arse. So spare me any comments about freedom and tyranny. You can save it for when this is all over.'

Atticus glared at him. 'You have me now, Centurion, but there will be a reckoning one day.'

'Sure.' Macro nodded. 'I'll make a note of it.'

'I'll have you!' Atticus spat. 'You pig!'

Macro suddenly lashed out with a clenched fist, striking Atticus squarely on the temple. With a grunt, he collapsed into the grip of the soldiers on either side. Macro shrugged. 'So much for tyranny. Get him to the cistern, and make sure no harm comes to him on the way. He can stay there for a couple of days to cool off before we let him go.'

The small column of soldiers picked their way along the main street and back to the acropolis. Macro saw that Julia was standing by the gate as they marched up the ramp. He had sent some men into the town to find some clothes for her amongst the ruins and she was wearing a pale blue tunic that reached down to her ankles. Macro bowed his head in greeting.

'Morning, miss. Had a good night's sleep?'

'Yes thank you.' She smiled briefly. 'Is there any word from Gortyna?'

'Not yet. I sent a message yesterday. We should get a reply by nightfall. Should put your mind at rest.'

'I hope so.' Julia pulled at a strand of her dark hair. 'It's hard not to worry about my father and Cato. I'm sure that Cato would have sent word as soon as he could to say that they were safe.'

'If the situation here is anything to go by then I expect they're up to their necks in it over at Gortyna. But I'm sure they'll send news the first moment that they can. Don't fret, Miss Julia. Your dad's a tough one, and Cato's as smart as new paint. They'll be fine, trust me.'

Julia nodded a little uncertainly and was silent for a moment before she continued. 'How long do you think we'll be here?'

Macro stepped aside from the column of soldiers and undid the strap of his helmet before removing it and wiping his brow. 'Difficult to say. There's plenty of shipping that puts into Crete, so word of what has happened here will reach Rome soon enough.'

'I haven't noticed any new ships in the port since we arrived.'

'True,' Macro conceded. 'That wave must have had a wide effect. It's possible that it did for the ships close to the island. Perhaps there will be others who have heard the news and are wary of landing in Crete. But someone will put into one of the island's ports sooner or later. They'll get the story, and carry it onwards to Rome. Once the emperor grasps the scale of the damage that's been done here, then he'll be sure to send help.'

'Help? What kind of help?'

'Troops, food, and a replacement governor as soon as he appoints one. When they arrive, then your father and the rest of us can leave, and take the first ship back to Rome.'

'And how long will it be before help arrives?'

Macro frowned as he made a rough estimate of the distances involved. 'Realistically, I'd say it'd be two months before the first ship comes from Rome.'

'Two months? Two months!' Julia gestured towards the tents. 'With the amount of food we have, those people aren't going to last two months. There has to be some quicker way to get help. What about the closest provinces? Egypt, Cyprus or Greece?'

'They will do what they can. But the trouble is, I imagine they'll be wary of doing anything without requesting permission from Rome.'

Julia shook her head. 'That's madness.'

'That's bureaucracy, miss.'

'But we have to help these people.'

'We are helping them. What they need is order, and that's what I am giving them. Once that is established then I can deal with the food and make sure that everyone is fed as well as our stocks allow. It's going to be tough, on all of us. Mollycoddling a civilian mob is not the kind of situation I'm used to handling, to be honest, miss.'

'So I can see,' Julia responded in an acerbic tone as she nodded towards the column escorting Atticus. 'That was very well handled. I'm sure that little incident has helped to win the people round.'

'Now that is out of order.' Macro frowned. 'I'm not standing for election, miss. I just want to do the best for those who have survived. I want to give them a decent chance to live through this and get back to some kind of normal existence. If that means I have to use methods that don't go down well with the mob, and troublemakers like Atticus there, then that's just tough.'

'On you? Or them?'

'On all of us.' Macro repositioned his felt skullcap and put his helmet back on. 'If that's all, miss, I have work to do.'

He strode off after his men, still fastening his helmet straps. Julia watched him for a moment, knowing full well that she was in the wrong. She had been acquainted with Macro long enough to know that however direct and harsh his methods might seem, his purpose was always well-meaning and fair. By the time she had decided to make her apology, Macro had already entered the headquarters building and disappeared from sight.

Julia slapped her hand against her thigh, furious with herself, and then turned away from the acropolis and gazed out across the tented slope. The crowd that had gathered to hear Macro's announcement was slow in dispersing, and little knots of people still clung together, no doubt voicing their anger. Macro had authority over them for the moment, she reflected, but when the food began to run out, hunger and despair would tear apart the present fragile order. She shuddered at the prospect, and then slowly made her way back through the gate into the acropolis. There was nothing for her to do. She had volunteered her services to help the cohort's surgeon tend the wounded, but he had rebuffed her curtly, saying that the hospital was no place for a senator's daughter. When she had tried to argue the case, pointing out that she had performed such duties during the siege at Palmyra, the surgeon had bitterly remarked that the people of the east were barbarians. Different standards applied in Crete.

Much as Julia hoped the surgeon was right, she had seen enough of the world to know that any civilisation was only ever a few meals away from anarchy and the bloody chaos that would inevitably follow. The thought immediately made her long to be reunited with her father and Cato. She felt a pang of longing for Cato and wished he was with her, making her feel safe.

'I hope you haven't called me here to waste my time,' said Macro as he placed the torch in an iron bracket and sat down on the bottom step of the cistern to look at Atticus. The Greek was chained by the ankle to the rock wall. His white tunic was streaked with filth. He had been in the prison for only one night, and the dark, the damp stench and the isolation had acted on him with impressive speed. 'You told the sentry it was important.'

'It is. I want to offer you a deal.'

'Really?'

Macro smiled thinly. 'What kind of a deal? Are you going to promise to be a good boy if I let you go?'

'Yes. I'll behave.'

'I see, and why should I trust you to behave? You see, I have no more faith in your word than you have in mine.'

Atticus licked his lips nervously. 'I know where to find food.'

'So do I; we keep digging in the ruins.'

'I mean, I know where we can find a lot of food. Enough to feed the people for many days.'

'Oh. And where would this food be?'

'The farming estate of a friend of mine.'

'Where?'

'On the coast, not far from here. The estate belongs to Demetrius of Ithaca.'

'We've already tried there. I sent a patrol yesterday. They came back empty-handed. It seems the slaves, or their brigand friends, had got there ahead of us and emptied the grain pits.'

Atticus smiled. 'That's what you think. Demetrius is a cautious man. Being close to the sea, he was always worried about raids from pirates. So he kept his valuables, and nearly all his produce, in a small compound a mile or so from the main estate. The entrance is easily missed, and the compound is protected by a palisade. I dare say that Demetrius will have headed there the moment the earthquake ended.'

'Assuming he survived.'

'I don't doubt that he did. He's a resourceful man.'

'I assume that you could lead us there.'

'In exchange for my freedom . . . and a reward.'

'Once you give me the directions to this compound,' Macro responded. 'If you're right, then I'll think about letting you out.'

'Nothing doing. You either let me show you where it is and let me go, or you can starve for all I care.' Atticus gestured casually. 'Of course you could always torture me to reveal the location and then have me quietly killed.'

Macro nodded slowly. 'Not a bad idea, that. A red-hot poker up the arse is usually pretty good at loosening tongues. I could give it a go, if you like.'

Atticus looked hard at Macro, trying to gauge if the other man was joking, but there was a dangerous glint in Macro's eyes and the Greek swallowed quickly. 'I'll show you where it is, and then you can set me free.'

'I'll think about it.'

'I won't co-operate unless you guarantee my release,' Atticus said with as much defiance as he could manage.

'It's too late to strike a deal, my friend. You've already told me you have something I want. I don't suppose for a moment that you want to take that knowledge with you to the grave. So, it's just a question of torturing you until you give it up. And if, by some miracle, you are a much tougher bastard than I take you for, then you might die before spilling your guts. I shan't complain if there is one less mouth to feed . . . once we've finished pulling you to pieces, a bit at a time.' Macro sat back and scratched his chin nonchalantly. 'So then, what's it to be? Tell me what you know, or let me prise it out of you?'

Atticus gritted his teeth as he let out a long hiss of breath. 'All right, I'll take you to the compound. Then will you release me?'

'You play fair by me, and I'll do the same for you,' Macro replied. He stood and turned to climb back up the steps.

'Hey! What about me?' Atticus called after him.

Macro paused and looked back. 'Tyrant you called me. That, I can live with. Pig, on the other hand, takes a little time to get over. Another night in here will do wonders to help you develop a due sense of deference. Sleep tight.'

CHAPTER NINE

The small column left Matala at daybreak. Macro took forty men armed with spears from his fighting century to escort four wagons, all that could be drawn by the available horses and mules. A handful of civilians had volunteered to drive the wagons and act as porters. Atticus, unshaven and blinking, was taken out of the cistern and chained to the driver's bench of the leading wagon. He scowled at Macro as the latter strode past and took position at the head of the leading section. Centurion Portillus had already provided him with directions to the estate and Atticus would direct them from there to the compound. Macro had left Portillus to command in his absence. With Centurion Milo, the other five sections of the fighting century, and the men detailed as rescue parties, he should have more than enough strength to deal with any trouble from the refugees in Macro's absence.

Macro took a last look down the column to make sure that every-one was ready, then waved his hand and swept it forward. The leading sections stepped out, their nailed boots grinding the loose chippings on the dried-out surface of the road. Behind them came the steady clop of the horses and mules and then the deep rumble of the wagon wheels. At the tail of the column the remaining two sections paced forward as a few refugees looked on. They watched the convoy for a short while, then returned to the daily struggle to search the ruins for food and anything of value that could be hoarded until after the crisis was over and normal life could begin again.

The road climbed a short distance inland before joining the main route that stretched along the southern coast of Crete. A milestone marked the distance to Gortyna, and Macro led the column in that direction. There had still been no word from Cato and Sempronius, and Macro was beginning to worry. Something might have happened to them on the road to the provincial capital, but short of sending out a search party, or travelling the same route himself, there was no way of knowing for sure. He tried to thrust the concern from his mind as he took in the surrounding countryside. As the road reached the fertile plain that stretched across much of the southern side of the island, a vista of farmland spread out on either side, dotted with the hovels of smallholders, the much larger structures of estates, and here and there a small village. They came to a junction beside a milestone and, following the directions given to him by Portillus, Macro led the column off the main road and down the lane towards the estate of Demetrius. The column tramped along the peaceful lane as insects droned lazily between the flowers that fringed the route.

'Sir.' One of the auxiliaries in the leading section suddenly pointed ahead.

At first Macro saw only an untidy bundle of rags, then quickly realised it was a body. He threw up his arm and called out, 'Halt!'

While the men and wagons ground to a stop, Macro cautiously made his way down the stony lane, warily glancing from side to side as he approached the body. It was a man who must have had an imposing physique when he was alive, despite his sparse grey hair and worn features. The body lay curled up on its side in a ball. The skin was livid with bruises and cuts. Beneath the skin, lumps and swellings indicated where bones had been broken, and the once strong jaw had been pulverised so badly that the misshapen face would have been barely recognisable to anyone who had known him in life.

Macro squatted down to examine the body, wrinkling his nose at the ripe odours of decay. The tunic was of a good quality and the belt was decorated with silver fittings. The man wore army boots, old but well looked after, and a tough leather whip was wrapped tightly about his throat. His tongue protruded from his swollen lips and his eyes bulged in their sockets. The brand of Mithras was clearly visible on the forehead, and Macro realised that he was looking at a legionary veteran. Discharged from the army, he had taken a job as an overseer of slaves. The hard life of the legions made such men well suited to the task, and also made them the first target of the wrath of slaves if they rose in rebellion.

Slipping his hands under the body, Macro rolled it off the road and into the grass at the verge. Rising back to his full height, he waved the column on and the men trudged past the corpse, briefly glancing over it as they went by. The more experienced and nervous of the men began to survey the surrounding landscape warily now that they had seen this first sign of danger. A short distance from the body, the lane passed through a grove of olive trees and then emerged before an extensive sprawl of buildings and empty grain pits. Immediately in front of them was an imposing gateway leading into the villa of the estate owner. A quarter of a mile away lay the slave compound. There were large gaps in the wall through which Macro could see the remains of the long barrack blocks in which the slaves were locked up each night. There was no sign of life there now.

The bitter tang of burning wafted through the air, and Macro halted the column once more outside the gate.

'First section, with me!'

His fist tightened round the handle of his sword as he warily approached the entrance to Demetrius's villa. One of the gates was still in place but the other had been thrust open, and Macro warily led his eight auxiliaries inside. There was a large open courtyard surrounded by a colonnade, which had supported a tiled roof before the earthquake. Now the shattered tiles lay in heaps about the columns. Opposite the gate stood the burned-out shell of the main residence. Blackened walls and charred timbers stood stark against the clear sky. In the centre of the courtyard lay the remains of a large bonfire: a tangle of burned wood, unrecognisable black lumps of matter and ashes. Around the remains of the fire were three tall beams and crosspieces. A body was nailed to each, facing the fire. The rear of each body was unharmed, and coloured cloth still clung to the corpses. However, on the side facing the fire they had been slowly roasted. The cloth had charred and the skin was black and blistered. Their lips had been curled back by the heat, exposing the teeth, which now seemed to grin at the horrified soldiers standing beneath them.

Macro picked up the lightly burned end of a shaft of wood and prodded the charred debris.

'Looks like someone went into the fire.' He turned and scanned the ground until he saw the hole into which the fourth beam had been dropped. The end of the beam still protruded from the remains of the fire. 'There. Looks like the slaves pushed one of their victims into the flames.'

'Fucking awful way to die,' muttered one of the auxiliaries.

Macro dropped the shaft and glanced round the inside of the courtyard. 'Well, there ain't a good way to die. Come on, lads. We've seen enough. Nothing to be done here.'

Outside, the men who had remained in the column looked curiously at the ashen expressions of the section Macro had taken inside. He made his way over to the wagon where Atticus was chained to the bench and ordered the driver to remove the shackles. Atticus rubbed his ankles and nodded towards the villa.

'Any sign of Demetrius?'

'Wouldn't know what he looks like. In any case, it's impossible to tell who any of them were.'

Atticus looked at him quickly. 'What happened in there?'

'Looks like the slaves decided to take revenge on their master and his family. Cooked 'em alive.'

'Sweet gods . . .' Atticus swallowed, then looked round anxiously. 'Do you think the slaves are still nearby?'

Macro shook his head. 'Not if they're sensible. You know the law – if any slave kills his master, then every slave in the household has to be executed. My guess is that once they realised what they'd let themselves in for, they ran for the hills.'

Atticus's expression hardened. 'Then they must be hunted down and killed.'

'All in good time,' Macro replied evenly. 'Right now I want you to take us to Demetrius's food hoard.'

'Yes, of course.' Atticus took one last glance at the villa gates, then drew a deep breath and pointed to a narrow track heading away from the buildings towards a distant line of pine trees. 'Over there.'

The column continued forward, eager to be away from the stench of the burned villa. Just before they reached the trees there was a shout from one of the wagons, and Macro turned to see the driver pointing across the open ground towards a jumbled cluster of rocks half a mile away. Three figures were standing on the highest rock, watching them.

'Slaves,' Atticus muttered through clenched teeth. 'We should take them. Centurion, send your men after those murderous bastards.'

There was grumbled agreement from the nearest auxiliaries, but Macro shook his head. 'Nothing doing, Atticus. We can't spare the men for a chase. Besides, my lads can't outpace them in full armour. In any case, they'll know the ground around here. Chances are they'll lead our men into a trap.'

'You're letting them get away?' Atticus said with a shocked expression.

'Can't help it. Right now we have more important things to deal with. The slaves can wait for the moment.' Macro cleared his throat and called out harshly, 'Keep moving! Move, you idle bastards!'

They entered the pine trees and the track wound its way through the dappled light. Macro scanned the route ahead, and the shadows on either side, as they progressed for over half a mile.

'You had better be right about this food hoard,' he said quietly.

'I know the way,' Atticus replied. 'I just hope the slaves haven't been there and taken it already. Chances are that quite a few of them knew of it.'

Macro nodded. 'Let's hope they thought better than to burn it down. The slaves have got to eat too.'

The track turned sharply to the left and descended into a gorge with steep sides, a perfect spot for an ambush, Macro decided, as he glanced up at the boulders strewn across the slopes. If those were tumbled down on to the column they would smash the wagons to pieces, and crush any man or horse in their path.

'How much further?'

'We're there.' Atticus raised his hand and pointed. 'Through the trees, see?'

Macro squinted and saw that the track began to open out into a clearing a hundred paces ahead. On either side the slopes of the gorge spread out. As the column entered the clearing he saw a sizeable wooden stockade, twice the height of a man. There was a watchtower at each corner and a stout pair of gates where the track ended. A number of bodies lay in front of the wooden walls, struck down by arrows and light javelins.

'Seems that the slaves paid a visit after all,' said Macro. 'Someone was here to see them off.'

'Stop there!' a voice called out from the stockade, and Macro saw that several men had appeared above the sharpened stakes that formed the wall. Each man carried a javelin, and there was further movement in the nearest watchtowers as bowmen climbed the ladders. A figure above the gate cupped a hand to his mouth and called out again, 'I said stop where you are!'

'Halt!' ordered Macro. He stepped forward and raised a hand in greeting. 'We're from Matala. Twelfth Hispania. Centurion Macro.'

'Centurion Macro? Never heard of you.'

'I arrived shortly after the earthquake.'

'How convenient!' the man above the gate replied caustically. 'Begone! Before I order my men to shoot you down.'

Macro looked back over his shoulder. 'Atticus! Come forward!'

The men parted as Atticus eased his way through the front ranks of the auxiliaries and stood beside Macro.

'Do you know that man up there?' Macro pointed.

Atticus strained his eyes for a moment and then smiled. 'Why, yes! That's Demetrius.' He stepped forward and called out. 'Demetrius of Ithaca, it's me, Atticus!'

There was a brief pause before the man above the gate responded in a relieved tone. 'Atticus! You survived. No surprise there. Who's your friend? I know the officers of the Twelfth, but I don't recognise him.'

'He arrived after the earthquake, like he says.'

'Fair enough . . .' Demetrius turned to call down into the stockade. 'Open the gate!'

With a faint creak from the ropes that acted as hinges, the gates swung inwards and a moment later Demetrius emerged, smiling, as he advanced on Atticus and Macro. After clasping arms with his friend, the estate owner turned to examine Macro.

'A relation of Atticus?'

'I think not,' Macro snorted.

'Well, you could be mistaken for a brother.'

'Really? Well, that's something I shall just have to live with.'

'A prickly friend you have here, Atticus.'

'He's no friend.' Atticus shook his head. 'What happened here? We passed what was left of the villa. When we saw the bodies I feared that you had been killed.'

Demetrius frowned. 'Bodies? What do you mean? What has happened to my villa?'

'Surely you know?'

'If I did, I wouldn't be asking. Tell me.'

Macro cleared his throat. 'The place has been burned down by the slaves. We found the body of an overseer a short distance from the villa, and four more bodies inside.'

The blood drained from Demetrius's face. 'When I brought my family down here I left my steward in charge with a handful of men I could trust.'

'What happened back there?' asked Macro. 'After the earthquake?'

Demetrius was silent for a moment, as he collected his thoughts. 'The slaves had been working late that evening, and had only just come back from the estate when the earthquake struck. I was with my family in the garden. If we had been inside, then we would have shared the fate of the kitchen staff, and been crushed and buried alive. As it was, they were the only ones we lost. I left orders for the slaves to repair as much damage as possible while we took shelter down here. My steward reported to me on the first evening after the earthquake, and said that the slaves were being kept in their place by the overseers and the repairs to the compound wall were under way. So I thought all was well, until he failed to report the following evening, and the one after. That was when they appeared.' He indicated the bodies. 'Turned up at dusk and demanded that I open the gates. When I said no, they charged the gate. I told my men to stop them, and as you can see, that did the job. They melted away into the trees. We've been keeping a close watch for them ever since,' Demetrius concluded wearily. 'Whoever they are.'

Macro nodded towards the bodies. 'Those aren't your slaves?'

'One or two of them. The rest are strangers.'

Macro stared at the nearest bodies for a moment, deep in thought. 'That's worrying. I had hoped that this was a local uprising. But it seems that your slaves must have been led on by outsiders. Possibly brigands from the hills who have come to stir things up and grab some loot, or slaves from another estate. Either way, your slaves are in open revolt now. They'll have to be dealt with when I get the chance.'

'Dealt with?' Demetrius looked alarmed. 'But I have a fortune invested in them.'

'Well, it seems that your investment has just turned sour,' Macro responded flatly. 'Sour enough to burn down your villa, and roast your steward and some others into the bargain.'

'When I find the ringleaders, I'll make them pay dearly,' Demetrius said bitterly, and then quickly looked at Macro. 'But why have you come here? To rescue us?'

'No, but you and these others are welcome to join us when we return to Matala.'

'So why are you here?'

'I've come for whatever supplies of grain, olives and any other foodstuffs you have in your stockade.'

Demetrius's eyes narrowed. 'You've come to take my property?'

Macro nodded. 'I am here to commandeer it. Due note will be made of everything we take away on the wagons, and you can apply for compensation once order is restored to Crete. Now, if you don't mind, I want the wagons loaded as quickly as possible. If there are rebellious slaves on the loose we should return to Matala before dark.' Macro turned to call an order back to the waiting column. 'Get the wagons into the stockade and load 'em up!'

'Wait!' Demetrius grasped Macro's arm. 'You can't take my property. I forbid it.'

'The people in Matala need feeding. There's not enough food in the town and we need yours. Sorry, but there it is.' Macro lowered his gaze to the Greek's hand. 'Now, if you don't mind stepping aside, my men can get on with it.'

'No. No! You can't. I won't allow you to.'

Macro sighed. 'I see. Well then . . . First section! Arrest this man. Disarm his followers. If anyone tries to resist, then knock 'em on the head.'

'What?' Demetrius stared about wildly as he was seized by two of Macro's men. The rest of the column marched on into the stockade, together with the wagons. As Macro had suspected, without

Demetrius to lead them, his retainers meekly surrendered their weapons and stood in a little group, under guard, as the soldiers and volunteers began to load the first sacks of grain and jars of olives on to the beds of the wagons. Demetrius continued to complain, loudly, until Macro drew his sword and patted the flat against the palm of his hand.

'Do be a good man and pipe down, eh? Otherwise I'll have to make you.'

'You wouldn't dare,' Demetrius spat back defiantly.

'He would,' Atticus interrupted. 'Believe me. Best do as he says. For now.'

The estate owner stared at his friend for an instant, and then his shoulders slumped as he gave way and sat heavily on one of the piles of grain sacks that stood between the low storerooms that filled the stockade.

'That's the spirit.' Macro smiled reassuringly.

The wagons were loaded as fully as possible, and the axles creaked and groaned under the load as the drivers steered them out of the stockade and back up the track towards the villa. Macro made a last attempt to persuade Demetrius to come with them, but the landowner was adamant that he wanted to protect what was left of his stock of food supplies. With a brief show of reluctance, some of his men opted to go with the column. A handful remained behind with him and watched as the column gradually disappeared into the pine trees that grew on the sides of the gorge.

As they headed back up the track, Macro turned to Atticus and muttered, 'Your friend is a fool. He might have driven the slaves off the last time. But if they grow in strength they'll be far more determined next time. Demetrius and the others will end up like those I saw at the villa, in all likelihood.'

'You really think so?'

'Hard to be sure,' Macro conceded. 'But it seems that the slaves are beginning to organise. If that's the case, then we may have quite a problem on our hands. Things could get pretty rough, right across the island.'

Atticus was silent for a moment. 'I hope you're wrong.'

'So do I,' Macro replied quietly, surveying the sides of the gorge as the heavily laden column slowly made its way along the track. As they emerged from the gorge he let out a sigh of relief. A short distance further on, the track began to pass through a thicker concentration of pine trees, and then, a little way ahead, it emerged from the trees on to open ground. In the distance Macro saw the remains of the villa. As he turned to Atticus, to make some joke about being out of the woods, there was a faint crack as a stick broke, somewhere off in the trees. Macro's eyes shot round to stare into the shadows beneath the branches.

Figures emerged from the gloom, stealthily closing in on the column from both sides. Macro drew his sword, snatched a deep breath and bellowed, 'Ambush!'

CHAPTER TEN

There was a sudden shout from the trees, and the cry was taken up on all sides as the attackers swarmed out of the shadows, charging towards Macro's column on the track. Macro planted his leading foot towards the nearest enemies and braced his shield up in front of him, sword arm drawn back ready to thrust.

'Form up! Face 'em!' he shouted to his men above the din. Most reacted swiftly, turning to confront the enemy, spear tips lowered. A handful were momentarily dazed by the suddenness of the attack and stumbled back in the face of the onslaught.

'Keep the wagons moving!' Macro ordered the leading driver.

As the attackers raced out of the shadows, Macro saw that they were dressed in old tattered tunics, most of them barefoot, and armed with an assortment of knives, hatchets and pitchforks. Only a handful had swords or spears and they clearly had no idea how to use them. They waved them around above their heads, wearing frenzied expressions of hate and terror on their faces, as they charged in. There was no time to take any more in as the first of them, teeth gritted and eyes wide and staring madly, slashed at Macro with a scythe. Macro took the glancing blow on the side of his shield and then pivoted on his leading foot to knock the slave off balance as he stumbled past. As the slave tried to retain his balance, Macro stabbed him in the side of the chest, driving the blade home, before ripping it free with a gush of blood. The man doubled up, releasing his grip on the scythe and clasped his hands over the wound as he slumped to the ground and curled up with a deep groan of agony.

Macro looked up. More slaves were pouring from under the trees. He could not estimate their strength, but they clearly outnumbered the men in Macro's column. However, the auxiliaries were trained fighters, and well armed. As Macro glanced round, he saw that his men were holding their own, cutting down the slaves as they came on in a disorganised rush. A sudden snarl snapped Macro's attention back to his front as a slave leaped towards him, swinging a meat-cleaver. He just had time to throw his shield up as the heavy blade slammed into the edge, cutting through the bronze trim and splintering the wood beneath, where it stuck fast.

'My turn!' Macro snarled, slashing at the side of the man's head, and the blade jarred as it bit through skin and skull with a wet crack. As the man dropped to his knees with a stunned expression, Macro withdrew his sword and knocked the cleaver free with the guard. Just then he felt something grasp his ankle and looked down to see that the first man had dragged himself towards his boot and, having grabbed it, was preparing to sink his teeth into Macro's calf.

'Don't you dare!' Macro kicked the hand free and stamped on the man's wrist with his nailed boot. Then he swung the lower edge of the shield at the slave's head, knocking the stricken man out. 'When I put you down, you stay down!'

Macro edged along the track, keeping pace with the leading wagon. He glanced to his left and saw that some of his men were too intent on the fight to realise that the wagons were continuing forward.

'Keep moving!' Macro yelled. 'Protect the bloody wagons!'

Even though they were poorly armed and being hacked down in droves, the slaves continued their ferocious assault, as if they had no fear of death. Macro saw one spitted by a spear as he hurled himself at the auxiliaries. The bloodied tip of the spear exploded through the back of his tunic and the slave heaved himself along the shaft as he clawed at the auxiliary's head. The soldier released his grip on the spear and snatched out his sword, thrusting it into the slave's throat. With a bloody gurgle of rage the slave flailed at his opponent, spattering the auxiliary with blood before his strength gave out and he slumped to his knees, still pierced through by the spear. The auxiliary backed away, hastily looking round to make sure that he was keeping a loose formation alongside his comrades as they paced along the road, doing their best to stay close to the wagons. The ground on either side was strewn with bodies, and still the slaves came on. Macro struck down a toothless man, old enough to be his father, and the man cursed him as he died.

A hand grasped Macro's shoulder and he spun round, ready to strike, until he saw Atticus and just managed to stay his sword in time.

'Give me a weapon,' Atticus pleaded. 'Before they tear me to pieces!'

Macro looked round and saw a pitchfork lying beside the body of a slave, no more than a boy. 'There! Take it.'

Atticus snatched the pitchfork up and grasped the shaft firmly as he lowered the prongs at a thin man racing towards him with a nailed club. The slave swung the club in a vicious arc, aiming at Atticus's head. The latter ducked the blow and then thrust his prongs into the slave's stomach, and with a grunt of brute strength carried the wiry slave up off the ground. The slave screamed as his weight carried him further down the sharp iron spikes that impaled him. Atticus twisted the shaft to one side and the slave crashed to the ground. Placing a boot on the man's chest he wrenched the prongs free and immediately went into a crouch as he looked round for another threat.

'Good job,' Macro said grudgingly.

The leading wagon rumbled out of the wood on to clear ground and continued towards the ruined villa, the driver cracking his whip over the heads of the horses and mules as he urged them on. Ahead of him, a couple of auxiliaries were forced to scramble to the side of the track before they were run down. Macro ground his teeth furiously as he trotted after the wagon.

'Not so bloody fast, you fool!'

The driver carried on heedlessly, and the others followed his example as the wagons emerged from the wood, leaving the auxiliaries and volunteers scrambling to keep up as they tried to fight off the slaves swarming round the column like angry wasps. One of Macro's men, at the rear of the last wagon, stumbled and fell, sprawling across the gravelled track. At once several slaves leaped on him with bloodthirsty howls of triumph and hacked and stabbed at him as he struggled on the ground. He let out a piercing shriek, before it was savagely cut off as axe blows rained down on his head.

Macro could see the danger clearly enough. If the men in the column could not stay together then they would be overwhelmed and butchered one by one. He had to slow the leading wagon. With a curse he released his grip of the shield handle and tossed it to one side so that it would not weigh him down. Fortunately there had been no time to find any greaves for his legs, and the scale armour was not heavy enough to stop him breaking into a run. He sheathed his sword and ran as fast as he could to overhaul the leading wagon, passing the heavy rear wheels. As it lurched over a bump, a jar of olive oil tipped over the side, narrowly missing Macro, and shattered on the stony track. He leaped over the shards of pottery, and as he drew level with the driver, grasped the side of the bench and launched himself up on to the foot rail. The driver glanced down in panic, before he saw it was one of his own side, and then cracked his whip again.

Macro did not waste time with any more words and struggled to his feet, driving his fist into the man's stomach so that he doubled over with a grunt, dropping the whip and traces as he slumped across the bench, gasping for breath. Macro snatched the traces up and pulled them sharply, dragging back on the horses' bridles.

'Whoa! Whoa there!'

With frightened whinnies the horses drew up and the slight incline of the track slowed the wagon at once. Macro settled them on a steady pace and then glanced round. He saw Atticus close by, still brandishing his pitchfork as he kept two slaves at bay. Now that the column was in the open, Macro had a far better view of his situation. Scattered across the field on either side were two or three hundred slaves. After witnessing the fall of so many of their comrades in the first moments of the attack, the rest were now more wary, and they hung back from the column, waiting to pounce on any stragglers, or charge into any gaps between the wagons and the men defending them.

'Atticus!' Macro shouted to him. 'Over here!'

Atticus thrust at the slaves nearest to him and trotted warily up along the side of the leading wagon. Macro leaned towards him, clasping the man's hand and hauling him up on to the driver's bench.

'Here, take the traces. Keep the speed down so that the rest of the wagons and the men can keep up. Is that clear?'

Atticus nodded, still breathing raggedly from his exertions. He took the traces in one hand, and kept a tight grip on the shaft of his weapon with the other. Macro waited a moment to be sure that he had the right pace, and then jumped clear of the wagon, landing heavily. At once he straightened up and drew his sword again.

'Twelfth Hispania! Stay with the wagons!'

The auxiliaries and those volunteers who had snatched up weapons from the dead and injured formed a loose cordon around the wagons as the column continued up the track at a measured pace. The slaves stayed with them, but kept more than a spear's length away, to one side of the wagons. Some had begun to snatch up stones and small rocks from the ground, and hurled them at the Roman soldiers. The uneven rattle and thud of the makeshift missiles accompanied the column all the way to the remains of the villa. Having cast his shield away, Macro did his best to duck any stones he saw coming, but one still crashed off his shoulder. Some of the unprotected volunteers were not so fortunate, and Macro saw one take a blow to the head. The man cried out, clasping a hand to his temple as he staggered away from the track. At once a slave with a mallet leaped forward and smashed it down on his head, crushing the skull in a welter of blood and brains.

They passed the villa and continued up the track towards the junction with the road to Gortyna. The slaves kept with them, stooping to snatch up stones and rocks to keep hurling at the column. For their part, the auxiliaries kept their shields raised and, when the chance permitted, threw missiles back. The path of Macro's column was marked by dead and injured slaves, with a handful of civilians and soldiers amongst them.

'How long do you think they'll keep this up?' Atticus called out from where he crouched low by the driver's bench.

'Until they get tired of it,' Macro replied tersely as he ducked to pick up a shield from one of his men who had fallen at the head of the column. A large rock had shattered the auxiliary's knee and he gritted his teeth as he sat on the ground. Macro turned to the nearest of his men.

'Get him on to a wagon!'

While they hauled the soldier up and dragged him, crying out in agony, to the rear of the leading wagon, Macro hefted the shield and held it high to cover his body. The rain of missiles eased off and he saw that the slaves were pulling back. Two hundred paces away, standing on a stretch of wall, stood a figure shouting orders to them. Unlike the others he was wearing leather body armour, with wrist guards, and a leather skullcap. A sword hung from a strap across his shoulder. Behind him stood several other men similarly equipped. As the slaves gathered in a loose mob in front of him, the man continued to give his instructions. With deliberate gestures he pointed in the direction of the road, and at once a body of his followers ran off in that direction. The rest turned back towards the convoy and continued to bombard it with stones and rocks. But this time they had picked a new target. Their fire concentrated on the leading wagon.

'They're going for the horses and mules!' Macro called out. 'Cover them!'

The men closed up along the flanks of the leading draught animals, protecting them as best they could. But the targets were too large to miss, and every so often one of the beasts would whinny and leap in its traces as it was struck. Atticus did his best to keep control of them, but the frequent stops slowed the pace of the column to a crawl. Macro gritted his teeth in frustration, well aware that the other group of slaves had raced ahead of them to the main road, no doubt with some plan in mind to renew the attack. Glancing up at the sky, he also realised that it was well past noon. If they did not quicken the pace there was a chance that they would still be on the road to Matala, surrounded by their attackers, as night fell. If that happened, then they could easily be rushed in the darkness.

He looked towards the slave leader again. The man was walking alongside the track, a hundred paces away, pausing now and then to watch the progress of his followers as they kept up their harassment of the wagons.

'You're not going to have things your own way for ever, mate,' Macro growled, then turned to the men following him. 'When I give the word, first three sections follow me. Go in hard and fast with as much noise as you can make. Get ready . . .'

Macro tensed his muscles as he walked slowly along the track, watching and waiting as the slaves grew more bold in their attack. Some, grinning with contempt, ran up to within ten feet before throwing their rocks and snarling insults at the auxiliaries. Macro waited until there were several of them close by, hurling missiles and defiance. Then he filled his lungs.

'Charge them!' He sprang to the side, pumping his legs as he threw himself at the slaves. 'Get 'em, lads! Kill 'em all!'

With a throaty roar, his men turned on the slaves and charged after their commander. The nearest attackers turned and fled, some knocking into their comrades in their haste, sending three of them sprawling in the coarse grass. Macro paused briefly to stab his blade down as he passed one of the slaves struggling to rise up on his hands and knees. The sword went in deep between his shoulder blades and the slave fell flat as Macro yanked the blade free and charged on, bellowing at the top of his voice. Even though they were not encumbered by armour, as the auxiliaries were, some of the slaves were aged, and for others the harsh conditions under which they had toiled for years had sapped their strength, and they were run down and killed without mercy as they tried to escape. Macro and his men chased them across the open ground beside the road, slashing at any of their enemies that came within reach.

Ahead of them the leader of the slaves unsheathed his sword and was shouting at his followers to turn and fight. The armed men who had been standing behind him closed up on each side, swords held ready as they made their stand. As the first slaves reached his position, the leader began to rally them. Faced with his ferocious harangue, they turned to confront the Romans, forming up in a crude line as they made ready to fight with their assortment of weapons. Some only carried the rocks they had picked up and others stood with bare hands as they confronted the auxiliaries.

Macro realised that the three sections had achieved all they could with their sudden charge. If they carried on they would be blown by the effort of the pursuit, and now that the slaves were turning on them, the advantage was lost. Macro drew up, panting heavily.

'Twelfth, halt! Form on me, lads!'

The first of his men ceased their pursuit, and hurriedly edged towards Macro. A handful of hotheads carried on a bit further, before they saw the solid body of the enemy waiting for them. Then they stopped and retreated to a safe distance before trotting back to the rest of their comrades, forming a line on either side of the centurion.

'Hurry it up!' Macro yelled at them. 'Quick as you can!'

One of the slaves shouted an insult after the Romans, but the sense of it was lost due to the blood pounding through Macro's head. More voices joined in, and a moment later the air was full of the cries of contempt, jeers and whistles of the slaves as they watched the Romans retreat. Macro could not help a wry smile as he steadily backed away towards the rest of the column. Despite their noise, the slaves did not seem to be in much hurry to turn the tables on the Romans and chase them back to the wagons. Their leader must have felt the same, sensing the opportunity to counterattack slipping from his grasp. Calling to his immediate entourage, he strode through the milling ranks of the slaves and towards the auxiliaries, beckoning the rest to follow him. One by one they drifted forward, and then as a mass, closing on the outnumbered Romans.

'Shit,' Macro muttered irritably. 'Thought it would take them a bit longer to get their balls back.'

Glancing over his shoulder, he saw that the column had moved on since he had led the wild charge. Now they were abreast of the last wagon, and the other sections of the century were continuing with their orders, staying close to the animals pulling the wagons.

'Right then, lads!' Macro called out. 'When I give the order, break and run to the last wagon. Then we'll form the rearguard . . . Now!'

They turned and ran across the fifty paces of open ground separating them from the tail of the column. Behind them the slaves let out a great shout and broke into a charge, leaping over the bodies of their stricken comrades as they surged after Macro and his men. As soon as the auxiliaries reached the last of the wagons, Macro turned and presented his shield. The others fell in on either side, forming a tight shield wall as they braced themselves for the impact of the charge. The first of the slaves struck at Macro's shield, hammering at the surface with a crude club. An instant later all his men were engaged, blocking blows and stabbing back as they gave ground, staying close to the wagon. Macro glimpsed the slave leader to his right, duelling with a thickset auxiliary. The slave sought for a gap between the shields to strike with his weapon, a finely decorated gladiator's sword that glittered in the afternoon sunshine. The auxiliary struck out, and the slave nimbly leaned to one side, before thrusting his point back at the auxiliary, narrowly missing his face as the tip glanced off a cheek guard. The slave looked up and caught Macro's eyes for an instant.

There was a flicker of recognition there, Macro was certain of it.

Then the slave launched into a furious series of blows that battered his auxiliary opponent against the side of the wagon. Too late the auxiliary saw the danger, and the solid timber disc of the wheel knocked him down and rolled over him, crushing his hips and snapping his spine, leaving him looking startled. As his mouth opened and shut and his arms flailed uselessly, he began to die in agony.

The one-sided nature of the melee told once again as the ground behind the wagon was littered with fallen slaves and only three of the auxiliaries. The leader of the slaves called his men off, and they ended their pursuit of the Romans and stood, chests heaving, glaring after the column as it rumbled its way up the track towards the Gortyna road. Macro waited until the gap had opened up to a hundred paces before he sheathed his sword and strode along the column to check on his men and the condition of the horses and mules. The rocks and stones had caused numerous minor injuries to man and beast alike, but they still continued steadily along the track.

'Not far to the road now, lads!' Macro called out cheerily. 'Those bastards have learned their lesson. They won't be bothering the Twelfth Hispania for much longer.'

He spoke too soon. Once a safe gap had opened up between the wagons and the slaves, their leader led his men forward again, keeping level with the Roman column. Macro regarded them warily, but when they made no attempt to close the gap, he took satisfaction in the knowledge that every step along the track was taking them closer to the safety of Matala. Now that he thought about it, he felt there was a good chance his column might get through after all, and the people of Matala would be fed for a few more days at least from the stocks piled on the wagons.

'Sir!'

Macro turned towards the voice and saw one of his men on a

slight rise in the track at the front of the column. He was waving his spear to attract Macro's attention.

'What is it?'

The first wagon ground to a halt as it reached the rise, and Atticus stood up on the driver's bench and stared ahead along the track. Macro trotted forward, past the other wagons.

'What's the bloody hold-up? What the fuck are you stopping for?'

'Look!' Atticus thrust out his arm.

As Macro drew level with the leading wagon, he looked in the direction Atticus indicated. From the higher ground he could see the junction with the Gortyna road barely a hundred paces ahead, where the track had been built up to meet the height of the road. Across the junction stood the slaves who had been sent to cut off the column. They had torn up some of the stone slabs from the road. With these, and some hurriedly felled trees, they had constructed a crude barricade. Macro estimated that there were over two hundred men waiting for them, with another two hundred behind the wagons. It was a neat trap, he admitted ruefully. The barricade would give little enough protection from Macro's auxiliaries, but it would stop the wagons from making any further progress before the way was cleared. The banked track meant there was no chance of driving the wagons round the barricade. Not without them toppling over on the slope. The choice was simple. Either Macro would have to abandon the wagons and retreat to Matala empty-handed, or he must continue the advance into the teeth of those defending the obstacle and try to cut a path through, while those behind attacked the rear of the column. If the column became stuck, Macro and his men would be surrounded and cut down one by one.

'What do we do?' asked Atticus. 'Well, Macro?'

'Shit,' Macro muttered under his breath. 'We keep going. We take the barricade and clear it away and fight our way through. The food has to get to Matala. Advance!'

Atticus took a deep breath and flicked the reins. His wagon lurched forward. After a short pause the others followed and the auxiliaries trudged on, shields held close to their sides. As they neared the barricade, Macro could see the slaves grimly preparing to defend it. Rough-hewn spears and pitchforks were lowered, ready to receive the Romans. Some collected more rocks to hurl at the men and horses approaching them. Glancing over his shoulder, Macro saw that the other party of slaves had already quickened their pace to catch up with the convoy. It was going to be a bloody business, he reflected, and the odds were lengthening against getting the wagons, the food and his men back to Matala. But there was no helping it, he thought resignedly. The only route to safety was through the barricade. He hunched his neck down a little and tightened his grip on his sword and marched steadily towards the enemy.

Suddenly, the slaves on the left of their line turned away from the approaching wagons and stared down the road towards Matala. An instant later some were backing away, and then the first of them threw down their weapons and ran diagonally across the field away from the road, making for the nearest grove of olive trees. The panic spread along the line, and before the Romans even reached the barricade the last of the slaves had fled.

'What the hell?' Macro turned to look down the road as the wagons halted. Once the rumbling of the wheels and the grinding tramp of boots had stilled, he could hear a new sound, the distant thunder of horse hooves pounding along the road. Around a corner in the road came the first of the horsemen, wearing red tunics and Gallic helmets, urging their mounts on. They carried spears, and shields were slung across their backs, except for the rider at the head of the column. He was dressed in scale armour and wore the helmet of a centurion, his crest swept back as he led his men towards the junction.

'They're ours!' Macro beamed. 'Ours!'

Behind the wagons the second party of slaves was melting away. Except for their leader and his companions. He stared at the approaching horsemen for a moment and then back at the wagons. When he saw Macro, he raised his sword in a mock gladiator's salute and then turned to follow the rest of the slaves running for the safety of the olive trees.

Macro turned his attention back to the approaching horsemen as they slowed to a trot and approached the barricade. The leader reined in, and steered his mount round the obstacle to the wagons on the other side.

'Centurion Macro,' a familiar voice called out. 'What on earth have you been up to?'

'Cato!' Macro laughed. 'Thank the gods. What the bloody hell are you doing here?'

CHAPTER ELEVEN

'Sempronius sent me back to fetch you and Julia,' Cato explained as he slipped down from the horse's back, wincing as he jarred his injured leg. He strode stiffly towards his friend and clasped Macro's hand. 'He needs us in Gortyna.'

Macro had noticed the limp and nodded at Cato's leg. 'You all right, lad?'

'Some bastard stabbed me in the thigh, but I'll live.' Cato glanced past Macro to the wagons, and saw that some of the animals and men had been injured. 'I spotted the slaves as we rode up. Looks like they've been giving you some trouble.'

'That's putting it mildly.' Macro grimaced. 'They were throwing themselves at us. I'd never have believed slaves would fight so hard. Anyway, Gortyna's the other way. You came from the direction of Matala.'

Cato nodded. 'I went there first. Centurion Portillus told me where you had gone. The senator and I passed here a few days ago and saw there was trouble. I thought it would be as well to make sure you were all right.'

'Well, we are now.' Macro pointed towards the cavalry squadron on the other side of the barricade. 'Who are that lot?'

'Fourth Batavian, stationed outside Gortyna. They lost half their mounts in the earthquake, as well as over a hundred of their men. Given the dangers on the road, the senator decided on an escort.'

'Dangers? I take it this isn't the only place the slaves are making trouble, then?'

'No.' Cato lowered his voice. 'There are uprisings all along the southern side of the island. Mostly on the big estates, but many of the slaves have run away from the towns as well. It's only to be expected that they would take advantage of the situation. There have been several reports of them attacking farms and smaller settlements. They even attacked a small detachment Sempronius sent to an outpost to guard the estates along the road from Gortyna.' Cato gestured towards the column behind Macro. 'But this? You must have nearly a hundred men with you.' He glanced towards the trees, where the slaves had taken shelter. Already a handful had reappeared along the fringe and were watching the Romans warily. 'They're getting ambitious. We'd better get your column on the road to Matala as quick as possible.'

While some of the Batavians formed a screen opposite the olive trees, the rest dismounted and helped Macro's men clear the barricade away from the road. A short time later the column was trundling along the road to Matala, the Batavians riding a short distance out on either flank to deter any further attacks. Cato had ordered one of his men to lead his horse as he marched alongside Macro.

'How are things at Gortyna?' asked Macro.

'Not good. The city wasn't as badly damaged as Matala, but just about every senior official and officer was killed or wounded when the governor's banquet hall collapsed.'

'Is the governor still alive?'

Cato shook his head. 'He died a few hours after we arrived. Might have been better if he had been killed outright.'

'How so?'

'The poor bastard was in agony, but the real problem is that he had handed power over to one of his men, Glabius.'

'Let me guess. Glabius is enjoying the opportunity, and isn't keen on having to move aside for Sempronius.'

Cato smiled thinly. 'Exactly. And since he has surrounded himself with friends, and a small army of bodyguards, he's in a good position to dictate his terms. So the senator has had to compromise. He is sharing power with Glabius for now. Glabius has authority over Gortyna, while Sempronius has taken charge of the rest of the province.'

'Great.' Macro frowned. 'Just what we need. A bloody turf war between two politicians while the world around them goes to the dogs.'

'True, but it won't last,' Cato continued. 'Sempronius has sent messages to every cohort and garrison detachment on the island informing them of the situation in Gortyna, and that he has taken temporary command of all available military forces. Once they're on our side, I don't think Glabius is going to cause any trouble. Then we can deal with the slaves and restore order.'

'That's easier said than done. If the rest of the slaves on this island are anything like that lot back there, then we've got a hard fight ahead of us, Cato. Believe me. If they get properly armed and organised then they're going to be a tough nut to crack.'

'Sempronius doubts it,' Cato replied. 'He reckons they won't amount to much unless they acquire some kind of leader.'

'But they have. I saw him.' Macro recalled an image of the man he had seen giving orders to the slaves. 'He looked like a hard case. A gladiator possibly. There's something else.'

'Oh?'

'He seemed to know me.'

'Really?' Cato raised his eyebrows.

'Yes. He looked at me. As sure as day, he recognised me.'

Cato was quiet for a moment. 'Do you know him?'

'I don't think so.' Macro frowned. 'I don't know. We may have met some time, but I can't place him. It certainly wasn't in the legions. He was young. No older than you, I'd say. From the scars on his face he's been in a fight or two.'

'Then perhaps he is a professional fighter, possibly a gladiator. There won't be many of those on the island, so we should find out who he is quickly enough, once we get back to Gortyna and put the word about. Still, if he is a gladiator, and he is leading that band of slaves who attacked you, then you're right, we've got a problem.'

'A problem?' Macro laughed drily. 'We're in a province devastated by an earthquake and the largest wave I have ever fucking seen. The governor and nearly all his lackeys are dead. The people are going to get very hungry unless someone sorts out a proper supply of food. There's only a handful of decent soldiers left alive on the island and now we've got a budding Spartacus on the loose . . . and you suggest we have a problem. Well, I'm simply delighted that the legions are still recruiting the brightest and the best. That's all I can say.'

Cato shrugged. 'Could be worse.'

'Could it? How exactly?'

'We could be back in Britain.'

Macro was silent for a moment before he pursed his lips and conceded, 'There is always that.'

'The question is, what does our gladiator friend hope to achieve from his rebellion?' Cato mused. 'For the moment he's free, and so are those who follow him. The first impulse would have been to run to the hills to avoid recapture and punishment. They would know that it would only be a matter of time before a powerful force was sent to hunt them down. But the earthquake has changed everything. Now there's a lot more to play for.'

'What do you mean?'

'You said it yourself, Macro. We've only a handful of men to take them on. We have the remains of towns to protect, and our hands are full keeping order and trying to feed the survivors. We're in no shape to take on a slave rebellion, small as it is right now. If this gladiator can persuade more runaways to join him, not to mention all the other slaves who have stayed behind, then who is to say how ambitious the man might become?'

Macro digested the suggestion and puffed his cheeks out. 'Are you suggesting he might make a play for the whole island?'

'Who knows? He might. But he might try and cut a deal with Sempronius for his freedom, and the freedom of his followers.'

'He won't make that one fly!' Macro snorted. 'If Rome starts setting slave rebels free in Crete, then who knows where that might end? Sempronius would never agree to it.'

'Quite. And when he doesn't, our gladiator is going to be faced with some difficult choices. If he surrenders, then the ringleaders will be crucified. That will be just the start of the reprisals. So he will have to find some way to escape from Crete, or take us on. That's the real danger. Unless we get reinforcements, then he will have the upper hand. If he wipes us out—'

'Bollocks! That's not going to happen.' Macro laughed. 'Once Rome hears what's happened here, they'll send out an army to crush the rebellion in double time.'

'No doubt. But by then the damage will be done. Word will go right round the empire that the slaves of Crete rose up and seized it from the hands of their masters. Now that's an example that might just inspire other slaves in every province under Roman rule. There's the problem. Sempronius can't afford to let this get out of hand. Neither can we, for that matter. If things go pear-shaped, you can be sure that the emperor will be looking for people to hold responsible. Do you really think he would stop at the senior political figure in Crete? Sempronius would be the first for the chop and my guess is we wouldn't be far behind.'

'Shit . . . you're right,' Macro muttered and glanced towards a distant hillock where a small band of slaves was still shadowing the column. 'Why is it always us that land in the shit? Always us.'

Cato looked at his friend and smiled. 'I asked you that question once.'

'Really? What did I say?'

'You looked at me, in that barely tolerant way that you do, and said,' Cato cleared his throat and did a passable imitation of the tone of voice Macro adopted with the thickest of his recruits, '*Why us? Because we're here, lad. That's why.*'

Macro stared at Cato. 'I said that?'

'You did. Quite a good aphorism I thought, at the time. Very stoic.'

'Load of shite, more like. If I say anything like that again, then feel free to kick me up the arse.'

'If you insist.'

There were no more attacks on the column as it approached Matala. In the gathering dusk the slaves who had been watching them turned away and vanished into the shadows stretching across the landscape. There was one last precaution for Macro to take before they returned to the town. He ordered a brief halt as the chains were replaced on Atticus and he was secured to the driving bench. One of the auxiliaries took over the reins. Atticus glowered at Macro and raised his foot to shake the heavy iron links from side to side.

'What is the reason for this, Centurion? I don't deserve this. Not after all I have done today.'

'You have been useful,' Macro agreed. 'But you're a proven

106

troublemaker, and right now I can't afford to let you stir the shit up amongst the people of Matala.'

'I risked my life to obtain the food in these wagons.'

'Sorry. You know how it is with leopards and spots. I don't think I can trust you. Not just yet.'

'Then when?'

'When I decide, and not before.'

'I suppose you will say that my being held in chains is for the good of my people?'

'Your people?' Macro chuckled. 'When did they become your people? You are your own mouthpiece, not theirs. Now then, do be a good prisoner, eh? I would hate to have to convince you to behave.' He held up a clenched fist. 'If I make my point clear.'

'Your merest threat of violence is powerfully eloquent,' Atticus replied coolly. 'You have me for now, Macro, but when I am released I will pay you back, with interest.'

'Of course. I'll look forward to it.' Macro slapped the rump of the nearest horse from the team drawing the first wagon and the animal jolted forward. The auxiliary cracked his whip and the rest of the team broke into a walk. As the wagon lurched forward, Atticus toppled backwards on to the sacks of grain piled behind the driver's bench, causing Macro to laugh.

'Bit hard on him, don't you think?' asked Cato.

'Perhaps.' Macro shrugged. 'But I'm not taking any risks, not until we have the situation in hand.'

'Who knows how long that will be?'

The column trundled round the last bend in the road, and there before them lay the ruins of Matala and the refugee camp. As the people caught sight of the loaded wagons with the wounded perched on top they began to call to their friends and family and hurried through the tents and shelters towards the road. As he watched the surge of humanity sweep across the slope, Cato glanced round at the thin screen of soldiers and cavalry.

'Decurion!' he called out to the commander of the squadron. 'Have your men close up round the wagons. Keep those people away.'

'Yes, sir!' The decurion saluted and turned to pass the orders on to his men. The riders nudged their mounts in towards the side of the road so that the wagons were protected from the approaching crowd. Cato glanced ahead. There was still half a mile to go before they reached the ramp leading up to the acropolis. The first people drew up across the road, fifty paces ahead of the front of the column. Macro hauled himself up beside the driver of the leading wagon and cupped a hand to his mouth.

'Make way there!'

After a moment's hesitation, the townspeople shuffled aside, and stood and stared at the laden wagons with hungry eyes. More and more people arrived to swell their ranks, and inevitably the pressure from behind forced those at the front back towards the road. The driver of the first wagon instinctively allowed his horses to slow down for fear of running into the nearest civilians.

'Clear the way!' Macro shouted again. 'Move back, damn you!'

As those closest struggled to do as they had been ordered, there were angry shouts from the back from those who feared they would miss out on any food that might be distributed. Macro turned to the decurion.

'Take eight of your men, and clear the road.'

'Yes, sir! You men, follow me.' The decurion dug his heels in gently and walked his horse forward, followed by his men, fanning out either side of their leader. As they closed in, Cato could see the frightened expressions of the people in the crowd as they pressed back. The fear spread through the packed ranks like wildfire and they recoiled from the horses as the decurion led his men down the road. Macro turned to the driver and muttered, 'Keep up with them.'

With a crack of the whip the wagon lurched forward again, rumbling over the worn paving stones leading up to where the town gate had once stood. Cato, the auxiliaries and volunteers increased their pace to keep up, and to his side he saw the hostile faces in the crowd as the column passed through.

'Bloody Romans!' a man in a torn tunic shouted, and raised his fist. 'They're going to keep it all to themselves!'

His anger was taken up by others and the air was filled with jeers and shouts. A mother raised her infant up for the passing horsemen to see and cried out in a shrill voice that her baby would soon die unless he was properly fed. Cato was tempted to offer some reassurance, and promise that they would receive a fair share of the rations, but realised it would be a pointless gesture. His voice would be drowned out by the din assaulting the column on all sides, and it would only make him look weak.

Distracted by the baying of the crowd, he failed to notice Atticus edging his way along the grain sacks piled on the leading wagon. When he came to the end of his chain, Atticus stopped and continued on his stomach until he could reach the end of the wagon. Cato's gaze turned away from the crowd and he started as he saw Atticus lying full length.

'What's he doing?' asked one of the auxiliaries marching beside Cato.

Bracing his feet, Atticus thrust his arms against the rearmost sacks of grain.

'Stop him!' Cato shouted, springing towards the wagon. But it was too late. The first of the sacks on the top of the pile tipped over the end and toppled on to the road. It landed with a soft thud and split. Grain exploded across the road with a swift, soft hiss. A second sack was already falling as Cato caught up with the wagon and hauled himself up. He saw Atticus struggling to push yet more of the grain on to the road, and stamped down hard on his arm. Atticus cried out as the nailed studs bit into his flesh and snatched his other arm back to try to shift Cato's boot. Leaning down, Cato hauled the third sack back so that it was in no danger of falling. Before he could think to do anything else, there was an excited shout from the crowd and a man darted between the horses and went down on his knees to claw the grain into a fold in his tunic. At once others followed suit and the auxiliaries were shoved aside as people frantically pressed through to get at the spilled grain.

Leaning down, Cato glared into Atticus's eyes and clamped a hand round the man's throat. 'Try anything else, and I swear I will cut your throat where you lie. Understand?'

Atticus was gasping as he nodded. Cato clenched a little tighter for a moment to emphasise his threat before he released his grip and turned towards the chaotic scene behind the wagon. The vehicle was still moving forward, behind the gap cleared for it by the decurion and his men. But the desperate surge of the crowd towards the grain had split the column in two, forcing the following wagons and their escort to stop.

Cato turned to Macro and called out, 'Keep going! I'll take charge of the rest.'

As Macro nodded, Cato jumped down and drew his sword, bracing his feet to maintain his balance as he was jostled by the crowd. He forced his way through to the rear half of the column, standing stationary before the heaving mass of civilians scrabbling away at the grain.

'Auxiliaries! On me! Form a wedge!'

Cato took up position in the middle of the road, and the men of the Twelfth formed up at his back in a chevron. When he saw that the men were ready, Cato took a deep breath and called out, as loud as he could, 'Shields front, present spears!'

There was a clatter as the shafts of their spears rapped against the shield rims, and an arrowhead of sharp iron points faced the crowd.

'Advance!' Cato bellowed and then called the time: 'One . . . two . . . one . . . two!'

The wedge tramped steadily forward and faces in the crowd began to look up in the direction of the approaching formation. Some snatched a last handful of grain and then turned to push their way to safety.

'They'll murder us!' a shrill voice cried out, and there were panicked shouts as the civilians scrambled out of the path of the on-coming soldiers. Cato called back over his shoulder, 'Get the wagons moving! Don't stop for anything until we reach the acropolis.'

As the wheels rumbled into life behind him, Cato continued the advance, the boots of the auxiliaries grinding over the scattered grain. Before them an old man had slipped to the ground and was struggling to rise to his feet. One of the soldiers thrust his shield out, knocking the man on to his side. He landed heavily on his knee and then rolled into a ball, hugging the joint as he groaned in agony. The auxiliary lowered his spear tip and Cato thrust his sword out towards the man.

'No! Leave him be and step over him.'

The old man was left on the ground as the formation passed over him, and then looked up in terror as the ground trembled under the weight of the heavy wheels of the wagons. The horses stepped nimbly over the prostrate form, but the wheels were insensitive to his plight, and Cato glanced back at the sound of the thin cry of dread to see the old man wriggle to one side at the last moment. Cato continued to advance along the road as the other civilians hurried to get out of the way of the lethal spear points.

Just before the column reached the remains of the gate, a stone flew out of the crowd and clattered off the side of a cavalryman's shield. Moments later more followed, mixed with mud and turds, spattering the men around the wagons.

'Ignore them!' Cato shouted. 'Keep moving!'

The rear of the column entered the town and continued along the main route, now cleared of rubble by the work gangs Macro had organised. Some members of the crowd followed them a short distance, still throwing missiles, before they gave up and backed off, shouting final insults before returning to their shelters. Macro was waiting for them on the ramp leading up to the acropolis. As Cato approached, brushing filth from his shoulder, Macro smiled ruefully.

'Like I said, we're always in the shit.'

'It wasn't pretty, but at least we got the wagons through,' said Cato. 'There's enough supplies for a few more days.'

'And then we have to go out and repeat the whole thing all over again.' Macro turned towards the first wagon and stabbed his finger at Atticus. 'Nice work, mate. You almost got some of your people killed. Happy now?'

Atticus shook his head. 'Not my fault.'

'Oh, but it was. If you hadn't played your fancy trick back there, there wouldn't have been any trouble.' Macro gestured to two of his men. 'Take him back to the prison. No rations for him for the next two days.'

'What?'

'The price you pay for the grain that you caused to be wasted.'

As Atticus was unchained from the wagon and led away, Cato surveyed the refugee camp and shook his head wearily. 'It's bad enough having to deal with the rebels, without making enemies of the civilians.'

'We're in a thankless job here, Cato old son,' Macro agreed, and waved the rest of the column forward up the slope to the gates of the acropolis. 'Even so, we have to do what we can to save these people.'

'Yes,' Cato replied, and was silent for a moment before he continued quietly, 'I hate to say it, but unless we get some help from outside, and get it soon, the province is going to collapse into complete chaos. It'll be a bloodbath and there's precious little we can do to prevent it.'

CHAPTER TWELVE

'Do you think Portillus is up to the job?' asked Cato as they rode out of Matala the following morning. Behind the two centurions followed the cavalry escort. Julia sat alongside the driver on a small cart halfway along the column of mounted men.

'He knows what he has to do,' Macro replied. 'I gave him his orders last night. Keep the people fed. Keep the rebel slaves at bay. Simple enough. Even Portillus can handle that. Anything else comes up, then he sends a message to Gortyna and asks for instructions. And at least he won't have to contend with Atticus.' Macro nodded to the rear of the column, where the Greek troublemaker was riding between two burly men.

'What do you intend to do with him?'

'He's tough and has courage, and provided he keeps his mouth shut I reckon we can put him on the strength of one of the cohorts at Gortyna.'

'What if he disagrees?'

'In that case, I'll offer him a choice. Atticus can wear the uniform, or he can wear chains.'

'Fair enough.' Cato nodded, then his thoughts returned to Matala. The situation in the town was sound enough. Even though there was no question of defending the refugee camp, Portillus had sufficient men under arms to defend the acropolis, and there was room enough for the townspeople to take shelter from any danger. Cato frowned at himself for admitting the possibility that the rebel slaves might consider an attack on the town. Yet every eventuality had to be anticipated. Even that. 'I'm sure he will manage.'

As the column made its way warily along the road to Gortyna, the sun climbed into a clear blue sky. Once in a while, the riders glimpsed movement in the distance and saw ragged figures watching them pass by. There was no sign of any bands of rebels, and once Cato was confident that there was no immediate danger, he reined in and waited for Julia's cart to catch up before walking his horse alongside.

'I wondered when you would honour me with your presence.' Julia smiled. She lowered her voice, but continued in the same light-hearted tone. 'Given the, ah, encounter last night, I feared you might have turned out to be the love-them-and-leave-them type. Like your friend Macro.'

Cato turned to meet her sultry gaze and could not help smiling at the thought of the previous evening. They had sat in a small neglected terrace garden that must have been the pride and joy of one of the previous commanders of the garrison, homesick for his villa back in Spain. Below them the ruins of the town were dark and shapeless where once they would have been illuminated by torches and the wan twinkle of lamps, accompanied by the sounds of revellers in the inns of the streets around the forum. Now there was silence, and even the refugee camp was quiet and still, until a small cluster of figures surrounding one of the camp fires slowly broke into a song, whose cheery melody drifted faintly across the ruins. Julia had leaned into his shoulder as Cato wrapped his cloak around them both.

'It's strange to hear them singing.' She spoke softly. 'After all that they have lost.'

'I suppose so, but perhaps song is one of the few things the wave and the earthquake couldn't take from them.' Cato turned his head and kissed her brow gently, shutting his eyes as he slowly breathed in the scent of her hair. He felt her tremble. 'What's wrong?'

'Nothing.'

'Nothing? I know you better than that.'

Julia shifted round and stared up at his face, dimly lit by the stars. She cupped his cheek in her hand. 'Cato, my love, I nearly lost you the night of the wave. I thought we were all finished when the water closed over us. In the cold darkness of the sea I gave in to terror. In the last moments I drew some comfort that at least we would be together in whatever afterlife there is.' She swallowed and continued. 'Then, when the ship rose back out of the sea, I saw that you were gone. I still lived, but you had been taken from me.' She glanced away, quickly wiping her eye. 'At that moment I felt like my heart had been ripped from my body. I remember thinking that I wanted to die. To throw myself into the ocean so I could be with you. For a moment, that was all I wanted to do.'

'Then I'm glad you didn't.'

'Cato, that's not funny. I mean it. I had no idea how much you meant to me until that moment when I thought you were dead.'

'But I didn't die,' he kissed the palm of her hand, 'thank the gods. We're still very much alive, my love, and we have everything to live for.'

'I know.' Julia nodded. 'Perhaps knowing that means some good has come out of all this.'

They looked across to the refugee camp on the side of the hill opposite the acropolis. Some more people had gathered round the fire where the singing had begun and added their voices. The tune was clearer now, and Cato and Julia listened to it for a while. He could not help feeling moved by the juxtaposition of the burden of so much tragedy and the cheerful lightness of the song that pierced the shadows of the night lying heavily upon the hilly landscape. He held Julia close to him and spoke softly in her ear.

'I want to make love.'

'Now?' she whispered. 'Here?'

'Yes.'

She looked at him for a moment before kissing him on the lips, slipping her hand gently behind his head and drawing him towards her as she eased herself back on to the cool grass of the terrace garden. Cato felt a warm rush to his loins as he began to harden. They kissed a while longer, revelling in the touch, the scent and the warmth of each other. Then Julia opened her legs either side of him and said, 'Now, my Cato. Now. I want you inside me. But watch that leg of yours . . .'

Cato felt a fresh tingle of ardour as he recalled it all again. He smiled at Julia trundling alongside him in the cart.

'I know what you're thinking,' she laughed.

'Is it so obvious?'

'Trust me. You're a man. Of course it's obvious.'

They both laughed. The nearest troopers of the mounted escort turned to look at them with curious expressions, before turning their attention back to the surrounding landscape, watching for signs of danger.

They approached Gortyna at dusk, without incident, and caught sight of the city as the road rounded the curve of a hill. After his experience of Matala, Macro was surprised to see that the province's capital appeared to have suffered far less damage than the port. To the side of the road leading to the main gate was a marching camp. A section of auxiliary troops guarded the entrance. Macro pointed to them.

'Who are they?'

Cato reined in as he drew alongside. 'Detachments from the Fifth Gallic and Tenth Macedonian, from the garrisons of Cnossos and Axos. The reports from the north of the island said that there had not been nearly as much damage there, so Sempronius sent orders for reinforcements to be marched to Gortyna. There should be more men coming from the other cities over the next few days.'

'Well that's something.' Macro nodded. 'As long as they aren't as out of condition as the boys of the Twelfth Hispania. We're going to need some good men to sort things out. What I'd give for a few cohorts from the Second Legion right now.'

'Not every auxiliary unit is like the Twelfth,' Cato countered. 'Those men we commanded at Bushir and Palmyra were fine soldiers. You said so yourself. As good as legionaries.'

'True enough,' Macro conceded. 'But that was only because we worked them hard, Cato. Drilled 'em hard and drilled 'em regularly. We made them ready for war. Trouble with garrison units is that most of their officers let them go soft. In time they're little better than the layabouts of the town watch. I'd lay good money that most of the auxiliary cohorts on Crete are cut from the same cloth.'

'Perhaps. But we can't know for sure.'

Macro looked at him. 'Really? Care to make a bet that there's not one man amongst that lot fit to take his place in the Second Legion?'

Cato considered the wager for a moment and shook his head. 'I can think of better ways to waste my money.'

They left their escort at the city gates, and the decurion, with orders to induct Atticus into one of the infantry cohorts, marched his men away towards their camp on the far side of Gortyna. Macro and Cato dismounted and led their horses along the main street as Julia's cart followed behind. Inside the walls, makeshift tents and crude shelters filled the ruined quarters of the city. They passed several gangs of slaves at work clearing rubble and making repairs to temples and business premises. Cato noticed that the slaves were securely chained to each other and were closely watched by overseers armed with heavy clubs. The poorest dwellings of Gortyna had been left to their owners, who picked over them, still gleaning for valuables and whatever food remained that had not gone off in the hot days following the earthquake. Armed men stood outside the larger houses and storerooms surrounding the city's forum.

'Seems that Glabius is looking after his own,' Macro commented quietly.

'For now,' Cato replied. 'But I don't imagine Sempronius will put up with this for long.'

'Why not? The rich have always been good at looking after each other.'

'Why not?' Julia interrupted. 'Because my father is no fool, Centurion Macro. He knows that if a wedge is driven between the local people, then it can only harm efforts to rebuild the province, and help the cause of the rebel slaves. That's why not.'

Macro scratched the stubble on his chin. 'If you say so.'

'Trust me,' she continued. 'He will do the right thing. He always has.'

Cato could believe it. The senator had a strong moral streak and a sense of duty to Rome that overrode any self-interest. Which was why he had never been granted any rank higher than quaestor. If he had been prepared to make and take bribes, then he would have been appointed a provincial governor years before.

They continued through the forum, where a handful of stalls had been set up by traders desperate to earn hard currency to buy food for their families. Even though it was late in the day, long past the usual time they closed up for the night, the traders were still waiting patiently for custom, though the area was almost deserted. A short distance from the forum stood the entrance to the governor's palace. The two Roman officers and the cart were waved through, and as they entered the courtyard Cato noted that the palace was guarded by auxiliaries. There was no sign of the town guards and the private bodyguards, who had remained loyal to Glabius.

Macro called over one of the governor's household slaves. 'You, where's Senator Sempronius?'

'Over there, master.' The slave bowed his head as he pointed towards the stable courtyard.

'Take the horses,' Macro ordered, handing the reins to the slave. Cato helped Julia down from the cart and the three of them made their way across to the entrance of the stables. There was no longer a restless crowd demanding treatment, and a calm sense of order prevailed in the buildings and store sheds on each side of the court- yard. The rooms to the right were still serving as a makeshift hospital, and Sempronius had commandeered those to the left for his head- quarters. As Macro, Cato and Julia were shown into a tack room, the senator glanced up from the desk that had been set up by the far wall. A pile of reports on waxed slates lay before him and he lowered the brass stylus in his hand as a broad smile creased his weary features. Releasing her hold on Cato's hand, Julia ran across the room and embraced her father.

'Easy, my dear!' he chuckled, kissing her tenderly on the cheek. Macro and Cato stood by the door in an awkward silence until Sempronius beckoned to them to approach. Julia straightened up and went to sit on the clerks' bench to one side of the desk.

'Good to see you again, gentlemen,' said Sempronius. 'Have a seat. How are things at Matala, Macro?'

'Not too bad, sir. The food is being rationed and there are supplies for some days yet. The people aren't happy, but we're keeping them in line, for now.' He glanced briefly at Cato. 'The chief difficulty is the slave rebellion.'

'Rebellion?' Sempronius frowned. 'I doubt a few minor skirmishes amount to a rebellion.'

'It's gone beyond a few skirmishes, sir.' Macro briefly recounted the attack on his column and the fact that the slaves were being led by the man in the leather skullcap.

'A gladiator, you say?' Sempronius mused, once Macro had finished his report.

'That's my guess, sir. If I'm right then he should be easy to identify. I'll give your clerks the details that I can recall of the man, and we'll see if anyone recognises him from the description.'

'Someone might, but what good will that do us?'

Macro was surprised. 'Well, sir, knowing your enemy is always something of a help.'

'But you said he seemed to know you already.'

'That's how it looked to me. Can't say I recalled him, though. Not yet. If I can learn something about him, then perhaps I can place this man and have some idea of how much of a threat he poses.'

Sempronius considered this briefly and then nodded. 'All right. I'll make sure his description is circulated. Though I don't see how one gladiator is going to upset my plans to restore order to Crete. He's no more of a threat than any other slave amongst that rabble skulking in the hills.'

Julia leaned forward. 'Father, this wouldn't be the first time that Rome underestimated the danger posed by an escaped gladiator. Centurion Macro is right to be concerned.'

Sempronius frowned, and then shook his head with a small laugh as he understood her point. 'This is Crete, my dear, not Campania. Gladiator schools are somewhat thinner on the ground here than they are around Capua. There is no danger of another Spartacus. Besides, I doubt that any slave in the empire can be unaware of the dreadful fate that befell those who followed Spartacus. They might run and hide, but any runaway slaves will be too terrified of being involved in a general uprising. They'd sooner be captured, returned to their masters and punished.'

Macro sucked in a breath as he recalled the fanaticism with which the slaves had attacked his column. 'Truly, sir, I hope you're right.'

'I am sure of it.' Sempronius softened his expression. 'Now, there are slightly more pressing problems to be faced before we worry too much about this gladiator of yours.'

119

'Really?' Macro raised his eyebrows.

'Yes, really,' Sempronius replied testily. 'We still have to contend with that fool Marcus Glabius. I've managed to persuade him to hand the governor's palace over to me, but he's occupied the acropolis, and keeps himself surrounded by bodyguards. He has also taken charge of the food supplies and had them moved to the storerooms in the acropolis. And while he controls the food, he controls Gortyna, and to a degree the troops under my command, since I am required to go to him for the men's rations. Now, I might have been prepared to overlook such issues if Glabius was feeding the people and helping them recover from the earthquake, but he isn't. He has been protecting the property of his friends, and openly permitting them to exploit the food shortage by hoarding supplies, while he uses the provincial treasury to buy grain and meat at vastly inflated prices for distribution to the poor. Some of the grain is ruined and the meat is rotten. It's an intolerable state of affairs,' Sempronius concluded.

'Then why do you tolerate it, sir?' asked Cato.

'Why?' Sempronius rose from his desk and made for the door to the courtyard. 'Come with me and I'll show you why.'

He led them into the centre of the stable courtyard and turned to point at the acropolis built on a nearby hill that dominated the centre of the city. A narrow track wound its way up the steep slope to the gate, which was protected by sturdy towers on each side. 'As you can see, Glabius has picked himself a safe spot to sit out the crisis. It would take an army to seize the acropolis, and he has all the provisions to withstand a siege while I have none to mount one. Besides, it would be madness to use force to bring Glabius to heel, given the problems we already face.'

'So what is your plan, sir?' asked Macro.

'My plan is to gather enough soldiers here to ensure that there is no popular uprising provoked by the ineptitude of Glabius. Also, I intend to restore order to the farms and estates of the southern part of the island, and round up those slaves you seem so concerned about. Once that has been achieved, then I will settle matters with Glabius.'

Cato shook his head. 'I doubt that would be a good idea, if you don't mind my saying?'

'Oh?'

'Glabius is a tax collector, sir. You know how well connected they are back in Rome. You would risk making some dangerous enemies if you took him on.'

'And I risk losing control of the province if I don't.'

'That's true,' Cato conceded. The senator was in an impossible position.

Sempronius stared up at the acropolis with a weary expression before he continued. 'I sent a full report on the situation here to Rome this morning. I said that I would wait for further instructions before dealing with Glabius.'

Macro and Cato exchanged a quick glance. The senator was taking the easy way out by waiting for orders; disowning responsibility for affairs in Crete. It might take as much as two months for a reply to reach Gortyna. In that time Glabius would be free to continue exploiting the situation, endangering the security of not only the province but the rest of the empire as well, once news of the collapse of authority on the island leaked out across the Mediterranean. It was essential that the senator realised the need to remove Glabius. Even if that made him enemies back in Rome, Cato reflected.

He cleared his throat. 'Sir, I don't think we can afford to wait for instructions from Rome. We will have to act long before then. Before Glabius stirs up too much hostility amongst the local people.'

Sempronius cocked an eyebrow. 'What do you propose we do then?'

The shift in authority from the senator to his subordinate was not lost on Macro, and he had to force himself not to show his surprise as Cato made his reply.

'We have to take control of the food stocks up there, sir. That means we have to arrest Glabius, and disarm his bodyguards. Once that's done, we can be sure that the people will be on our side.'

'While we make enemies of Glabius's friends?' Sempronius paused. 'Both here and back in Rome.'

'Can't be helped. Besides, the mathematics of the situation is quite clear, sir. There are more hungry people than there are friends of Glabius. Who would you rather have on your side?'

Sempronius pressed his lips together and glanced at the others, before turning to stare helplessly at the walls of the acropolis. Julia cleared her throat and gently took her father's hand. 'Cato's right. You must act. Soon.'

The senator was silent for a moment before he nodded slowly. 'Very well. Glabius will be dealt with.'

CHAPTER THIRTEEN

The following morning, Senator Sempronius met with his senior military officers. In addition to Macro and Cato, there were the commanders of the three auxiliary cohorts. The prefect of the Batavian cavalry, Marcellus, was a slender, hard-looking veteran with silver hair and piercing dark eyes. The detachments of the two infantry cohorts were led by centurions, Albinus and Plotius, men who had served with their units since first signing up. Unfortunate, since Macro had hoped they might have been promoted to their present rank from the legions.

'Pity,' he muttered to Cato as the senator made the introductions. 'But we'll have to make do.'

Sempronius glanced at him irritably as he continued. 'Macro is the acting prefect of the Twelfth Hispania at Matala. Centurion Cato is serving as my military aide and chief of staff.'

Marcellus looked searchingly at Cato for a moment. 'Might I ask the substantive rank of Macro and Cato?'

'Of course.' Sempronius nodded. 'Both hold legionary rank, pending reappointment to new units once they return to Rome.'

'I see.' Marcellus nodded with a small smile of satisfaction. 'Then, as prefect, I am the senior officer present.'

'You are, technically,' Sempronius replied in an even tone. 'However, as the senior office-holder in the province, I have the final word in matters of command. For the present I am content to permit Macro to retain command of our forces.'

'I have to protest, sir. Macro is only an acting prefect. I am a permanent holder of that rank. Therefore I should be in command.'

'Your protest is noted, Prefect Marcellus; however, I have made my decision. Prefect Macro will lead my men.'

'I see.' Marcellus nodded. 'I'd like that noted in writing, sir.'

123

'Would you?' Sempronius looked surprised for a moment, before he recovered. 'Are you sure about that?'

The other man returned his stare steadily and then shook his head. 'I suppose not. After all, what difference does it make? There aren't likely to be any rewards handed out to the commanders as a result of our actions in this crisis.'

'Quite,' Sempronius replied. 'This is a simple policing matter, gentlemen. Our goals are to enforce order, feed the people and recapture the slaves who have run away from their masters. That is all.' He glanced round at his subordinates. 'Having considered the situation, I have made the following plans to achieve our goals. The Batavian horse and the Fifth Gallic will be tasked with hunting down the fugitive slaves and any brigands that are preying on the people and property of this province.' He paused, and chewed his lip for a moment before continuing. 'Prefect Marcellus will command this force.'

Macro cleared his throat. 'Begging your pardon, sir. I thought you said I was your choice for commander.'

'I did.'

'Then shouldn't I lead this column?'

'Your particular talents are required here, for the present.'

'Sir?'

'I will explain later.' Sempronius turned to Centurion Plotius. 'The Tenth Macedonian will remain in Gortyna, to keep order and to help with reconstruction. Centurion Cato will assign work details for your men.'

'Yes, sir.' Plotius nodded.

'Any questions?'

Marcellus spoke. 'Yes, sir. It will take my men some days to carry out their job, and we will need adequate provisions. The thing is, Marcus Glabius has not been forthcoming with the supplies he has hoarded up there on the hill.'

'So I've heard.'

'Well, the truth of it is that he has been giving me half of what I need for the men and horses, and he's been doling it out on a daily basis. I will need at least ten days' supplies, and I will need it in full rations.'

'I've already requested that,' Sempronius replied. 'However, Glabius has sent me word that he must put the people of Gortyna first. He will only grant you – those are his words – five days' supplies, at half rations, for you and your horses.'

Marcellus's expression darkened. 'That won't do, sir. In any case, who is he to tell you what he will provide from his supplies?'

'Who indeed?' Sempronius smiled weakly. 'Glabius is the man sitting on the food chest. He's also the man sitting pretty up there in the acropolis. Until the situation changes, the allocation of supplies is in his hands. In the meantime, you and your men will take what rations he provides for us, and when they are exhausted you will have to live off the land.'

Cato leaned forward. 'Begging your pardon, sir?'

'What is it?'

'Prefect Marcellus and his column will not be campaigning through hostile territory. At least, it won't be hostile to start with. The local people have little enough food as it is, and if our men turn up and start seizing what's left, then we are hardly going to keep their loyalty, and that's something we're going to need in full measure in the days to come.'

'Well, what of it?' Sempronius responded in an exasperated tone. 'Our soldiers have to be fed.'

'That's true, but it would be best if they take as little as possible from each settlement they pass through, and also they must pay their way.'

'Pay?' Marcellus snorted. 'We're bloody army, not traders. We don't pay our way.'

Cato pursed his lips. 'As things are, I would recommend that we pay for the food, sir. Unless we want the peasants, slaves and brigands making common cause.'

'Let them try,' scoffed Marcellus. 'I'll ride them into the ground.'

'I'd rather you didn't,' said Sempronius. 'I would imagine the emperor would not be pleased to lose any more tax-payers in this province than is wholly necessary. You'll do as Cato says and pay for your supplies, and don't leave people to starve in your wake. Is that clear?'

'Yes, sir.'

'Good, then I want you and Centurion Albinus to prepare your men to march at first light. Your orders will be sent to you later on. I will want regular reports on your progress, Marcellus. Every other day.'

'Yes, sir. Is that all?'

Sempronius stared at him for a moment and nodded. 'Yes. The briefing is over. You may leave, except for Centurions Cato and Macro.'

They remained in their seats as the other three officers scraped back their chairs and rose to salute and leave the room. Once the door was closed behind them, and the sound of footsteps had receded across the flagstones of the stable courtyard, Macro cleared his throat and leaned forward belligerently.

'Might I ask why I am not being entrusted with command of the column being sent to deal with the slaves?'

'It is not a question of trust.' Sempronius sighed. 'Rather, it is not a question of my faith in you so much as my lack of trust in Marcellus.'

'Eh? I don't follow you, sir.'

'You saw what he was like. Ambitious, and resentful. Marcellus has been serving in Crete for long enough to favour an insider like Glabius over me. I could be wrong about him, but I won't take the risk. I'd rather he was kept away from Gortyna while we deal with Glabius. Chasing down the runaways and enforcing martial law will keep him occupied for a while. Besides,' Sempronius smiled, 'I meant what I said about requiring your talents here, Macro.'

'Sir?'

'I think it is time I resolve my differences with Glabius and persuade him to retire from his current post. I have no intention of setting Marcellus loose on the southern part of the province short of rations. So, we must get our hands on the supplies up in the acropolis as soon as possible.'

Macro glanced at Cato and winked. 'Now that sounds like my kind of proposition.'

Cato looked at Sempronius. 'What do you have in mind, sir?'

'A little subterfuge, which we will put into effect once Marcellus is a safe distance from Gortyna. Tomorrow afternoon should do.' Sempronius could not suppress a small chuckle. 'And then we shall see if Glabius has any backbone to back up his bluster. That's all for now, gentlemen.'

Macro and Cato were at the door when Sempronius called after them. 'One other thing. I've found out who this gladiator might be. It seems that the governor's wife bought him on a trip back to Rome a few months ago. Apparently he was a rising star and Antonia paid a small fortune for him.'

'Why?' asked Cato. 'I mean, of what use is a gladiator to a Roman matron?'

Macro and Sempronius glanced at each other, and Macro raised his eyes.

'Oh.' Cato blushed. 'I see. Anyway, what is his name?'

'I didn't get his real name,' said Sempronius. 'Only the one he fought under – "The Iron Thracian". Not much help, I'm afraid. Still, if he survived the earthquake, he might be the man who is leading the slaves.'

As the sun began to sink behind the mass of the acropolis, Sempronius, accompanied by two men in the plain tunics of clerks, with the bags containing their writing materials slung from their shoulders, made his way up the path leading to the main gate of the acropolis. He had sent a message to Glabius earlier in the afternoon requesting a meeting to discuss the provisioning requirements of his troops. Glabius had consented, and agreed the time that Sempronius had suggested for the meeting.

The shadows were lengthening on the slope leading up to the acropolis, casting gloom over the narrow alleyways between the houses that clustered there. Up on the wall that ringed the top of the hill, a handful of Glabius's men patrolled along the sentry walk, dark shapes against the brilliant glare of the sky. Sempronius was wearing a white tunic, fringed with the broad red band that signified his social status. Across his shoulder was a sword belt, from which hung a richly decorated scabbard and hilt – a weapon that had been in his family for generations and survived the capsizing of the *Horus*.

As the gradient steepened and the route began to zigzag up the slope, Macro turned to Cato and mumbled, 'This is never going to work. We shouldn't have let him talk us into it.'

'The plan will work, *if* we keep quiet.' Cato tapped his mouth with a finger.

Macro clamped his lips together and shook his head in resignation. He walked a little awkwardly, thanks to the knife bound against his spine under the tunic. Cato also moved warily, and with a slight limp, as he was still recovering from his wound. He wore a felt skullcap to help conceal his identity if they encountered any of Glabius's men who might have visited the senator's headquarters. He had met Glabius once, and the man was sure to recognise him when they came face to face, but by then it would be too late for the tax collector to do anything about it.

A vague movement to his side drew Macro's attention and he saw a file of auxiliary troops stealing along the narrow alleys that threaded the houses and small shops crowding under the looming mass of the acropolis. This part of the city had not suffered nearly as badly as the rest, but even so, Centurion Plotius and his men would be forced to pick their way quietly over the occasional heaps of rubble in order not to alert the sentries on the walls above them.

The two guards at the gate rose to their feet and hefted their spears as the senator and his followers approached. Cato saw that they were big, heavy men with the broken noses of boxers, or perhaps from time spent in the street gangs that were a feature of every large city across the empire. They moved to bar the way to the closed gate and one raised his hand to halt Sempronius.

'State your business, sir,' he said bluntly.

'I'm here to see Marcus Glabius. He is expecting me.'

The guard smiled faintly as he replied. '*Governor* Marcus Glabius left word to admit you, sir. He said nothing about any companions.'

Sempronius bit back on his anger. 'These men are my personal secretaries. I need them to make notes at the meeting. Now let us through.'

The senator took a step towards the gate. The guard whistled and the other man on duty blocked their path.

'Get out of my way,' Sempronius growled.

'Not so fast, sir,' said the first guard. 'I have to search these bags before I let you enter.'

He turned to Macro and Cato and nodded towards their haver-sacks. 'Put 'em on the ground and step back two paces.'

They did as they were told and watched as the guard knelt down, opened each bag in turn and rummaged through the waxed slates and styli before flipping the flaps back and stepping away. 'Pick 'em up.'

Cato could sense Macro bristling with anger at his side as they retrieved their bags, and willed his friend to control his temper. The guard approached the gates and bellowed out the order for them to be opened. There was a dull grating from inside as the locking bolt was slid aside, and a moment later one of the doors groaned on its hinges as it swung inwards. The guards stepped aside as Sempronius clicked his fingers and led Macro and Cato into the acropolis.

Like many Greek cities, the acropolis was dominated by temples and shrines to those gods most revered by the local people. In addition, there were a number of administration buildings and barracks built close to the walls that ran around the edge of the hill. There were no priests in view. A handful of men dressed in comfortable tunics were sitting in the shade of a grove as they drank wine from a slender-necked amphora.

'Seems like the quality of Gortyna are doing all right,' Macro muttered.

A large group clustered around a game of dice outside one of the barrack blocks, and another six men were patrolling along the walls, occasionally glancing down over the city, or out across the plains in the direction of Matala, and up into the hills behind Gortyna. The earthquake had flattened one of the smaller temples, and large sections of the roofs of the others had fallen in. The two-storey administration building was largely intact, save for the portico, which had collapsed and now lay in piles of rubble on either side of the entrance.

As they passed the Temple of Jupiter, Best and Greatest, Cato saw that it was the newest structure on the acropolis, and the least damaged. Through the columns that surrounded the building he could see sacks of grain and racks of amphorae piled high along the outer walls. The main doors were open, and more supplies were visible in the dim interior. Cato quickened his pace, caught the eye of Sempronius and nodded towards the temple.

'Enough there to feed the people for a while yet, not to mention our men.'

'I know,' Sempronius replied coolly. 'Damn Glabius.'

He led them towards the administration building, where another one of Glabius's hired men stood on guard. Sempronius explained his business once again and the guard nodded and escorted them inside with a curt gesture. They passed through the main hall, which was filled with fine rugs, furniture, statuary and boxes of scrolls. The contents of Glabius's house, Cato surmised, carried up to the acropolis for safe keeping until the crisis was over. On the far side, a door gave out on to a small colonnaded courtyard. A staircase on the far side climbed up to a second level of rooms, built directly on top of the wall. The guard led them up the stairs and along a narrow corridor until they reached a door at the end. He stopped and rapped on the frame.

'Come!' called a high-pitched voice from inside, and the guard lifted the latch and swung the door open before stepping aside to let Sempronius and his men pass. The room was long and narrow, with windows along one side giving fine views out over the city. Smaller windows, high up on the opposite wall, allowed the afternoon sunlight to fill the room with an amber hue. Glabius sat behind a desk beside one of the windows. A pile of waxed tablets lay before him, with one open on the desk. As they entered, he hurriedly made a final mark in the wax and closed the tablet.

As he strode across the room, Macro studied the man they had come to see. Marcus Glabius was short, a head shorter than even Macro, and heavily covered with fat and flesh that made his cheeks pendulous and quivery. Although his wrinkled face indicated advanced years, Macro was surprised to see that Glabius had fine curly black hair, and then realised that the tax collector was wearing a wig. He wore a silk tunic and soft doeskin boots that laced up to just below his knees. He struggled to his feet and bowed towards his guests.

'Welcome, Senator.' He glanced shrewdly at Macro. Cato had manoeuvred himself to stand behind Sempronius's shoulder. 'I had not expected you to bring company. Witnesses to our discussion, perhaps?'

'These men are my secretaries, not witnesses,' Sempronius replied coldly. 'They are here to take notes.'

'Both of them? Surely one would suffice?'

'For a lesser official, perhaps,' Sempronius countered. 'But as a senator, and as acting governor of the province, it is for me to choose how many men I need.'

'Acting governor?' Glabius smiled. 'You have no right to that title, alas. My poor friend Hirtius made that quite clear in his last hours.'

'Nevertheless, I have assumed the governorship, and have written to Rome to seek confirmation.'

A quick frown flitted across Glabius's features, before he smiled again. 'How strange. I have written to my good friend the imperial secretary, Narcissus, to ask for confirmation of my own claim to the post. Ah well, we shall soon see who Rome acknowledges. Anyway, I believe you are here to request rations for your men.'

Macro knelt down and opened his bag. With one hand he began to rummage through the contents, while the other stole slowly round, behind his back. The senator cleared his throat and answered the tax collector clearly.

'No.' Sempronius shook his head. 'Not this time. I have finished with requests, Glabius. Nor will I condone any more payments, at your profiteering rates, for the rancid stocks that you supply to my men. I have come here to demand that you surrender control of the supplies gathered here. Furthermore, I want you, your friends and your hired thugs to quit the acropolis immediately.'

For an instant, Glabius's eyes widened with a stab of anxiety. 'Sadly, I am unable to comply with your wishes.' He stepped out from behind his desk so that he had a clear line to the door at the end of the room. 'Now, if you don't mind, I think I might need a few, er, witnesses of my own in here.'

He opened his mouth to draw a deep breath and call for his guards as Sempronius turned to Macro and nodded. 'Now.'

Macro surged to his feet, dagger in hand, and hurled himself at Glabius, knocking him back against the wall and driving the breath out of him in an explosive gasp of pain. Before the tax collector could react, Macro spun him round, grabbed him under the jaw with his left hand and thrust the edge of the dagger against his throat.

'Don't move a muscle,' he hissed in Glabius's ear. 'The blade's sharp, and will cut through your throat at the slightest pressure.'

Glabius attempted to wriggle, and Macro clamped his left hand tightly about the man's windpipe. 'I said, don't move. And if you make a sound without my say-so, it'll be the last thing you do. Understand?'

Glabius made to nod, but wisely changed his mind and whimpered, 'Yes.'

Cato leaned across the table and turned the tablet that Glabius had been working on round to face him. He flipped it open and ran his eyes over the columns of figures under some clearly marked headings. He let out a low whistle. 'Looks like you're making a small fortune on the commissions on the grain purchases. What am I saying? It's a bloody huge fortune. I think I'll hang on to this.' He turned to Sempronius for permission. 'Sir?'

'Take it. Put it in your bag. I'm sure Narcissus will be delighted to find out how well his friend is doing out of the provincial treasury.'

'Yes, sir.'

'Good.' Sempronius smiled as he stood in front of Glabius and crossed his arms. 'Now that I have your attention, and your co-operation, I want you to listen carefully. You will do exactly as I say. If you manage that, then you will live. If you mess up, or try to make a run for it, or shout a warning, then Centurion Macro will kill you on the spot. So listen. This is what you're going to do . . .'

A short time after Sempronius and the others had entered Glabius's office, they re-emerged. This time the tax collector accompanied them, following the senator, while Macro and Cato walked behind Glabius. Macro held the dagger in his right hand, concealed in the shoulder bag, which had a small slit to the front through which the point of the blade projected, just enough for him to keep the tip in Glabius's side as they walked steadily along the corridor and down the steps into the courtyard. The guard who had shown the visitors up to the office was waiting in the shade of the colonnade and hurriedly rose to his feet at their approach. Glabius slowed to a stop and beckoned to the man.

'Over here!'

The guard drew up in front of the small party and eyed them curiously, until Glabius started to give his orders. 'I want the men summoned to the side of the Temple of Jupiter, at once.'

'Yes, sir.'

Macro gave Glabius just the lightest of prods, as a little reminder.

'Oh yes,' Glabius added hurriedly. 'Make sure they are all there, including the men at the gate and on the walls.'

'All of them?' The guard could not conceal his surprise at the order.

'Yes, all of them!' Glabius replied harshly. 'D'you hear me? All of them.'

'But sir, the gate? Who will guard it?'

'That's not important now. I want everyone by the temple, for a . . . a . . .' Glabius bit his lip, and then started as Macro applied some pressure to his back. 'A reward! Yes, I want to reward you men. For your loyal service. For all the hard work you have done to help the people of Gortyna come through the dark time that has afflicted us!'

Macro leaned a little closer and whispered under his breath, 'Easy does it. Let's not go overboard, eh?'

Glabius nodded ever so faintly as he cleared his throat. 'Just summon the men. Tell them I want to address them, them and all my family and friends in the acropolis. Send word to them as well, at once. Go!'

The guard bowed his head and turned to stride away.

'Don't walk, run!' Glabius called after him, after another prod from Macro. With a last glance back, the guard stumbled into a trot as he hurried away to carry out his orders. As the clatter of footsteps faded, Glabius swallowed nervously and glanced at Sempronius. 'Do you think he believed me?'

'You'd better pray he did.'

Glabius stared intently at the senator. 'I don't know what exactly you think you are doing, but you won't get away with it.'

'We shall see. You just play your part and we'll take care of things.'

'What are you up to?'

'You'll see. Now then, let's get moving again. As far as the entrance. And then we wait there while your men assemble.'

With Macro keeping a close eye on Glabius, they slowly made

133

their way back through the hall and halted just inside the building. Keeping to the shadows, they watched as the bodyguards and hired thugs began to drift across the acropolis and assemble to the side of the colonnade of the Temple of Jupiter. Sempronius had noted the area on a previous visit, and saw how the bulk of the temple concealed the line of sight to the main gate. They waited and watched as a small crowd of the tax collector's guests ambled around the corner, carrying the wine amphora with them and chatting cheerily as they found a shaded corner to sit down in and wait for their host. All the while Macro kept the point of his blade lightly pressed into the small of Glabius's back. Once, when he swayed forward a fraction, Macro grabbed the back of his tunic and gave him a harsh tug.

'You even think about trying to run for it, and I'll have you.'

'I wasn't thinking about it! I swear. I'm just . . . just scared.'

Macro winked at Cato as he replied in a growl, 'Good. Being scared might just keep you alive.'

Glabius swallowed and nodded.

They waited until the last of Glabius's followers appeared to have answered the summons, and then Sempronius turned to him. 'Are you clear on what you have to do?'

'Yes. Absolutely.'

'Then let's do it.' Sempronius took a deep breath and placed his hand on Glabius's shoulder as they walked slowly out of the entrance and started to cross the paved area towards the temple. As they walked, Sempronius muttered to Cato, 'Carry on, Centurion.'

'Yes, sir.' Cato saluted and turned to stride towards the main gate, a waxed tablet clutched under one arm to reinforce the impression that he was a menial clerk going about his business.

Glabius glanced round. 'Where's he off to?'

'Never you mind,' Macro said from behind. 'Just concentrate on what you have to do.'

They continued forward towards the small crowd beside the temple. At their approach the men stopped milling about and turned to Glabius and the others expectantly.

'This will do,' said Sempronius, drawing up. 'Right then, it's your show.'

With Macro standing behind and just to one side of him, and Sempronius on the other flank, Glabius took a deep, nervous breath and raised an arm.

'My friends! Faithful retainers! I am delighted to announce that Senator Sempronius and I have reached an agreement about the governance of the province. I have decided to—'

'Not so fast,' Sempronius said under his breath. 'Spin it out, like I told you.'

As Glabius continued, the senator glanced to his side and saw that Cato was halfway to the gate. Glabius had to keep his men occupied for a little while yet.

'I have decided to, ah, firstly thank you for your friendship and your service. You have been a great source of support in the troubled days since the gods brought down their wrath on our fine city of Gortyna . . .'

Cato looked back and was relieved to see that Glabius had the attention of his followers. No one seemed to be taking any interest in the clerk Senator Sempronius had sent on some errand. He continued striding away from the temple, trusting that everyone had answered the summons. Ahead of him was the gate, abandoned by the sentries. The locking bar was securely in place, a heavy wooden beam capped with bronze at each end. As he reached the gate, Cato paused to look round, but there was still no sign of life at this end of the acropolis. He dropped the waxed slate in his shoulder bag and slipped the strap over his head before lowering the bag to the ground. Then he hurried to the locking bar and grasped the handle, heaving it to one side. The beam shifted a tiny distance and he relaxed his grip for a moment so that he could adjust his footing and brace his shoulder against the handle. Taking a deep breath, he gritted his teeth and threw his weight behind the handle, grunting as he strained his muscles to shift the beam. It slid a little further, this time accompanied by a dull grating as it began to move.

Cato rested briefly and continued, and the beam slowly eased towards the iron hoops through which it passed on either door. At last it came free of the left-hand door and slid into the receiver channel. He eased it a little further, past the fine shaft of daylight that separated the doors, and then let go of the beam, which settled back into its brackets.

Grabbing the empty hoop, Cato leaned back, boots seeking purchase on the worn paving stones. With a squeaky groan that sounded deafening to his ears, the door began to swing inwards. It had opened about a pace when a leather curtain that formed the door in a nearby latrine shed was flung to one side and a man emerged, pulling down his tunic. A scabbard was tucked under one arm, the belt straps dangling down to his sandals. He glanced towards the gate and froze when he saw Cato.

'What in Hades . . . ?'

Cato threw his weight back with renewed effort.

'Stop! Stop that!' the man yelled, releasing the hem of his tunic and drawing his sword and discarding his scabbard in one fluid motion. 'Get away from the fucking door, you!'

Cato ducked through the gap and cupped a hand to his mouth as he bellowed down the road leading into the city. 'Tenth Macedonian! On me!'

There was a scraping sound, and he turned to see that the man was heaving against the edge of the door.

'No you don't!' Cato snarled, fumbling through the slit in his tunic and ripping out the dagger that was tied there. He clenched his fist round the handle and threw his weight against the door, stopping it dead. The impact drove the man back a step, and Cato seized the advantage to thrust again at the door, pressing it open another couple of feet before he sprang through the gap. The guard backed off a short distance, crouched low and readied his sword. He glanced at Cato's dagger and sneered.

'Run, boy! While you still have a chance.'

Cato felt a wave of rage flush through his body. Then he heard a shout from down the slope as Centurion Plotius ordered his men forward. Unless Cato stood his ground, the door would be closed before they reached the gate. He swallowed nervously and shook his head.

'No,' Cato replied. 'You run.'

'What?' The guard looked surprised for a moment, then his teeth clenched as he stepped forward to attack. As soon as he was in range, he lunged straight at Cato's stomach. Cato leaped nimbly to the side, hissing a curse at the pain in his leg as the blade cut through the air close by. As the guard snatched back his sword, Cato slashed at his arm. It was a desperate attack, and the dagger struck the sword blade with a sharp scraping ring. At once the guard drew his weapon back and now slashed at Cato in a swinging arc. Cato had no choice but to go down on one knee and duck as the glittering edge swished overhead. The guard had put his full strength into the blow, and the momentum of the blade carried his arm round and momentarily unbalanced him. Cato threw himself forward, striking at the man's booted foot, and felt the dagger pierce the leather straps, then flesh and bone. There was a shriek of agony as he yanked the handle free and rolled to one side, and over again before scrambling back on to his feet.

Blood was gushing from the guard's foot as he rolled his eyes and roared with rage and pain. Then his eyes flickered back towards Cato, wide and terrifying. With another meaningless shout he staggered forward, swinging his sword wildly. Cato knew that any blow that connected would cripple him if it did not kill him outright. He held the dagger out in front of him, ready to attempt to parry the sword. The first blow missed its target, but the second, a vicious backhanded slash, connected with the dagger with such force that it was wrenched from Cato's hand and flew through the air, spinning end over end, until it clattered across the flagstones some distance away.

'Right, you skinny bastard,' the man growled, backing Cato against the closed door. 'Time to die.'

There was a series of shouts from the direction of the gate, and several of Glabius's men turned their heads at the sounds. After a moment Glabius paused and looked to his left. Until Macro prodded him in the buttock.

'Keep talking.'

Glabius let out a small yelp and lurched half a pace forward before he recovered his wits.

'Better keep their attention,' Sempronius urged quietly. 'Get on with it.'

Glabius nodded, drew another breath and did his best to ignore another shout from the gate as he continued. 'My friends, let me just say that, having conferred with the senator, I have agreed to relinquish the post of governor, for the sake of unity and the safety of our people. So, I salute Senator Gaius Sempronius, acting governor of the province of Crete!' He thrust his fist into the air. There was no response, just shocked expressions from his friends and followers, some of whom were edging forward so as to see what was causing a disturbance at the main gate. The silence was broken when one of the bodyguards took a step forwards and stabbed his finger at Glabius.

'Who's going to pay us then, eh?'

'He's right!' cried another. 'We'll be out of a bloody job.'

There was a chorus of angry shouts before a voice piped up. 'We don't need that fat bastard! Let's choose ourselves another governor, boys! Time for a bit of democracy, like.'

There was a roar of laughter and Glabius raised both hands to appeal to them, calling for silence. 'You have to do as I say! I pay you!'

'Not any longer!' a man called out, and then bent down to scoop up a pebble and hurled it at the tax collector, striking him on the shoulder.

'Ow!' Glabius flinched.

Macro spoke quietly to the senator. 'We're losing it, sir. We stay here much longer and that lot will have our bollocks for breakfast.'

Cato's eyes were focused on the tip of the blade as it advanced towards him, gleaming and deadly. The guard would make no mistake this time. In the distance he could hear the drumming of boots on the street as Plotius and his men raced towards the open gate. The guard heard it too, and hesitated, glancing back over his shoulder.

There was no time for thought. Cato acted instinctively. He leaped forward, going low, under the blade, reaching out to grab the guard around the legs and use his weight to throw the man off balance. The impact drove the guard back a pace, but he was solidly built and managed to keep his balance as he glared down at Cato. His blade was still pointed up, so he smacked the pommel down on to Cato's head.

Cato felt his teeth clash heavily as the blow landed with blinding impact. He felt his grip loosen on the guard's legs, even as he willed his fingers to clench into the man's flesh. But for a moment his body was numbed, and he collapsed on to the ground, landing heavily on his side. As his vision began to clear, he squinted up into the light, and saw the silhouette of the guard as he leaned over Cato, sword raised as he shouted, 'You are fucked!'

There was a confusion of sounds: boots, the groan of the gate hinges and a sudden grunt and groan of pain. Cato blinked. The guard had gone and he was staring up into a clear sky, and then another blurry shape intervened.

'Centurion Cato! Sir, are you all right?'

'What?' Cato clenched his eyes shut for a moment, willing the dizzy nausea to abate. He felt hands haul him to his feet and hold him there.

'Sir?'

Cato opened his eyes and the anxious expression of Centurion Plotius swam into focus. 'I'm fine. Bit dazed, but I'm fine.'

The auxiliaries were pressing through the gate and spilling on to the open ground inside the acropolis. Cato thrust his arm out towards the Temple of Jupiter, where he could see Macro and the others backing away in the face of a shouting mob. 'Plotius, get your men over there at the double!'

Plotius nodded and swept his drawn sword up as he shouted to get his men's attention. Cato saw a crimson ribbon along the edge of the blade, and glancing down he saw the guard at his feet, the side of his face laid open by a sword cut.

'Tenth Macedonian!' Plotius bellowed. 'Follow me!'

He charged across the flagstones, towards the temple, and his men pounded after him, shields up and spears held ready. Cato ran after them in an unsteady lope, as his sense of balance had not yet recovered from the blow to his head.

Stones were raining down on them now, and Macro and the others had to raise their arms to protect their heads. Glabius turned to run, back towards the administration building. There was a roar from the mob at the sight, and then they surged forwards.

'Sir!' Macro called to Sempronius. 'Run for it!'

The two Romans turned and sprinted after Glabius, pursued by the tax collector's erstwhile employees. At the back of the crowd, his friends and cronies hung back with terrified expressions. Glabius puffed into the entrance and ran on, heading towards his office, as if that might save him. Macro was close behind, and realised at once that they would be hounded and killed if they continued. The entrance was a natural choke point. He drew up abruptly and turned round as Sempronius swerved to one side to avoid him.

'Grab that post, sir!' Macro pointed at a broken length of timber in the rubble.

Sempronius snatched it up, hefting it quickly to find a good handhold, and the pair of them faced the mob surging towards the building. Macro spread his feet and held out his dagger, his lips curled into a snarl. There was one man out in front of his comrades, the one who had thrown the first stone, and he slowed as he reached the entrance, then stopped, staring at Macro and Sempronius uncertainly. The next two men followed his cue and the mob reined in, momentarily quiet as they faced the two Romans.

'Throw down your weapons and back away!' Sempronius ordered.

There was no response, and the crowd glared at him in open hostility. The senator risked a glimpse to his left and saw the first of the auxiliaries running towards the temple.

'Let's kill 'em!' a voice shouted from the back of the crowd. 'Kill 'em now!'

'Wait!' Sempronius thrust out his hand. 'You lay a finger on us and you die! It's all over for you now. My men are coming. Look!' He stabbed his finger towards Plotius and his men dashing towards the temple. 'Drop your weapons before it's too late. Those men have orders to kill anyone who resists! Do as I say, drop your swords!'

The crowd was still for a moment, uncertain, and for a moment Macro feared that they might fight, and begin by slaughtering him and the senator. Then there was a clatter as the first sword hit the ground. Then another, and then all the men were dropping their weapons.

'Now back off!' Sempronius called. 'Over there, beside the temple!'

There was a ripple of movement as the men edged away, glancing anxiously at the approaching auxiliaries. By the time Plotius and his men reached the entrance, the ground in front of it was clear.

Plotius saw the scratches and cuts from the stones on Macro and Sempronius's arms. 'You're injured.'

Sempronius shook his head. 'We're fine. Nothing serious. See to the prisoners. Get them off the acropolis as soon as you can. Take them to the amphitheatre. Let them sweat it out tonight and then set them free in the morning. Except Glabius. Find him a nice quiet cell of his own up here and keep him isolated.'

'Yes, sir.' Plotius saluted.

Cato pushed his way through the ranks of the auxiliaries, anxiously looking for Macro. He smiled as soon as he saw his friend and clapped him on the arm.

'I saw them go for you. For a moment there I feared the worst.'

'Feared the worst?' Macro snorted with derision. For a moment he was tempted to make light of it, but instead he shook his head and puffed out his cheeks. 'Fuck, that was close.'

CHAPTER FOURTEEN

Over the following days, Cato was charged with organising the feeding of the inhabitants of Gortyna, and those refugees camped in the ruins and outside the walls. Having gone through the inventory of the food supplies stockpiled on the acropolis, it was clear that the population could be fed for at least a month. Each morning wagons left the acropolis for distribution points across the city to hand out rations to the waiting queues. The wagons were escorted by sections of auxiliaries, who protected them and ensured that all waited their turn to be given their allotted share of the food.

At the same time, the stocks of food held privately by Glabius's friends were confiscated and the inedible grain and meat that they had been selling was burned in a pit outside the city. At first the merchants had protested, demanded compensation and threatened to present their claims to Rome. Cato coolly invited them to proceed with their threat, and added that he would be sending his own report on their corrupt appropriation of imperial funds, with the collusion of Glabius. The merchants quickly backed down, and some, more mindful than their companions of the harsh justice meted out by the emperor, even offered to repay the small fortunes they had made from the sale of overpriced and spoiled food supplies.

In addition to the food stocks of the merchants, Cato sent strong patrols on to the farmland that sprawled across the southern plain, searching for further supplies of food to add to those held on the acropolis. With the inventory fluctuating every day, he needed help in keeping track of the consumption and supply of food, and one evening, as Sempronius dined in his new headquarters on the acropolis, Julia volunteered to take on the task. It was the usual affair of the senator, his daughter, Cato and Macro, each one on a couch, in front of a low table. Sempronius and his daughter sat side by side with Macro to the senator's left and Cato to Julia's right. The meals were simple, as the senator felt duty bound to share the privations of the inhabitants of Gortyna to an extent. The handful of small dishes presented by those kitchen slaves that remained were as artfully presented as anything served at a great banquet, and were consumed with great gusto by Macro.

'Lovely!' He smiled, licking a smear of sauce from his lips as he set down a small bowl of shredded pork in honeyed garum. 'I could eat that all night.'

'And so could most of the people outside these walls,' Sempronius observed as he chewed slowly. 'But we have to lead by example, as any centurion of your experience should know.'

'Well.' Macro sucked through his teeth. 'There's a time and place.'

'This is it, alas.' Sempronius swallowed and considered the situation for a moment. 'We need more food, and soon.'

'What about Egypt?' asked Cato. 'Surely they have more than enough grain to spare?'

Sempronius nodded. The crops that grew along the Nile were famous for their yield, and were the largest source of grain for the teeming multitudes of Rome who had come to depend on regular, free handouts paid for by the emperor. 'I know the legate there well. Gaius Petronius. We served together on the Rhine. Petronius was one of the equestrian tribunes – a good man. I could ask him, but the chances of any emergency food aid from that quarter are slim. Rome has the first, and only, call on Egyptian grain. The truth of it is that we have to make do with what we have for the present. That means that you must keep a close eye on our level of supplies.'

'True. I could use some help with the books, sir. If you could spare some of your clerks.'

'I'm short-staffed as it is. But I'll see what I can do.'

Julia lowered her plate and shifted round on her couch. 'What about me, Father? I could help Cato.'

'You?' Sempronius raised his eyebrows.

'Why not? You have paid some of the finest teachers in Rome to educate me. I'm sure I could manage to book-keep easily enough.'

'I'm sure you could, but I didn't pay those fine teachers just so that you could do the work of a humble clerk.'

'I'm sure.' Julia smiled mischievously. 'But whatever happened to leading by example? Surely that applies to all of us in this crisis? It would show the locals that Romans, no matter how high born, share their burdens. A shrewd political move, if nothing else.'

Sempronius stared at her for a moment, and then shook his head ruefully. 'Gentlemen, if I have one word of advice for you, don't have children. Or at least, if you must, then never overindulge them, else they will be your masters by and by.'

'I'll drink to that!' Macro laughed, as he helped himself to a goblet of wine and drank half of it down in one gulp.

Julia frowned. 'Have I ever failed to show you the respect that you are due, Father?'

'Well, now that you mention it . . .'

They stared at each other for a brief moment, before breaking into light laughter. Julia swatted his arm and then reached for an apple. Her father smiled fondly at her for a moment before he continued softly, 'Sometimes you remind me so much of your mother. By the gods, I miss her.'

Abruptly he lowered his eyes and coughed, then swiftly picked up his cup and held it out to Macro. 'Fill it up, Centurion. I'll join you in that toast.'

As their cups clinked together, Julia turned to Cato and took his hand, caressing the back of it with her thumb as she smiled. 'At least we can spend more time with each other this way.'

'We can, as long as we make sure that we do our duty first.'

'Call it what you like,' she whispered, and then laughed as Cato shuffled with embarrassment.

Sempronius looked round. 'What's up with you, my girl?'

'It's nothing, Father. A private joke.'

'I see.' Sempronius glanced at Cato. 'Make sure she works hard.'

'Yes, sir.'

There was a lengthy silence, then the senator turned back to Macro. 'How are the men coming on?'

As soon as he had taken charge of the forces remaining in Gortyna, Macro had begun a rigorous training programme for the auxiliaries. At first Sempronius had not been convinced that it was a good use of their time. They were needed to police the streets and the refugee camp, and help with the gangs of volunteers and the remaining slaves as they cleared rubble and made repairs to buildings, the sewers and the small aqueduct that supplemented the city's water supplies. But Macro recalled all too well the ferocity of the slaves he had fought in defence of Matala's supply wagons, and was adamant that the men be made ready to fight as quickly as possible. Therefore the soldiers of the Tenth Macedonian had been divided into two groups, and alternated between carrying out their work in the city and drilling on the training ground outside Gortyna.

Macro paused a moment to think before he replied. 'Truth to tell, the lads of the Tenth are willing enough, and morale is good, which is surprising given the circumstances. The trouble is they have been on a garrison posting for too long and have grown soft. There's hardly a man who would be able to march fifteen miles in full kit and make a fortified camp at the end of the day. They change formation too slowly and are sloppy with it. Still, I'm making steady progress. Another month or so and they'll be more than a match for any band of slaves.'

'So I should hope. From the reports I receive from Marcellus, it seems that the slaves don't present much of a danger. He's swept the plain and driven them into the hills. Now he aims to starve them out, or at least weaken them enough to attempt to pursue them into the mountains, track them down and crush any resistance.'

Macro nodded approvingly. 'Seems the right way to proceed. Good luck to him. Though I can't help thinking that the slaves seem to have lost their spirit. They were keen enough to fight when I encountered them.'

'Perhaps you and your men discouraged them. After all, your report said you had inflicted heavy casualties on them.'

'That we did,' Macro said flatly. He took no pride in the slaughter of the poorly armed and untrained slaves. But it was them or him, and there had been no time for pity.

'So, we have them contained,' Sempronius concluded. 'We have got rid of Glabius and his cronies and we have sufficient food to see the immediate crisis out. I have a feeling we are over the worst of it. The emperor will be happy with us, and once the province is settled and a new governor sent out from Rome, we can resume our journey home.' He smiled contentedly at Macro and Cato. 'I think we should be pleased with ourselves, gentlemen.'

'Another toast?' Macro raised his cup.

'Indeed.' Sempronius laughed. 'To success.'

Their cups clattered together and then the senator turned to Cato. 'What? Not joining in? Raise a cup, Cato.'

Cato forced a smile. 'If you say so, sir. To success.'

He drank, then lowered his cup. Julia squeezed his hand. 'Why the long face?'

'I'm not sure.' Cato shrugged. 'Force of habit, I suppose. I just can't help feeling that we've not seen the back of our problems here.'

Julia looked disappointed. 'And there I was, taking you for an optimist, full of the joys of youth.'

'I'm young enough,' Cato conceded. 'But I have seen more of this world than most men my age, and many who are much older. Something tells me we're not through this yet. You mark my words.'

'It's a fucking javelin, not a bloody crutch!' Macro bawled into the auxiliary's ear as he savagely kicked the butt away. The javelin clattered down, and with a gasp of surprise the exhausted soldier lost his balance and crashed to the ground in a cloud of dust.

'What now?' Macro bent over the man, hands on hips, as he continued to shout. 'Asleep on my parade ground! You 'orrible little man. Who do you think I am, your bleeding mother come to wake you in the morning?' He kicked him in the ribs. 'On your feet!'

Macro snapped upright and continued down the length of the century, which had just returned to the parade ground after he had taken them for a run twice round the city. Having witnessed the fate of the first man in the line, the others hurriedly shuffled to attention, chests heaving as they held their javelins and shields tightly to their bodies and stared straight ahead. Macro, in the chainmail vest, greaves and helmet he had taken from the stores of the Twelfth Hispania, was in far better shape than the men, and breathed easily as he strode down the first line, inspecting the Macedonians with a contemptuous expression. The only man amongst them with the kind of spirit he wanted to see was Atticus, who had turned out to be one of the best recruits Macro had ever encountered: tough, and with a natural talent with weapons. Macro had already earmarked the Greek for promotion to optio.

'I've seen a sewing circle of old women who looked more warlike than you lot! You are pathetic. How in Hades can you look so clapped out after a nice little trot like that? Right then, after javelin practice we'll do it again, and if any man falls out, or fails to stand properly to attention when we get back here, I will kick his arse so hard he'll be coughing his balls up. So help me.'

Macro reached the end of the line, pivoted round and pointed out the ten straw figures fastened to stakes thirty paces away. 'There's your target, one section to each. If you can't hit a still target like that on a nice neat parade ground then you are going to be no fucking use to me on a battlefield soaked in blood and covered in bodies. You will throw your javelins until every man has scored five direct hits. I don't care how long it takes, because I am a patient man and nothing makes me happier than the prospect of spending all evening at javelin practice. Form section lines!'

The men hurriedly shuffled into position. Most sections had fewer than eight men, as some had been lost in the earthquake and others were sick or injured.

'First man!' Macro bellowed. 'Make ready your javelin!'

The leading man in each line stepped forward, grasping the javelin in an overhead grip and swinging the throwing arm back. They were using light javelins, more slender than the standard weapon that sometimes doubled as a spear. Macro waited until every man was ready and had had a brief chance to take aim.

'Loose javelins!'

With a grunt each man stepped forward and hurled his javelin. They arced through the air towards the targets. There was a brief explosion of straw on two of the dummies; three went wide and five failed to make it even as far as the targets.

Macro folded his arms and glared at the men who stood empty-handed. He took a deep, calming breath before he called out, 'That was the most miserable display I have ever seen! Your best chance of survival on the battlefield would be to make the enemy die laughing at your utterly shit efforts. To the back of the line, ladies. Next rank!'

As the practice session wore on, the men failed to improve to anything close to the standard that Macro required of them, much to his exasperation. It was one thing to threaten to keep them at it until they got it right; quite another to have to endure it alongside them. Some of the men were adept with the javelin, most could hit the target half of the time and a handful were so hopeless that Macro feared they would have missed the dummies even if they stood within spitting distance.

At length he saw Cato making his way out of the nearest city gate and heading towards the parade ground. They exchanged a salute as Cato joined his friend. As another wave of missiles mostly missed their targets, Cato clicked his tongue.

'Glad to see you haven't lost your touch as an instructor.'

'Ha fucking ha,' Macro grumbled. 'What are you here for? Assume you didn't come out here just to take the piss.'

'As if.'

'Anyway, you're no bloody good with a javelin. Seem to recall that you nearly skewered me that time in Germany.'

'I was just a raw recruit then,' Cato responded defensively. 'I've mastered it now, of course.'

'Really?' Macro's eyes twinkled. He turned towards his men. 'Ladies! I am delighted to announce that we have a proper soldier here who is only too happy to show you the art of javelin throwing.'

'Macro . . .' Cato growled.

'You there!' Macro pointed to the nearest man. 'Hand your javelin to Centurion Cato!'

'Macro, I really haven't got time.'

'Bollocks. Let's see who has lost their touch, shall we?' Macro waved a hand invitingly towards the javelin the soldier was holding out. 'Be my guest.'

Cato's eyes narrowed furiously. He snatched the weapon and strode to the front of the line. Turning to face the target, he focused on it intently as he flipped the weapon in his hand and caught it in an overhead grip. He placed his leading foot carefully, eased back his throwing arm and sighted the target along his left arm, lining it up with his middle finger. Then, taking a deep breath, he tensed his muscles and hurled the javelin forward with all his strength. The weapon arced up, reached the apex of its trajectory and then dipped down and punched through the centre of the dummy's body.

Cato spun round towards Macro, hands balled into fists as he hissed triumphantly, 'Yessss!'

At once he forced himself to recover his composure and strolled back towards his friend, trying hard to look casual, as if hitting the target was all in a day's work. Macro nodded his head in admiration.

'Nice throw.'

'Eat your words, Macro.'

'Not bad at all, except that you somehow managed to throw the bloody thing the wrong way round.'

'What?' Cato turned quickly to look at the target. Sure enough, the point of the javelin was protruding from the chest while the butt sagged on to the ground on the other side. 'Shit . . .'

'Well, never mind.' Macro patted his shoulder. 'It's a useful demonstration in improvisation, if nothing else.'

Cato scowled. 'Ha fucking ha.'

Macro laughed. 'Now then, what brings you here?'

'Message from Sempronius. A section of the sewer has collapsed and needs to be dug out. He wants you and your men to see to it.'

'Oh, thanks. Just what I needed.'

Cato smiled as he saluted Macro again. 'What goes round comes round, eh? I'll see you later on. Right now I have to get back to the acropolis, and the delights of record-keeping. Have fun.'

The sunlight was streaming through the windows high on the wall in the office next door to the one recently vacated by Glabius. Here too there were windows overlooking the city, and Cato was staring out over the damaged buildings and ruins, now washed in a pale orange hue. His mind gradually drifted back to the concern that was consuming him. Over the previous days, Marcellus's optimistic reports on his progress were being countered by fragments of news and rumours arriving at Gortyna that told of numerous raids by the slaves on isolated farms and estates. Then, the previous day, a cavalry squadron sent in search of a patrol that had not reported in returned to inform Cato that they had discovered the bodies of the missing men. The cavalrymen had also passed through a village where every man, woman and child had been slaughtered and left in a pile of mutilated bodies in the centre of the village, scarcely three miles from Gortyna.

'Hey!' Julia called out from the other side of the desk. 'Would you mind keeping your attention on the job?' She tapped the slate in front of her with a stylus. 'My father wants the revised figures tonight, and we still have to account for the supplies on those wagons that turned up at noon.'

'Sorry.' Cato flashed a smile. 'Just thinking.'

He picked up the inventory of the first wagon and prepared to add up the ticks for each sack and announce the total to Julia to note down.

There was a sudden sharp rap on the door, and Cato turned round.

'Come in!'

The door opened, and one of Sempronius's clerks entered. 'Sorry to interrupt, sir, but the senator wants to see you at once.'

'At once?' Cato glanced at Julia and saw her frown. 'Very well, I'll come.'

He pushed his chair back and stood up, pausing a moment. 'We'll continue later on.'

Julia nodded wearily.

Cato followed the clerk out of the office. He wondered why Sempronius had summoned him so peremptorily. They were not due to meet until the evening briefing. At the end of the corridor, the door to the senator's office was open and the clerk stopped to knock on the frame.

'Centurion Cato, sir.'

'Very well, show him in.'

The clerk stood to one side and Cato strode past him into the office. Sempronius was sitting at his desk. To one side stood an officer. Cato recognised him as one of Marcellus's centurions. The man was in armour, and a bloodstained rag was tied round his sword arm. His face was covered with stubble and he looked exhausted and strained. Sempronius glanced at Cato with a drawn expression. 'I have sent for Macro. He should join us shortly. Meanwhile, do you know Centurion Micon?'

Sempronius indicated the other officer, and Cato looked at him briefly and nodded as he crossed the room and stood in front of the desk. 'I take it you have a report from Prefect Marcellus?'

Micon looked to the senator for guidance.

'Just tell him,' Sempronius said wearily. 'Tell him everything.'

Cato turned to Centurion Micon, as the other man cleared his throat. 'Yes, sir. Centurion Marcellus is dead.'

'Dead?'

'Yes, sir.' Micon nodded wearily. 'Him and all his men.'

CHAPTER FIFTEEN

The Parthian glanced up as he held the needle and lamb's-gut thread poised over the wound. A sword cut had laid open the gladiator's thigh. Fortunately the wound was shallow and clean and had bled nicely to keep it clear of dirt and grit. The muscle was superficially torn and would mend without causing any handicap. The gladiator was standing in front of him, stripped down to a loincloth. His torso bore several scars, some of which looked like they might have killed or crippled a lesser man. Although he had been strong and fit before he had become a slave, two years of hard training had left him with a superb physique. The Parthian had never seen the like in all his days tending the warriors of his master's bodyguard.

It had been a good life, he reflected briefly, before the border skirmish that had led to his capture and then being sold on as a surgeon to the family of a wealthy Greek merchant. Since then, it had been an endless succession of slaves with boils, sprained ankles and wrists, and venereal diseases amongst the girls of a brothel the merchant owned in Athens. The Parthian had been travelling with his master when the earthquake had struck Crete. He had been outside the inn where the Greek and his retinue had been staying when the earth roared and rumbled beneath him, throwing him to the ground. When the earthquake had passed and he stood up, there was nothing left of the inn, and not a sound came from beneath the heap of rubble.

The Parthian had taken the chance to flee into the hills, where he wandered for two days, growing steadily hungrier, until he came across the gladiator and his band of slaves. At first he was content to accept the scraps of food that were freely given to him, and resolved to travel to the coast and find a ship heading east on which he could stow away. But then he had come to know the gladiator. There was something about him that reminded the Parthian of his master back home. An inextinguishable aura of authority and determination that would brook no obstacle. Once the gladiator had learned of his medical expertise, the Parthian was asked to remain with the slaves and tend to their needs. For the first time in his life he had been offered a choice, and as he pondered the novelty of deciding his own fate, he saw the gladiator watching steadily, waiting for his reply. At that moment he knew that his choice had been made.

In the days that had followed, the gladiator's band of followers had swelled as more slaves flocked to his side, begging to be given the chance to take up arms against their former masters. The gladiator had taken them all, selecting those who were fit to be part of his growing war band. The rest were sent to the large, flat-topped hill that served as their base. Already the approaches to the summit had been protected by earthworks and palisades, and thousands of slaves lived on the hill in a variety of crude shelters, or even in the open air. Despite the hardships and the ever-present fear of Roman soldiers and recapture, they were happy and savoured every day that they remained at liberty.

The Parthian leaned closer to the wound and examined it briefly. Three stitches would suffice to reattach the severed muscle. Another nine or ten stitches would be enough to close the wound, the Parthian decided. He glanced up.

'This is going to hurt. Are you ready, Ajax?'

'Do it now.'

As the gladiator stood still, the surgeon leaned forward and probed into the wound, drawing the two ends of the muscle together. Then he pierced the tissue, pressed the needle through and sewed his stitches, before cutting off the spare thread and knotting it securely. He glanced up. 'All right?'

Ajax nodded, keeping his steely gaze on the vista below him. He stood on the cliff above the defile, bathed in the warm glow of the morning sun. The sun had risen an hour earlier, and the first shafts of light had shone down the length of the defile, illuminating the corpses of Roman soldiers sprawled and heaped along the narrow path. In amongst them were the bodies of horses and hundreds of the slaves who had closed in to finish off the Romans caught in the ambush. It had been a bloody fight, Ajax recalled vividly. The desperate courage of his men against the training, armour and weapons of the Romans. The last of the enemy had been hunted down and killed just before dawn. Now his men were picking the bodies clean of anything that would serve the needs of his growing army. Before, they had a miscellany of swords, knives, scythes, spears, pitchforks and clubs. Now they had proper kit, and Ajax knew how to use it. Several of his followers had once been gladiators themselves, and had already started to train the best of the slaves in the ways of combat. Soon, they in turn would train other slaves, and before the month was out, Ajax would have thousands of men under arms, and nothing would stand in the way of his revolt.

He winced as the surgeon pinched the open mouth of the wound together and pushed the needle through his skin, deftly pulling the thread tight before returning the needle back through the flesh in the opposite direction. The pain was hot and made every nerve in his leg shriek with agony, but he kept his jaw clamped shut and fought down the temptation to show that he was suffering. Pain was proof of life, his first trainer had told him at the gladiator school outside Brindisium. The bearing of pain was also the measure of a man, the trainer had continued as he had walked down the line of new recruits, striking every man in the face as he passed in each direction. Those that flinched or whimpered he struck again and again, until they collapsed on the ground, bloodied and broken. The next day he repeated the exercise, and the next, and by the end of the first ten days, they could all stand and take his blows without any expression crossing their faces.

So Ajax stood steady as a rock as the Parthian surgeon worked unhurriedly on his wound and he did not look down until at length he heard the Parthian ease himself back and stand, bloodied fingers holding the needle in one hand as he reached for a cloth from his bag with the other.

'There, it is done. I will check the wound again tonight. Try not to exert the leg too much today, or the stitches may tear.'

The gladiator offered one of his rare smiles. 'There is no need for exertion today, Kharim. The slaves have won their victory; now let us celebrate. Once we have tended to our wounded and buried our dead, we return to camp. We'll slaughter and roast a herd of goats, break open the wine and have a banquet worthy of the gods.'

'Which gods? Mine or yours?'

Ajax laughed and clapped his hand on the Parthian's shoulder. 'Neither, or both. What does it matter? As long as we are free men, who cares which gods we worship? Life is good, made sweeter still by the defeat of those bastard Romans.'

'Yes.' Kharim nodded as he wiped his hands clean on the rag and peered down at the bodies below. He was silent for a moment. 'It was a shame about the boy.'

Ajax's smile faded as he recalled the youth who had led the Romans into the trap. 'He knew what his fate would be. Pollio was as brave as they come.' Ajax slowly balled his hand into a fist. 'He will not be forgotten. He bought us this victory with his life. I shall honour Pollio by killing more Romans.'

The Parthian glanced at him uneasily. 'Why do you hate the Romans so much?'

'Simple. They made a slave of me.'

'They are no worse than other slave owners. Yet you do not hate others as you hate Rome.'

'You are right.' Ajax smiled faintly. 'In truth, I have my own reasons for hating the empire, and a handful of Romans in particular. But it does not matter. As long as my hatred feeds my desire for freedom, yours and that of all the slaves who follow me, then let me indulge it, eh?'

They shared a smile, and then Ajax frowned as he caught sight of a small party of escorted prisoners being led along the top of the cliff towards him. The leader of the escorts was a young man, tall and broad, and grinning as he approached his commander. Ajax maintained a stern expression as he folded his arms and stood, stiff-backed, as the prisoners were brought to him.

'Chilo, what is this? I gave the order that there were to be no prisoners.'

'Yes, Ajax, I know. But this one,' Chilo turned and grabbed one of his prisoners by the shoulder and roughly shoved him forward so that he stumbled and nearly lost his balance, 'is a centurion. I caught him, with these others, hiding beneath a wagon at the rear of their column. They didn't put up any fight, and threw down their swords. And there was me thinking that centurions were supposed to die rather than surrender.'

Ajax stared at the Roman officer. 'Is this true?'

The centurion lowered his eyes and nodded.

'Why? Tell me why you dishonour yourself, and these men you lead.'

'Why?' The centurion looked up nervously. 'We were beaten. There was no point in further resistance.'

'Coward!' Ajax shouted. 'Coward! There is always a point to resistance! Always. That is why I stand here as your victor. And you bow in defeat. You are humiliated, Roman, the more so because you chose shame rather than death. A slave lives a life of shame, of obeisance, always in fear. In this he has no choice, and death is merely a release from humiliation and pain. That is the lesson I learned when Rome made me a slave.' He paused and then sneered at the centurion. 'That is why these slaves beat you, Roman. They know that liberty is the only thing worth dying for. Yet you, and these other curs, you chose to surrender your liberty rather than die. And that is why we defeated you. That is why we will defeat every Roman soldier in Crete. Because our will is stronger than yours.'

The centurion stared back, terrified by the intensity of Ajax's glare. There was a tense pause before the gladiator took a deep breath and continued. 'What is your name, Centurion?'

'Centurion Micon, sir. Second squadron, Second Batavian Mounted Cohort.'

'Well, Centurion Micon, it appears that there is no Second Batavian Mounted Cohort any more. Therefore it has no need of a centurion.' Ajax swiftly pulled out a dagger and grabbed Micon by the harness that covered his chainmail vest, and which marked him out as an officer. Three medallions were attached to the harness: campaign awards. Ajax slipped the blade under the leather shoulder strap of the harness, smiling as the Roman flinched, and cut the strap with a quick jerk. He cut the other shoulder strap, and then the tie that bound the harness around the centurion's waist, and wrenched the harness and its medallions away from Micon. He held it up for his men to see and then contemptuously hurled it into the ravine. There was a roar of approval from the slaves who had been watching the little drama.

'You are no longer a centurion,' Ajax sneered. 'You are nothing more than the last scrap of your precious cohort.'

He turned to Chilo. 'Take your prisoners to the edge of the cliff and throw them off, one by one.'

Chilo grinned. 'Yes, General! It will be my pleasure.'

'No!' one of the Batavian auxiliaries shouted. 'You can't! We surrendered!'

'How foolish of you,' Ajax replied coldly. 'I wonder if you would have spared me had I begged for mercy on the sands of the arena. Chilo, get on with it.'

Chilo and two of his men grabbed the nearest auxiliary and dragged him roughly towards the edge of the cliff that dropped into the ravine. The Roman shouted and screamed for mercy, writhing in their grasp. They struggled towards the edge, and stopped a safe distance back, before holding the captive's wrists firmly. Chilo stood behind him, then, bracing his boot in the small of the auxiliary's back, thrust him forwards as his men released their grip. With a terrified scream the Batavian lurched over the edge of the cliff, arms flailing. Then he was falling in a lazy tumble as he clawed at the air. His screams were cut off a moment later as his head struck an outcrop of rock and exploded like a watermelon. His body bounced off the cliff and fell with a heavy crunch on to the boulders at its foot. One by one his comrades suffered the same fate, as the slaves cheered each man, and jeered those who struggled most as they were led to the edge.

At last only Micon remained. He had slumped to his knees and was trembling pitifully as his captors came for him. Chilo had him dragged towards the cliff, but just before they reached the edge Ajax called out:

'Stop!'

Chilo and his men turned towards their leader with questioning expressions.

'Not him.' Ajax waved them back from the edge. 'That one lives. Bring him here.'

The shaking Roman was thrown to the ground before the gladiator and Ajax bit back on his disgust as he stared down at the man, pathetically mumbling his thanks.

'Silence, you dog!' He kicked the Roman. 'Hear me out. I want you to go back to Gortyna, and tell your superiors – tell everyone you meet – all that you have seen here. You tell them that the slaves will be free, and that we will destroy, with sword and fire, any who come between us and freedom . . . Now stand up, you cowardly vermin. On your feet! Before I change my mind.'

Micon scrambled up and stood trembling before Ajax.

'Do you understand what you have to do, Roman?'

'Y-yes.'

Ajax turned to Chilo. 'Find him a horse, then escort him away from here, a safe distance so our people won't be tempted to chase him down and cut his throat. Then set him free. Is that understood?'

Chilo bowed his head. 'Yes, General. As you command.'

That night fires flared into the starry sky to warm the slaves as they celebrated their victory. At the heart of the patchwork of mean shelters and tents that formed their camp was a large open space in front of the tent of Ajax and his closest companions. Scores of fire pits had been dug, and as darkness fell, mutton carcasses on spits roasted over heaps of glowing embers, filling the air with the rich aroma of cooking meat. For slaves, used to an unvaried diet of gruel and whatever small animals they might snare, this was the height of luxury. The kind of feast that their former masters enjoyed, and which they had only ever dreamed of. Wine, bread and fruit taken from the kitchens of the estates that had been sacked by the slaves were freely distributed on the orders of Ajax.

As his followers feasted, Ajax made his way from fire to fire, congratulating those who had fought in the ambush, and listening patiently as they boasted of their part in the battle. It did his heart good to see how the ragged, cowed fugitives who had joined his struggle against Rome were now so full of fight. Where he led in battle, they would follow, unquestioning. He had been used to the adulation of the mob that came to spectate at the games in Rome, but this was altogether different. These slaves, these people, did not follow him because he won them bets, nor because he excited their bloodlust. They followed him because they shared a common burden. And now, he mused, they shared a common destiny.

He had nursed their ambition with small raids on estates and villages, and then attacks on Roman patrols. Only when he had been sure that they were ready did he plan the previous night's ambush. He had watched the Roman column ever since it had set out from Gortyna. Skirmish by skirmish he had lured the commander towards the hills, and then, when the trap was set, he had sent in the boy. The child had not hesitated for an instant when Ajax had asked Pollio to carry out the task that would almost certainly lead to his death. The boy's father had been killed by an overseer, and his mother sold to a brothel. All he lived for was revenge. He had gone to his death willingly and Ajax had been glad for him to go, knowing he would have done precisely the same if their positions had been reversed. He had long grown used to the conviction that there was nothing he would not do if it aided his desire to defy and destroy Rome and all it stood for. In time, his followers would come to share his vision as fully as he did, as the boy had, and Rome would tremble as it beheld a tide of those it had treated as little more than things rise up to overwhelm the empire.

Ajax allowed himself a moment to indulge in the dream of Rome being crushed beneath his heel. Then he reined in his imagination and focused on the immediate future. A small battle had been won. Now was the time to exploit the victory, before the Romans could recover from the shock of the defeat.

As the fires died down, the slaves finished the last scraps of their feast and drank the last of the wine. Some began to sing, fragments of songs remembered from the time before they or their forebears had been slaves. Songs from every corner of the empire, and the melodies and rhythms, often strange to his ear, moved Ajax deeply. Truly there was no corner of the earth that had not felt the scourge of Rome. Once more his heart was filled with cold, cold rage and a thirst for revenge.

Returning to the centre of the camp, he climbed on to a wagon piled high with captured equipment and stood atop the driver's bench, sword in one hand, the standard of the Batavian cohort in the other. He clattered the blade against the silver disc bearing an image of the emperor. The surrounding crowd turned towards the sound and began to fall silent, watching their leader expectantly. Ajax lowered his sword and stared out over the sea of faces, dimly lit by the wavering glow of the dying fires. Filling his lungs, he began.

'You have feasted on the best meat, the best wine and the best delicacies that we have taken from those who were our masters. Tell me, what is it that has the best taste tonight?'

'Roast mutton!' a voice cried, and scores of others called out their agreement.

'Garum!' cried another.

'Figs!'

'My girl's cunt!' someone shouted, and there was a roar of laughter.

Ajax clattered his sword against the standard again to silence them. 'You are all wrong! I'll tell you what tastes best and sweetest to every one of us tonight . . . Liberty! Liberty!'

The crowd cheered, thrusting their fists into the air as they echoed the cry. 'Liberty!'

When the cheering had died down, Ajax continued. 'My friends, we have won the first of many fights. But not without cost. We fought with clubs and farming tools against men in armour with swords and spears. Now their weapons are ours, and when we next fight the Romans it will be on far more even terms. No! The next fight will be on *our* terms. They have grown fat and complacent on the back of our labour and suffering. They cannot match the determination of those who fight for their freedom. That is why they will lose. That is why we shall triumph!'

More cheering greeted his words. Ajax indulged them a moment before he raised his sword and called for quiet.

'My friends, we have tasted liberty, and now victory, but our work is only just beginning. I have a plan. We will demand that our freedom be recognised. We will demand that the Romans give us safe passage out of their empire. Now, it is just possible that they may be inclined to refuse such a reasonable request . . .'

The crowd laughed and jeered for a moment before Ajax continued.

'So, my friends, we must teach them a lesson, to prove how serious our demands are. Tomorrow I will lead an army off this hill and out on to the plain. Within days I will show the Romans that their defeat last night was no accident. I will give them another defeat that will shatter their arrogance and humble them. In a few days they will learn just how terrible our revenge can be . . . Then they will be forced to meet our demands. If they don't, then I give you my word that we shall slaughter every last Roman on the island.' He thrust his sword into the heavens. 'Death to Rome! Death to Rome!'

The crowd took up the chant, and it thundered out into the night, strident and challenging, daring Rome to defy them.

Ajax climbed down from the wagon and strolled over to Chilo. 'Time to complete the night's entertainment, I think. Have the men bring out my little pet.'

'My pleasure.' Chilo grinned. He turned away, gesturing to a handful of his men, who followed him inside Ajax's tent. They emerged a moment later carrying an iron cage. As the crowd saw the cage they edged forward, forming a loose circle around it. As Chilo and his men set it down in the glow of the cooking fires, Ajax stepped up to the cage and looked through the bars. Inside he could make out a human form, visible in the slats of orange light passing through the bars. The figure was naked and bruised and sat with her arms hugged round her knees as strands of matted hair hung down over her fleshy body.

'My lady Antonia, thank you for joining us,' Ajax mocked. 'I am sorry that you have missed the feast, but you have not missed all the entertainment. I have saved the best until last, in your honour. I know your pleasures well enough. All those months I had to service you like some rutting bull. You have no idea how much the thought of you and your soft, weak, fat body has revolted me. You have wasted my seed, and soiled me. Now it is your turn to be soiled.' He clicked his fingers at Chilo. 'Get her out!'

Chilo cut the ties that fastened the door to the cage and reached in to drag the former governor's wife out. She put up a pathetic struggle and then collapsed on the ground at the feet of Ajax as some of the crowd wolf-whistled.

'I'll be kind.' Ajax smiled coldly. 'I'll let you choose. On your back, or on all fours.'

She stared up at him with terrified eyes, her lips quivering. 'I beg you, spare me. Please.'

'No.'

'Then why did you save me? When the earthquake struck, you came for me in the garden. Why?'

'For this moment, my lady. Yes, in a way I saved you. I saved you so I could have my revenge for the indignity of being your toy. I saved you for these men.' Ajax indicated Chilo and his companions, who were grinning cruelly. 'Take her, use her in any way you want, and when you're done, throw her body down into the ravine with the others.'

Ajax turned away and strode back towards his tent. Behind him the crowd looked on as Chilo had two of his men hold the Roman woman face down on the bare ground. A moment later the first of her shrill screams of terror and agony filled the night.

CHAPTER SIXTEEN

Macro arrived at Sempronius's office carrying with him the faint odour of the work he had been supervising in the city's sewer. He nodded a greeting to Cato and saluted the senator, before casting a curious eye over Centurion Micon.

'Now that we're all here, take a seat.' Sempronius folded his hands together. 'Then Centurion Micon can make his report. I take it you know nothing of what has happened yet, Macro?'

Macro glanced at Cato and shook his head. 'I'm not aware of anything. Apart from some shouting from the forum as I headed up here.'

'Shouting?'

'Yes. Didn't sound like they were celebrating.'

'Our friend Centurion Micon was unwise enough to break his news in the forum before he came to find me. It'll be all over Gortyna before nightfall.'

'News?' Macro frowned. 'What in Hades is going on, sir?'

'There's been a defeat. Marcellus and his column have been wiped out by the rebel slaves. Centurion Micon managed to escape. But you'd better hear it from Micon.'

'I should think so.' Macro eyed Micon coldly. 'The story of how a band of slaves carved up the best part of a thousand men has got to be worth hearing.'

Sempronius leaned forward. 'Just listen.'

Macro raised his hands and leaned back as he nodded at Micon. 'Please tell us.'

Centurion Micon was unsettled by the critical tone of his superior and took a brief moment to compose himself before he cleared his throat and began.

'It happened yesterday, at dusk, thirty miles to the east of Gortyna.

163

As you know from Prefect Marcellus's reports, we were tracking down bands of slaves and driving them before us. All the time they were pulling back, away from Gortyna and into the hills. We were sure we had them on the run. We'd cleared them out of the plain, and once they were forced up towards the mountains, the plan was to trap them and finish them off once and for all. Marcellus was confident that the campaign would be over in less than a month. Then, three days ago, one of our patrols captured a slave. A young lad, no more than twelve or thirteen. He was brought in and questioned, and told us that the leader of the slaves was a great gladiator who had pledged to lead the slaves to freedom or die. Our men scoffed at this, but then the boy claimed to know the gladiator, said that he was one of the gladiator's servants. That was when he realised he'd said too much and clammed up. But it was too late. The decurion in command of the patrol took the boy to Marcellus. At first he refused to talk, then the prefect called in the interrogators.' Micon paused and looked round at the other officers. 'You know how good they are at loosening tongues. Well, it took them the best part of an hour before they broke the boy. They'd beaten him badly and used heated irons, then they brought out the gouges. First sight of those did the trick. Even so, never seen guts like that in a youngster,' Centurion Micon mused. 'Or a slave.'

'Please continue,' Sempronius cut in.

'Yes, sir. Anyway, the lad told us that he knew where the rebels were camped, and he would take us there if Marcellus promised that he would be sent back to his master without any further harm. Naturally, the prefect gave his word. Marcellus sent for his officers. He gave us wine and said he'd lead us back in triumph, herding thousands of captive slaves, while their leader was dragged behind in chains.

'The next morning he gave orders for all patrols to be called in and the men prepared for an attack on the slave camp the following night. Centurion Albinus suggested that a report be sent back to Gortyna, advising them of the attack, but Marcellus said that it would be better if we simply returned with our captives once the attack was over. Nothing is as eloquent as success – those were his words. So we set off into the hills, guided by the boy, who was tethered to

Marcellus's horse. At first the going was easy, along a broad path, and even as dusk settled and it became dark there was enough moonlight to see our way as the track narrowed and became steeper. Then, after perhaps two or three hours, we saw a faint glow above a hill a mile off. That was the camp, the boy assured us. We continued forward more carefully and Marcellus sent scouts on ahead. All was well for a while, until we were within half a mile of the camp. Then one of the scouts came back and reported that the track passed through a narrow ravine before rising steeply up towards the top of the hill. Marcellus was suspicious and ordered the column to halt while he questioned the boy again. The lad was adamant that it was the only way up to the camp without taking a wide detour that would mean we wouldn't reach it before daybreak. Marcellus ordered us forward again.

'The ravine was barely twenty feet across, with steep sides, too steep to climb, and we did our best to advance quietly as the sounds echoed off the rock faces on either side. Just as the head of the column began to emerge into the open, there was a sudden flaring up of light along the crests on either side. They had faggots drenched in oil, which they lit up and threw down on to us.' Micon paused again as he recalled the horror of the previous night. 'There was fire everywhere, and the faggots exploded into blazing fragments all around us. The horses panicked and ran into each other and trampled the infantry. By the light of the flames the enemy – the slaves, I mean – started to roll boulders down on to us. Boulders, and also logs into which they had driven iron spikes and hooks. It was carnage, sir. Marcellus was one of the first to be struck down, but not before he'd drawn his sword and cut the boy's throat. That was the really terrible thing. The lad just stood there and laughed as it happened. He spat into Marcellus's face before he died. An instant later, the prefect was crushed by one of the logs. Killed outright. There was no one in command, and some men charged forward to get out of the trap. Others turned back, and some just huddled under whatever shelter they could find.'

'And what did you do?' asked Macro.

'I turned back,' Centurion Micon confessed. 'What else could I do? I called what was left of my men to me and we rode back through the column the way we had come. Only the slaves had closed that off, throwing abatis across the track. Some of our men tried to clear them away, but they had slingers on either flank and our men went down like flies. But they opened a gap, and I charged my men through it.' Micon glanced at the other officers furtively. 'We went after the slingers, to give the others a chance to clear the rest of the barricade away and make good their escape. But that's when the spearmen came up out of the ground. They'd been lying down behind the slingers, and as soon as we charged up, the slingers melted away and we rode straight on to their pikes. I turned away, after the last of my men was cut down, and rode back down the track towards the plain, breaking through a handful of slaves covering the track. I didn't stop until I had put the best part of a mile between us. Then when I did rein in, I looked back and saw the flames glowing in the ravine. I can still hear the cries and screams of our men echoing off the rocks. The slave spearmen formed up at the edge of the ravine, and slaughtered every one of our men caught in their trap.' Centurion Micon lowered his head. 'The column didn't stand a chance, sir. I didn't know what to do . . . Charge back into the fight, or do my duty and report back to you.'

'So you decided to save your skin,' Macro snorted. 'Instead of going to the aid of your comrades. Typical bloody auxiliary.'

Cato leaned forward. 'There was nothing Centurion Micon could do.'

'He could have died like a soldier, and not run like a bloody whipped cur and abandoned his mates.'

'Then who would have been left to make his report to us?'

Macro sucked a breath in through his teeth. In the legions, it was a dyed-in-the-wool tradition that centurions never gave an inch in battle. Clearly a different standard applied in the auxiliary cohorts. 'Well, surely he could have found someone to ride back and break the news.'

Sempronius rapped his hand on the desk. 'Enough! This is not getting us anywhere. The question is what do we do now? This defeat has changed everything at a stroke. Marcellus had the best of our men, and now he's thrown them away. All we have left are a few small detachments on the north of the island, the Tenth Macedonian, and the cohort at Matala. What's that? Six hundred men at most.' Sempronius shook his head. 'How the hell could these wretched slaves have done this to us? How could they have defeated trained soldiers? I underestimated the slaves, and this gladiator who is leading them.'

Cato kept his mouth shut and fought back a surge of anger and indignation. It was the senator's responsibility for not taking the slave threat seriously enough. Cato, and Macro to a lesser extent, had both been aware of the dangers, but their concerns had been dismissed. It was tempting to exact some recognition of who should bear the blame, but now was not the time. Any bitter divisions amongst those left in charge of the province would only make their perilous situation worse.

'So,' Sempronius continued, looking at Macro and Cato, 'you're the ones with military experience. What should we do?'

'What can we do?' Macro answered coldly. 'It seems we're outnumbered, outwitted and we've been given a good kicking. Best thing to do is send for help and hold out here until it arrives.'

Sempronius did not appear to like what he had heard and turned to Cato. 'And what do you think?'

'Macro's right, sir. With so few men, we have no choice. It would be madness to send what's left against the slaves. Gortyna must be defended.'

'Defended?' Sempronius raised his eyebrows. 'How? There must be twenty or thirty breaches in the walls where the earthquake shook them down.'

'That's true enough, sir. But we have to repair them before the slaves take it into their heads to march on Gortyna.'

'Do you really think they will?'

'I would, if I was in their place. Now they have us at their mercy, they can make their demands, or threaten to wipe us out.'

'Then we have to fix the walls, at once.'

Macro shook his head. 'That's not possible, sir. The damage is too great. Even if we set every man, woman and child to work repairing the breaches, it would take us too many days to do it.'

Cato thought a moment. 'Then we must abandon Gortyna. We have to bring everyone up here on to the acropolis.'

'Is there room for everyone?' asked Sempronius. 'There are over fifteen thousand people out there. The conditions would be appalling.'

Cato looked at him directly. 'They either come up here, or take their chances with the slaves.'

'What about Matala?' Macro interrupted. 'We could send some of them there. If they left now, they could reach the port before this slave army moves in from the east.'

'No. It's too risky. The slaves might already have patrols out in the surrounding countryside. We'd need to send a strong detachment to protect the civilians. We need every man here, to defend the province's capital.' Cato paused. 'However, we have to send a warning to Centurion Portillus and tell him what has happened. He'll need to protect the people of Matala. It would be best if he was ordered to move them up inside the acropolis there as well.'

Sempronius sagged back in his chair. 'My gods, these slaves have us on the run. They'll have us trapped like rats in a hole. When Rome hears of this, I'm finished.'

Cato cleared his throat and spoke softly. 'If we don't do what we can to save what's left, then we risk losing the entire province, sir. That's something the emperor would never forgive.' He let his words sink in and then continued. 'The thing is, we were never supposed to be here in the first place. It was just blind chance that our ship was passing when the wave struck.'

'So?'

'So I don't see how you can be called to account. The situation could hardly have been worse, and you've done all you can to restore order.'

'Kind words, Cato, but I doubt the emperor will agree with you. Regardless of what we might have achieved, we are the ones he will hold responsible if these slaves succeed in humbling Roman interests.'

Macro puffed his cheeks. 'Then you're going to have to bloody do something about it – sir.'

'Do?' Sempronius said helplessly. 'What can I do?'

'Get more men. More soldiers.'

'How? I can't just conjure them out of thin air.'

'Get them from Egypt,' Macro said tersely. 'You said that you know the emperor's legate there, right? Gaius Petronius. He's a member of the equestrian class.'

Sempronius nodded.

'And you're a senator. So you outrank him. Order him to send reinforcements.'

Sempronius considered this for a moment before responding. 'And if he doesn't?'

'Then you must tell him that if Crete falls to the slaves you will make damn sure that Rome knows that you asked him for help and he refused. You won't be the only one who draws down the emperor's wrath.' Macro forced a smile. 'I can't see him turning down the chance to avoid being in Claudius's bad books.'

'Macro's right, sir,' said Cato. 'You have nothing to lose from pressing the Egyptian legate for help. If you head to the coast and take the first available ship, you could be in Alexandria in a matter of days, and back here with the reinforcements inside a month. If you can get enough men, I'm sure we can quickly crush the revolt.'

'You think it's that easy?' Macro glanced at him in surprise.

'Why not? As long as we don't follow the example of Marcellus.'

Sempronius cleared his throat. 'I'm not leaving Gortyna. It's out of the question.'

'Why?' Cato stared at him.

'Think about it, Cato. The slaves have annihilated most of our forces and have the province at their mercy. Just at that point the acting governor decides to quit Crete for the safety of Egypt to fetch reinforcements, while his subordinates and thousands of civilians are left to face the rebels. It's not the most edifying display of leadership, is it?'

'That's for others to say, sir. You have to put that possibility aside for the moment. You have to go to Egypt. You know the legate. Only someone with your authority can persuade Petronius to send reinforcements.'

'That's true,' Sempronius conceded, and nodded slowly as he contemplated the problem. Then a smile formed on his lips and he looked up at his officers. 'Of course, if I was to send someone in my place, authorised to act on my behalf, then we might get our way. Obviously, the person in question would have to be up to the task of talking the legate round.'

At the same moment both the senator and Macro fixed their eyes on Cato. With a sudden surge of alarm, Cato sat back and shook his head. 'No. Not me.'

'Why not?' asked Sempronius.

'I'm too young,' Cato admitted. 'The legate would take one look at me and wonder if he could take me seriously as a centurion, let alone the envoy of the governor of Crete. Send Macro.'

'What?' Macro started, and then glared at Cato. 'Thanks.'

Sempronius smiled briefly. 'With all due respect to his abilities as a politician, Macro's talents are best utilised in defence of Gortyna. The man I need in Alexandria has to be a powerful advocate for our request for reinforcements. I think you are that man.'

'Yes,' Macro added with a smirk. 'I know you, lad. You could argue the hind leg off a donkey, and then debate the moral justification for doing it. The senator's right, it has to be you.'

Cato felt the situation slipping out of his control and made one last attempt to protest. 'Sir, please reconsider. I'm one of the most junior centurions in the army. Even if Petronius accepts my arguments, he's hardly going to entrust me with a force large enough to crush the slaves.'

'Then I will just have to promote you,' Sempronius decided. 'Temporarily, of course. For the duration of the emergency.'

'Promote me?' Cato was stunned by the idea, until he realised it made sense. Up to a point. 'If I go in as a prefect, then it will look even more ridiculous than me holding the rank of centurion, sir. Besides, the Legate of Egypt would still have seniority.'

'Who said anything about being a prefect? I'm sending you to Egypt with the civil rank of tribune.'

'Tribune?' Now Cato was truly shocked. The tribunate was largely an honorific title in Rome, but was still occasionally conferred upon officials sent out to the provinces to act with the authority of the emperor and his senate. Cato gently chewed his lip. 'Can you do that?'

'I am the acting governor of this province, having assumed

authority in the emperor's name. It's worked so far. And, as you said, what have I got to lose? I'll draw up the document, and seal it with the governor's ring. In fact, you'd better take my family ring with you to prove that I sent you. That, and your quick wits, will carry the argument.'

'They'll have to,' Macro added. 'Otherwise we're all in the shit.'

'Quite,' said Sempronius. 'If we win the day, then I'll just have to hope the emperor overlooks the fact that I've overstepped the mark in conferring the rank on you.'

Cato smiled bitterly. 'And if he doesn't, then I'll be had up for acting without proper authority. Men have been condemned for treason for doing such things. I think I'd rather stay here and face the slaves.'

'Then you're dead either way.' Sempronius shrugged. 'What have you got to lose?'

Cato's shoulders drooped in resignation. 'All right, then. I'll go.'

'Good man!' Macro slapped him on the back. 'Get to Alexandria, and find us those men. And don't go and fuck it up.'

'Thanks for the encouragement.'

'You're welcome.' Macro grinned. 'Anyway, you've got it easy. It's us who'll be having to cope with those slaves and that gladiator they've got leading them. Which reminds me.' He turned to Centurion Micon, who had been keeping as still and as quiet as possible during the preceding discussion, no doubt hoping that invisibility was his best hope in escaping the shame of fleeing the battlefield that had claimed the lives of his commander and all but a handful of his men. He wilted before Macro's gaze.

'Sir?'

'This gladiator. Did that boy you captured mention his name?'

'Yes, yes, he did, sir.' Micon nodded. 'He said he was a Thracian, called Ajax.'

'Ajax?' Macro scratched his chin, and then his fingers froze as his eyes suddenly widened. 'Ajax!' He turned to Cato. 'What do you think? Is it possible?'

'Does the name mean something to you?' asked the senator.

'It does. At least I think it does. The man I saw recognised me, I'm certain of it. But there's only one Ajax I can recall meeting, and it's hard to belive it can be the same man.'

Cato took a deep breath. 'If it is, and he knows that we're on the island, then we're in even more danger than I thought. Ajax won't rest until he's had his full measure of revenge.'

'Revenge?' Sempronius hissed with frustration. 'Would you mind telling me what's going on? Who is this Ajax, and what has he got against you?'

'It's a long story,' said Macro. 'But he has his reasons for hating us. His father used to command a pirate fleet operating out of the coast of Illyria. Until Cato and I put paid to his activities. We captured Ajax, his father and most of the pirates. We had orders to make an example of them.' He shrugged. 'Cato and I were the ones who crucified his father and had Ajax sold into slavery.'

CHAPTER SEVENTEEN

Two days after the news of the defeat reached Gortyna, Cato arrived at the small fishing village of Ciprana on the south coast. The port had been recommended to him as being virtually cut off from the rest of the island by the sheer mountains that surrounded it. Only a little-used track linked Ciprana to the plain, picking its way along steep slopes and ravines. It was unlikely that the slaves had even heard of the place, let alone knew how to find the port. There should be some craft there capable of carrying Cato across the sea to Alexandria.

He travelled on horseback with an escort of four picked men, all wearing scarlet tunics and cloaks that marked them out as Roman soldiers. Cato had been provided with an expensively embroidered tunic from what was left of the wardrobe of Governor Hirtius. He also wore the man's fine calfskin boots, which were a little on the large side, but comfortable enough after years of wearing the heavy nailed boots of the legions. In a sealed leather tube that hung from a thong around Cato's neck were two documents and the senator's family ring. The first letter appointed him to the temporary rank of tribune, signed and sealed by Senator Sempronius in the name of the Emperor Claudius. Both Cato and the senator hoped that the document would impress the legate in Egypt enough to persuade him to send aid. The second was a detailed report of the situation in Crete, which clearly outlined the dangers facing the province. Sempronius concluded with a request that Legate Petronius send a squadron of warships and a military force powerful enough to put down the slave revolt.

It was an ambitious demand, Cato reflected. There was every chance that Petronius might refuse, or delay sending the reinforcements while he sent a message to Rome asking for Sempronius's instructions to be approved. Such a delay would prove fatal to all concerned, and the senator had impressed upon Cato the need to use all his persuasive skills to ensure that Petronius complied. He would be armed with bluff and argument, Cato mused. Hardly an inspiring thought.

As Cato and his escort followed the shepherd who had been sent along to guide them to the port, his mind was fixed on the peril that Julia and Macro faced at Gortyna. The people had been terrified by the news of the ambush, and some had chosen to pack what belongings they could and flee to the north, over the high mountains that formed the spine of the island. With neither food nor protection, they would be at the mercy of the weather and the bands of brigands that preyed on travellers from their strongholds. There had been no reasoning with those who had chosen this course rather than face the prospect of being massacred by the rebel slaves.

Macro had been unmoved as he watched them trickle out of the city. 'Less mouths for us to feed, at any rate.'

'That's true.' Cato watched the refugees a moment longer before turning to his friend. 'Do you really think you can hold Gortyna if the slaves attack?'

Work had commenced on repairing the walls and gates of the city as soon as the remaining inhabitants could be organised into labour gangs. Gaps were filled with rubble and topped with crude breastworks. It would not keep the enemy out for long, Macro had informed the senator, but Sempronius had quietly pointed out that it would be best to keep the people occupied and offer them some hope, rather than sitting and waiting in fear.

'We'll make a show of manning the walls. I'll have all the spare kit distributed to able-bodied men, so at least we'll look like we have the numbers to put up a good fight. If Ajax calls our bluff and attacks, then we'll fall back to the acropolis and hold out there. We should be safe enough.'

'I hope so.'

Macro glanced at his friend and saw the young man's concerned expression. 'You're worried about Julia.'

'Of course I am.'

'I'll make sure she's safe. If it looks like the acropolis is going to fall, then I'll do my best to protect her and get her safely away.'

'And if you can't?'

'Then I will protect her until they cut me down.'

Cato was silent for a moment. 'I wouldn't want them to harm her. If there was any risk of the slaves taking her alive . . .'

'Look here, Cato,' Macro began awkwardly. 'I'm not prepared to prevent her falling into their hands. If that's what you mean.' He paused and cleared his throat. 'Not unless you really want me to.'

'No. I wouldn't ask that of you, or anyone. That's her choice.'

'I suppose.' Macro poked his vine stick at a crack in the stonework. 'She's a brave one, and proud too. She'll do what's right, if the time comes.'

Cato felt his stomach lurch. This conversation did not feel real. They were talking in the calm, measured tones of men who might be casually discussing the solution to some kind of technical problem. The image of Julia, powerless and terrified before the faceless rage of the vengeful slaves, filled his heart with a pain he had not known before. At the same time, he could not bear the thought of her being put to death, even to spare her a worse fate before death eventually came. He felt sick and gripped the edge of the parapet with his fingers. It was tempting to abandon his journey to Alexandria and remain in Gortyna to defend Julia. After all, the Legate of Egypt would probably deny them the forces needed to put down the revolt. It was a fool's errand.

He took a deep breath to calm his growing anxiety and pushed himself away from the wall, and straightened up. 'Well, let's hope that it doesn't come to that. I'll return as soon as I can.'

'You do that.'

They clasped arms and then Macro nodded towards the administration building. 'Have you said goodbye to Julia yet?'

'No. I've been putting it off. I don't know who she is more angry at, me for going or her father for sending me.'

Macro chuckled and slapped Cato on the shoulder. 'I warned you, old son. A soldier should never let himself get too involved with the fairer sex. It unmans him, and preoccupies his mind when it should be focused on other things.'

'Too true,' Cato replied. 'Too bloody true. Anyway, here I go.'

He raised his hand in mock salute. 'Those who are about to die salute you!'

Macro laughed as he turned away and made his way along the wall towards the gatehouse, where some of the auxiliaries were struggling to mount an old ballista that had been discovered in the acropolis's armoury.

Cato climbed down from the rampart and wearily made his way across to the administration building. Julia was in the office, head bent over a table of figures. She did not look up as Cato entered the room.

'What do you want?'

Cato swallowed nervously. 'I've come to say goodbye.'

'Is that all?' she replied quietly, still not looking up. 'Well, you've said it, so you can go now.'

Cato stood in the doorway, torn between leaving the fraught atmosphere, and never wanting to leave her presence ever again. Then he saw a falling twinkle of light, caught by the sunshine pouring through the window and realised it was a tear. At once his heart was filled with the warm ache of compassion, and he swept across the room and wrapped his arm around her shoulder as he tenderly kissed the back of her head.

'Julia, my love, don't cry.'

'I'm not crying,' she mumbled even as her slight frame trembled. 'I'm not.'

Cato gently drew her up from her seat and put his arms around her, holding her close to his chest as she buried her face in the folds of his cloak.

'It's not fair . . . We should never have ended up here. We should have been in Rome by now, planning our future. Not here, in these ruins.'

'We're here because we're here,' said Cato. 'There's nothing we can do to change that, Julia.'

'I know that. I'm not a fool.' She looked up, eyes red-rimmed and glassy. Her lip trembled as she continued. 'But why do you have to leave me?'

'Because I must. Your father has ordered it.'

'Why didn't he send Macro instead?'

'He thought I was best suited to carry out the task. He needs me to do it. He's depending on me, Julia. And so are you, Macro and everyone else here. If I succeed, there's a chance we may defeat the rebels and go to Rome as we planned. But if I don't go, we will have no chance.'

She stared at him and then nodded reluctantly.

'You must be brave.' Cato lifted her chin and kissed her. 'I will return.'

'Swear that you will be careful.'

'I will be careful, I swear by all the gods.'

They looked into each other's eyes and then kissed again, before Julia abruptly broke free of his arms and eased Cato back. 'Then go, my darling. Now.'

Cato almost felt a pain as she separated from him and nearly gave way to the impulse to hold her again. One last time. But he nodded slowly, and then turned towards the door and strode steadily out of the room, along the corridor and down into the courtyard without once looking back. He did not trust himself to.

The shepherd paused as he reached a bend in the track and pointed towards the sea. As he drew level with the man, Cato reined in and looked down on the fishing village. To call it a port was a bit of an overstatement, Cato reflected as he scrutinised the scattered handful of dwellings that fringed a narrow curve of grey sand between two rocky headlands. The water was clear all the way out past the headlands that protected the bay. The wave that had destroyed the port at Matala had swept past Ciprana, causing much less damage. A few houses closest to the shore had been destroyed, but those built on the slope well above the sand had survived intact. Most of the fishing boats and the nets that had been drying on frames by the shore had not been so fortunate. They had been washed away and smashed against the rocks of the headland. Some of the least damaged boats had been salvaged and were being repaired on the beach. Only one was drawn up on the sand ready for use.

'Come on.' Cato waved to his escort and they continued in single file. A short distance further on, the track began to wind its way down the hill in a long series of zigzags. As the small party began its descent, a few of the villagers had emerged from their homes and were watching the approaching strangers cautiously. Cato saw one of them run towards the largest of the buildings, and a short time later a group of men emerged and made their way across to the place where the track entered the village and waited for the Romans.

Cato raised a hand in greeting as he approached the men. Behind him, the guide and Cato's escort looked round warily.

'Stop there!' one of the villagers called out in Greek as he stepped forward and pointed at Cato. 'Who are you?'

'Tribune Quintus Licinius Cato, from Gortyna.'

'Really?' The villagers' leader was a broad-shouldered man with short, powerful legs and tightly curled grey hair. He cocked his head on one side and continued in a suspicious tone. 'What brings you here, Roman?'

'I am on imperial business. Urgent imperial business.'

'What business?'

Cato reined in a short distance from the man. 'I am carrying a message from the governor of the province to the Legate of Egypt. I need a boat to take me and my men to Alexandria.'

'Why would such an important official come here for a boat?'

'Because Ciprana is probably one of the only ports on the south coast that has not been completely destroyed by the wave, or the slaves. Have any of the rebels been here?'

The man shook his head. 'Very few people bother to cross the mountains to visit us. Why should the slaves be any different?' He paused. 'How do I know that you are not part of the rebellion?'

'Do I look like a slave?'

'No,' the villager admitted. 'But for all I know you could have murdered some Romans and taken their clothes, and are trying to escape from the island.'

'What?' Cato shook his head irritably. 'Nonsense. I am who I say I am, and we have come here to seek passage to Alexandria.'

'Sorry, Tribune. We can't help you. You'd best try somewhere else.'

'There isn't time to try somewhere else,' Cato said firmly and pointed towards the beach. 'I need that boat, and a crew at once. We will pay our fare, and leave you these horses.'

'Can't help you. We need that boat for our catch. It's the only seaworthy craft that we have left, the only means of feeding ourselves. You can't have it.'

'I can pay you enough to buy your village some new boats,' Cato responded. 'Name your price.'

'We can't eat money, it is of no use to us now. That boat is all that stands between us and starvation. I'm sorry, Tribune. It's not for sale.'

Cato leaned forward in his saddle and stared intensely at the man as he continued. 'We need that boat, and we will have it, along with the best sailor in your village. As I said, you will be amply rewarded. If you are short of food here, then I suggest you take any valuables you have and set off for Gortyna. If you still want to protest, then you can make your case to the governor. Now, I have no further time to waste.' Cato slid from the saddle and reached into his saddle bag for a pouch of the silver coins that had been issued to him from the provincial treasury on Sempronius's orders. He tossed it to the villager, who fumbled the catch and nearly dropped the money.

'There's three hundred denarians in there,' Cato explained. 'More than enough for you to buy some new boats for the village.'

The villager hefted the bag for a moment and shook his head. 'I told you. We have no use for it.'

Cato strode up to him with a menacing expression and growled, 'I don't have time for debate. Find me a man to sail that boat at once. If I don't get to Alexandria as soon as possible, then the slaves will take over the island. Do you want that?'

'We keep to ourselves,' the villager persisted. 'Why should they bother us?'

'Because they will not rest until they control Crete. No matter how many they have to kill. I can offer you protection if you lead your people to Gortyna.'

'Protection?' The villager smiled as he stepped away from Cato. There was a flicker of polished metal, and Cato glanced down to see that the man had drawn a small, delicately curved knife. At once the others followed suit. 'We don't need protection. But you might, Roman.'

179

Cato glanced round quickly. There were eight men in front of him, but half of them looked old and frail. Several more men stood around the confrontation. Some carried clubs and one had a barbed fishing spear.

'Put those knives away,' Cato ordered. 'Don't be a fool. My men and I are professional soldiers. If you want a fight, then you'd better understand that even though you outnumber us, we would still kill most of you, before even one of us fell.'

The leader of the villagers was silent for a moment, and then spat to one side. 'That's quite a claim, Roman.'

Cato flicked back his cloak and grasped his sword handle. 'Want to put it to the test?'

Behind him, there was a metallic rasp as the men of his escort drew their weapons. Behind them, the shepherd backed away a few steps then turned to run back up the track away from the village. As the sound of his footsteps died away, the two groups of men stared at each other in silence, waiting for the other to make a move. Then the fishermen's leader smiled slowly.

'All right then. There's no need for everyone to get themselves killed. Let's keep this between you and me, Roman. A straight fight. If you win, you can take the boat and the best of my men to sail her. If I win, then your men leave the village and find themselves a boat somewhere else.'

Cato thought quickly. Even though the leader of the villagers was powerfully built, he was not a trained fighter and was more likely to have used his blade for gutting fish than for fighting. It would be a risk, but it would save a much greater loss of life if a more general fight broke out between the two sides. He nodded.

'You have a deal. Swords or daggers?'

'I'll stick with this blade.' The villager grinned. 'It's served me well enough in the past.'

'Very well then.' Cato stretched his stiff legs for a moment. Then he unclasped his cloak and slipped his sword belt over his head, and turning to the nearest of his escort handed them over.

'Here, take these.' He leaned slightly closer and lowered his voice. 'If anything happens to me, the governor's message is here.' Cato patted the leather tube under his tunic. 'Grab one of their

180

men and make for the boat. Whatever happens, that message has to get through to Alexandria. Whatever the cost. Understand?'

'Yes, sir.'

Cato turned back to face the leader of the villagers. Drawing his dagger, he paced warily towards the man and stopped a safe distance away.

'We have agreed the terms. If you lose, then the boat will be mine, yes?'

The fisherman nodded. 'That's right. Lads, make sure he has what he wants, if he wins.'

Cato went into a crouch, blade held out slightly to one side, as he had been taught by Macro in the early days of his time in the Second Legion. Opposite him the villager did the same, while his companions backed away and formed a loose arc behind him. As he stepped closer, Cato saw for the first time a scar on the brow of his opponent, a crude sun motif burned on to the skin. In a horrible moment of realisation, Cato knew that this was no mere fisherman after all. There was no time for further thought as the man suddenly lunged forward, slashing at Cato's knife arm. Cato whipped it back, turned slightly to his right to retain his balance and thrust back at the other man's arm. He leaped back out of range, with a grin.

'Good reactions, Tribune,' he muttered, in Latin, and for an instant Cato froze.

There was another blur of motion as the man lunged again. Cato moved to parry the blow, but quick as lightning the man's blade changed direction and cut in and up towards Cato's throat. Cato threw his head to one side, and the tip of the blade sliced through the air and nicked his ear, then the man jumped back.

The small cut burned and Cato felt a warm trickle flow down his neck. He shook his head and crouched, ready to attack or defend, as he spoke quietly. 'A soldier, then?'

The villager smiled. 'Once.'

'From the brand of Mithras, I'd say a legionary.'

The villager said nothing.

'So you're a deserter.'

'What does it matter?' The man smiled. 'And don't think you can goad me. You're bleeding, Tribune. How does it feel, rich boy? I'm going to cut you down to size a piece at a time.'

Cato watched him intently, his mind racing. The man had been a professional soldier. The chances were that he knew as much, if not more, as Cato did about knife fighting. There was no technical advantage to be had then. But there was some hope. His opponent took him as some son of an aristocratic family and no doubt thought him soft and inexperienced.

'Try it, you scum,' Cato sneered haughtily. Immediately he sprang forward, slashing out wildly with his blade, all the time keeping his arm extended and his body out of range of the other man's knife. The villager easily ducked the attacks or deflected them with swift parries that clinked and scraped as the two men duelled. Cato stumbled back, breathing heavily, as the blood continued to drip from his ear.

'You're soft, Tribune,' the other man sniffed. 'Just like all you aristocratic mother's boys. Playing at soldiers. I'm going to enjoy this.'

He stepped forward, feinting again and again, laughing as Cato frantically tried to block each thrust as he gave ground. Then, with a cry, Cato stumbled and fell back. At once the other man sprang forward, crouching as he came on, knife poised to strike into Cato's chest. Cato spun to one side and lashed out with his boot, catching the other man hard, behind the knee. His momentum and the loss of weight-bearing on the leg Cato had struck, caused the man to lose his balance, and he crashed heavily to the ground, face first. Cato jumped on to his back, snatching a clump of hair in one hand, while he pressed the tip of his knife into his opponent's throat so that it just cut the flesh. Leaning forward, he hissed into the man's ear:

'You're right. Amateurs should never, ever try and fuck with professionals.' He eased himself up. 'Give in, or I'll cut your throat where you lie.'

'Bastard . . .'

Cato pulled on the man's hair. 'Last chance. Submit or die.'

'All right, you win,' grunted the man.

'Louder. So everyone can hear it.'

'I give in! I give in. The Roman wins!'

'That's better.' Cato released his grip and let the man's head slump into the dirt. Rising up warily, he backed away and sheathed his dagger. His defeated opponent rolled over and sat up, rubbing the small cut in his neck. He stared at Cato with a puzzled frown.

'You're not like any tribune I ever met. Where were you raised, in the slums of the Subura?'

Cato shook his head. 'No, in the imperial palace, as it happens.'

'What?'

'It doesn't matter. I need that boat now.' He paused and thrust his finger at the man. 'And I want you to sail it.'

'Me?'

'You were a soldier once. You're a bit rusty now, but useful in a fight. You'll do. What is your name, soldier?'

'Yannis. That's what I'm called here.'

'Fair enough.' Cato held out his hand, and after a brief hesitation the fisherman allowed him to help him back to his feet.

'If you're the head man here, your people will need a replacement. You'd better appoint one. If taking the boat means they may go hungry, then their best chance is to make for Gortyna. They should tell the men on the city gate that Tribune Cato sent them there. Whatever happens, your people need to stay clear of any bands of slaves they see.'

Yannis nodded. 'All right then, Tribune. As you say.'

He turned away to talk to his followers, while Cato watched him closely for any sign of treachery. A short time later Yannis exchanged farewells with his men and gestured to Cato and his escort to follow him down to the beach.

'Have you no wife or woman here?' asked Cato as he caught up.

'What's it to you?' asked Yannis curtly. Then he shrugged. 'She was killed by the wave.'

'I'm sorry. So many people have suffered such a loss. That's why I must reach Alexandria. To get more men to help restore order.'

'To help defeat the slaves, you mean.'

'It comes to the same thing.'

The fishing boat was perhaps twenty-five feet long, with a mast stepped slightly forward of the centre of the craft. A steering paddle was attached to the side and a pair of oars lay in the bottom. It stank of fish.

'Will that get us to Egypt?' one of Cato's escort asked doubtfully.

'As well as any vessel,' Yannis replied, then turned as several men emerged from the village carrying water skins and strings of dried fish. They placed the meagre supplies in small lockers either side of the mast, and then Yannis turned to Cato.

'Get in.'

The Romans clambered aboard and quickly sat down as Yannis barked an order. The fishermen heaved the boat into the calm waters of the bay and pushed it out until they stood chest deep. Yannis pulled himself over the side, and indicated the oars.

'One man on each of those; place them in between those pegs there. That's it.'

With the oars in place, the soldiers clumsily propelled the craft out towards the entrance to the bay, while Yannis sat with the handle of the steering oar in his hands. Looking back, Cato saw that many of the villagers were standing watching the last of their boats head out to sea. Their sense of resignation and despair was palpable. A sudden lurch beneath the keel made Cato grasp the side.

Yannis laughed. 'It's just a swell, Tribune. Wait until we reach the open sea. Then you'll be panicking.'

Cato forced himself to let go of the side and sat staring out beyond the bows as his men stroked the fishing boat clear of the bay. As soon as they reached open water, the small craft bobbed up and down on the swell and Cato swallowed nervously as he tried to maintain an untroubled expression. When they were well clear of the land, Yannis gave the order for the soldiers to stop rowing and stow the oars in the bottom of the boat. Meanwhile he undid the ties fastening the sail to the spar and hoisted it up the mast. As soon as the sheets were fastened securely around the cleats, the sail filled and the boat surged forward, away from the coast.

'How long will it take to reach Alexandria?' asked Cato.

Yannis frowned as he thought for a moment. 'Perhaps three days to the African coast, and then another three along the shore if the wind remains fair.'

'Six days,' Cato mused unhappily. Six days crammed into this small boat with just two feet of freeboard. The constant motion of the water around him was frightening. He had thought that the short-lived voyage on the *Horus* was unnerving, but being at sea in this open fishing boat was terrifying. Yet there was no avoiding it. Macro, Julia and all the others were depending on him to get through to Alexandria.

He continued to gaze back at the land for some time, wondering if he would ever see his friends again.

CHAPTER EIGHTEEN

In the days that followed Cato's departure, Macro kept the people hard at work repairing the city's defences. In addition to filling the breaches in the walls, one of the gatehouses had collapsed in the earthquake and Gortyna's surviving stonemasons cannibalised the stones from a nearby wrecked temple in order to rebuild it. Macro's preparations extended outside the walls, where work gangs equipped with army tools picked away at the hard, stony ground, digging defensive ditches in front of the most damaged sections of the wall. Given the difficulty of the ground, there was no question of excavating a ditch the entire circumference of the city. So Macro turned to other methods of slowing down any enemy attack.

Summoning some of the city's blacksmiths to his headquarters on the acropolis, he introduced them to one of the legions' favourite defensive weapons. There had been a small box of caltrops buried away at the back of the armoury, and Macro picked one out for his small audience to see. He held the four-pronged piece of iron up and then dropped it on the desk in front of him, where it landed with an alarming thud that made the blacksmiths jump.

'There.' Macro pointed. 'See how it lands with one point facing up? It'll do that every time, and if you scatter those in grass the enemy will not see 'em until they tread on them. The spike goes through the foot and cripples the victim. It'll break a charge almost every time.' Macro gazed at the caltrop fondly. 'Lovely piece of kit. Saved my neck more times than I care to mention.' He looked up. 'The question is, can you make these in quantity before Ajax and his mob turn up?'

One of the blacksmiths came over to the desk to have a closer look. He picked it up, felt the weight and nodded. 'Easy enough to make, but can I suggest a refinement?'

'Be my guest,' Macro invited, intrigued to know how the Greek could hope to improve on the Roman design.

'As it is, the points are fairly easy to remove. While you will have injured your enemy, he might not be incapacitated.'

'Really?' Macro cocked an eyebrow. 'I should think that having a fucking great spike shoved through the bottom of your foot might just take the smile off your face. Wouldn't you say?'

'Oh yes,' the Greek agreed. 'I'm sure it would. The thing is, the victim of this device might yet be able to limp into a fight, or off the battlefield. But what if we barbed the ends? Then it would be almost impossible to dislodge and the enemy would have to stop and cut it out, or wait to be carried from the battlefield.'

Macro shook his head. 'No. If the bloody thing is barbed, then it's removed from play with the casualty. What's the point in that? If it does its job and is discarded, then it is still on the battlefield ready for the next victim. See?'

'That's true,' another blacksmith interrupted. 'But you're ignoring the fact that the removal of a casualty requires at least one other man. Thus, a barbed caltrop will rob an enemy of a minimum of two men.'

The first Greek clicked his fingers. 'And what if those who were helping the man from the field were also to tread on these things? Why, the increase in the casualty rate would be exponential.'

'Expo-what?' Macro blinked, then held up his hands. 'Stop right there! Look here, I just wanted you to tell me if you could make some more of these. That's all. Can you do it?'

'Of course we can do it. The Greek looked offended. 'But why not improve on it at the same time? That's my point.'

'We could form a design committee,' someone suggested helpfully.

'No!' Macro protested.

'If we tested a few designs I'm sure we could provide you with a far more efficient weapon, Centurion.'

'There's no time.' Macro was getting exasperated. 'And the bloody thing works well enough as it is. Right?'

The Greek pursed his lips unhappily. 'Within limits, I suppose.'

Macro clenched his eyes shut for a moment and then opened them, stabbing his finger into the blacksmith's chest. 'Just make them. As many of them as you can. To this design and no other. Is. That. Perfectly. Clear? No, don't talk, just nod.'

The blacksmiths assented meekly.

'Thank you.' Macro breathed a sigh of relief. 'Then please get on with it. Send word the moment you have the first batch ready. Now go.'

Macro strode to the door and wrenched it open, ushering them out of his office. As soon as the last one had gone, he shut the door, returned to his desk and sat down, gazing at the caltrop as his temper began to subside.

'Greeks . . .' he muttered. 'Never use one word when a thousand will do.'

In addition to the improvements to the city's defences, Macro took charge of recruiting men to supplement the fighting strength of the auxiliaries. At first Sempronius had appealed for volunteers, but when fewer than a hundred of the city's menfolk turned up at the parade ground Macro had marked out a short distance beyond the wall, sterner measures were called for. Several sections of auxiliaries were sent out to scour the city for fit men and have them marched out to the parade ground. There, they were brought before Macro, where he made his selection of those he would use to bolster Gortyna's garrison. Details of each man's name, family, home street and occupation were carefully noted before he was presented to Macro, sitting at a campaign table under an awning.

It was dispiriting to see a succession of unhappy or angry men who were capable of bearing arms but resented the opportunity to defend their families and their city. One such was a tall, well-muscled young man in an expensive tunic. His dark hair was neatly cut and a finely trimmed beard graced his jawline. At first Macro could not place him, then in a sudden flash he recalled that he had been amongst Glabius's coterie up on the acropolis the day the tax collector had been deposed.

'Name?'

'Pandarus, son of Polocrites.'

Macro glared at him. 'From now on you call me sir. Is that understood?'

'I see no need to call you sir, Roman.'

'And why is that?' Macro smiled invitingly.

'Because I am not a soldier, nor will I ever be. Furthermore, I will protest about my treatment here through the highest channels. My father has political contacts in Rome. Once they are informed that a lowly officer has dared to pluck a free man from his home and forcibly conscript him at the point of a sword, there will be no limit to the retribution that is brought down on your head.' Pandarus was pleased with his brief monologue and offered a placating smile to Macro. 'It's not too late to put an end to this sad little drama of yours. Comedy, more like.' He turned and gestured to the line of men standing in the sun, waiting to be seen by Macro. There was a muted chorus of support. 'Let us all go, and I will do you a favour, Roman, and not report your criminal activities to your superiors in Rome.'

He drew himself up and crossed his arms as he stared down at Macro. The latter stared back for a moment and then lowered his stylus on to the wax slate with a weary sigh.

'Have you finished, Pandarus?'

'Finished?' Pandarus frowned, then became angry. 'You don't think I'm serious, do you?'

'Oh, I'm sure you're serious; it's just that I am not inclined to take you seriously,' Macro replied. 'I mean, look at you. Dressed up like a cheap tart. Is that perfume I can smell?'

'It is a male scent. An extremely expensive scent.'

'So you look like a male tart, and you smell like one. That I can forgive . . . just about. What I cannot forgive is that people like you think you're too good to get your hands dirty by taking up a sword and defending what's yours: this city, your family and your friends – assuming you have any. What makes you so fucking special that you should be excused from taking your place alongside the other men who are prepared to fight?'

'My father pays his taxes,' Pandarus protested. 'He pays them so that his family doesn't fight, and we can leave that to little people like you.' He could not resist the sneer, yet the moment the words were spoken he realised he had made a mistake. 'What I meant to say was—'

'Shut your mouth!' Macro shouted into his face. 'You miserable little coward! You're the little people. You and all those others who have so little heart, so little courage, so little sense of honour and duty that they think that money can buy them everything. Well, money is the least of your worries now. There's an army of slaves out there who are waiting for their moment to launch an attack on this city. Do you really think they are not going to butcher you and your family because you have connections in Rome? Fucking idiot.' Macro shook his head in anger and exasperation. 'There is only one way we are going to survive this, and that's if every man who can fight is up there on the wall, ready to kill or be killed. Right now I could not give a toss whether you are some dandy pervert or the son of the emperor himself. You will take up a sword with the rest of the men in the line. You will be trained to fight with the auxiliaries. You will fight like a lion to keep those rebel bastards out of the city, and if need be you will die like a bloody hero, sword in hand, spitting curses into your enemy's face. Do I make myself clear?'

Macro thrust his face forward, inches from that of Pandarus, and the latter nervously backed off a step.

'I m-meant no offence.' Pandarus flapped his hands.

'Sir!' Macro shouted, hooking his booted foot behind the young man's heel and then thrusting him hard in the chest so that he stumbled back and crashed to the ground. Macro pounced on him, knee on Pandarus's chest as he snatched out his dagger and thrust the blade to within an inch of the other man's eyes. 'Last time I say it. You call me sir when you address me. Got it?'

'Yes, yes, sir!' Pandarus whimpered.

'Better!' Macro eased himself up. 'Now get your kit, and report to the centurion on the drill ground with the other recruits. Get up! Get moving!'

Pandarus scrambled to his feet and scurried off towards the wagon where an optio from the auxiliary cohort and four of his men were busy issuing sword, helmet, armour and shield to each man sent their way. Macro turned back to the line of waiting men. Most were ordinary townspeople, but there were some better dressed amongst them. He walked down the line inspecting them, then returned to the shade of the awning.

'Is there anyone else who takes exception to fighting at my side, and the side of our heroic friend Pandarus? Well?'

The men refused to meet his glare and stood in silence. Macro nodded. 'Good.'

He turned and made his way back to his stool, then sat down at the desk and picked up his stylus.

'Next man!'

Eight days after Cato had set off for Alexandria, Macro joined Senator Sempronius and his daughter for dinner: a thin stew of pork and beans served with bread by one of the few remaining slaves of Hirtius. The rest had run off to the hills, or to swell the ranks of Ajax's rebel army.

The slave was an elderly man, stooped and frail-looking. He had long been conditioned to being silent and avoiding the eyes of his masters. Macro watched him for a moment, wondering what it must be like to live as a slave. He had been used to seeing them on the streets of Ostia and Rome as a child, and so had never really considered what it must mean to be one. Since then, he had spent long years in the army, where the slaves he had encountered had mostly been when he was off duty. There had also been a handful of occasions when he had seen proud enemy warriors taken captive, chained up and marched away into slavery. Indeed, he had profited from his share of such prisoners, and the money he had gained had rather obscured the fates of those who had thus enriched him.

As the slave finished serving and retired to stand still against the wall, Macro continued to examine him while he casually dipped a chunk of bread into the steaming bowl before him. It was tempting to ask the man what he thought of Ajax. And what he thought of the Romans and Greeks who were determined to defeat the rebel gladiator and his followers. If indeed he thought anything about them.

Macro paused. How could a slave not think about the revolt,

191

when there was little other topic of conversation in the city? Could this slave, so taciturn, be harbouring deep hatred for his masters and a yearning to be part of the uprising? Might he be listening alertly to any conversation to which he was privy, and then wait for a chance to escape and reveal his information to Ajax? What if his plan was more treacherous still? It would not take much effort to procure sufficient poison to kill all three of those to whom he had just served their evening meal.

Macro glanced down at his stew with a look of suspicion. He lowered his bread, dripping with gravy from the stew, on to his platter and turned towards the slave.

'You there, step closer.'

The slave started forward nervously, eyes flickering round the Romans lying on their couches around the table. Sempronius glanced at his daughter and Julia raised a quizzical eyebrow.

Macro wiped the smears of gravy from his lips. 'Slave, you have heard the news about Prefect Marcellus's defeat, I take it.'

The slave nodded quickly.

'Do you take comfort from this news?'

'Master?'

'I asked you if you took comfort from the news. You're a slave. So what is your view of the rebels' victory? Do you rejoice at it?'

The slave glanced down and shook his head.

'Look at me,' Macro ordered, and the slave reluctantly raised his head enough to meet Macro's gaze. 'Surely you are on the side of those who would set you free? Well? Speak up, man.'

The slave's anxiety was clear as he struggled to make a reply. Macro waited patiently, and at length the slave spoke. 'Master, I want freedom. So do many slaves. But I have savings and I plan to buy my freedom one day. It is the only way for me. Those slaves who join Ajax may have their freedom now, but I think they must live in dread of being returned to slavery. That is not freedom. When I eventually have my freedom, I shall want to be free from fear as I am free from slavery.' He paused, and looked round at his masters. 'I have made my choice. Those who follow the gladiator have made theirs.' He turned back to Macro. 'Is that all, master?'

Macro thought for a moment, then nodded. 'Leave us.'

The slave bowed his head and backed away from the table.

'He's lying,' Macro muttered.

'Well, what did you expect?' asked Sempronius. 'A frank admission that he sympathises with Ajax? It was unfair to put him on the spot like that.'

'Perhaps.' Macro pushed his plate away.

'I wonder how Cato is faring?' Julia intervened. 'He must have reached Alexandria by now. What do you think, Father?'

Sempronius thought a moment and then nodded. 'I'd have thought so, provided all has gone well. Which I am sure it has,' he added hurriedly, before dipping his spoon into the stew, fishing out a piece of meat and popping it into his mouth. At once, his face contorted in agony. Macro jumped to his feet and stepped towards the senator, glancing at the slave as he did so.

'Sir! What's the matter? Are you all right?'

Sempronius held up a hand to stay Macro and nodded. He swallowed, then reached for his wine to quench the pain in his mouth. 'Damn, that stew's hot!'

Macro let out a sigh of relief and returned to his couch.

Julia was looking at him curiously as she delicately blew across her spoon. 'What is up with you?'

'It's nothing. I just thought . . . Never mind.' Macro quickly changed the subject, with a forced smile. 'I'd be willing to bet that Cato is even now sitting at a fine banquet with the Legate of Egypt, busy talking him out of his entire garrison. You know what he's like.'

Julia smiled. 'Yes, he can be most persuasive.'

Sempronius frowned and Macro burst into laughter before he could stop himself. For a moment the senator continued frowning, then gave way to the impulse and joined in. With all the strain of the previous days and the grave concerns over the arrival of the slave army before the hastily repaired walls of Gortyna, it did both men good to laugh. When it had died away, Macro topped the other man's cup up with wine and raised his own in a toast.

'To Cato. May he prove big enough for a tribune's boots, and return to us at the head of a great army.'

'I'll drink to that.'

'And me.' Julia raised her cup. She took a sip and then spoke softly. 'By the gods, I miss him so much.'

Macro nodded. He didn't want to say anything for fear of seeming to miss a comrade more than was properly acceptable. All the same, he mused, he would rather have Cato at his side as he prepared the hotch-potch of defences and defenders to face the enemy.

Sempronius drank from his cup and then set it down. 'How are things coming along, Macro? Those new men proving to be of any use?'

'They're doing well enough. Most have managed to work out which end of a sword to hold. They'll never make good soldiers, or even adequate ones, in whatever time we have available to us before the rebels decide to attack. I've appointed Centurion Micon to command them. It'll give him a chance to redeem himself. All in all they won't amount to much, but they'll be better equipped than most of the slaves they'll encounter.'

'Although you can be sure that this man Ajax will have distributed the kit he recovered from the bodies of Marcellus and his men.'

'That's true,' Macro conceded. 'In which case, I give Centurion Micon's lads no better than an even chance when it comes to a fight.'

Sempronius sighed wearily. 'Not a great help, then.'

'I can only hope they prove me wrong.'

The conversation was interrupted by three distant blasts on a trumpet, the alarm signal that Macro had arranged. He rose quickly to his feet, followed by the others, and abandoned the meal as they made their way out of the administration building and across the acropolis to the tower above the main gate. Men were stumbling out of their barracks, kit in hand, and racing to their positions on the wall. Macro ran up the worn stone stairs and emerged on to the platform, hurrying across to the parapet. Below him the city sprawled across the plain. One of the men who had been on watch thrust his arm out towards the west.

'Over there, sir.'

Macro shaded his eyes as he stared into the setting sun. At first the glare concealed the approaching enemy from sight. He was surprised that the rebels were coming from the west. Marcellus's column had been massacred away to the east. Where had they been? he wondered. Then he dismissed the concern as his eyes began to pick out the details of the enemy marching across the plain towards the city. There were two columns, one making directly for Gortyna and the other angling to the south to march round the city and take up position to the west, Macro guessed.

'Ajax has finally decided to take the bull by the horns.'

'Yes,' Sempronius replied, panting as he caught up. 'So it seems. An apposite metaphor, by the way.'

'Really?' Macro glanced at his superior.

'This is the island where bull-leaping had its origins, Macro. In the old times, that was the phrase used to describe the moment when the acrobat was ready to face a charging bull and grabbed its horns at the last moment before somersaulting over the bull's back.'

Macro stared at the senator for a moment. Cato was going to have a lot in common with his prospective father-in-law. The two of them were sure to spend many long winters' evenings together swapping such useless nuggets of information. He sighed. 'That's fascinating, sir.'

Julia glanced sidelong and smiled at Macro as her father continued.

'The trouble is that the metaphor is the wrong way round. It is we who are facing the bull, not Ajax. And I fear that unless we are all as nimble and determined as the proverbial acrobat, we are going to be ground into the dust by the first charge.'

Macro shook his head. 'No, sir. I ain't going down that easy. The rebels are just slaves. They lack training and there's no question of them having any siege equipment. For the moment, we have the advantage.'

'I hope you are right.'

They continued to watch as the slave army deployed around the city. The clouds of dust kicked up by their feet and the hooves and wheels of the sprawling baggage train filled the air with a warm orange haze. Sempronius told his daughter to remain on the acropolis while he and Macro made their way down to the city gate to inspect their opponents more closely. Macro made a hasty calculation of the size of the enemy force before the light made estimation too difficult. The slaves marched in loose bands of varying size, and here and there amongst them the rays of the setting sun gleamed off burnished helmets, armour and weapons.

'There must be over twenty thousand of them, sir.' Macro spoke quietly so that his words would not be overheard by the nearest sentry. 'Maybe as many as thirty thousand.'

Sempronius puffed his cheeks out as he beheld the multitude settling around the city's walls. 'They would never believe this in Rome. An army of slaves? The idea is preposterous.'

'Yet there it is, sir.'

'Quite.'

As they watched the slaves fall out of their columns and begin to make camp, a sudden movement caught Macro's eye. He turned his head slightly to see a party of horsemen emerge from the slave host, trotting casually towards the city. Sempronius saw them a moment later and muttered, 'Ajax?'

'Who else?'

They watched as the party of riders reined in some distance beyond the range of any archers on the wall. A single man came forward. Thin and sinewy, he wore the scale armour vest of a Roman officer over a light blue tunic. One of the garrison's handful of archers casually strung an arrow and began to take aim.

'Lower that bow!' Macro bellowed at him. 'No one is to shoot without orders!'

The rider slowed his horse to a walk a short distance away and turned it to make his way along the wall, one hand resting on his hip as he surveyed the faces of the defenders with haughty disdain. Macro silently gave thanks that he had not yet given the order for the caltrops to be sown in the grass around the city. That was one surprise he most definitely wanted to save for the right moment.

'General Ajax sends his greetings to his former masters!' the rider called out in a clear, pleasant voice.

Sempronius turned to Macro with an amused expression. '*General* Ajax? It seems the gladiator has aspirations.'

The slave called out to the defenders again. 'The general wishes to speak with the man who calls himself the governor of the province, Senator Sempronius.'

Sempronius sniffed with irritation.

Macro smiled. 'And he's well informed. I wonder what he wants to discuss?'

There was a moment of silence before Sempronius gave a resigned shrug. 'There's only way to find out.'

He turned away from the parapet and made for the stairs that led down to the gates.

CHAPTER NINETEEN

Ajax, in the company of Kharim, watched the progress of his envoy carefully. Chilo had proved himself brave enough since he had joined the small band of fugitives that had attached themselves to Ajax since the first days of the revolt. But there was a certain carelessness to his bravery that Ajax had noted during the very first skirmish they had fought with a Roman patrol. It was almost as if Chilo had no fear of death, even as he loved his new life, free from the terrible constraints of slavery. In the ranks of Ajax's closest lieutenants, Chilo was clearly the most popular with the rest of the army. Chilo had been born free, the son of an Athenian merchant. When his father's business partner disappeared with every last piece of silver just before the annual taxes were due to be paid, it had ruined the family. The tax collector, as was his right, had duly compelled the merchant to sell himself and his family into slavery. Chilo had been five at the time, and was separated from his family at the slave market when he was bought by a Roman official and sent to serve as a household slave on his estate in Crete.

All this Ajax had learned over the camp fire as he led his growing band of runaway slaves across the ruined province. But of his years of servitude Chilo had said little, and when he did speak of them his eyes burned with an intense hatred – a sentiment that Ajax could readily understand. He had long since come to understand the difference between men who were born slaves and those who had become slaves. There was a degree of acceptance of their condition in the former. They had joined his army to be sure, and fought well enough, but the majority lacked the fanaticism of Chilo and the others who had borne slavery as a mark of shame. Every slight and injustice that they endured had burned its way into their souls. It was like a slow poison, Ajax had realised once, when reflecting on his own experience.

His father had commanded a small fleet of pirate ships that had defied the Roman navy for many years before they had finally been trapped and destroyed in a bay on the Illyrian coast. His father had paid the price for defying Rome by being crucified. Ajax and the others who had been captured were sold into slavery. It was ironic that he had been bought by the owner of a gladiator school and trained as a fighter, and now he was repaying his former masters for the skills he had learned in the arena by causing them as much suffering as possible. Every Roman he killed, every estate he sacked and every breath of free air that he drew slowly drained away the poison of slavery.

The only concern that troubled his mind was the uncertainty of the future. He had not remotely considered attempting to launch a revolt when he had made his escape from the governor's palace following the earthquake. There had been only the innate desire to run, to be free, to escape from Crete and find his way to some quiet corner of the world where the stain of slavery could gradually be erased. He had been with the governor's wife when the building began to tremble, amid the grumbling roar as Poseidon brought down his wrath on the island. They were in one of the storerooms off the back of the kitchens, where she had summoned him. Antonia had been leaning against the wall, with him inside her, while her long nails and bejewelled rings had raked the flesh of his back. As the walls shook, she screamed and thrust him away, and in that moment Ajax had resolved to be free. Free of her, free of the indignity of being her sexual play thing and free of slavery. One blow to her head had knocked her cold. Lifting her fleshy body into his arms, Ajax had left the collapsing palace, fleeing from the governor's compound into the streets, no one paying any attention to a man helping a stricken woman to safety.

Once he had escaped from the city, Ajax had been tempted to finish Antonia off. To strangle her, or crush her skull with a rock. Then, as he considered his revenge, it occurred to him that she should suffer as he had suffered. She would come to know the shame of being a slave before she was allowed to die. So, hands bound, and a leather collar and lead fixed about her neck, the fat patrician woman had been dragged along with her captor as he sought refuge in the hills behind Gortyna. Ajax was far from the only slave seeking refuge. On the first night of his new-found freedom, he came across several ragged men and women who had escaped from one of the estates. They welcomed him to their fire, shared their food and within a day looked to him as their leader. They too had wanted to kill Antonia, and Ajax had been tempted to let them, but in the end decided that she had not suffered enough just yet.

Other slaves, singly and in groups and larger bands, swelled his ranks, bringing with them a handful of other men with gladiatorial experience, even a few ex-soldiers who had fallen on bad times or been condemned to slavery. These he set to work training the slaves to fight. Initially there had been few weapons, but they had improvised by tying knives to staves, using pitchforks and scythes, and eagerly snatching up any swords and spears that they came by in the estates and villages they had started to raid.

At first Ajax was content to lead the slaves only until he had satisfied his need for revenge, and then he would carry out his original plan to leave the island and find a home far from the eyes of his former masters. But the more the escaped slaves looked to him to lead them, and the more it became clear that they were devoted to him, the less inclined he was to desert them. There was a bond of loyalty between them, he realised and accepted. A quality that he had not experienced in the years he had been a slave.

If he could not leave them, then it was his duty to see that they were saved from being returned to the living death of their former condition. Gathering the best men around him, Ajax made each the commander of a band of slaves. They were to be responsible for showing their men how to use weapons, how to take up position in simple formations and also for organising the distribution of rations and spoils. From the outset Ajax had made it clear that any food that was captured was the property of all. He addressed the ragtag mob from the top of a broken wall and told them that he would lead any who accepted his rules. He promised them that they would have revenge on their masters, and that he would lead them to freedom. Only a handful of bitter or timid spirits had refused his conditions and left the rebel camp. The crowd that remained clamoured to fight their former masters to the death.

The first of their fights had been against a small Roman foraging column that had ventured out from Matala. Despite the heavy losses, Ajax had been impressed by the fearlessness with which his rebels had charged the spears and shields of the Roman troops. Later their courage had been repaid with the destruction of the column that had arrogantly allowed itself to be led into an ambush. And then, only three days ago, they had achieved an even greater success. Ajax smiled. One which he would relish telling these Romans about, provided they had the guts to emerge from their defences and speak with him.

'Look there!' Kharim nodded towards the city. 'It seems that the Romans are falling for Chilo's charms.'

Ajax stared towards Gortyna, and saw one of the doors in the gatehouse begin to open. Several figures emerged, auxiliaries. They trotted out and formed a skirmish line a short distance in front of the gatehouse. A moment later two more men emerged, and took up position behind the soldiers. Chilo, alerted to their appearance, turned his horse and trotted towards them, reining in right in front of the nearest enemy soldier, who nervously backed off a few paces. There was a brief exchange of words before Chilo wheeled his mount and galloped back towards Ajax and his companions.

Dusk was settling over the plain as he drew up, scattering dust and stones.

'General,' he grinned. 'It seems they're willing to talk.'

'Talk?' Ajax responded disdainfully. 'Oh yes, they'll talk all right. But will they listen?'

'If they want to live then they'll listen,' Kharim said quietly. 'Do you want me to bring the wagon forward?'

Ajax nodded. 'Keep the cover on, and keep it back fifty paces.'

'Yes, General.'

Kharim wheeled his mount away and galloped back towards the baggage train. Ajax took a deep breath and waved at Chilo to ride with him. The six men, all ex-gladiators, whom he had chosen for his bodyguard, eased their mounts into a trot and followed their leader, warily watching the waiting Romans for any sign of treachery. Ajax was under no illusions about the possibility that the enemy might not abide by the usual rules of parley. He reined in beyond javelin range of the Roman skirmishers and halted his men. ~

'Chilo, you and the others stay here. If they play any tricks, then come for me.'

'General, you can't trust them. Make them come to us.'

'No, I want them to see I am not afraid.' Ajax clicked his tongue and edged his horse forwards. 'You stay put, Chilo. That is an order. When Kharim brings the wagon up, I want you to have it halted behind my bodyguards.'

'Yes, General.'

Ajax walked his horse across the open ground at an easy pace. The men ahead of him were clearly visible in the rays of the setting sun, washed in the same red hue that burnished the scrub grass and stones outside the city. The auxiliaries were squinting into the light, some having grounded their spears to shade their eyes. He knew that he would appear as a dark silhouette to them, seemingly larger than life and threatening as he approached. It might make him a clearer target, but any Roman attempting to hurl a javelin, or even a spear, would be forced to squint, and their aim was sure to be spoiled. He stopped twenty paces from the nearest of the auxiliaries. The horse snorted and pawed the dusty ground with its hooves.

'Who are you?' A man called out from behind the Roman line.

'Ajax, general of the army of free men.' He swept his arm back towards the host making camp for the night. 'I am here to state our demands. To the governor in person. To his minion, if the governor is too fearful to speak with me.'

'I am not afraid,' the man responded haughtily. 'Not of you, nor your band of rebels.'

'Then prove it! Come forward and face me.' Ajax thrust his arm down, pointing at the ground. 'Here, beyond the protection of your men.'

The two figures standing behind the skirmishers strode boldly towards him, passing through their men and drawing up ten feet away. One wore armour, a scarlet cloak and a helmet, and he hefted his centurion's vine cane as he scrutinised the commander of the slave army. Ajax felt a cold chill tickle his neck. He recognised the face. This was the officer who had led the foraging column. But he had seen him before, somewhere else, he was certain of it, yet for the present could not place him. He turned his attention to the other Roman, who was taller and wore a white tunic with a broad red stripe. He crossed his arms as he drew himself up to his full height to confront Ajax.

'Say your piece, slave.'

Ajax bit back on his irritation. 'I no longer count myself a slave, nor do any of the men and women in my army.'

'Army? That is no army. Merely a rabble.'

Ajax could not help smiling. 'That rabble slaughtered a thousand of your best men, Sempronius.'

The Roman clamped his lips together.

'Besides,' Ajax continued, 'my army now controls most of southern Crete. We go where we will, while you Romans hide behind your defences and pray for deliverance. But your gods have deserted you. There is nothing that stands between you and certain death, except me.'

'I see, you've come to save us,' Sempronius sneered.

'I have come to offer you a chance to save your lives and the lives of every man, woman and child inside the walls of Gortyna.'

'And how can I save them?'

'By giving us our freedom and by ensuring that we are given free passage from this island to the eastern frontier of the empire.'

Sempronius chuckled bitterly. 'Is that all?'

'It is a fair exchange for your lives, wouldn't you say?'

'No. It is out of the question. I don't have the authority to do that.'

'But you are the governor. You act in the name of the emperor and the senate. You could grant us freedom.'

'What's the point?' Sempronius sneered. 'I thought you said you were no longer slaves.'

'I want it in writing,' Ajax said firmly. 'I want it guaranteed in the name of Rome.'

'Why?' Sempronius insisted. 'What difference does it make?'

Ajax smiled. 'I know what sticklers you people are for paperwork. I want our freedom to be official.'

Sempronius was silent for a moment. 'You want to rub our noses in it, you mean. This is about revenge.'

'Yes . . .' The image of his father nailed to a crossbeam and left to die appeared in Ajax's mind – raw and painful. 'I deserve revenge for the suffering I have endured at the hands of your people. So do all those who now follow me. Your emperor should count himself lucky that my demands are so modest.'

'But you must know that Claudius could not possibly concede to this. The senate would not stand for it. Nor would the mob. If he gave in to the demands of a common slave the mob would tear him to pieces.'

'I think you will find that I was a most uncommon slave, Governor,' Ajax said tersely. 'Otherwise we would not be here.'

'All right, then. Let's say, for the sake of argument, that I agree to your demand. What makes you think that any other Roman official will honour it? In any case, you have no means of finding sufficient ships to carry your people away from Crete. How do you think you will be able to compel Rome to keep to her side of the bargain?'

'It's simple. I will take you, and every Roman, and the city's leading families as hostages. You will come with us every step of the way. When we reach the frontier, and not before, we will release you. If the emperor, or any of his subordinates, attempts to hinder us, then I will start killing my prisoners, beginning with you.'

Sempronius took a sharp breath. 'That won't work. I've told you, Rome cannot agree to your demands.'

'Then it is up to you to persuade the emperor. I take it you were trained in rhetoric as a youth. No doubt by some expensive Greek slave. Now's the chance to put your skills to good use. Your life depends on it.'

'This is absurd. I cannot accept your demands. You know it.' Sempronius paused and drew a deep breath. 'Now, let me tell you what my demands are. One: you lay down your arms and surrender. Two: you identify all the ringleaders to me. Three: all other slaves are to return to their owners at once. In return, I will send you and the other ringleaders to Rome to be sentenced before the emperor and the senate. Furthermore I will do all that is within my legal power to limit the punishment of the slaves who freely return to their masters.'

Ajax stared at the Roman with a cold expression. He had expected such disdain from Sempronius, and a refusal of his demands. It was time to demonstrate to these Romans that their danger was very real.

'Senator, your demands are no more acceptable than mine. Yet the difference between us is that you are in no position to make demands.' Ajax turned in the saddle and called back towards his men. 'Chilo! Bring the wagon here!'

The line of horsemen parted and four oxen trudged forward, drawing a heavy covered wagon behind them. A driver sat on the bench, with another man who was covered in filth. His tunic was in tatters, exposing skin that was streaked with grime and blood, and marked with cuts and bruises. He was chained to the wagon by his hands and ankles and his head was bowed.

'What's this?' asked Sempronius.

Ajax turned back. 'I suspect you have been wondering why we did not advance on Gortyna immediately after the ambush. The answer is in the wagon. You see, my army bypassed Gortyna during the night eight days ago. We made for Matala instead. The commander of the garrison there proved every bit as arrogant as you, Sempronius. He managed to herd most of his people on to the acropolis. Those that remained in the refugee camp we put to the sword. I sent a messenger to the gate to demand the surrender of the acropolis. I told your Centurion Portillus that I wanted the food on the acropolis, not him and his people. When he surrendered, they could all go free. If he did not submit within two days, then I would take the acropolis and slaughter every person inside its walls. I am glad to say that Portillus saw reason, and surrendered the very next day.' Ajax paused as the wagon rumbled up, turned to one side and halted behind him. He caught a waft of death and decay and heard the buzzing drone of flies as he continued. 'Sadly, as far as the people of Matala are concerned, it was necessary for me to make an example of them in order that you would believe me when I came here to make my demands to you.'

'What have you done?' asked the centurion behind Sempronius.

'I did what was necessary. I had the garrison and townspeople marched out of the city and then I told my men to kill them.'

Sempronius shook his head. 'You're lying.'

'Yes, I thought that would be the reaction. So I brought proof. Chilo, remove the cover.'

Wrinkling his nose in disgust, Chilo edged his horse towards the side of the wagon and grasped one corner of the cover. With a savage heave, he wrenched it away and let it fall to the ground. A swirling mass of insects rose into the evening air. Sempronius covered his mouth with a hand and stepped back. The nearest of the auxiliaries squinted at the contents of the wagon and then turned to one side to vomit. Ajax watched their reactions with quiet satisfaction as they gazed upon the severed heads heaped on the bed of the wagon.

'That is what is left of the soldiers of the Twelfth Hispania. The rest we left out for the carrion and the dogs.' Ajax turned to the driver of the wagon and pointed at the man chained beside him. 'Release him! Then leave the wagon and get back to the camp.'

'Yes, General,' the driver replied and then ducked down to release the pins that fastened the shackles to the wagon. As soon as he had done that, he roughly pushed the man off the bench and he tumbled on to the ground beside the wagon with a thud and lay there groaning.

'Get up!' Ajax ordered. Chilo leaned down from his saddle and grasped the prisoner's hair and hauled him to his feet. With a thrust from Chilo's boot, the man stumbled towards Ajax and the two Romans.

'You may not recognise him now,' Ajax stared at the men in contempt, 'but I believe you know Centurion Portillus, lately the commander of the garrison of Matala. I thought I might spare him so that he could confirm what I have told you. Here, Senator, the prisoner is yours.'

Chilo goaded Portillus towards Sempronius, who could not help recoiling at the soiled, stinking creature that confronted him. The senator swallowed and forced himself to control his voice as he addressed Portillus.

'Is it true?'

'Yes, sir,' Portillus mumbled, barely able to meet his superior's eye.

'Are they all dead?'

'Yes, sir.' The centurion's voice quavered. 'I saw them die. All my men. All the civilians, every last one of them, even the infants.'

'I see.' Sempronius glared at him. 'And is it true that you surrendered without a fight?'

'We had no choice,' Portillus protested. 'They threatened to put us to the sword. You heard.'

'It seems they did it anyway.' Sempronius's expression became severe. 'You have disgraced yourself.'

'Don't be too hard on him,' Ajax intervened. 'I betrayed him in turn. He wasn't to know.'

'Wasn't to know what?' Sempronius spat back. 'That you should never trust the word of a slave?'

'What does my word matter? Or yours?' Ajax paused a moment. 'All that matters is that you know what the consequences are if you refuse to meet my demands. For the last time, Senator. You will surrender Gortyna to me. If you do not, then you and everyone else will share the fate of the people of Matala. You have until noon tomorrow to decide.'

He turned his horse towards the camp, then paused and turned back, gesturing at Portillus. 'I return this man to you. I have no further need of him.'

Sempronius looked briefly at Centurion Portillus and then cleared his throat. 'I don't want him. Neither I nor my men will be contaminated by his cowardice.'

Ajax shrugged. 'So be it. Chilo!'

'Yes, General?'

'Finish him.'

Chilo nodded and dismounted. He pulled out a broad-bladed dagger from his belt and advanced on Portillus with a cruel smile. The latter's eyes widened in terror and he lurched towards Sempronius, the chains causing him to tumble to his knees.

'Spare me! For pity's sake, don't let him!'

Sempronius stepped back nimbly. 'Don't you dare beg me, you cur!'

Chilo stood behind Portillus and grasped him under the chin with one hand, and before Portillus could make more than a strangled whimper, the blade slashed across his throat. A great rush of blood spurted out and splashed on the ground. Chilo released his grip and stepped back. For a moment Portillus frantically clasped his hands to his throat, then he slumped back and rolled on to his side, his body trembling as he bled out.

Chilo wiped the blade on his tunic.

'Bastard,' the centurion who had accompanied Sempronius growled. He drew his sword and stepped forward.

'Put that sword away!' Sempronius shouted.

The centurion ignored him and advanced towards Chilo. 'Let's see how good you are against a man who can fight back!'

'Leave him!' Sempronius grabbed the officer's shoulder. 'I gave you an order, Centurion Macro! Leave him.'

Ajax froze. He was still for an instant, then twisted round in his saddle and stared at the Roman officer. 'Macro? Centurion Macro?'

His heart was filled with a rush of emotions. Bitter hatred, rage and a strange joyful exultation. His limbs trembled with excitement and there was an almost inhuman desire to throw himself on Macro and tear the Roman to pieces. Blood pounded through his veins as he raised his hands, fingers clawed, as if he would wring the other man's neck. Then the moment passed, and self-control struggled to control his thoughts. Not now. Not while there were higher stakes.

'Ajax, the pirate's son.' Macro nodded slowly, sword raised and braced to defend himself against any sudden attack. 'You remember me, then?'

There was a keening groan in Ajax's throat as he fought to restrain his rage.

'I remember you well enough, lad,' Macro continued. 'And I remember your father. When this is over, you'll share his fate. By the gods, I swear it . . . Unless you want to fight me now. Come on!' He raised his sword. 'Man to man.'

Ajax was breathing deeply. His senses were heightened to a feverish pitch of sound, sight and smell, just as they always were in the arena when the signal to fight was given. Slowly, slowly he forced himself to calm his desire to hurl himself at Macro. Instead he eased his sword hand to his side, and sat erect, still staring fixedly at the Roman.

'We will have our fight, Centurion. Not here, not now. But the time will come. No god, no fate, no person would deny me the right to kill you with my own hands.'

Ajax abruptly turned his horse away and kicked his heels in, galloping back towards his army. His heart was filled with overwhelming resolve. When Macro was defeated, he would learn what it meant to die in the most humiliating, agonising manner, just as Ajax's father had done.

CHAPTER TWENTY

'Just what did you think you were doing back there?' Sempronius snapped the moment they reached his headquarters in the acropolis. 'You were goading him. You saw his expression at the end there. He was insane. For a moment I thought he'd go for you with his bare hands.'

'Might have been better for us if he had, sir,' Macro replied coolly. 'Then I could have had him. With Ajax gone, how long do you think that ragbag army of his would hold together?'

Sempronius gave him a calculating look. 'What makes you think you could have beaten him? The man looked as tough as any fighter I have ever seen in the arena, and he's been trained to kill.'

'So have I. And I've had rather more experience at it. Besides, what good would all that gladiatorial training have been if he had lost his head and thrown himself into a fight?'

Sempronius nodded. 'I see. That's what you were counting on. That's why you provoked him.'

'Of course, sir. First rule of war – always try and get the enemy to fight on your terms.'

'Well then, I owe you an apology. For a moment I thought you had lost control of yourself.'

'Me?' Macro looked pained. 'Lose control of myself?'

'In any case, thanks to your intervention, I doubt that Ajax is going to be predisposed towards sparing anyone if he does take Gortyna.' Sempronius sat down behind his desk and turned to gaze over the city. Macro had given orders for torches and braziers to be lit along the wall, in case the rebels made any attempt to attack under cover of darkness. The usual watch had been doubled and the rest of the men were quartered in houses close to the walls. Some half-mile outside the city were clusters of camp fires, arranged in a great arc that enclosed the hills to the rear of it. As soon as night had fallen, several sections of men had been sent out from Gortyna to start sowing the caltrops along the approaches to the weakest lengths of the wall. Now there was a tense stillness as the defenders beheld the enemy host and waited.

Sempronius turned away from the window. 'If the city falls, he will take his hostages and kill the rest. I am sure of it.'

'Then we must make sure that we hold Gortyna.'

'Easily said, Macro. We have to think through all the choices open to us.'

Macro's eyes widened. 'You're not seriously considering surrender?'

'No,' Sempronius replied. 'But it is an option, none the less. We'll have to put the situation to the ruling council. They have to be told.'

Macro shook his head. 'Sir, if we let a bunch of civilians have their say, well, it's obvious they'll take the offer to save their skins.'

'Then we must persuade them that Ajax is not to be trusted.'

'Why ask them in the first place? Just tell them we ain't giving in, and we'll fight the rebels until the last man, or until Cato returns with reinforcements.'

'We have to keep them on our side even though I doubt that the idea of fighting to the last man is going to win much support. We'll have to play up the idea of the city being relieved.' Sempronius yawned and ran a hand through his grey-streaked hair. 'Either way, we must assemble the council and explain the situation. I'll have them brought here within the hour. I want you with me.'

Macro's shoulders slumped for an instant. 'It'd be better if I remained on the wall, sir. In case the enemy try anything on.'

'No. You'll be here. That's an order. If this city can be defended, then they'll need to hear that from a professional soldier. We have to talk them out of considering surrender, so you'd better be persuasive, Macro. The last thing we need is a divided city at our back when we face the rebels.'

The city's councillors entered the office with anxious expressions and took their places on the benches that Sempronius had ordered for them. He had considered making them stand, but had decided that it would be better if he stood and they sat. It was an old technique for establishing authority that he had learned from his Greek tutor of rhetoric. As the last of them entered and settled on to the benches, Sempronius glanced at Macro sitting on a chair in the corner of the office. The centurion was leaning forwards, elbows on knees and fist supporting his chin as he stared down at the floor with a resigned air. Sempronius frowned briefly, then turned back to his audience, who were talking in muted tones.

'Thank you for coming, gentlemen . . .' He waited for them all to fall silent and focus their attention on him. 'As you are no doubt aware, the rebels have arrived to lay siege to Gortyna. Some of you will have heard that my senior military officer and I met their leader, Ajax the gladiator, at dusk. He gave us his demands, namely freedom, and free passage out of the empire for him and his followers.'

'Then why don't you agree to his terms?' One of the councillors, a fat merchant, leaned forward. 'Give him what he wants and get him away from us.'

Several of his companions nodded and muttered their agreement.

Sempronius fixed his gaze on the man. 'Polocrites, isn't it? Olive oil exporter.'

The man nodded, and folded his arms, as Macro muttered to himself, 'Like father like son. No stomach for a fight.'

'It isn't as simple as that, Polocrites. Even if I agree to his demands, Ajax wants to take hostages to ensure that we keep our side of the deal. To that end he wants us to surrender the city and hand ourselves over to him. It is his intention to keep his hostages until he has made good his escape from Roman territory.'

As the import of his words sank in, another of the councillors spoke up. 'That's preposterous. He can't hope to take the entire city with him. How would he feed such a multitude? How could the rebels stop them escaping?'

'Ajax does not intend to take everyone hostage. Just the Romans . . .'

Polocrites nodded. 'That's fair.'

'And the richest families of Gortyna,' Sempronius continued.

Polocrites glared. 'That's an outrage! This gladiator's fight is between him and Rome. We have nothing to do with it.'

'Why don't you go and tell him that?' asked Sempronius. 'Now be quiet and hear me out. Ajax wants high-value hostages. He hopes that the emperor will think twice before reneging on any deal I may make regarding freeing these slaves if it means putting our lives at risk. I have to tell you that I do not think for a moment that Claudius would permit a mass revolt of slaves to succeed. Indeed, I think he will do everything in his power to have Ajax and his followers tracked down and destroyed. If that means we are killed, then that's a price he will be prepared to pay.' He paused, steeling himself to continue. 'And there's worse news. It is my belief – my conviction – that if Gortyna is surrendered to the rebels, they will take their hostages and put the rest of the population to the sword.'

'How can you possibly know that?' Polocrites scoffed.

'It's quite simple. Some days ago the garrison and people of Matala surrendered to the rebels and now they are all dead.'

For a moment there was complete stillness and silence in the room, before one of the councillors asked, 'Dead? All dead? How do you know?'

'Ajax told us.' Sempronius indicated Macro. 'He brought us the heads of the men of the Twelfth Hispania, and had their commander confirm the details before being murdered in front of our eyes. If you don't believe me then you can see for yourself at first light. Ajax left the heads in front of the main gate. He said he wanted to provide us, and those back in Rome, with proof of his ruthlessness. It's possible that he also needed to burn his bridges to make sure that his followers realised there was no going back. Not after they had massacred an entire town. For the slaves there is, from now on, only freedom or death.'

'If he has proved his point, then he does not need to kill our people,' said Polocrites.

'I disagree. After Matala, he is no longer restrained by fear of the consequences.' Sempronius recalled the wild rage and hatred he had seen in the gladiator's eyes, and his cruel pleasure at the death of Portillus. 'I'd go further. He has a taste for death and an insatiable thirst to get revenge on those who were his masters. It would be madness to trust him, and little short of suicide to place ourselves in his hands.'

'What are you suggesting we do then?' Polocrites opened his hands helplessly.

'We must defend Gortyna. We must not submit to his demands.'

'How can we defend Gortyna against that host?' Polocrites rounded on Macro. 'You're the soldier here. What chance have we got of holding the city?'

Macro looked up. 'About as much chance as surviving if the rebels take us hostage.'

The councillor's jaw slackened, then he turned to his companions. 'Did you hear? The situation is hopeless.'

'It's not hopeless,' Macro countered sharply. 'I didn't say that. It depends on a number of things. The enemy have more men, but they haven't got much good kit, and they're not trained soldiers. They don't have any siege equipment, and they're going to have to learn how to attack a city from scratch. On the other hand, given the length of the wall we have to defend, and the fact that sections of it are weak where we've had to rush the repairs, numbers may well win the day. However, if we can hold them off long enough for Cato to return with reinforcements, then the day is ours.'

'And how likely is it that your friend has succeeded in reaching Egypt?'

Macro had his doubts. There would have been dangers on the road to the fishing port, then Cato would have had to cross the sea to the African coast, where there might be pirates picking off lone merchant ships. Even if he reached Alexandria he would have to face the sea again on the return journey. Macro's breath escaped with a frustrated hiss. 'Centurion Cato . . .' he paused and glanced at Sempronius, 'I mean Tribune Cato, is one of the most resourceful officers in the Roman army. If any man can get through to Alexandria and get us the men we need to end this rebellion, it is him.'

'I see. And how long do you think it will be before he can return with an army powerful enough to destroy the gladiator and his followers?'

'Hard to say.' Macro pursed his lips. 'Another ten days at the earliest, but more likely to be nearer twenty.'

Polocrites stared at him for a moment before shaking his head with a chuckle. 'For some reason I am not encouraged by this news.'

He rose to his feet and turned to the other councillors. 'There is another way to save Gortyna. To save our people.'

'Then tell us,' said Sempronius. 'I'm sure we would all be delighted to discover the means to our salvation.'

Polocrites ignored him steadfastly as he addressed his companions. 'Ajax must know that he will lose many hundreds of his men, perhaps thousands, if he is forced to assault Gortyna. It may also take several days. All of which will dispirit his followers. Every day they are forced to fight us will feed their bloodlust. There will be no mercy if they take the city. We will be put to the sword. Our women will be raped and tortured and our children butchered.'

Macro nodded. 'All the more reason to fight to the last man.'

'No,' Polocrites responded sharply. 'All the more reason to find another way out of the peril we are placed in.' He continued in a crafty tone. 'What if we were to offer to hand over the Romans to Ajax? If we were to co-operate in providing his hostages, then surely he would be grateful to the people of Gortyna for sparing his men the need to assault the city, and saving the rebels the time and effort of mounting a siege.' Polocrites paused briefly, then concluded, 'I think we can make a separate peace with the rebels.'

There was an uncomfortable silence before Macro laughed. 'You cheeky Greek bastard! For a moment there I thought you were serious.'

Polocrites turned to him with a deadpan expression. 'I am serious.'

'No you're not.' Macro smiled. 'Because if you were, that would make you a dirty little back-stabbing traitor. And if that was the case, then I'd have no choice but to cut your throat and hurl your worthless carcass over the city wall and into the ditch for the dogs to feed on.'

'You wouldn't dare,' Polocrites said quietly.

'Sorry.' Macro shrugged. 'Like I said, I'd have no choice. It'd be regrettable but necessary. I'm sure you would understand . . . But since you're having a joke with us, and you really wouldn't even contemplate dishonouring yourself in such a cowardly manner, there's no harm done. Now, you've had your fun. There's no question of surrender, and no question of negotiating with Ajax.' He paused and casually pulled out his dagger, and carefully edged the point under a fingernail to dislodge some dirt. 'I do have that right, don't I?'

The councillors watched Polocrites closely as the man stared at Macro and gauged his chances of escaping the fate Macro had mentioned.

'I'm sorry.' Macro looked up from his manicure. 'Did you say something?'

'No.'

Macro frowned and slowly rose from his chair.

'I meant yes.' Polocrites backed off a step.

'Yes?'

'Yes,' Polocrites said hurriedly. 'I was joking.'

'Good.' Macro nodded and carefully replaced his dagger. 'That's that then.'

'Well,' Sempronius cleared his throat uneasily, 'it seems that we are agreed on where we stand, gentlemen. It is important that we present a united front to the defenders and people of Gortyna. There will be no talk of negotiating with the enemy. It is our joint resolve to defend the city, to the end if that is necessary. I trust that is understood by you all. Now, on that note of agreement, I am calling this meeting to an end. Thank you for your attention, and your continued support.' He bowed his head and then indicated the door. Polocrites was the first to leave, sweeping past the others as he strode swiftly out of the room. The rest followed his lead, some shooting nervous glances in Macro's direction as they departed. When the last of them had gone, Sempronius sighed and slumped back down on to his chair.

'Hardly an inspiring display of unity.'

'No, sir.' Macro chewed his lip. 'But I think they'll keep their mouths shut for a little while.'

'I hope so.' Sempronius rubbed his temple and shut his eyes. 'It all comes down to Cato in the end, doesn't it?'

'Yes, you're right.' Macro went over to the window and rested his hands on the frame as he stared out towards the main camp of the rebels. 'I meant what I said about him being the best man for the job. The trouble is, being the best is not enough sometimes. He's pushed his luck in the past and it won't last for ever.'

'Don't write him off too quickly.' Julia's voice carried across the room.

Both of the men turned and saw her at the door. She stared at Macro for a moment and then made her way down the gap between the benches and sat on the one nearest her father's desk.

'I wasn't writing him off,' Macro explained. 'I'm just concerned for him.'

'We all are,' Sempronius added. 'With good cause. I hope he won't let us down.'

'He won't,' Macro said firmly.

Sempronius turned to his daughter. 'What brings you here?'

'I came to report on the day's food consumption. Your guards said there was a meeting. I waited outside until it was over.'

'I take it you heard everything.'

'Most of it.' Julia nodded. 'Can't say I'm very impressed with the locals. What do you intend to do about them, Father?'

'Do? Nothing. Not unless they start making trouble for us. If that happens, they can join Glabius in the acropolis cells.'

'I'd have that man Polocrites closely watched if I were you.'

'She's right,' said Macro. 'The man's trouble. Might be better to lock him up now, before he can spread any more of his poison.'

Sempronius considered the suggestion for a moment before he shook his head. 'We'll leave him be for now. I can't afford to be making enemies inside the city when we have a far greater danger to deal with. We're already in enough peril. Which is why I've come to a decision.' He leaned forward and looked steadily at his daughter. 'I want you to leave Gortyna.'

'Leave?' Julia shook her head in surprise. 'What are you talking about? I'm staying here. With you.'

'That's impossible. It's too much of a risk. There is a good chance that Ajax and his army will take Gortyna. If the city falls, I could not bear the thought of what might happen to you.'

'Father, it's not as if this is the first time we've been under siege.'

'No, but last time I had no option. We were trapped in Palmyra. There is still time for you to leave Gortyna and make it to the north of the island. You can wait there for news.'

'I will not go,' Julia replied firmly. 'I will stay by your side. I will

217

wait for Cato. And if the city falls, then I will die by my own hand before any of the rebels can touch me. I swear it, Father.'

Sempronius looked pained at her suggestion. He stared at her while he fought with his fear for her safety. 'Julia. You are my only child. You are the most important thing in my life. I cannot let you remain here where your life is in danger.'

'Er . . .' Macro shuffled awkwardly. 'Would you like me to, ah, leave the room?'

'No,' Sempronius replied. 'Stay.'

Julia smiled fondly and reached forward to take his hands. 'Father, I know what I mean to you.'

'No you don't. No child does, not until they have children of their own.'

She returned his gaze for a moment and shook her head sadly. 'I cannot go. I do not want to leave you, and I must be here when Cato returns.'

He leaned wearily back in his chair. 'I have made my decision. You will leave Gortyna.'

Julia glared at him, then lowered her head and stared at her hands. When she spoke, there was no hiding the strain in her voice. 'When do you wish me to leave?'

'Tonight. I suspect that Ajax will want to cut the city off the moment he realises that we will not be agreeing to his demands. If you leave under cover of darkness, you can put some miles between you and Gortyna before dawn. I'll send a small escort with you. The rebel scouts will miss you if you go quietly and head north into the hills. Make for Cnossos.' He turned to Macro. 'I want you to pick some good men to escort my daughter from the city.'

'Sir?'

'You are to go with them until they have reached a safe distance from Gortyna. Then you can return here.' A brief look of embarrassment crossed the senator's face. 'I know there's a chance that you might have some trouble getting back, so I won't order you to do this. I ask it as a favour, to a friend.'

'Don't worry, sir,' Macro replied firmly. 'I'm happy to do it. For you, and for Cato.'

'Thank you.' Sempronius stood up and crossed the room to the window, where he clasped Macro's arm. 'You're a good man. One of the best.'

'I said I'd do it, sir. You don't have to go on about it.'

Sempronius laughed. 'Very well. Go now. Take your pick of the men, the best of the horses and enough rations for the journey. Report back to me as soon as you return.'

'Yes, sir.' Macro nodded, and Sempronius released his arm. As Macro made for the door, Julia stepped forward to embrace her father. Sempronius kissed the top of her head. He held her tight for an instant and then let her go. She turned away and hurried from the room without looking back.

Sempronius listened to the light patter of her sandals, soon lost under the harsh clatter of Macro's nailed boots, then both died away as they left the building. He took a deep breath to calm the pain in his heart and gazed out towards the twinkling sprawl of fires that marked the rebel camps.

'Cato, my boy,' he muttered to himself, 'for pity's sake don't fail me now.'

CHAPTER TWENTY-ONE

As dawn broke, Yannis woke Cato to point out a trailing column of smoke rising into the sky above the horizon. To their right, the Egyptian coast was two miles off, low-lying and almost feature-less, apart from the occasional cluster of small huts and fishing boats. They had been sailing along the coast since putting in briefly at Darnis to take on water. There were no roads along the coast and Cato had been advised to continue the journey by sea. Once he had learned the rudiments of sailing, Cato and Yannis had taken it in turns to steer the fishing boat while the other Romans did their best to keep out of the way in the small, cramped and stinking craft. The weather had been fine and a westerly breeze meant that they made good time. There had been no need to put in to land each night after leaving Darnis since the moon had lit their way, sparkling dully off the sea. Even though they had made good progress, Cato was fretful, his mind constantly occupied with concern for his friends back in Gortyna. Indeed, he had been dozing, thinking of Julia, when Yannis had shaken his shoulder gently, and now the fisherman looked amused as Cato stirred, wondering what he had just muttered.

'Yes, what is it?'

'We're in sight of the lighthouse. I thought you'd want to know.'

Cato scrambled stiffly up from the side of the boat and balanced his feet against its motion as he stood beside Yannis. He saw the column of smoke at once, and the faint gleam of a polished surface at its base. 'How far away are we?'

'I've heard that it's possible to see the top of the lighthouse from twenty or thirty miles away. I've been to Alexandria a few times, when I was a soldier. See that sparkle? That's a huge curved piece of brass, regularly polished. By day it reflects the light of the sun, and at night the flames of the fire that burns at the top of the tower.'

Cato had read of the great lighthouse at Alexandria and felt a tingle of excitement at the thought of seeing such an architectural marvel. From what he recalled, the lighthouse was only one of the landmarks of the city founded by the greatest general in history. Alexandria was also filled with the most brilliant minds in the world, drawn to the vast collection of books in the Great Library. If there was time, Cato firmly resolved to see something of the city.

With a full sail bulging under the pressure of a stiff breeze, the fishing boat surged across the swell, and as the sun climbed into the sky, the other Romans stirred and watched the distant structure slowly crawl above the curve of the horizon. The hours passed and Cato pulled on his felt cap and tipped the fringe down to shield his eyes from the glare of the sun. By noon the port itself was clearly visible, and beyond, the vast expanse of the city. At the heart of Alexandria were the various complexes of temples, markets, palaces and the Great Library, huge edifices worthy of a city that had a population almost as great as that of Rome. Yannis pointed out the two harbours, the nearest of which had to be approached cautiously due to the dangerous shoals and rocks that lined its entrance. Scores of ships lay at anchor, or moored to the quay, where a multitude of tiny figures laden with cargo toiled between the ships and the long row of warehouses that faced the wharf.

Yannis steered the boat around Pharos island towards the second, smaller harbour. It was only as they approached the lighthouse built on to the end of the island that Cato fully appreciated the scale of the structure, built on the orders of the second Ptolemy. A vast square base with walls and low towers served as the platform for the main tower, which soared into the sky, over four hundred feet in height. The first level was square, pierced with rows of windows. Above it was an eight-sided section leading up to the final, smallest level, which was round. The fire was housed in the upper floors of the highest level, and above that gleamed the huge brass reflector. There was a tiny flurry of white specks swirling about the top of the lighthouse as one of its keepers hurled scraps of food to the gulls. Cato and the other Romans were stunned by the building. In all their lives they had seen nothing to compare to it, not even in Rome, with all its grand buildings. Yannis laughed at their awed expressions.

'Somewhat humbling, isn't it? Not so sure that Rome is the centre of the world any more?'

'I had no idea it was as magnificent as this,' Cato admitted. 'How on earth could they have built it?'

He had been raised with the idea of Roman omnipotence. Rome was the greatest city, its people the greatest race, and its gods were the most powerful. He had not been fool enough to take this smugness at face value, but he had travelled the empire from Britain to Palmyra and seen nothing to compete with the magnificence of Rome. Until now.

The boat passed the end of Pharos island and a short while later Yannis altered course and headed into the port that opened out beyond the lighthouse. The wind was now abeam the fishing boat, and it heeled as Yannis adjusted his mainsheets. The main concentration of shipping was over to the right, and Cato saw a fleet of large vessels heading directly for them. Yannis altered course to avoid them.

'The grain fleet,' he explained.

Cato nodded as he examined the vessels more closely. They were built like the *Horus*, but on a larger scale, with high sides that bulged outwards. A purple pennant rippled from the top of each mast. He watched them as they sailed past with almost stately grace, as the faint swell had almost no effect on them. Each vessel was filled with grain destined for Rome, where it would feed the common people for the next four months while the fleet returned to Alexandria for the next consignment. Ever since the Emperor Augustus had finally annexed Egypt and made it into a Roman province, the fertile fields watered by the great river Nile had become the breadbasket of Rome. Unfortunately the mob had come to rely on the free handout, and successive emperors had not dared to put an end to the dole, no matter how much gold it cost them.

The courses of the fleet and the fishing boat diverged as Yannis steered the craft towards a small port at the base of the peninsula that protected the harbour. A fleet of Roman warships lay at anchor in the sheltered waters, and beyond them steps and ramps rose up from the sea towards a large palace complex.

'That's the old royal port,' said Yannis. 'And the palaces built by the

Ptolemies. Except for that building to the right. That's the Great Library.'

Cato looked towards the building Yannis had mentioned. He had assumed that it was yet another palace, but now that he looked more closely he could see a steady stream of people moving in and out of the vaulted entrance. More were visible on the balconies on the upper floors, scanning racks of scrolls or talking in small groups.

As the fishing boat approached one of the ramps that emerged from the sea, Yannis uncleated the mainsheets and thrust them into the hands of two of Cato's men. 'Let them go the moment I say.'

He judged the approach carefully, and when the boat was no more than fifty feet from the shore he called out, 'Now.'

The sail flapped up and billowed freely in the wind, and the fishing boat rapidly lost way through the water. Just before it grounded, Yannis heaved on the steering oar and the craft surged round and bumped gently on the stone ramp a short distance below the surface. Their arrival had been noticed by some of the sentries guarding the steps up to the palace, and a section of legionaries led by an optio came marching down the ramp.

'What's all this then?' the optio called out. 'You gypos know you ain't allowed to land here. Off limits. Military only, so piss off.'

Cato felt his temper rise. After eight mostly sleepless days of being confined to the small fishing boat, he was desperate to be on dry land again. He was about to tear a strip off the optio for insubordination when he realised that he was so tired he was not thinking clearly. His clothes, and those of his men, were grimy, and they had not shaved since leaving Gortyna. It was no wonder the optio had mistaken them for common fishermen.

'What are you waiting for?' The optio folded his arms. 'Get lost before I have the lads give you a good hiding.'

Cato cleared his throat. 'A word to the wise, Optio. Best to check the lie of the land before you blunder into it. I'm Tribune Quintus Licinius Cato, and these men are my escort.'

The optio's eyes narrowed as he scrutinised the bedraggled men standing in the boat. He shook his head. 'Bollocks you are.'

Cato reached down for his leather tube, pulled the lid off and took out his letter of commission, signed and sealed by Sempronius. 'Here. Read it.'

The optio glanced at the sea lapping a short distance from his boots and shook his head. 'No, you bring it here. Just you mind. Those others stay in the boat for now.'

Cato eased himself over the side and splashed down into the knee-deep water. He surged ashore and thrust the letter at the optio. The other man took the document, unrolled it and scanned the contents for a moment before he looked warily at Cato. 'Tribune Cato?'

'That's what it says. I have to see Legate Petronius immediately.'

'Now just wait a minute, sir. What is going on?'

Cato fixed him with a firm stare and there was iron in his tone when he replied. 'Optio, do I really have to explain myself to you?'

The optio chewed his lip a moment and then saluted. 'Sorry, sir. I am at your command.'

'That's better. Now, I want my men fed and rested. Have your section look after them. You will take me to the legate.'

The optio nodded, then detailed his companions to help secure the boat and escort the arrivals to the garrison's barracks. He turned back to Cato and bowed his head. 'If you'd follow me, sir.'

He led Cato up the ramp and through a towering arch decorated with a frieze of Egyptian deities. On the far side was a large courtyard with an elegant colonnade running around three sides. Opposite the arch, a hundred paces away, a wide flight of steps rose up to the entrance of the main palace. A section of legionaries stood outside, shields and javelins grounded as they took their watch in the blazing sunshine. Another arch to the right opened out on to a busy thoroughfare of considerable breadth that was thronged with people and pack animals. The din of the street was partly muted by the colonnade, but even so, the hubbub of a teeming population reminded Cato of Rome.

The optio turned to him as they strode across the courtyard, smiling at the wobbly gait of the tribune. 'Been at sea a few days then, sir?'

Cato nodded.

'Mind telling me what you and your lads were doing in a fishing boat?'

'Yes.'

'Oh?' The optio was puzzled for an instant before he got the point. He clamped his mouth shut and they continued in silence, climbing the dazzling white steps towards the palace entrance. The sentries advanced their javelins in salute as the optio passed, and tried to look straight ahead and not pay any attention to the bedraggled man, reeking of fish, who accompanied him. Inside the entrance was a large hall, filled with petitioners waiting for their chance to put their grievances to the legate or one of his officials. At the end of the hall was a large doorway, flanked by eight more legionaries. A table stood in front of the doors, seated at which was a centurion in a light tunic. His vine cane lay in front of him. He was reading through one of the petitions when the optio and Cato approached the desk.

'Yes?' he said without looking up.

The optio stood to attention. 'Beg to report the arrival of Tribune Quintus Licinius Cato, sir.'

'Yes, just wait a moment,' the centurion muttered automatically, before he realised what had been said. He looked up, glanced at the optio and then switched his gaze to Cato. 'Him – a tribune? What nonsense is this?'

'It's true, sir. He showed me his letter of appointment.'

'Did he? Let me see.'

Cato impatiently produced the document again. The centurion read carefully through it, then examined the seal closely before he puffed his cheeks out and finally returned it to Cato. 'Seems genuine. What brings you here, Tribune? Shipwreck and rescue by a fishing boat from the smell of it.'

'I am here to see the legate, on a matter of the gravest importance. I have been sent by Senator Sempronius, acting governor of Crete.'

'You want to see the legate?'

'At once.'

'That's tricky, sir. He's in his private bath suite. Left orders that he was not to be disturbed.'

'That's too bad. I have to speak with him now.'

The centurion weighed up his orders against Cato's obvious impatience, and nodded. 'Very well, sir. Optio, take him up to the roof garden. Legate's private baths.'

'Yes, sir.' The optio saluted and gestured to Cato to follow him as the centurion returned to his petitions, working out which ones might provide him with the best chance of earning a hefty bribe. The sentries opened the doors to admit Cato and the optio, and on the far side they entered an inner hall. Corridors stretched away to the right and left, and directly ahead a staircase led up into the sunlight. Cato followed the optio as he mounted the steps. They emerged on to a wide-open space flanked by tall walls. The sounds of the city were muffled and competed with the light splash of fountains. Palms grew in geometrically arranged flower beds and provided occasional shade over the paved walkways that bisected the roof garden. Against the far wall Cato could see a suite of buildings and the shimmer of a plunge pool. Smoke wafted up from the furnace that provided the heat for the steam and hot rooms of the legate's private bath suite.

As they approached the pool, Cato saw that a small party of men was sitting in the water chatting idly. Two more lay on cushioned benches as slave masseurs worked on their backs, gleaming with scented oil.

'What's this?' one of the men called out as he saw Cato and the optio striding towards the pool. 'We have visitors! Legate, one of the men has found himself a tramp.'

There was some laughter and the officers looked round curiously as the optio halted and stood to attention, saluting one of the men being massaged. 'Sir, beg to report that Tribune Cato wishes to speak to you.'

The legate rolled his head round towards the optio, and a brief flicker of anxiety flitted over his face as he looked at Cato. 'Tribune Cato? Never heard of him. Are you his slave? Tell your master to make an appointment to see me through the usual channels. That is, via my clerks' office. Now go.'

Cato stood his ground with a determined expression. 'I *am* Tribune Cato.'

'You, a tribune? I don't believe it.'

'I have already presented my written authority to two of your officers. I can produce it again, if you wish.'

'Later. First, tell me what a tribune is doing in Alexandria. Who sent you? Narcissus?'

Cato could not help smiling at mention of the emperor's private secretary. Aside from being Claudius's personal adviser, Narcissus also ran a formidable network of spies and assassins to protect his master.

'I haven't come from Rome, sir. I sailed here from Crete.'

Petronius's nose wrinkled. 'You stink of rotting fish.'

'A fishing boat was all that could be found to bring me here. Now send these people away, Legate Petronius. We must talk.'

'Send them away? How dare you?'

'I must speak with you alone, on a vital matter. I have been sent here on the orders of the acting governor of Crete.'

'Acting governor? Has that fool Hirtius been replaced?'

'Hirtius is dead, along with the majority of the senior officials of the province.'

'Dead?' The legate pushed the masseur away and rolled round to sit on the bench facing Cato. 'How?'

'There was an earthquake on the island. He was entertaining his officials and local dignitaries when it struck. Much of the palace collapsed, burying Hirtius and his guests.'

'Earthquake?' The legate raised his eyebrows. 'There have been rumours in the city about Crete being destroyed by a giant wave.'

'The island's still there. But there was a wave, and between it and the earthquake nearly every city and town has been reduced to ruins.'

'So who's in charge now?'

'Senator Lucius Sempronius. We were travelling together when the wave struck. The ship was forced to head for the nearest port, and that's when we learned that the disaster had struck the island. He took charge of the situation.'

'Sempronius?' the legate mused. 'I knew him once. A fine officer. So he's taken charge in Crete? Well, good for him. But forgive me, how can I be certain that you speak the truth? You've just washed up from the sea with some fanciful tale of disaster. Why should I believe you?'

Cato took the ring from the leather tube around his neck and handed it to Petronius. 'There, recognise the crest?'

Petronius held it up and examined the design, a wolf's head over crossed forks of lightning. He nodded. 'It belongs to Sempronius. All right then, why has he sent you here?'

Cato looked meaningfully at the other guests, all of whom had been listening to the preceding conversation in avid silence. 'Sir, I really must insist on speaking to you alone.'

'Alone, eh?' Petronius stared at Cato for a moment before he clapped his hands. 'Out! Leave us! At once.'

His officers and other guests hurriedly climbed out of the pool and, picking up their robes from the benches and seats that surrounded it, made off towards the far corner of the garden, where a terrace overlooked the harbour. Once the last of them was out of earshot, the legate waved the optio away. 'Stand over there, at the end of the pool. If I call for you, come running.'

'Yes, sir.' The optio saluted and strode away.

Cato could not help a small smile at the legate's precaution. 'I had no idea that being the Legate of Egypt was such a dangerous job.'

'A man in my position must always be cautious,' Petronius sighed. 'Egypt is an imperial province. The legate is appointed by the emperor in person. Therefore he is always the target of envious senators, and at the same time he is in grave danger of disappointing the emperor, and you know how that ends.'

'Indeed.'

'So,' Petronius took his linen tunic from the end of the massage couch and pulled it over his head, 'what does Senator Sempronius want of me? Emergency supplies, some engineers to help with the clear-up?'

'Those would be welcome, sir, but the situation is rather more serious than that. There is a full-scale slave rebellion in Crete. For the moment it is confined to the southern half of the island, but we've lost control of things. The slaves have wiped out the force sent to deal with them, and the remaining soldiers and officials are bottled up in a handful of cities and towns.'

'Sounds bad.' Petronius stroked his chin and looked at Cato shrewdly. 'I imagine you are about to ask me for some men to help put these rebels down.'

Cato nodded. The time to deploy his persuasive skills was on him, yet his body was still coping with the giddy effect of so many days at sea and his mind was dull with fatigue. He opened the top of the leather tube and extracted the second scroll from inside. 'This is from the governor.'

He handed the letter to Petronius, who broke the seal and opened it. Before he began to read he glanced at Cato. 'I expect you could use a drink? Something to eat?'

'Yes, sir.'

Petronius indicated the tables vacated by his officers. Several platters of fruit and delicacies lay half eaten, together with silver jugs of wine. 'Sit over there and help yourself while I read this.'

'Thank you.' Cato walked over and helped himself to some grapes and oranges, relishing the taste after days of chewing dried fish and hard baked bread. He sat down on a cushioned stool and poured himself a cup of the watered wine, sipping it as Petronius read through the brief report on the situation in Crete. At length the legate rolled the papyrus up and strode over to join Cato, sitting down opposite him and pouring a cup of wine for himself.

'I always find that a massage leaves me feeling thirsty.' He smiled. 'In fact almost anything one does in Egypt makes a person thirsty. At least the climate is bearable here in Alexandria. But further down the Nile it gets unbearably hot, and almost nothing lives in the deserts on either side. You have it good in Crete.' He stopped and tapped the scroll. 'At least you did.'

'Can't say I've been there long enough to notice,' Cato replied. 'It was our bad luck to be sailing past the island when the earthquake struck.'

'Unlucky for you maybe. Lucky for Crete that such high-ranking officials just happened to be on the scene to take charge.'

'I suppose,' Cato said carefully. So far the legate had not questioned his rank, and it was necessary to convince him to come to Sempronius's aid before his mind was clouded over the question-able status of Cato's elevation to the rank of tribune.

'Sempronius mentions the need for military support but does not say how many men he requires. Do you know what he has in mind?'

'Yes, sir.' Cato took a deep breath. The senator and his two senior

229

officers had carefully considered the forces required to guarantee victory over the rebels. 'One legion, two cohorts of auxiliary infantry and two cohorts of cavalry, as well as a squadron of warships to provide transport and support any coastal operations.'

Petronius stared at him, then laughed. 'You can't be serious. That's nearly half the garrison of this province. We're thinly stretched as it is.'

'But you're not engaged in any campaigns at the moment?'

'No,' Petronius admitted.

'And are there any uprisings to contain?'

'No. But that's because I have enough men to keep the locals in their place, and the desert Arabs at bay.'

'I understand that, sir, but Sempronius will only need the use of your forces while he puts down the slave revolt. As soon as Ajax—'

'Ajax?'

'The leader of the slaves, sir. A gladiator. As soon as he is crushed, the forces can return to Egypt at once. The governor gives his word on that.'

'That's reassuring.' Petronius took an exasperated breath. 'Look here, Tribune, I'm happy to do what I can to help out in another province, but what Sempronius asks is impossible. I have two legions here. The Twenty-Second is down at Heliopolis. The Third Cyrenaica is dispersed along the coast, and my auxiliaries are garrisoning towns across the delta. It would take some days, months even, before I could concentrate such an army as Sempronius requires. By then your revolt will probably have fizzled out.'

'I doubt that,' Cato responded. 'It is growing in strength every day. Sir, I can see you don't grasp how critical the situation is. The slaves slaughtered one thousand of our men in a single attack. Somehow Ajax has managed to fashion an army out of them, and I fear he has ambitions to free every slave on the island.'

'Then let Rome deal with it. If the situation is that critical, then the emperor will need to assemble an army to put the rebellion down.'

'But he won't have to if we act now.' Cato paused and decided to try a new tack. 'Sir, if you fail to send help to Sempronius, then Crete will be lost. As you say, it will require a large army, and perhaps years to recover the island and stamp out every last nest of rebels. The cost to the emperor will be vast. But what if he realises that the revolt could have been crushed if forces had been available to intervene earlier? You said it yourself: being the emperor's man in Egypt is a tricky business. If you fail to act now, you are sure to disappoint the emperor, and, as you say, we know how that ends.'

Petronius glared back. 'Are you threatening to blackmail me?'

'No, sir. Neither I nor Sempronius will have to. The lost opportunity will be apparent to everyone, and sadly the mob does like to have someone to blame whenever there is bad news.' Cato paused a moment. 'Act now and you could emerge as the man who saved Crete.'

The legate sat back and folded his arms. 'And what if I so denude Egypt of forces that a rebellion breaks out here in my absence and we lose this province? How do you think the mob will react to *that*, Tribune?'

'That is a remote possibility,' Cato conceded. 'But you have good order here at the moment. It's not likely to happen.'

'But if it did?'

'Then you are dead either way, sir. The best thing to do is save Crete, and save it quickly, then have your men return to Alexandria.'

'You make it sound so easy.'

'I am merely stating your options as I see them, sir.'

Petronius stood up and walked slowly around the pool, head bent in thought, hands clasped behind his back. By the time he returned to the table, his mind was clearly made up. 'I can't leave Egypt. If anything happened in my absence, the emperor would have my balls for breakfast. And I'm not prepared to give you all the forces you ask for. So let's compromise, Tribune. I have eight cohorts of the Third Legion here, with an auxiliary and cavalry cohort in a camp twenty miles from the city. If I keep two of the legionary cohorts in Alexandria I should be able to maintain order. As for the other units, I will have to shift men around the delta region, but it should be possible to manage. That's my offer then. Six cohorts of legionaries, and one each of cavalry and auxiliaries. In addition to the naval squadron. Take it or leave it.'

Cato considered. Would two and a half thousand legionaries and a thousand auxiliaries be sufficient to destroy Ajax and his army of slaves? There was no question that quantity was no substitute for quality and the heavily armed legionaries could carve a path through the poorly equipped ranks of the slaves. Even so, they would be massively outnumbered. There was little point in committing a force that lacked the strength to see the task through. On the other hand, if Sempronius could strike quickly enough, he might inflict a victory on the rebels before they grew too established. Cato cleared his throat.

'That is a generous offer, sir. I am sure Senator Sempronius will be eternally grateful to you.'

'Bollocks to Sempronius. I just want Narcissus kept off my back. Now, if that's agreed, I suggest you get some rest. Make sure you have a long bath and a good shave while you are at it. I'll give the orders for my forces to concentrate in Alexandria. I suspect my staff officers are going to be kept busy over the next few days. That's no bad thing. Do them good to get back to some soldiering for a change.'

'Yes, sir.' Cato felt as if a great burden had been lifted from his shoulders. 'Thank you.'

'Don't thank me. Not yet. I don't think any of us can rest easy until that gladiator is captured and nailed to a cross.'

CHAPTER TWENTY-TWO

T he first attack on Gortyna took place only a few hours after Ajax returned to his camp. His closest comrades had never seen him so angry as he swept past his bodyguards and into the half-ruined farmhouse that he had chosen for his headquarters. He tore off his cloak, and hurled it to one side as he made for the jug of wine and hunks of bread and cheese that had been left out for his supper. There were some of his men who made every effort to enjoy the finest foods that they had been able to loot from the wealthy villas that the slave army had sacked. Ajax did not begrudge them such indulgences. After a life of servitude, they had every right to taste freedom in all its forms. He preferred a simple diet, one that would feed his body and not spoil it, and he made no secret of his plain fare, knowing that it would bind his followers closer to him.

Now he forced himself to sit down at the table and pour himself a cup of wine. He drank it deliberately and then poured another and dipped his bread in before chewing it methodically, staring at the cracked wall in front of him. The owner of the farm had obviously been a man of some wealth, but limited taste. The walls of this, his dining room, had been covered with murals depicting a bacchanal orgy. Directly in front of Ajax was an image of a pair of gladiators, a secutor like Ajax himself, in a wary crouch as he faced a net-wielding retiarius. Arranged around them were the guests, drinking and gorging and laughing as they urged the gladiators on. One of the women, heavily made up, was holding the penis of a man as she watched the fight with an excited expression. In the centre of the party sat the host, a fat, jolly bald man wearing a leaf crown awry on his shining pate as he raised a cup in the air, filled to overflowing.

'Bastards!' Ajax roared, snatching up the jug and hurling it against the wall with all his might. The jug exploded, sending shards of pottery and jets of wine in all directions. The mural was instantly covered in dark liquid that ran down the wall so that the images were distorted by a red film. Ajax's heart was pounding as he stared at the wall with wide, terrifying eyes. Behind him there was a creak as the door swung on its hinges.

'General? Are you all right?' Chilo asked anxiously. There was a pause as he saw the remains of the jug and the wine on the wall. 'General?'

For a moment Ajax remained still, fighting back the rage that burned in his heart. The memory of his slavery was still like an open wound, and above all thought of the indignities and pain that he had suffered was the image of Centurion Macro, one of those responsible for the crucifixion of his father, and the cause of Ajax being sold into slavery. Macro, and that other one, the tall, thin officer his own age, and the legate who had commanded them, Vespasian. Even if the others were beyond his reach, serving elsewhere in the accursed empire of Rome, Macro was at hand, and at his mercy. Ajax muttered an oath to every god he held sacred that he would avenge his father, he would avenge himself and he would make sure that Macro was made to suffer every torment that could be conceived before he was allowed to die.

Chilo coughed. 'General? Is there anything I can do?'

Ajax sucked in a deep breath and turned round. Chilo commanded the best men of the slave army. They had been equipped with the pick of the captured armour and weapons. 'Yes. Summon your men. Have them formed up. We have some ladders, I recall.'

'Yes, General, some, but they are in sections and will need to be securely lashed together before we can use them on the walls of Gortyna.'

'Then see to it. At once. We will attack as soon as they are ready.'

'Attack?' Chilo could not hide his astonishment. The openness of his character was one of the reasons Ajax had chosen him to be one of his closest comrades. He could not hide anything from his general, especially any sign of doubt or treachery.

'But General, the men have marched most of the day. They will be settling in for the night.'

'That's too bad. Besides, the Romans will have seen us make

camp. They won't be expecting any attack so soon after we have arrived. That's why we must do it. To catch them unawares.' Ajax thought a moment. 'We'll make for that section close to the main gate. It's been repaired, but it looks weak, and they haven't been able to raise it back up to the level of the rest of the wall.' He nodded to himself. 'Yes. We'll attack there, out of the darkness.'

The gleaming helmets of the sentries were clearly visible by the light of the flames flickering along the wall as Ajax thrust his hand up to halt the column behind him. Chilo repeated the gesture and the men drew up, still and silent as shadows. Ajax had ordered them to leave all unnecessary kit back at the camp, and anything that might make a noise that would give them away. Half a mile back, the much larger war band of Kharim stood ready to charge in if a breach was secured, or the gatehouse seized. His men were armed with an assortment of weapons and carried little or no protection. But their hearts were filled with determination to throw themselves at their enemy if the chance came.

Chilo's men were barefoot and wore scale armour and helmets. They carried shields and spears with daggers thrust into their sword belts. Ajax waved his hand and the men gently eased their shields down and crouched beside them. Ajax lowered his own shield and spear to the ground and removed his helmet, softly ordering Chilo to do the same.

He gestured to Chilo to accompany him and they crept towards the walls, no more than a hundred paces away. They kept low and moved slowly, edging towards the glow cast by the light of the torches up on the wall. The gatehouse was just to their right, and the flames of a brazier mounted on the squat tower over the gate flared into the night, occasionally sending up small swirls of bright sparks that quickly flickered and died. Ajax was keen to get as close to the wall as he could to see where the repaired section looked weakest. If they could rush the wall and break into the city, then the gatehouse could be quickly taken and the gates opened for Kharim and his men to finish the job. He was about to creep further forward for a closer inspection of the defences when Chilo suddenly seized his arm and held him back.

'What?' Ajax hissed fiercely as he glanced round.

'Look there.' Chilo released his grip and pointed into the grass two feet ahead of them. At first Ajax could see nothing out of the ordinary, and then he spotted it, a dark spike, unnaturally straight and unlike the blades of grass surrounding it. He reached forward cautiously and felt the object. Cold metal. He picked it up and drew it back for a closer look. He was holding the object by one of four prongs, each the length of his finger and ending in a sharp spike.

'Very clever, our Roman friends,' he whispered. 'They've sown the approaches with these . . . things. They'd break a charge beautifully.'

He stared at it a moment and then tossed it to one side. 'We have to clear a path before we bring the men forward.'

Chilo nodded, then suddenly froze, straining his ears. He turned his head to the right and pointed. 'There.'

Ajax squinted in the direction indicated and saw a dark figure backing away from them, hunched over a wicker basket, which he dipped into, tossing something to one side.

'Should we wait until he's gone, General?'

'No. He might see us, or come back this way. Wait here,' he ordered, and pulling out his dagger he half rose and slowly circled round to his right. The enemy soldier continued with his task, occasionally pausing and raising his head to glance towards the rebel camp, at which Ajax froze until the Roman returned to his work, and then moved on again. Once he had crept round behind the man, he closed in, step by step; then, clenching his fist around the handle of the dagger, he sprang forwards, sprinting the last few feet. The Roman heard the rustle of grass and glanced back just as Ajax slammed into him, knocking him down. He clamped his hand over the man's mouth and thrust his head down against the ground as he smothered the Roman's lighter frame and brought the tip of the dagger up under the soldier's chin. By the faint glow of the torches he saw that his enemy was aged and scrawny, a veteran auxiliary close to the end of his enlistment.

'One move, one sound, and you're dead.' He pressed the blade so the man would realise his peril. 'Understand?'

The man nodded slightly, eyes wide with terror. He winced as the point bit into his skin.

'Good,' Ajax whispered, then slowly lifted his hand from the man's mouth. 'Are you out here alone?'

'N–no. Don't kill me.'

'You'll live if you answer me truthfully.' Ajax inched his knife back. 'Now then, how many more of you are there?'

'Four. There are four of us. Two on the other side of the gatehouse and one going in the other direction.'

'Will he come back this way?'

The Roman thought briefly and shook his head. 'Not for a while. He had more ground to cover.'

Ajax nodded towards the basket the man had been dragging. 'Those things you're sowing on the ground.'

'The caltrops?'

Ajax half smiled – so that was what they were called. 'Yes, the caltrops. How deeply have you laid them?'

'Over ten, fifteen feet.'

'I see.' Ajax suddenly clamped his hand down and thrust the dagger up through the Roman's throat and into his skull, twisting the blade left and right, scrambling the man's brains. The soldier spasmed violently, but he made no sound apart from a light gasp, then he went limp. Ajax lifted his hand from the man's mouth and pulled the dagger out, feeling a warm rush of blood spurt over his fist. He eased himself off the body, and wiped his blade on the man's tunic before sliding it back into his belt and making his way back to Chilo.

'There's another of them over to the left.' He spoke softly as he knelt down. 'Send one of your men to deal with him. Then you and I have to clear a path through to the wall.'

Ajax crept back and took spears from four of his men before returning to the first caltrop. He thrust two of the spears into the ground, twenty feet apart, and then went down on his hands and knees and groped through the grass until he found the next caltrop. He tossed it to one side and edged forward until he found and disposed of the next. Chilo joined him to the left, together with another man, and worked through the grass towards the wall. They were about halfway through the task when there was a strangled cry from their left and they froze for an instant, staring towards the city to see if there was any sign of alarm. Ajax watched the nearest sentries, but they seemed not to have heard the noise and continued the patrols along their allotted stretch of the wall.

'Back to work,' Ajax whispered and edged himself forward in the grass, cautiously extending his hand to feel for the next spike. He breathed a sigh of relief that the alarm had not been raised. At that moment there was a shout from further along the wall, relayed from sentry to sentry, and then the shrill blare of a horn cut through the cool night air. Ajax jumped to his feet and ran back to retrieve his shield and spear. He swung the point towards the wall and bellowed to Chilo's men, 'Charge! Charge 'em and show the bastards how well a slave dies!'

Chilo sprang towards him. 'We haven't finished removing the caltrops! General, you must stop the men!'

It was too late. The ladder parties came running forward out of the darkness. Ajax indicated the spears. 'Between those. Make straight for the wall!'

They ran past, carrying the hastily assembled ladders under their arms, and crossed over the belt of the Roman defences. All made it safely through, except one of the men from the last team, who suddenly screamed in agony, released his grip on the ladder and collapsed on to the ground, howling as he pulled the spike out of his crippled foot. Ajax ignored him as he stormed after the ladder parties and raced on towards the wall. Behind him came the rest of the men, urged on by Chilo, as he bellowed at them to get forward and pass between the spears.

Ahead of the rebels the defenders were pointing them out and shouting their cries of warning. More Romans spilled out on to the battlements above the gatehouse, and a moment later there was a flare of gleaming flames and a bundle of oil-soaked rags arced over the parapet and roared as it tumbled down the wall and rolled away from the base towards the ditch. In the light of the bright flames the ladder parties were easily observed and sentries began to heft their javelins, ready to hurl them into the figures streaming out of the night. The shrill notes of the trumpet had been taken up by others across the city and up on the acropolis, and Ajax knew that time was against him now.

He reached the ditch and paused near the edge to wave the ladder parties on. 'Get over! Fast as you can!'

The first four men carrying their ladder stumbled and slid down the slope into the ditch, crossed the bottom and began to scale the far side, each using his spare hand to scrabble for purchase on any tufts of grass or exposed roots. The head of a javelin buried itself in the soil by Ajax and he instinctively raised his shield and hunched down, watching for danger. There were more men appearing along the top of the wall all the time, and he felt the first cold stab of anxiety in his guts over the fate of the attack. Should he have taken this risk? Was this more about finding and killing that centurion than attempting to take the enemy by surprise?

The other ladder parties rushed past him, scrambling across the ditch and up the other side before making straight for the base of the wall to set their ladders in place. More burning faggots flared down from above, clearly revealing the ladders and the men in the lurid orange hue of their flames. The rebels made easy targets now, and Ajax saw the first man fall, skewered by a javelin that passed through his back and on down deep into his leg. The man released his grip and dropped to the side in terrible agony. His hands groped round to the shaft of the javelin and feebly tried to pull it free, only to cause fresh agonies that made him scream. A second man was killed under the first ladder as a large stone crushed his head.

There was a sudden rush of men past Ajax as the rest of Chilo's war band surged across the ditch and up the far side before making for the ladders held in place by their comrades. Now, many more missiles were being thrown down from above and could hardly fail to find a target in the wave of rebels racing towards the wall.

'Keep going!' Ajax bellowed. 'Up the ladders!'

Springing forward, Ajax joined the rush struggling across the ditch. He kept his shield up, and it slammed back into him as a body fell against the front. He threw his weight to one side, over his steady foot, in order to keep his balance, then thrust hard to make sure the body fell away. He continued, gritting his teeth once as a stone cracked off the corner of his shield. Then he was at the base of the ladder, heart pounding.

'Move aside!' he shouted into the face of the man about to climb the first rung. One more was ahead of him, halfway up already. On either side more men had reached the ladders and were starting to ascend the wall. Ajax transferred his spear to his shield hand, grasped the side of the ladder and began to scale the rungs one at a time. In front of him he could see that the stones had been crudely laid without mortar and he cursed the fact that his army had no siege weapons of any kind. He imagined a catapult or a covered ram would make short work of the hastily repaired wall. There were shouts from above as the Romans became aware of the danger of the men climbing up towards them. Glancing up, he saw the dim shapes of heads leaning over the parapet and there was a thud as another stone glanced off his shield.

'Target those men on the wall!' Chilo called out. 'Use stones! Rocks! Anything they throw at us!'

Some of the rebels stooped to pick up whatever came to hand and hurled it up at the enemy, driving some of them back. Some missiles clattered back down, falling on the men below, but did little harm as they bounced off the armour that had been taken from the bodies of Marcellus's men. The man ahead of Ajax reached the last rung as the ladder gave out close to the parapet. He swung his leg up and over and disappeared from view as Ajax climbed up into his place. His heart was beating wildly and he felt a heightened sense of vulnerability and fear that went beyond the normal tense anxiety of the arena, or any battle he had ever fought in. His right hand groped up the rough stonework until his fingers reached the edge. Sliding his hand over the parapet, he grasped the inside of the wall and heaved himself up, swinging his foot up as he went. Even though he had a firm purchase with his hand and foot, it still took some effort to lift his weight, burdened by armour and the spear, over the parapet and on to the wall.

Ajax landed lightly on his feet, and quickly transferred his spear back into his right hand as he sheltered behind his shield. He rose up, glancing to both sides. The man who had climbed the wall ahead of him was battling to the right, desperately defending the foothold he had gained at the top of the ladder. Ajax turned the other way and saw a section of Romans struggling to dislodge the ladders further along as they stabbed down with their javelins and tried to lever the ladders away from the wall. Luckily they had been preoccupied with the threat immediately in front of them and had not seen him. Down in the city he saw scores of the enemy piling out of side streets into the base of the gatehouse and making for the stairs to reinforce their comrades facing the rebels.

Ajax lifted his spear and switched to an overhand grip, resting the head of the shaft on the shield rim as he moved towards the defenders. He took a quick glance back and saw that another man had reached the wall.

'Follow me,' he ordered as he advanced along the narrow walkway. He closed to within ten feet of the nearest Roman before he was noticed. The man barely had time to turn before the gladiator was upon him, thrusting with his spear. The iron head punched into the hand thrown up in a vain effort to ward the blow off. The point passed through it and on into the man's throat, cutting through windpipe and spine before bursting out the back of his neck. Ajax thrust his shield out, knocking the body to one side as he wrenched the spear back, ripping it free before concentrating on his next opponent. A burly optio had succeeded in tipping one of the ladders back and now turned to face Ajax, snatching out his sword as he raised his shield.

For an instant the two men sized each other up. Ajax could tell at once that the optio was an experienced and able fighter. His balance was good and he had lowered himself into a crouch, from which position he could spring into a powerful attack the moment he saw his chance.

Lifting his spear slightly, Ajax feinted towards the optio's face. The man parried it easily and resumed his posture. Then, with a sudden snarl, he lunged forward, his point stabbing towards Ajax's groin. Ajax swung his shield round and deflected the blow, and instantly thrust again with his spear before the optio could recover. But the man was surprisingly nimble for one his size and he ducked under the strike. Ajax backed off a pace, and risked a quick glance to see how the fight was going. Beyond the section ahead of him, more men were spreading along the wall. Below, in the streets, the enemy streamed towards the steps leading up on to the wall. There was not much

241

time, Ajax realised. If the rebels could not get enough men on to the wall to make their numbers tell, then the assault was doomed.

The optio clattered his sword against the edge of his shield and sneered. 'Had enough, then?'

Ajax could not help laughing. Such an obvious taunt was beneath even the greenest of gladiators. He moved forward again, determined to cut the man down and clear a path for Chilo and his men. The optio's shield came up, ready to take the next spear thrust. Ajax feinted high, forcing the Roman to raise his shield still further, then the gladiator went down on one knee, angling the edge of his shield forward and smashing it against the other man's leading shin. There was a sharp crack at the impact and the optio bellowed in pain and rage as he collapsed. Ajax recovered, rising over his victim, and struck home, taking the man under the armpit, driving through his side into his chest. He stamped his foot down on the Roman, then yanked the spearhead free and stepped over the body. With the death of the optio, the other Romans backed away, crowding back towards the first of their comrades who had climbed the wall to aid them.

The gladiator glanced over his shoulder. Ten or more of his men were on the wall now, together with Chilo. As three of them came running along the walkway, Ajax stepped into the parapet to let them pass.

'Keep 'em busy!' he ordered. 'Don't let them press you back.'

He retreated a few paces before turning and hurrying towards Chilo, and thrust his arm out towards the gatehouse. 'That way! Keep the men going that way. We must take the gate, quickly!'

Chilo nodded, calling to his men, 'Follow me!'

Together with several of his companions, Chilo ran along the wall towards the open door leading from the walkway into the gatehouse. He was no more than a spear's length from the opening when a Roman stepped out, then stopped in surprise as he saw the rebels pounding towards him. The next moment Chilo slammed into him and they crashed back through the doorway into the gatehouse. His men crowded in behind him and the sounds of shouts and the clash of shields and blades carried outside to Ajax. He had already transferred his bloodied spear to his shield hand and was helping a man over the rampart and thrusting him towards the gatehouse. 'Go!'

As he waited for the next man, Ajax looked back along the wall and saw that only two ladders were still standing. In the streets, the sound of nailed boots was deafening as more and more Romans rushed towards the endangered section of their defences, and he knew that the rebels could not get enough men on to the wall to hold it for much longer. Already one of the three men tasked with holding the walkway further along was down, doubled over as he curled round a wound to his groin. His comrades were forced back and a moment later the man was dead, killed by the first Roman to step over him.

Another man came over the rampart and Ajax grabbed his arm. 'With me!'

He hurried forward to help the two men faced by impossible odds. Four might stem the enemy tide long enough for Chilo to take the gatehouse. They stood, shields presented to the Romans, stabbing overhead with their spears. Another of the defenders went down, clutching his throat as he toppled off the wall. Then the enemy were up close, shield to shield, grunting with the effort of pressing the rebels back. Step by step, Ajax and the others were forced to give ground, falling back past the top of the other remaining ladder. Then one of his men collapsed, caught by the blade of a short sword rammed through a gap in their shields. Behind him he heard renewed sounds of fighting from the gatehouse and then Chilo ordering his men to fall back.

'No!' Ajax shouted at the top of his voice. 'Chilo! Hold fast!'

But his voice was drowned out by another, cutting through the night as a Roman officer bellowed, 'Kill the bastards! Cut 'em down! Come on, lads, on me!'

Ajax felt a nudge at his shoulder as another man who had climbed the ladder joined the desperate struggle. He let the man by to take his place and turned to see how Chilo was faring. There was a sick feeling in his gut as he saw that a fresh wave of Romans had already pushed the rebels out of the gatehouse and was forcing them back towards the remaining ladder. The fight was lost, Ajax realised at once, and instantly knew he must do what he could to save his men.

He leaned over the wall. 'Back! Fall back!'

The upturned faces below him were dimly visible by the fading glow of the burning faggots, and their looks of despair cut into his heart like knives, but there was nothing else he could do. 'Fall back, I said! Now!'

The first of them turned and retreated towards the ditch.

'General!' Chilo came up to him, panting and face spattered with blood. He nodded towards the remaining ladder. 'You first.'

For an instant Ajax was tempted to refuse, before his reason took over. The attack had failed and his men would need him alive.

'All right. But you and the rest get down as fast as you can.'

'Yes, General.'

Ajax swung himself back over the parapet and felt for the top rung with his bare feet. He let his spear drop to the ground below and clambered back down. As he reached the bottom, the first of Chilo's men came after him.

'Don't let them get away!' the Roman officer shouted above the din of the fight on the wall, and Ajax felt his guts tighten at the sound. He looked up and snarled through clenched teeth, 'Macro . . .'

One by one his men came down the ladder and fled back across the ditch. From the other side there were cries of shock and pain, and Ajax realised that some of them must have run over the belt of caltrops in their haste to get away from the wall. Chilo landed heavily beside him.

'You the last?'

'Two still up there.'

There was nothing that could be done for them. Ajax clapped Chilo on the shoulder. 'Let's go.'

They turned and ran towards the ditch as there was a brief, final clash of weapons on the wall. Then a voice boomed out:

'AJAX!'

He hesitated and looked back. In the light of a torch blazing a short distance along the wall, he saw the Roman centurion. He had a javelin drawn back in his right hand as he took aim at the rebel leader. Then, with a grunt, he hurled the weapon down. His aim was true and the dark shaft swept towards Ajax. Before he could react, a body slammed into him, knocking him to one side. The javelin struck with a sound like a pick driven into wet sand and there was an explosive grunt of air. Ajax's gladiator's reflexes served him well as he rolled back into a crouch. At his feet lay Chilo, staring up and gasping as his fingers felt the shaft that pinned him to the ground through his stomach.

'General, go,' he managed to groan.

Ajax grasped the shaft and wrenched it out. Then he grabbed Chilo, lifted him on to his back and scrambled down the ditch, across the bottom and up the other side. There was another shout from the wall.

'Don't just stand there, you dozy bastards! Get him!'

Another javelin struck the earth close by as Ajax struggled over the edge of the ditch. Several more followed as he staggered on, watching the ground as carefully as he could to make sure he did not step on one of the caltrops. Once he was sure that he had passed through them and was out of range of the javelins, he sagged down and lowered Chilo to the grass. Chilo rolled on to his back with a sharp cry of pain and clutched a hand to the wound.

'Oh . . . fuck, fuck, it hurts,' he muttered.

Ajax saw some more of his men a short distance off. 'Over here, now!'

Even though they recognised the sound of their general, they hesitated briefly before they did as he ordered. Ajax indicated the stricken Chilo. 'Get him back to my headquarters and send for Kharim. Understand? Then go, now!'

They picked Chilo up and made off into the night. Ajax's heart was still pounding from his exertions and he stood breathing hard as he stared back towards the wall. The crest of the centurion was plainly visible amongst the other men behind the rampart. There was a derisive whistle, then jeering from the enemy, and Ajax spat to clear his throat.

'Macro!' He cupped a hand to his mouth and called again. 'Macro! When I take the city, I will cut your heart out with my own hand! This I swear!'

CHAPTER TWENTY-THREE

'**B**ugger it!'

Macro thumped his fist down on the parapet, and winced as the pain shot up his arm. His javelin would surely have killed or crippled Ajax had it not been for that other man, damn him. With Ajax out of action, Macro had little doubt that the morale of the rebels would have been stricken, and even if a new leader emerged to save the revolt, the loss of Ajax would have won a few days' reprieve for the defenders. He turned away from the retreating rebels and examined the scene around him. Bodies lay sprawled along the walkway and some of the parapet had been pulled away by the enemy as they came over. It had been a close thing. The men on watch had been one of the units raised from the city's population. They were under the command of optios and centurions appointed from the ranks of the auxiliary cohort. Had it not been for them, the rank and file might have fled.

Macro pointed to the nearest centurion. 'Flaccus!'

'Sir?'

'Clear the walkway. Have our dead taken to the burial pit.'

'Yes, sir.' Flaccus paused. 'And the other bodies?'

Macro jerked his thumb over the wall. 'Might as well leave them in full sight of the rebels. Might help to put them off their stride.'

'Yes, sir.'

Leaving Flaccus and his men to carry out the work, Macro descended to the street and made his way along the inside of the wall to the next tower. It was fortunate that he had taken the decision for troops to be quartered near the wall as soon as the rebel army set up camp outside the city otherwise the surprise attack would have succeeded. Macro had chosen the men for Julia's escort earlier in the evening and ordered them to have their mounts ready to leave at the fourth hour of the night. He had just retired to an inn for an hour's rest when the alarm sounded. As it was, he had snatched up his armour and sword as he raced towards the gatehouse, and arrived just in time to steady the men attempting to fight their way up the stairs on to the wall. Even though the rebels had been lightly protected and outmatched by the defenders, their fierce determination had almost won the day. Macro had thrust his men back into the gatehouse, shouting encouragement as he forced his way through their ranks to lead from the front. By the time he had reached the wall, the rebels were in retreat. Only a few remained to defend the top of the ladder as their comrades descended, and they were quickly cut down. Then he had seen a handful of figures running from the wall and snatched a javelin from the nearest man before he called out the gladiator's name. There had to be a chance that Ajax would be there, leading the attack. In the thin red light cast by the faggots, Macro had recognised him at once when Ajax looked back.

It had been a good throw, he mused bitterly. A fine one, in fact. Ajax should be dead. For some reason the gods had spared him for now. But next time, gods or no gods, Macro resolved to kill the gladiator and put an end to his butchery. Muttering a quick prayer of apology to Jupiter and Fortuna for his brief impiety, he went to check on the other sections of the wall before he reported to Sempronius.

The senator was sitting in his office when Macro arrived. A single oil lamp provided the only illumination, barely enough to see the walls of the room by.

'Where have you been?' Sempronius asked coldly. 'The attack ended over two hours ago. You should already be on the road with my daughter.'

'I'm sorry, sir. I had to make sure the other sectors of the wall were prepared to fight in case the rebels made another attack.'

'That's as maybe, but we have lost too much time. I still want you to take Julia out of Gortyna as soon as possible tonight.'

Macro felt a weary weight descend upon his shoulders. 'Sir, it will be light within a couple of hours. I don't think it's safe to try and get your daughter out of the city any longer. She might be safer if she stayed.'

'Really? From the first reports it seems that the enemy nearly took one of the gates at the first attempt.'

'We saw them off easily enough, sir.'

'Perhaps. But what if the next attack succeeds? Then we will be trapped up here on the acropolis. Thousands packed in together. We won't endure that for long before someone betrays us, or the people decide to turn the Romans over to Ajax. I will not subject my daughter to that. She must leave the city now, while there is still time.'

'Sir.' Macro spoke gently. 'I understand your concern for Julia, but I think it is already too late to try to get her away from Gortyna.'

'Why?'

'The rebels are determined to close the net around the city as soon as they can. Tonight's attack proved that. Even though they are camped out on the plain, there is a good chance they will have patrols out on all sides of the city before long.'

'All the more reason to get my daughter out of here now. Before these patrols of yours begin. Go now, while the route through the hills to the north is still open.'

Macro stared at the other man, exasperated. 'Sir, I tell you, this is not a wise course of action. Trust my judgement on this.'

'I'm sorry, Macro. I think you are wrong. I doubt that the slaves will be organised enough to already have patrols in the hill. Even if they did, there are so many routes through the hills that they could not cover more than a fraction of them. There is a risk, I'll not deny it. But in my judgement, the risk to Julia is far greater if she remains here. Besides, I cannot concentrate on defending Gortyna while my daughter's life is at stake. Please understand me.'

Macro shrugged. 'As you wish, then, Senator.'

'Good. I am grateful to you, Macro. More than you can know. Now, my daughter is waiting for you with her escort. Get her out of the city and away to a safe distance before you return.'

'Yes, sir.' Macro rose wearily to his feet, saluted and turned to leave Sempronius's office. He made his way down to the stables beside the governor's palace. The ten men he had chosen stood up at his approach. Each man wore chainmail under his cloak, and carried a sword at his side. A few days' provisions and a water skin were slung from their shoulders. The horses were saddled, and held by two handlers, with spare mounts for Macro and Julia. She emerged from the shadows and looked questioningly at Macro.

'Your father hasn't changed his mind. Time to go,' he ordered. 'To the north gate. We'll lead the horses through the streets until we reach the wall. No sense in having one fall on any loose rubble.'

As the small column passed through the darkened streets of Gortyna, Julia asked softly, 'Do you think they will attack again tonight?'

'I doubt it. It's my bet that they took a chance that we would expect an attack at dawn, or on the morrow. They thought they'd catch us napping. To be fair, they almost did. But we gave them a hiding, miss. They lost a good number of men and will no doubt be licking their wounds. I doubt they'll be in a hurry to try anything whilst it's still dark. Not while they can't see the caltrops.' He smiled with satisfaction over his order to see that the iron spikes had been made and sown in time for the attack. 'As long as they direct their attacks towards specific points on the wall, we should be able to handle them. The problem will come when they realise we have too few men to defend the whole perimeter. If they launch a general attack around the city, then they will take the wall.'

'And then?'

'If I see such an attack coming, I'll get the people up on to the acropolis and we'll hold out there as long as we can.'

Julia glanced up at the gloomy mass of the hill that dominated Gortyna. 'How long can you hold the acropolis?'

'For several days. We'll be safe enough from rebel attacks up there. The problem will be the water supply and sanitation. Once the water runs low there will be thirst, and then sickness, and then we'll have to surrender.' Macro forced himself to smile and lighten his tone. 'But that's not going to happen, miss. Cato will have arrived on the scene long before then.'

'Yes, I hope so.' She took his hand and gently squeezed it. 'Look after my father for me.'

'Look after him?' Macro's eyebrows rose. The idea that Senator Sempronius needed any looking after was surprising. But he could sense her anxiety well enough and nodded. 'I'll keep an eye on him.'

They reached the northern gate, a small single-arched structure with a door that would only admit a small cart, or riders in single file. Macro halted the escort and climbed up the stairs to the platform above the gate. The duty optio saluted as he saw his superior emerge from the staircase. He had been alerted earlier that a party would be leaving the gate during the night.

'All quiet?' asked Macro.

'Yes, sir. No sign of any movement.'

'Good.'

'Sounded like quite a fight over towards the east gate.'

'Nothing to worry about,' Macro said calmly. 'Just some half-arsed attempt to rush the wall. Soon sent 'em packing.'

The optio was relieved and Macro clapped him on the back. 'You just keep your attention on the ground in front of you and let the others do their jobs.'

'Yes, sir.'

Macro glanced over the parapet. Below the gatehouse a narrow track rose up towards the hills behind the city. The dark ground was dotted with occasional black shapes of trees and bushes, but all seemed still. He turned back to the optio. 'Right then, I want you to remember that I'll be coming back this way. Hopefully while it's still dark. Make sure your sentries know. I don't fancy being skewered by some dozy sod taking me for a rebel.'

'No, sir. I'll see to it.'

'Do.' Macro nodded and returned down the stairs to Julia and the escort. He took the reins of his horse and cleared his throat to address the two men on the door. 'Open it up.'

They drew back the locking bar and hauled on the brass ring, and with a light grating sound the door swung inwards. Macro led his horse through the arch into the night. Julia and the others followed him out of the city. As soon as the last of them had passed through, the soldiers shut the door and rammed the locking bar home. Macro looked back at the escorts and spoke the order. 'Mount.'

As the soldiers hauled themselves up into the saddles, Macro went to help Julia. He cupped his hands together. 'Step up on that, miss.'

Once she was in the saddle and had tucked the end of her long tunic beneath each leg, she took the reins.

'Had much riding experience?' asked Macro.

She nodded. 'I used to ride when I was younger. I'm sure it will all come back to me once we get going.'

Macro nodded and then turned to mount his own horse. When he was settled in the saddle, he took a firm grip of the reins and raised his arm to attract the attention of his men. 'Forward.'

The small column trotted off along the narrow road. A hundred paces from the gate, the route began to climb towards the hills and became a well-worn track where countless mule trains had passed by before. When they reached the crest of the first hill, Macro turned in his saddle and looked back. The city was outlined by the ring of torches and braziers flickering along the wall. More torches and lamps twinkled amid the houses and ruins and up on the acropolis. On either side of the city sprawled the camp fires of the rebel army, and as Macro cast his experienced eye over the size of the enemy camps and quickly estimated their strength, he wondered if Cato's relief column would be strong enough to fight its way through to Gortyna, let alone launch a campaign to crush the rebels. When the real contest came, it would pitch the training and equipment of Roman legionaries and auxiliaries against overwhelming numbers and fanatical desperation. Macro could not guess at the outcome of such a conflict; it was quite unlike any other he had experienced.

They continued into the hills, and Macro's senses were finely strained as he kept glancing ahead and from side to side, all the time listening for any sound that might alert his suspicion. They had travelled perhaps five miles when he detected the first hint of dawn to the east; a faint luminosity in the night sky that outlined the mountains more clearly. The track had merged with a dried-out river bed. Steep rocky slopes rose on either side. Macro raised his hand. 'Halt.'

The others reined in as Macro turned his horse round and nodded to Julia. 'We've come a fair distance from the city. I doubt there will be any rebel patrols this far into the hills. There's nothing for them to scavenge up here. Good luck, miss.'

'Thank you, Macro,' she replied quietly and glanced towards the horizon. 'You should have turned back before now. It'll be light long before you return to Gortyna.'

'I'll be all right. It'll take them a while to get over the kicking we gave them earlier.'

'I hope so.'

There was a brief silence as they looked at each other, then Julia leaned across to kiss him on the cheek. 'Take care, Macro. Give my love to Cato when he reaches Gortyna.'

'I will.' Macro was still flushing from the embarrassment of being kissed in front of the escorts. 'He'll be glad that you're somewhere safe. As soon as it's all over, he'll come and find you.'

She nodded, and then Macro nudged his heels in and moved on towards the optio leading the escort. 'You clear about your orders?'

'Yes, sir.' The optio went on to intone his instructions. 'We make for Cnossos, and if the rebels come north we take a ship to Athens, where the senator's daughter is to be placed in the care of the governor.'

'Very good. Now you'd better get moving.'

They exchanged a salute, and Macro spurred his horse into a trot as he rode down the column. The optio gave the order to advance and Macro heard the horses' hooves clop forward again, but he did not look back. Julia was safe, and he was needed back in Gortyna. In truth he should have remained there, but the senator had insisted on his seeing his daughter on her way. Even though he resented the order, Macro realised that it would help put Sempronius at his ease, and the senator could ill afford any distractions now that Ajax and his rebel horde were camped before the walls of the province's capital.

He continued back down the river bed and up on to the track as it turned sharply round a large rock, passed through a small forest and began to descend. The air was cold and he breathed in the sharp scent of the pine trees as he calmly contemplated the danger he was riding back into. As soon as Ajax had got over the failure of his initial assault, he would be quick to realise that his best chance lay in stretching the defenders' resources. A co-ordinated series of attacks on the most damaged sections of the wall was bound to be rewarded with a breakthrough somewhere. One breach was all that the rebels would need; then they would flood into the city and massacre anyone who failed to reach the acropolis in time.

Macro was so intent on his thoughts of the coming siege that he heard the enemy scouts before he saw them. There was a sudden shout and he reined in abruptly and stared about in a moment of panic. The path was traversing the side of a hill and the trees fell away sharply to his left. A short distance ahead, the track bent round and zigzagged down the hillside. Two hundred paces below, Macro saw a large party of horsemen, perhaps as many as fifty of them, riding along the track, dressed in dull brown and grey tunics and cloaks. One of them had seen him and was pointing directly up as he called out to the others. They stopped and looked up, and located Macro's red cape in an instant. The leader shouted a command, and at once his men spurred into a gallop and raced up the track.

'Oh, shit,' Macro muttered. It was as he had feared, and for an instant a spark of anger flared in his breast. 'Damn Sempronius . . .'

For an instant he thought of leading them away from Julia and her escort. But there was nowhere to go. The slope on either side was too steep to ride on. He could only continue forwards, or turn back in the direction he had just come from. It took only a brief moment's thought for Macro to realise there was only one course of action. He had to ride back and warn the others, who would then have to spur their horses on and try to outrun their pursuers. Pulling savagely on his reins, he wheeled his horse round, and dug his heels in and galloped back up the track. Behind him he could hear the pounding of hooves and the cries of his pursuers.

He leaned forward, whipping the loose ends of the reins round the horse's neck while he shouted harsh encouragement and gripped hard with his thighs. Reaching the top of the slope, he rounded the rock again, dropped into the river bed and galloped along, spraying pebbles and loose stones into the air. He could see the way ahead of him for another few hundred paces before the route curved round a slope, and there was no sign of the escorts. He estimated that he had less than a quarter of a mile's start on the men behind him, and as he approached the bend their cries and the pounding of hooves echoed off the rocky slopes on either side. As the horse scrabbled round the bend, he saw Julia and the others a short distance ahead. The rearmost auxiliary turned in the saddle and looked back. As soon as he saw Macro, he called out and the escorts halted. Julia had turned her horse and was surprised and anxious to see Macro hurtling towards them.

'Macro! What's the matter?'

'We've got company!' he shouted as he rode up, reining in harshly. 'We must go, now! Follow me!' He spurred his horse on again, riding at the head of the line, following the river bed as it began to twist and turn more frequently as it led up into the mountains. He kept glancing back to make sure that Julia was keeping up, and saw her leaning forward as she rode along with the rest of the men, her expression one of determined concentration. The sound of hooves and the occasional shouts of the pursuers filled the still air. Above, the craggy skyline was illuminated by the first rays of the rising sun, but down in the river bed it was still gloomy and chilly.

As they turned yet another corner, the route split into two paths, both seeming to continue up in the direction of the ridge ahead. Macro halted the column, desperately sizing up the choice. The path to the right was narrow and sloped gently. The other route was wider and the incline more pronounced. Macro hoped that it might reach the crest more quickly and raised his arm.

'That way!'

They charged into the left fork and urged the horses up the slope, the leading mounts spraying dust and pebbles into the faces of those behind. Macro stayed at the head of the column, keeping just in front of Julia. On either side the slopes became steeper until they were in a ravine. Then, as they galloped round another bend, the path ended in a sheer cliff, forcing them to come to an abrupt stop. The snorting of the horses and the scraping of their hooves filled the air. Macro stared at the cliff, heart pounding.

'Fuck!' His spare hand balled into a fist and he struck his thigh. 'Fuck!'

'Macro.' Julia looked at him, afraid. 'What do we do?'

Macro turned round to face the escorts. 'Swords out! We're going to have to cut our way through!'

Some of the men briefly stared at him in surprise until the optio called out, 'You heard the prefect! Swords out! About face!'

Macro pointed to the nearest of the auxiliaries. 'Stay with the lady. If you see a chance to get her away during the fight, do it. Head for Cnossos.'

'Yes, sir.'

Macro edged his horse through to the front and raised his sword. 'Let's go!'

They spurred their mounts, thundering back down the ravine. Ahead of them the sounds of the pursuers were clearly audible, harsh and distorted as they echoed off the rock face. The two sides were suddenly upon each other as they met on a bend. Horse thudded into horse and the riders desperately held on before they hacked at their opponents. Macro and his men were equipped with the standard short swords, while the enemy carried a mixture of weapons: short swords as well as longer blades, the lethal crooked falcatas and some spears that were little use in the tight press of horseflesh and men in the confined space. The air was filled with the scrape of blades, wild snorts and whinnies, grunts as men struck blows, and cries of pain as they landed. The dust on the floor of the ravine swirled in clouds about the men locked in conflict.

Macro hacked a sword thrust to one side and opened up the face of the man as he withdrew his weapon for the next blow. From the corner of his eye he saw the first of the escort go down, run through with a battered-looking cavalry sword. The auxiliary doubled over, then rolled off to one side as his enemy yanked the blade free. A brief glance was all Macro could spare him as he turned to parry another blow and stab at the face of his next foe. The man threw himself back to avoid the thrust and tumbled off the back of his horse. Macro could see that the escort was hopelessly outnumbered and being steadily forced back. Another of his men was cut down with a savage blow to the head that shattered his skull in an explosion of blood and brains. A sudden surge of horses pressing forward into the melee found Macro squeezed back between his men so that he was close to Julia again.

She met his eyes with a questioning look. He pursed his lips and shook his head. There was no chance for them now. Macro turned his horse round. There was one last course of action to be contemplated. He needed a moment to prepare himself for the deed.

'Come with me.'

'Where?'

Macro did not answer. He nodded to the man he had assigned to protect her. 'Get stuck in, lad. Make every blow count.'

Then he led the way back up the ravine at a gallop, until they came to the end. There he dismounted and offered Julia his hand. When she was down beside him, she glanced round at the high rock surrounding them.

'There's no way out.' She looked up at him, lips trembling. 'Is there?'

'No, miss.' Macro looked at her sadly.

Julia glanced back towards the ravine, as the sounds of the fighting drew closer. 'What will they do if they capture me?'

Macro knew well enough. Almost certainly there would be no mercy, and plenty of suffering before they had finished with her. 'Best not to think about that.'

'What?' She stared at him and responded plaintively: 'I don't want to die. I don't want to suffer.'

'I know.' Macro put his arm round her shoulder awkwardly. 'This way.'

He led her to the cliff and they turned to face the ravine. With a last savage clatter of blades and a final cry of pain the noise of the fighting died away. Then there was the sound of horses coming their way. Julia pressed into Macro.

'I'm afraid. I don't want to die.'

'Of course not, miss,' Macro replied gently. 'It's only natural.'

'And you?'

Macro smiled. 'It's been a long time coming. I've grown used to the idea. I know one thing. They're not going to forget me in a hurry.'

The first of the enemy appeared, then another, and more of them emerged from the gloom. They came on at a steady walk, weapons held ready. Some bled from wounds and all of them stared at Macro and Julia fixedly. Macro stepped in front of Julia and raised his sword.

'Come on then, you bastards! See how a Roman dies!'

There was no response, just a deathly cold in their eyes as the horsemen clopped towards them. Julia took Macro's elbow and he felt her tremble as she spoke.

'Macro, don't let them take me. Please.'

He felt an icy sense of dread clench round his heart at her words.

There was no avoiding what he must do. Macro felt sick. He swallowed back the bile and turned towards her.

'I'm so sorry, miss.'

She glanced past him to the approaching men, then grasped his shoulders and stared into his eyes. 'Do it quickly!'

Macro's features twisted into an expression of agonised helplessness, then he nodded and lowered the bloodied tip of his sword to rest against her stomach, just under her rib cage. Her body was warm to the touch even though she was shivering. She clenched her eyes shut and took a last gasping breath as one of the men shouted a warning and they rushed forward.

'The gods save you, Cato my love,' she whispered. 'Macro, I'm ready. Do it.'

CHAPTER TWENTY-FOUR

It was taking far too long for the force to assemble, Cato fretted irritably as he made his way along the breakwater extending from the old royal quarter into the great harbour. To his left there was a mass of commercial shipping riding at anchor waiting for a berth, and beyond lay the Heptastadion – the long causeway stretching from the mainland to the island of Pharos. As he glanced at it, Cato could not help admiring the ambition of the Alexandrines once again. The city was full of wonders, as he had discovered while waiting for Petronius to assemble the relief force to be sent to Crete. The library had overawed him. Never before had he seen such a concentration of learning. In addition to the vast number of books on every conceivable subject, the place was filled with scholars quietly discussing shared interests, or locked in vehement dispute over some point.

He sat down on the steps of the Temple of Timon at the end of the breakwater. From there he had a good view of the fleet assembling in the royal harbour. In addition to a squadron of warships, Petronius had provided four light scouting ships of the same class that Cato and Macro had served aboard when they had been seconded to the fleet at Ravenna some years earlier. Besides these, there were eight large cargo ships to carry the horses and equipment allocated to the force. Counting the marine contingents aboard the warships, the legate had assigned nearly five thousand men to the force being sent to the aid of his old friend Senator Sempronius.

The decision of who to appoint as commander of the force had proved to be a delicate matter. In addition to the experienced officers commanding the legionary cohorts, as well as the auxiliary units, Petronius had a number of military tribunes on his staff who claimed the command for themselves. Cato had reminded the legate that

258

Sempronius would be making his own decision with respect to appointing a commander of the relief force when it reached Crete. Moreover, he had asked that Cato himself be the commander of the forces while they were en route to the province. In the end Petronius had appointed the senior centurion of the Twenty-Second to the post, until they arrived at Gortyna. Decius Fulvius was a scarred, bald veteran with the build of a boxer, who could bellow like a bull. Cato was impressed by his competence and aura of authority, and accepted the legate's decision.

Even though the commander had been appointed and the ships were ready, the auxiliary units were still on the march and would not reach the city for another day, Cato had been informed. The prefects, long used to the comfortable garrison duties of Egypt, had proved reluctant to be sent on campaign and had made every excuse to delay their departure, until the legate had threatened to replace them on his own authority and report the matter to the emperor. That had done the trick and the two cohorts had set off at once.

It had been several days since he had arrived in Alexandria, Cato reflected in a depressed mood as he found some shade on the steps of the temple and gazed out to sea. Somewhere out there lay the island of Crete, where his friends were in danger. They needed him and he was stuck here in Alexandria, dragging his heels until the relief force was ready to set sail. He thought longingly of Julia, and for a moment he closed his eyes and lifted his face to the sea breeze, letting it caress his skin as she was wont to do so lightly with her fingertips that it made his body tremble at the sensation. He could not wait to be in her arms again, to hold her body against his and kiss her.

Abruptly he stopped himself pursuing that line of thought. The consequences would be embarrassing in such a public space, and the agony of her absence would only depress him further and make him more anxious over having to wait for the fleet to set sail from Alexandria. As he opened his eyes, he felt the wind strengthen, and the awning over a nearby fish stall billowed up and snapped taut. The stallkeeper was already looking anxiously to the west as he began to pack his goods away into baskets to carry back down the breakwater into the city. Cato rose from the steps and walked round to the far side of the temple. The sky beyond the Heptastadion was dark and cloudy and the swell in the harbour was more noticeable. A storm was coming, blowing in from the west.

For a moment Cato watched the horizon, wondering if he should return to the quarters the legate had provided for him in the palace that had once been the home of the Ptolemaic pharaohs. There he would be forced to endure the empty conversation and mindless entertainments of Petronius's bored staff officers as the storm broke outside. The thought soured him, and he resolved to stay and watch. A fresh blast of wind buffeted him and he turned to see that the storm was almost upon him. Great waves were crashing against the foot of the lighthouse across the bay and bursting in massive clouds of spray swept on by the rising wind. Out to sea, a grey curtain of rain was sweeping towards the coast beneath dark clouds that smeared the sky along the horizon.

The rain began in earnest, stinging his face, and Cato could not help shivering slightly in the cold wind moaning around the temple. All at once there was a dazzling flash of light and a moment later the muffled metallic crash of thunder, as the storm struck the port. A cargo ship, a mile out, was battling to reach the harbour, almost all the sail reefed in as her bows burst through one wave after another. Suddenly the distant sail collapsed; Cato saw that the mast had snapped, and sail, spar, and rigging tumbled over the side. As the tangled wreckage hit the water, it acted as a brake, savagely dragging the ship over to one side as it turned its beam towards the great waves rolling in from the heart of the sea. For an instant Cato could make out the men crouching on the deck. Then a huge grey wall crashed over the ship, engulfing it. The keel broke the surface, like the spine of a whale, and settled in the water; then the next wave washed over it and the ship was gone. Cato stared at the spot, willing there to be some sign of survivors, but there was nothing, and the curiosity of before turned to horror at the sudden extinction of the ship and its entire crew.

'Poor bastards,' he muttered, then turned away and walked slowly towards the shelter of the temple, as the wind-fanned flames in the cupola at the top of the lighthouse flared brilliantly against the dark storm clouds scudding overhead. Once he was in the shelter of the tower, Cato took a last look towards the sea, his heart filled with pity for any ships out there in such a tempest.

Two days later, early in the morning, the fleet was ready to sail. Petronius came down to the dock in the royal harbour to bid farewell to Cato and First Spear Centurion Decius Fulvius. The storm had passed the day after it had struck and several ships had foundered in the commercial harbour. Fortunately the fleet had lost only one trireme, which had dragged its anchors and been holed when it struck the breakwater.

'Take good care of my men.' Petronius smiled faintly at Cato. 'I want 'em back in good condition once you have put down the slave rebellion. The gods know I'm taking a big risk in stripping so many men from the garrison of Egypt to help Sempronius out. Make sure he understands that.'

'I will be sure to pass the message on to the senator, sir.'

'Good, and tell my old friend that if he should ever need my help again in the future, then please hesitate to call on me.'

Cato smiled at the quip, but Fulvius just frowned for a moment and then shrugged before he saluted his commander. 'I'll look after the lads, sir. Shouldn't think a mob of renegade slaves will give me much trouble. Even so, I'll not take any unnecessary risks.'

'Good.'

Cato followed Fulvius across the gangway and on to the deck of the flagship, an ageing quadreme named the *Triton*. As soon as they were aboard, the marines hauled the gangway in and the men at the oars fended the vessel away from the dock. As soon as a sufficient gap had opened up, the navarch commanding the fleet gave the order for the ship to get under way, and the oars were unshipped and the blades lowered into the sea. The officer in charge of the rowers set an easy pace and the *Triton* glided across the still waters of the royal harbour and headed out to sea. The rest of the squadron took up station astern, as the troopships set sail and followed behind the warships. It was a fine spectacle, Cato reflected as he saw that hundreds of the local people had come out on to the Heptastadion to watch the fleet depart. The formation headed out past the lighthouse, and the *Triton's* bows lifted as they emerged into the swell of the open sea. The sudden motion caused Cato to grasp the side rail, and the image of the stricken ship he had seen during the storm jumped unbidden into his mind. The navarch chuckled as he glanced at him.

'Not much of a sailor, then?'

'Not much,' Cato admitted. 'I've had more than my share of sea travel recently.'

'Well, not to worry. The storm has blown itself out nicely.' The navarch scanned the horizon and sniffed the air. 'We're in for a fine spell, and will make Crete within three days at the most.'

'You can smell the weather to come?' Cato asked in surprise.

'No. But it helps calm my passengers if they think I can.' The navarch winked.

Cato made his way to the stern and stared back at Alexandria. By noon the city and the coastline had disappeared over the horizon, but the lighthouse was still clearly visible, and in the gentle breeze the smoke from its signal fire rose at an angle into the heavens.

In the fine weather the fleet made steady progress across the sea and sighted the coast of Crete on the evening of the third day. After carefully examining the coastline, the navarch was content that he knew where they had made landfall and gave the order to turn to the west and follow the coast towards Matala.

'We should reach the port tomorrow,' he announced to Cato and Fulvius as they shared a meal in his tiny cabin that night. He nodded at Cato. 'You say the port was hit hard by that wave. How bad was the damage, exactly?'

Cato finished chewing a hunk of bread and swallowed. 'There's not much still standing,' he recalled. 'The warehouses were flattened and much of the quayside was swept away. There's plenty of wrecked shipping along the shore and in the bay, but the beaches a little further out are clear enough. We could land our forces there.'

'Very well,' Fulvius agreed. 'As far as you're aware, we shouldn't be facing any opposition when we land.'

'No. Not unless something's happened to Matala.'

'Is that likely?'

Cato shook his head. 'I doubt it. If the rebels have paid a visit, the garrison had orders to take the people up into the acropolis. It's a fine defensive position. Without siege weapons the rebels would have had little chance of taking the place. No, we shouldn't have any problems putting ashore at Matala.'

'Glad to hear it,' said Fulvius. 'And once the column's ashore, we'll put paid to this gladiator of yours in double-quick time. You see if we don't!'

The sun was high in the sky as the *Triton* led the fleet into the bay. The navarch was taking no risks and had two men in the bows watching the water ahead of the warship for any obstacles caused by the wave or the earthquake. The marines and the additional legionaries from the Twenty-Second packed the sides of the ship and stared in curiosity and shock at the ruined port. For the first time since they had set off from Alexandria, Cato noticed that Fulvius looked a little shaken.

'Never seen anything like it,' the veteran muttered. 'It's like the port has been pulverised.' He turned to Cato. 'Seems you weren't exaggerating what you said about that wave.'

'No. And that's only the beginning.' Cato pointed inland. 'What's left of the city is up there, and once you see that, you'll have some idea of what's happened to the whole island.'

Fulvius shook his head slowly as he continued to survey the devastation.

As the warship eased its way further into the bay, Cato called to the navarch and indicated the *Horus*, still beached some distance along the shore. 'Head over there. The bottom's sandy and shelves gently.'

The navarch nodded and ordered the steersman to alter course, and the *Triton* swung gracefully round, oars dipping into the clear water in unison. Fulvius was still staring towards the ruins.

'Odd,' he said quietly. 'There's no sign of life at all. You'd think someone would have spotted us and called attention to the garrison commander. Or the other townspeople at least.'

Cato looked again at the port. 'You're right. I can't see a soul.'

'Best proceed cautiously when we get ashore then,' Fulvius decided. 'Just in case.'

They were interrupted by a bellowed command from the navarch as he ordered all the idle hands, marines and legionaries to move aft of the mast. As the men shuffled towards the stern, the ram slowly rose clear of the water, and after a few more strokes of the oars the navarch cupped his hands to his mouth. 'Ship the oars! Prepare to beach!'

The blades rose clear of the water and were run in as the warship continued forward. The deck shuddered slightly as the keel touched the sandy bottom, and carried on a little way before the friction killed the last of the ship's momentum.

'Marines forward! Lower the gangways!'

While the marines heaved the narrow ramps down from the gaps in the wooden side rails at the bow, the other warships began to beach on either side. Looking back towards the entrance of the bay, Cato saw the cargo ships cautiously approaching under minimal sail. They had too great a draught to beach and would have to anchor a short distance out and wait for the smaller vessels to ferry the men, horses and equipment ashore.

Centurion Fulvius had put on his helmet and was fastening the straps. He nodded to Cato. 'Best get your kit on. I'll have my lads ready to recce the city the moment we get on dry land.'

Cato struggled into a chainmail vest, strapped on his sword and put on his helmet before joining Fulvius and the legionaries assembling by the gangways. In addition to their usual complement, each of the warships was carrying two centuries of legionaries and the men were jostling to get ashore as quickly as possible after having spent the past few days crowded on to the open decks. The marines had already disembarked and run up the sand to form a skirmish line. When he was happy that his men were ready, Fulvius called out the order. 'Right then, boys, get ashore. One man on each gangway at a time, unless you want to land in the drink.'

Some of the men laughed or smiled at the warning as the first of them carefully made their way down the narrow gangways and on to the sand. Fulvius looked towards the port again. 'Still nothing. It's looking a bit worrying, I'd say.'

Cato did not reply, but inside he felt the familiar tightening of his guts as he let his mind contemplate the possible reasons for the stillness and silence of the port. He stood and waited his turn as the men disembarked, and then followed Fulvius down on to the beach. The optios were already forming the men up as they disembarked from the warships. Once the first cohort was ready, Fulvius gave the order to advance, and they began to march warily down the beach towards the port, following the same route Cato had taken when the *Horus* had limped into the bay after being swamped by the wave. The cohort had to break ranks to negotiate the rubble and debris when the men reached the edge of the port area. Despite the occasional shouted orders and the clatter of kit as nearly five hundred men picked their way forwards, no one came to investigate. The sense of foreboding was greater than ever, and Cato gripped the handle of his sword as he accompanied Fulvius up the shallow ravine towards the main town.

The streets were still and silent and Cato looked up as the acropolis came into view, but the walls were empty; not a single man visible on watch, or guarding the gates, which were wide open. The only sign of any life was a small swirl of dark birds over the acropolis.

'Where is everyone?' asked Fulvius. He turned to Cato. 'Could they have left? Has Sempronius ordered them to head for Gortyna maybe?'

'I don't know. I can't see why he would.'

They continued through the streets, towards the acropolis, and began to ascend the ramp. A faint breeze wafted down the slope, carrying with it a sickly stench. Fulvius, Cato and the leading section of the cohort stopped abruptly. Fulvius went to draw his sword, and then stilled his hand and swallowed hard instead.

'Keep moving,' he growled at his men, and they carried on up the ramp towards the open gateway. As they passed through the arch, the foul smell was overpowering. A handful of startled carrion birds squawked and flapped into the air as the first men into the acropolis drew up and stared at the ghastly scene before them. The entire space within the walls was covered with bodies, mottled and bloated with decay. The paving stones were dark with dried blood, and further away from Cato and the others, the carrion continued to worry at the corpses with their beaks and claws. Nobody had been spared. Not the old and infirm, not the women, nor the children. All had been hacked to death.

Cato covered his mouth and nose as he looked about.

'What the hell happened here?' Fulvius muttered.

'The rebels must have attacked and found a way in,' Cato guessed. 'That's why they're all in the acropolis, and not at the refugee camp outside the city.'

'I thought you said they would be safe up here.'

'They should have been. It doesn't make sense.'

Both men were silent for a moment as they gazed at the scene of the massacre. Then Fulvius scratched his chin nervously. 'If the rebels could take Matala, then we have to assume that Gortyna is also in danger.'

Cato felt an icy spasm in his neck. Gortyna . . . Julia and Macro . . . He felt sick with despair and uncertainty. He swallowed the bile rising in his throat and turned to Fulvius.

'We have to get the rest of the column ashore at once and make for Gortyna before it's too late.'

'It may already be too late.'

Cato was stung by the implication of the other man's words. 'In that case,' he responded with chilling intensity, 'we still march on Gortyna. We will not rest until every last one of the rebels has paid for this with their lives.'

CHAPTER TWENTY-FIVE

'Is there nothing that can be done to save him?' asked Ajax as they emerged from the farmhouse. Kharim wiped the traces of blood and pus from his hands with a linen rag, and then shook his head.

'I'm sorry, it's in the hands of the gods now. You might want to make a sacrifice to Asclepius and pray for his help. I have done all that I can for Chilo, but his wound has become corrupted. I've seen it before, as have you. It will fester and poison his blood and he will die. I'm sorry.'

'I see.' Ajax nodded with a weary air of resignation.

It pained Kharim to see the gladiator brought low by this, amongst all the other burdens of command that rested on his powerful shoulders. It had been five days since the rebel army had arrived before the walls of Gortyna and Ajax had launched his surprise attack. It had cost the rebels dearly. Over two hundred of Chilo's band had been killed or wounded, and many of the survivors had been crippled by running on to the caltrops as they retreated into the night. The mood in the rebel camp had soured, and though Ajax was determined to make another attempt to take the city by force, he was aware that his followers had been shaken by the failure of the first night.

It had been their first major setback since the outbreak of the rebellion, and Ajax was forced to realise that there were limits to what could be asked of men and women who had had no experience of the hardships of conflict. They had been intoxicated by freedom and fanatical in their defence of it. But fanaticism was not enough when what Ajax really needed was men trained in the art of siege warfare and disciplined enough to carry an assault through in spite of the dangers. Besides, fanaticism was a fickle thing, he had discovered. The initial fearlessness and ferocity of the early days of the revolt had begun to give way to a simple desire to live well and enjoy the luxuries they had looted from their former masters.

Ajax clasped Kharim's shoulder. 'I thank you for doing what you could for Chilo.'

'You don't have to thank me, General.' Kharim smiled sadly. 'Chilo is as a brother to me, as he is to you. His men love him. This has hit them hard. I wish I had the skills to save him.'

'I thank you anyway.' Ajax stared at his companion for a moment. 'I need a new man to take over from Chilo.'

It was the first mention of such a thing, and Kharim realised that his leader now accepted that Chilo would not recover.

'Who do you have in mind?' Kharim asked.

'I am not sure yet. My first thought was you.'

'Me?'

'Why not? You fight as well as you practise your healing skills. And you are loyal to me, are you not?'

'Do you have to ask?' Kharim responded with a pained expression.

'No. I am sorry, my friend. I did not mean to slight you. Sometimes I slip back into the blunt frame of mind of a common gladiator.'

'There is nothing common about you,' Kharim replied, and gestured to the camp surrounding them. 'Ask anyone. Do you know, I have even heard some of the women praying to you? As if you were some kind of a god, or a king.'

Ajax frowned. 'That is foolishness. We are free now, we are not beholden to anyone but ourselves.'

Kharim looked at him. 'You believe that, and that is why they love you and will follow where you will lead.'

The gladiator drew himself up and briefly surveyed the nearest cluster of tents and shelters where the former slaves sat at their ease. Some talked, some simply sat and looked at the world around them as if seeing it anew. A handful of children were playing around a cage to one side of the farmhouse, goading the prisoners with sticks. It was a peaceful scene of contentment, yet Ajax knew it could not last. He turned back to Kharim.

'Pass the word. I want the leaders of all the war bands to meet in the garden at dusk. We must talk. There are choices that must be made. Commitments to be renewed. You understand?'

'Yes, General. I will tell them.'

Kharim turned and strode away, towards the area of the camp where his war band had set up their shelters. Ajax watched him a moment and then turned to go back inside the farmhouse. He passed through the colonnaded hall with the shallow pond at its centre. Once that had been fed by rainwater from the roof, but the earthquake had left a large crack in the bottom, and now it was dry and filled with cracked plaster, dust and a handful of smashed tiles that had fallen in from the roof. He made his way towards the best bedroom in the house, where Chilo lay on a soft bedroll. Despite having the windows open on both sides of the room, the air was warm, and as Ajax approached, a sickening tang assaulted his nostrils. He hid his distaste as he knelt down beside Chilo.

Chilo's skin was waxy and glistened with perspiration. He lay with a fine robe covering his body as far as his chest, hiding his wound. Sensing the gladiator's presence, he opened his eyes, struggled to focus and forced a smile.

'General, I wondered when you'd come to see me.' He spoke softly, a slight rasp to his words.

'I was here just a moment ago.'

'Were you?' Chilo frowned. 'I can't remember.'

'It's the poison in your blood,' Ajax explained. 'It's playing tricks with your mind.'

'Ah.' Chilo reached out his hand and took that of Ajax. His touch was hot and feverish, and Ajax forced himself not to recoil. Chilo smiled. 'Well you are here now, at the end.'

'Yes.'

'It's been too short a time to have known you, my general.'

'And you, my friend.'

'Friend?' Chilo smiled contentedly. 'Thank you.' His eyes moistened and he looked away.

'There's no shame in tears, Chilo. We have seen enough suffering in our time to justify a river of tears.'

Chilo nodded. 'Suffering, and joy.'

'Joy?'

'I found you, my general. You gave me freedom, and revenge.'

Ajax felt his throat constrict with a slight burning sensation. He swallowed before he could trust himself to speak. He leaned forward slightly and stroked the lank hair plastered to Chilo's scalp.

Chilo suddenly clenched his eyes tightly shut and grimaced, and his body went rigid. His fingers clamped tightly round Ajax's hand as he fought the wave of agony burning through his body. Slowly it passed and he went limp. The pulse in his neck throbbed as sweat trickled from his brow. At length his breathing became calm and his gaze flickered back to Ajax.

'I'm sorry.'

'You have nothing to be sorry for.'

'I cannot fight at your side any more.'

'I know. I will not forget you.' Ajax paused. 'You saved my life. Why?'

'Why?' Chilo frowned. 'Because you are as a brother to me.'

Ajax nodded slowly. 'I must go now. I'll come back later and we can talk again.'

'Thank you.' Chilo glanced across the room to where his armour and weapons still lay against the wall. 'Before you go, could you bring those over here, beside the bed.'

Ajax glanced at the weapons. 'Why?'

'My sword still has Roman blood on it. If I feel strong enough, I might want to clean the blade.'

Ajax stared at him a moment and then nodded slowly. 'Very well.'

He collected the weapons, and Chilo's mail vest, and laid them gently on the floor beside him. 'There.'

'Thank you,' Chilo replied softly, as he stared fixedly at the ceiling.

With a heavy heart Ajax headed towards the door, pausing on the threshold. 'I will see you again, my brother.'

'Yes,' Chilo replied, and then whispered. 'In this life . . . or the next.'

Outside, Ajax stood still for a moment, wondering if he should go back to Chilo. It took all his strength of will to resist the notion. Chilo was in great pain and he was dying. If he chose to end his life then so it was. He was free to decide. That was what he had given his life for. Even so, there was a great heaviness in the gladiator's heart, which soon turned to bitterness and hatred. He looked towards the cage, where the children had given up poking the prisoners with sticks and now squatted down at arm's length to watch the Romans and laugh at their wretched condition.

'Get away from there!'

He started towards them and the children hurriedly rose to their feet and scampered off into the camp. Ajax continued on towards the cage, an iron construction six feet long by four feet in height and depth. There was not much room for the occupants, and there was no shelter from the elements. At night they shivered in the cold air, and by day they were tormented by the sun. Their clothes had been taken from them so that they now sat in their own filth. Ajax had ordered that they not be harmed, and they were fed and watered just enough to keep them alive. His nose wrinkled at the stink of their shit and piss as he rested a hand on top of the cage and leaned towards it so that he could watch the two prisoners, a man and a woman, sitting on opposite sides.

'How are my guests feeling today?'

The man looked up at him without replying and the woman drew up her knees as she stared fixedly at the ground. Ajax smiled at them.

'Oh come now, surely the accommodation can't be that bad? You know, when I was first sold into slavery I spent the first month of it in a cage smaller than this, with two other men. By now I think you can imagine what that must have been like. But imagining a thing is not the same as enduring it, as you are discovering.'

Neither of the prisoners stirred and Ajax stared at them for a moment, until the woman shuffled round and turned her back on him. Ajax laughed and then squatted down so he could stare across the cage into the man's face. His hair was dark and matted with a crust of dried blood from the blow to the skull he had received at the time of his capture.

'How is your head today, Centurion? Or should I call you prefect these days?'

Macro did not reply.

'You've obviously done well since we first met. A centurion of marines you were then, and now look at you. The commander of the garrison of Gortyna. Of course, your rise through the ranks has been

271

rather eclipsed by my own. From slave to general in a matter of days.'

'Some general.' Macro spat on the ground beside him. 'You're nothing more than a brigand. And you call this rabble an army?' He nodded to the camp outside the cage.

'Oh, we haven't done so badly. It's not as if you Romans have covered yourself in glory since the rebellion began. Wouldn't you agree?'

Macro stared back at him. 'You must know this can only end one way. An army will come to Crete and crush you and your followers. So far you have only faced men from the auxiliary cohorts, second-rate troops at that. You cannot hope to defeat the legions.'

'We shall see,' Ajax replied. 'Meanwhile, I am the master of Crete. Or will be, once Gortyna is taken and the governor joins you in this cage.'

'What do you intend to do with us?' Macro asked quietly. 'You must know that we are no use to you as hostages. Sempronius will not surrender if you promise to spare us.'

'I know that. I made the offer yesterday and he turned me down.' Ajax turned towards Julia. 'Not straight away, you'll be glad to hear. I could see him struggle over the decision. It's not an easy thing to lose a daughter . . . or a father.' He glanced back at the farmhouse. 'Or a friend.'

Macro followed the direction of his gaze. 'The man who saved your life. How is he?'

Ajax took a sharp breath and glared at Macro. 'Dying, or dead. What does it matter to you?'

'It's not personal, who I kill on the battlefield,' Macro explained. 'But we are not on the battlefield any longer. It was a brave thing he did. Admirable. I would be sorry to hear that he had died.'

'Of course, the professional respect of one soldier for another. But aren't you forgetting something? My friend was a slave, not a soldier.'

'Slave or soldier, what does it matter?' Macro responded wearily. 'When a man picks up a weapon and faces you in a fair fight, what else matters? Surely you of all people must understand that, Gladiator.'

'Don't call me that!' Ajax said fiercely. 'I am no longer a gladiator,

Roman. I fight for myself and I fight for my people. I would rather die than fight to entertain the mob again.'

There was a brief silence as Ajax fought to control his rage. The temptation to smash open the lock to the cage and drag the Roman out of his filth and slaughter him tested him sorely. He clenched his fists and shut his eyes and breathed deeply for a moment until the rage had passed. Then he stood up and turned to walk away.

'Wait!' Macro called out. 'Tell me, what are your plans for us? Me and the lady.'

Ajax half turned and smiled coldly. 'To let you suffer for as long as possible. When being confined in that cage has driven you half mad, then I will have you killed, Centurion. As slowly as I possibly can. I want you to die by inches, and I want you to feel the agony of every moment of that death. As for the woman, since she is of no use to me now that her father has abandoned her, she can suffer here with you, and then my men can have her. They have developed something of a taste for the flesh of well-bred Roman women.' Ajax looked at her and smacked his lips. 'Of course, if I am fortunate enough to capture Gortyna first, then I will make sure that your father, the good senator, is there to witness the shaming of his daughter.'

'Bastard!' Macro kicked out with his feet, crashing against the bars of the cage. 'You fucking coward! I swear to all the gods that if you touch one hair of her head, then—'

'What? Then what?' Ajax laughed. 'You'll come and haunt me? Perhaps I should make you watch as well, before I have you killed.'

Macro clenched his teeth and a low keening sounded in his throat. He grasped the bars of the cage and shook them with all his strength.

'Macro!' Julia suddenly snapped. 'Macro! Look at me!'

Macro tore his gaze away from the gladiator and fixed his eyes on hers.

'He's baiting you, Macro. Don't let him. Don't give him the satisfaction. We must be better than him. Stronger.'

Ajax smiled. 'You can play the brave aristocrat now, my fine lady, but we'll see how long you last once my men get their hands on you. Now I must go. I've enjoyed our little chat. Really I have. I'm sure we will speak again soon.'

He waved at them in mock farewell, and walked off to find a horse and begin his daily inspection of the defences of Gortyna.

When he returned to the farmhouse in the middle of the afternoon, Kharim was waiting for him.

'Chilo is dead,' the Parthian reported plainly.

Ajax lowered his head and nodded. 'Did he die by his own hand?'

'Yes.'

'That is what he wanted. Where is he?'

'Inside. I have given orders for his body to be wrapped in linen for burial, but I thought you might want to see him first.'

Ajax was still for a moment and then shook his head. 'He is dead, and I will remember him. That is enough. Give the orders for his burial. Find him a grave somewhere quiet, where his body won't be discovered by the Romans.'

Kharim stared at him, delicate brows slightly raised in surprise. 'You think they might beat us, then?'

'They might. Nothing in this life is certain, my friend. If the rebellion fails, I will not have his body treated as a trophy. Nor mine. Or yours.'

'I understand.'

'Good. Now, I need to eat. I'll be in the garden if anyone needs me.'

Kharim bowed his head. 'Yes, General.'

Ajax spent the rest of the afternoon there, sitting on a bench, leaning forward, elbows resting on his knees, hands clasped and supporting his chin. He stared at a small shrine to a household god in the corner of the garden as he reflected on the progress of the rebellion. The idea of leading a rebellion had never occurred to him when he had taken the chance to regain his freedom after the governor's palace had collapsed. In truth he could have escaped at any time since his arrival in Crete, but the prospect of being on the run for the rest of his life, and of a terrible punishment if he was caught, had dissuaded him from such a course of action. The earthquake had changed everything. At first he had thought it would be the perfect chance to disappear, to be thought lost amongst the ruins with so many others. He had planned to change his appearance, bide his time, and find a berth on a ship leaving the island. Instead he had stepped into the role as leader of a small band of runaway slaves and almost without any kind of plan had become the leader of an army of rebels. With this responsibility had come the opportunity to avenge himself on Rome, and Ajax now admitted he had been seduced by such a prospect. The question was, what could the rebellion realistically hope to achieve?

That arrogant aristocrat in Gortyna had refused to negotiate any agreement that resulted in the freedom of the rebels. If that could not be guaranteed, then what was the purpose of the rebellion? Centurion Macro was right. In time, Rome would send a powerful army to crush the slaves, and the consequent retribution would be terrible indeed. With a heavy heart Ajax realised that he must lay the matter before his closest followers. If the rebellion was to achieve anything, then he had to be certain that those who looked to him for leadership clearly understood and shared his aims.

When the commanders of the war bands arrived at the farmhouse, their mood was subdued. Word of Chilo's death had swiftly gone round the rebel camps and many openly grieved for him. They filed into the garden and sat on the spare benches, or squatted on the ground in a loose semicircle in front of Ajax. Kharim and some others had brought a small brazier out from one of the farm's store sheds and lit a fire in the middle of the garden. Ajax examined the faces of his closest men by the glow of the flames. They were all hard men, from widely differing backgrounds. Some were ex-gladiators, like him, while others had been gang leaders on estate farms or on the chain gangs that loaded ships, or had worked the quarries and mines of the island. One had been a stonemason, condemned to fashion the tombs of the wealthy while looking forward to the common grave of a slave pit when his own time came. Another had been the strong man of an entertainment party, delighting wealthy Romans with displays of his strength, little knowing that he would one day crack the skulls of their compatriots as freely as he crushed walnuts in his bare hands.

Despite the variety of their former lives, they were now united in a common cause, and all looked to Ajax to lead them to a better life.

He cleared his throat as he rose to his feet and ran a hand through his curly black hair. 'My friends, today we lost a man who was as a brother to us all. Forgive me, but my heart is heavy with grief, else I would welcome you here with wine and meat, and perhaps Chilo would have a song for us.' He saw that some of the men smiled fondly at the memory. 'But Chilo is gone and I am in no mood for pleasantries. My heart is made heavier still by the need to face up to certain truths. Truths that I must share with you this night.'

He paused briefly and sighed before he spoke again. 'The Romans will never give us freedom. Nor will they ever leave us in peace. That is certain.'

'Then we shall take our freedom,' the stonemason, Fuscus, growled. 'And if they object, why, then we shall just have to take their lives instead.'

There was a chorus of approval at these words and Ajax nodded. 'A fine sentiment, and one that has served us well so far, Fuscus. But I fear that we have already achieved as much as we could hope to. We have defeated the Romans in battle, we have sacked one of their cities, and the remaining Romans are bottled up behind their fortifications. We are the masters of this island. For the present. Now we must ask ourselves what is the true purpose of our rebellion.'

'You sound like a philosopher,' a voice called out, and some of the men chuckled.

Ajax forced a smile. 'I am no philosopher. I would rather act than think. Yet now is the time when we must think. We cannot avoid it any longer.'

Some of them were wearing puzzled expressions as Ajax folded his arms across his chest and continued, 'What do you want to achieve?'

There was a brief silence, then a voice called out. 'Freedom, General. That is all we have ever wanted.'

Ajax nodded. 'We have that, at the moment. But it will not last. The Romans will not rest until the rebellion is crushed, no matter how many soldiers it takes, or how long it takes. They are relentless. That is their way. I had hoped that we might escape this island, by using hostages, but the governor will not surrender Gortyna. Nor will we find sufficient ships to transport our people to other shores. So we must find a solution here on Crete, and we must find it before the Romans send an army to decide the issue. We have a limited time in which to negotiate from strength. In that time we must make the Romans think we present the gravest danger to them. That is why we must take Gortyna as soon as we can. We need as many Roman hostages as possible to bargain with. My brothers, we must keep on the attack.'

His words were met with silent disapproval. Fuscus cleared his throat. 'General, we lost too many good men in the first assault. And that was only against one gateway. If we are to take the city, we will have to attack in far greater strength. Next time we would lose thousands of men, not hundreds.'

'That is true. I won't deny it. But if we fail to take Gortyna and Rome won't negotiate with us, then we are all dead in the end.'

'But there is no need to attack the city,' Fuscus continued. 'We can starve them out.'

'And how long will that take? Do you imagine they were idle when we were dealing with Matala? My guess is that they took the opportunity to stock up with all the food supplies they could find. They might hold out for months. Long enough for an army to land in Crete and break the siege. Besides, how are we expected to feed our people for that long? Within a few days we will have exhausted the immediate area, and will have to send parties further and further afield to find food. We must take the city as soon as possible, whatever the cost.'

This time several of the men shook their heads and there were muttered protests. Another man spoke up. 'General, it is too much to ask of our men. They are brave and they have achieved great things so far. But it would take a trained army to capture Gortyna. I cannot ask my men to risk their lives in a reckless attack. Even if I agreed to it, I doubt they would follow my orders.'

Some of his comrades added their agreement to his view and Ajax glared at them in frustration. 'Then we might as well cut our losses totally and prepare for surrender now. If we are lucky we might get the governor to agree to generous terms if we offer to lay down our arms and end the rebellion. I'm sure that he would be willing to concede to just executing the ringleaders, and any others who could be identified as having raised their hands against their masters. It would not end there. You know the law. If any slave of a household is found guilty of killing his master, then all the slaves of the household are condemned to death. Those who survived would be lucky to escape with a flogging before being returned to their owners.' Ajax looked round the room defiantly. 'Shall we go down that road, my brothers?'

There was a tense silence before Fuscus dared to reply. He swallowed nervously as he addressed the gladiator. 'General, it seems that you are offering us a choice of death now, or death later. Our people are living for the moment. Every day of freedom is a gift to them. Can you wonder that they believe that life is too precious to be risked in an attack on Gortyna?'

Ajax felt his guts tighten into a knot. He wanted to scream at these fools. Had they not taken great risks and made great sacrifices already? Now was not the time to let their courage fail them. He forced his voice to remain calm.

'I am sure that Chilo thought his life was precious. Yet he gave it up for the rebellion, and died with no regrets.'

Fuscus looked down as he replied. 'I am not Chilo.'

'Evidently. And what about the rest of you? Would you betray his legacy?'

No one replied, and Ajax refused to break the guilty silence that tormented them. He was uncertain what to do, or what to say, and had to clench his fists behind his back and fight the urge to bellow his rage at them, to shame them. For a moment he resolved to attack the city by himself. He would stride towards the walls sword in hand and see how many of his people had the guts to follow him and see through the commitment they had made to each other by joining in rebellion against Rome.

But then a figure emerged from the door leading back into the farm, one of the leaders of the patrols that Ajax had sent to scour the island. He was breathing hard and sweat glistened on his skin.

'What is it?' Ajax demanded.

The scout glanced round at the assembled commanders of the war bands, and then back at Ajax.

'Speak,' he ordered. 'Make your report.'

The scout nodded, then licked his dry lips and began. 'We've found some ships, General. A whole fleet of them. They're in a bay three days' ride from here.'

'Ships? A fleet?' Ajax raised an eyebrow. 'Warships?'

'No, General. Cargo ships. Huge cargo ships, filled with grain. We captured one of their crew and questioned him. These ships are the grain fleet, sailing for Rome. They were caught in a great storm. Two of them sank. The rest were damaged and have put into the bay to make repairs. That's where we found them, beached while they wait for spars, cordage and sails to arrive so they can be repaired and continue sailing for Rome.'

Ajax thought quickly. 'How soon before the repairs are complete?'

'A while yet, sir. Our man reckoned that it would take several days to organise the spare parts and send them to the bay.'

'Where is this crewman?'

The scout nicked his throat with his finger. 'Sorry, General. I thought it was for the best.'

Ajax nodded. Already his mind was grasping the significance of this news. He smiled to himself and muttered, 'The grain fleet . . .'

Fuscus's eyes were wide with excitement. 'By the gods, we could feed our people for the best part of a year if we took their cargo.'

Ajax chuckled. 'You're missing the point, Fuscus. It's not our people who need the grain. It's the people of Rome. Without the grain fleet they will starve. There are over a million mouths to feed in Rome. How long do you think the emperor will be able to defy a starving mob?' Ajax nodded gently to himself. 'At last we have a weapon that we can hold at the throat of our enemy.'

CHAPTER TWENTY-SIX

The crews of the warships were left with the task of burying the dead of Matala, while Fulvius marched his column on to Gortyna. Cato rode ahead with a squadron from the mounted cohort, consumed with anxiety for the fate of his friends. He led the horsemen on at a gallop, thundering along the dusty road to the provincial capital, all the while terrified of what he might see when he finally arrived in sight of the city. The horses and men were only allowed to stop and rest when they were on the verge of exhaustion, and then Cato ordered them to walk on until he judged that the mounts had recovered enough to continue being ridden.

All the time his mind was a raging turmoil of images. In his mind's eye he saw Gortyna in smouldering ruins, streets littered with butchered bodies, leading all the way up to the acropolis, where . . . He clamped his eyes shut for an instant to force the image from his mind and turned instead to prayer, silently begging the gods to spare Julia, Macro and all the others. If they were safe, then Cato swore to be the servant of the gods – their slave – and live only to please them. If the price of his friends' lives was his own, then so be it.

An inner voice chided him for being a hypocrite. Since when had he ever placed so much faith in divine intervention? He felt torn between the two impulses, and then turned instead to thoughts of revenge. If Ajax had killed them, Cato resolved never to rest until the gladiator was hunted down and killed, whatever the cost. His heart filled with hatred that spilled into his veins and he was consumed with a burning intensity of purpose to destroy Ajax, to obliterate every fragment of his being. Until now, he had never tasted such a desire for revenge, and for a brief moment some part of his mind, still capable of rational thought, reminded him that this was the self-same revenge that fuelled the fire burning in the heart of Ajax.

'Fuck Ajax,' Cato muttered to himself through clenched teeth.

The decurion who was walking his horse beside him glanced at Cato. 'Sir?'

'What?' Cato glared at him.

'I thought you said something. An order, like.'

'No. It was nothing. Nothing.' Cato moved round to the side of the horse. 'Mount up!'

The horses' flanks were still heaving like bellows and the decurion looked at Cato ready to protest, then bit his lip. The rest of the squadron wearily pulled themselves back into the saddle and took up their reins.

'Get a move on!' Cato barked at the slowest of them. 'If we're too late, then the gods help you.'

'Sir,' the decurion edged his mount closer to Cato and lowered his voice, 'the lads are exhausted.'

'I don't bloody care. We have to reach Gortyna as soon as possible. D'you hear?'

'Sir, it will not make any difference how quickly we reach Gortyna.' He gestured to his men. 'There's only thirty of us. If the slaves are there, then we're not going to be able to do anything. If they've already dealt with the city, then . . .' He shrugged. 'We won't be able to change what has happened.'

'I don't give a damn,' Cato growled. 'I'm in command, and if we have to ride the horses into the ground to reach Gortyna before dark, we'll do it. Understand?'

The decurion took a deep breath and nodded.

'Then let's go.' Cato thrust his arm in the air, and swept it forwards as he spurred his horse into a trot. 'Advance!'

He increased the pace into a gallop and they pounded on down the road. Late in the afternoon, as the shadows were lengthening, the milestones indicated that the city was close. The crops on either side had been harvested, and the trees in the orchards and olive groves that they passed were stripped bare, as if a host of locusts had swept through the land. There were bodies too, sprawled beside carts and wagons that had been unable to outrun the slaves. Cato felt his guts knot in agony as he saw the evidence that Ajax and his army had gone before him. He was being driven to the edge of sanity by the dread of the sight that would greet them when they finally reached the city.

Then they passed the last milestone, as the road climbed over a slight rise, and the city was there before them. Cato reined in. 'Halt!'

As the horses snorted and the riders breathed heavily, Cato squinted as he scanned the landscape. The ground surrounding Gortyna bore the unmistakable signs of being the site of a huge camp. The remains of hundreds of fires had scorched the ground and left low piles of ash at their centre. Every tree, shrub and small building had been stripped for firewood and kindling. Here and there lay piles of animal bones picked clean by those who had fed on them and were now attracting small clumps of birds and rats who gleaned the bits of gristle that were left. There were some latrine ditches, but most of those who had camped here had simply defecated in mutually agreed areas where patches of their waste lay in clear view. A handful of figures were visible outside the city and more on the walls and in the towers along them.

'Ours or theirs?' muttered the decurion.

'Only one way to find out,' Cato replied, tightening his grip on the reins.

The decurion looked sharply at him. 'If they are slaves, then our mounts are too far gone to make much of an escape.'

'Then you had better pray that those are our men.' Cato waved the column on and urged his horse into a trot. They made their way across the plain towards the city. At their approach there was a thin blast from a horn and those outside the city hurriedly made their way back towards the nearest gates and sally ports. Cato slowed the pace as they came within quarter of a mile of the city's west gate and ordered the squadron's standard bearer to raise his staff so that the pennant would be clearly visible as they approached.

The decurion gestured towards the men on the gate. 'They're clearly ours, sir.'

'Too early to say,' Cato replied. 'The rebels have been helping themselves to the kit they took off our men. Keep your eyes peeled.'

As Cato walked his horse towards the closed gate, a figure stepped up behind the ramparts and raised a hand. 'Halt! You at the front, advance and be recognised.'

Cato clicked his tongue and edged forward. 'Tribune Cato! Returning from Alexandria with the reinforcement column. Open the gate!'

'Yes, sir!' the optio on watch replied, with evident relief.

Moments later the doors swung inwards and Cato spurred his horse into the city, followed by the rest of the squadron. As soon as he was through the arched gateway he slipped off the back of the horse and strode over to the optio, jerking his thumb towards the plain.

'Seems you had company whilst I was gone.'

'Yes, sir. Thousands of 'em.'

'Did they give you any trouble?'

'They made one attack the day they arrived, and paid a heavy price. After that they settled in to starve us out.'

'So where are they?'

The optio shook his head. 'No idea, sir. They were gone this morning. Must have marched off during the night and left the fires burning so we wouldn't catch on until first light. The governor's sent patrols off to search for them and see where they're headed.'

'The governor?' Cato frowned. 'Where's the prefect? Macro?'

'Macro's gone, sir.'

'Gone?' Cato stepped up to the optio and grabbed his harness. 'What do you mean, gone?'

'Captured, sir.'

'Macro taken prisoner? I don't believe it. How is that possible? You said the attack was beaten off.'

'It didn't happen then, sir. It was afterwards, while he was trying to get the governor's daughter to safety, away from the city.'

Cato swallowed and stared into the optio's eyes, unblinking. He lowered his voice. 'The governor's daughter, was she also captured?'

'Yes, sir.'

'How do you know this?'

'The leader of the rebels, that gladiator, had them brought forward in a cage when he tried to talk the governor into surrendering.'

Cato felt a flush of hope lighten his heart. 'So they're alive.'

'Yes, sir. Or at least they were when the gladiator showed them to the governor. That was several days ago though, sir. Last anyone has seen of them.'

Dread flooded back into Cato's heart. He looked down and saw his knuckles were white where he was holding the optio's harness so tightly. He forced himself to let go and step back, and gestured to the cavalrymen. 'Have these men taken to the stables at the governor's palace. Make sure horses and men get fed and find them a place to rest.'

'Yes, sir.'

'Does the governor still have his headquarters up on the acropolis?'

'Yes, sir.'

'Very well.' Cato breathed deeply to ease the tension in his chest. 'Carry on, Optio.'

Leaving his horse in the care of the decurion, Cato made his way through the streets towards the road leading up to the entrance of the acropolis. The townspeople forced to live in the ruins he passed spared him no more than a glance as they prepared for the evening meal. The weary resignation of their spirits was clear in almost every face. Only the children showed any signs of life and contentment as they heedlessly played amid piles of rubble between the surviving buildings.

The moment of hope that Cato had felt when he had heard that Macro and Julia were alive was now dashed by the knowledge that they were still in the hands of Ajax. While they served a purpose as hostages they would live, but the moment the enemy judged them worthless their lives would be forfeit. Worse still, if Ajax took it into his head to enact some kind of grisly revenge for the death of his father, then Macro and Julia would be subjected to every imaginable torture and torment before being granted the mercy of death. Cato felt sick at the idea, and had to pause in his stride for a moment before he could continue up the slope to the acropolis.

When he reached the headquarters he found Senator Sempronius in his office, sitting at the window as he stared blankly out across the city. A wine jug was on the desk and he was nursing a goblet in his hand when Cato rapped on the door frame.

'What is it now?' Sempronius said wearily. 'Anyway, I thought I gave orders that I was not to be disturbed.'

'It's me, sir.' Cato spoke gently.

Sempronius turned round quickly and his expression filled with relief. 'Cato! I feared we had seen the last of you. Come in, my boy. Sit you down!'

His words were slightly slurred. Cato could not tell if it was from exhaustion, grief or wine. Sempronius set his cup down on the table and refilled it before pushing it towards Cato. A small amount slopped over the rim and ran red down the side. The senator leaned forward on his elbows. 'Well, what have you to report?'

'Sir, I've heard what happened to Macro and Julia.'

Sempronius's shoulders sagged. 'Yes.'

'We have to believe they're still alive.'

The governor nodded, and for a few moments both men stared at each other in a shared grief that went beyond words. Then Sempronius cleared his throat and looked down at his hands as he spoke. 'Your report, please.'

'Yes, sir. Legate Petronius has provided most of the men you requested. We landed at Matala this morning. I rode ahead of the main force. The reinforcements will reach Gortyna by tomorrow night.'

'Good.'

'There are also warships and marines at Matala that we can call on. The reinforcements are under the command of First Spear Centurion Fulvius, of the Twenty-Second Legion.'

'Fulvius? Why not you, as I requested?'

'Legate Petronius decided I was too junior for such a command. He appointed Fulvius to lead the column until the reinforcements reach Gortyna, and then you are to assume authority over them. I had thought that Macro would take charge, sir.'

'Yes, well, that is no longer possible. We shall need a new commander.' Sempronius looked up. 'Do you still have that document authorising you to act as tribune?'

'Yes, sir.' Cato reached for the thong around his neck, and pulled the leather tube out of his tunic and offered it to the governor. 'It's here, together with your ring.'

Sempronius took the tube, pulled off the cap and tipped the contents out on to the desk. He placed his family ring back on his finger and then picked up the roll of parchment and tapped it gently on the desk as he thought. 'Macro is no longer with us. Therefore the command passes to you, Cato.'

'Me?' Cato shook his head in astonishment. 'Me? But, sir, I-I. . .'

Sempronius pushed the document across the table towards Cato. 'There. Your appointment still stands, which means that as tribune you outrank Fulvius. The command of the forces at Gortyna is yours. That is my decision, and my order. When the reinforcements arrive, I want you to take command of them, find Ajax and destroy his army. That is your priority, Cato. You are not to let any other considerations interfere with your orders.'

'Sir?'

'There will be no negotiations with the rebels. No deals with regard to hostages.' Sempronius swallowed. 'Do I make myself clear?'

Cato nodded. 'And if, in carrying out your orders, the chance to effect a rescue of the hostages does occur . . .?'

Sempronius stared at him, eyes moist and lips trembling. 'Then you get my daughter back, you hear? And save your friend Macro.'

'I will do everything in my power to save them both,' Cato replied. 'I swear it, on my life.'

The patrols that had been sent out to find and follow the slave army reported back to Gortyna the following evening, just as Centurion Fulvius reached the city with his tired, dusty column of legionaries and auxiliaries. While the men were found billets in the city, Fulvius and the commanding officers of each cohort were summoned to the governor's quarters on the acropolis, where Cato and Sempronius awaited them.

As the legionary centurions and the auxiliary prefects eased themselves down on to the benches set before the governor's desk, orderlies passed amongst them with cups of water flavoured with pressed lemons. Once they were refreshed, Sempronius slapped his hand on the table to bring them to order.

'Gentlemen, I know you are tired, so I will be brief. You have been sent to Crete to destroy the slave rebellion led by the gladiator Ajax. Our latest intelligence is that he is marching to the east of the island. He is estimated to have some twenty thousand men with him under arms, and as many camp followers.'

The officers exchanged concerned expressions as they considered the odds. Sempronius coughed. 'That is not the whole story, however. No more than a fraction of his men are properly armed and only a handful have any kind of military training, or fighting experience. Your men will have little difficulty in defeating them, provided you can pin them down and force them to battle. Once they are defeated, any last vestige of rebellious spirit encountered in the slaves is to be crushed without mercy.' He paused to let his words sink in. 'Any questions?'

Fulvius nodded. 'Do we know why they lifted the siege and marched east?'

'Not yet.'

'Do we know where they might be headed?'

Sempronius shook his head. 'No. I'm told there are no cities or major ports in their path. Just a quiet strip of coastline, near an abandoned town called Olous.'

'It's possible they may have arranged for some ships to meet them in the bay next to Olous,' Cato added, nodding towards a map of the island hanging on the far wall.

'Where would they find ships?' asked Fulvius. 'I thought most of them had been wrecked by the wave.'

'The slaves have looted plenty of gold, silver and other valuables,' Cato replied. 'I doubt they will find it difficult to find some ship owners with more avarice than principle to serve their needs. However, we have a squadron of warships waiting at Matala. If we send them to Olous we may well be able to catch the rebels between our ships and your soldiers. If we do, then they will have no choice but to turn and fight us.'

'All right, then.' Fulvius nodded. 'I'll send the order for the galleys to get moving. My men can begin the advance to Olous at first light.'

Sempronius cleared his throat and raised himself up in his chair. 'That will not be necessary, Centurion. My senior officer can give the necessary orders.'

'What?' Fulvius looked surprised. 'But I understood that Macro had been taken prisoner.'

'Yes. That's why I have selected a replacement for him.' Sempronius waved a hand at Cato. 'The tribune is to take command of the local forces and your reinforcements.'

'Him?' Fulvius stared at Cato. 'Sir, I must protest.'

'Your orders are clear enough, Centurion. You are to hand over command to me the moment you reach Gortyna. And here you are. I have chosen Tribune Cato to command our combined forces. You will serve as his second in command.'

Fulvius shook his head. 'Sir, with respect, the tribune is too young and too inexperienced to take command.'

'Really?' Sempronius leaned back in his chair, looking at Cato as he counted off on his fingers. 'Appointed optio in the Second Legion. Took part in the invasion of Britannia, where you were decorated for bravery. You and Macro rescued the family of General Plautius. You were involved in the capture of the enemy commander, Caratacus, and the subsequent defeat of the remnants of his army. Then you served with the Ravenna fleet in the pursuit and destruction of a pirate squadron operating from the coast of Illyria. After that you served in Judaea and put down a revolt. And then, when I first met you at Palmyra, you held the citadel until relieved and then went on to defeat the Parthians in a frontier battle.' Sempronius looked straight at Cato. 'Am I correct?'

'Yes, sir. But I cannot take the full credit for all that.'

Fulvius was looking at Cato with a frankly admiring expression, but then turned abruptly back to Sempronius. 'An impressive record, I'll admit, but given that Centurion Macro has been taken captive, I think I should refer this matter to my legate, sir.'

'Enough! You and Cato have your orders. There will be no further discussion of the matter. I charge you both with finding and defeating the rebels. The briefing is at an end. Tribune?'

Cato stiffened. 'Sir?'

'You have work to do. Carry on.' Sempronius rose from his chair, and all the officers hurriedly stood to attention as he strode towards the door. Once he had left the office, Cato stood at ease and there was an awkward silence as the other officers glanced from him to

Fulvius. Cato cleared his throat. 'You are all aware of our situation, gentlemen. Have your men get a good night's rest. We face something of a challenge in the days to come.' He smiled faintly. 'You are dismissed. Centurion Fulvius, remain behind.'

Fulvius nodded, and remained on his feet as the other officers filed out of the room and the last man closed the door behind him.

Cato took the chair vacated by Sempronius and met the other man's gaze steadily. 'I don't imagine you're too pleased with the governor's decision.'

'No, I'm not,' Fulvius agreed bluntly. 'I assume that list of your achievements is accurate.'

'It is.'

'You're obviously an impressive young officer,' Fulvius conceded. 'And I'm sure you will go far, in time. But ask yourself, is this the right moment to take such a risk and appoint youth over experience?'

'I thought the point of the governor's remarks was to prove that I *do* have experience,' Cato responded tersely. 'In any case, the question of who should command is academic. The governor has appointed me. Of course, I will be happy to hear any suggestions you might wish to make during the course of the campaign.'

Fulvius nodded, and Cato decided that he had better make sure that Fulvius did not take this as an invitation to undermine his authority. 'Be clear on one thing, Fulvius. I will not brook any attempt to contradict me in front of the other officers, or the men. Is that understood? If you disagree with any of my decisions, you may make your case in private only.'

'I understand.'

Cato took a deep breath. 'From now on, you will address me as "sir".'

Fulvius bit back on his irritation and saluted formally. 'Yes, sir.'

'Good.' Cato was relieved that the confrontation had been avoided, for the present. In truth he was not certain that he would be a better man for the job than Fulvius, let alone Macro. However, there was no avoiding the responsibility Sempronius had thrust upon him. Not without surrendering all of his authority to Centurion Fulvius, and he would not do that while Julia and Macro were still prisoners of the rebels. He paused, and smiled to himself as he realised that this was precisely why Sempronius had chosen him to command the force. He needed someone who would not put his daughter's life at risk. The only man who had as much stake in Julia's survival as her father was Cato. The extolling of Cato's record was merely a ruse to win Fulvius's respect, he decided bleakly. Be that as it may, he would do everything in his power to end the rebellion and save the lives of Julia and Macro.

Fulvius was watching him impatiently and Cato cleared his mind in order to consider the details of the coming campaign.

'We have to plan the advance, and co-ordinate with the warships. You'd better send for your headquarters staff. We've got a long night ahead of us.'

'Yes, sir.' Fulvius rose up, saluted and left the office. Cato stared after him for a moment, then sighed and reached for a blank wax slate and stylus to begin making his notes outlining the order of march for the men of his new command.

The column was already on the move as dawn lightened the eastern horizon in a watery pink glow. Two squadrons of cavalry rode half a mile ahead of the first cohort of legionaries. The mounted men were spread out in a screen to provide early warning of any possible ambushes, and to run down and kill or capture any rebel stragglers they might encounter on the road to Olous. Cato had made it clear to the decurions of each squadron that he wanted prisoners to question. More than anything he needed to know that Macro and Julia were still alive. There was little doubt as to the route the rebel army had taken. The country ahead of the Roman column had been ravaged by the enemy, and was marked by burned buildings, occasional bodies and the remains of fires. Cato was still puzzled by the decision Ajax had taken to abandon his siege of Gortyna so abruptly and make for the eastern coast.

Cato sat on his horse by the city gate and watched as the long column of legionaries, followed by the baggage train and then the auxiliaries, snaked out along the road that climbed towards the rolling hills on the horizon. In a few hours the warships at Matala should receive their orders and begin making their way along the southern coast. Even though the army had only sixty miles to march across the spine of the island and the fleet had to sail at least four times the distance, the ships would arrive first, with orders to seal the entrance to the bay and prevent any ships entering or leaving. If the rebels were thinking of escaping by sea, then that route would be closed to them and the approach of Cato's force would give them very limited room to manoeuvre, especially as they would be slowed down by their non-combatants.

As the tail of the column began to emerge from the city gate, Cato saw Sempronius pass through the small side arch and stride towards him.

Cato saluted. 'Good morning, sir. Come to see us off?'

Sempronius reached up and took Cato's hand. 'The gods protect you, Cato, and Julia and Macro.'

Cato nodded. 'I'll do whatever I can to bring them back.'

'I know you will.' Sempronius released his hand and stepped back a few paces as Cato tugged gently on the reins and dug his heels in, trotting the horse along the line of the auxiliary troops, burdened down by their marching yokes as they headed into the dust stirred up by those ahead of them in the column.

It took two days of hard marching to reach the hill town of Lyttus. The walls had been shaken to pieces by the earthquake and the rebels had pillaged the town and put most of the survivors to the sword. A handful of old men, women and children wandered through the ruins with numbed expressions. Cato gave orders for them to be fed and detailed a century to escort them back to Gortyna. Then, as the men made a makeshift marching camp out of the rubble from the walls, and settled for the night, Cato joined Fulvius and his staff in the small temple to Athena that had survived intact in one corner of the forum. One of the clerks was already lighting the oil lamps and distributing them to his colleagues as they sat cross-legged on the floor ready to carry out the usual compilation of strength returns and ration consumption. While Fulvius signed off each of the completed records, Cato began to read through the daily reports from the scouts that Sempronius had sent to follow the rebel army. They confirmed that Ajax was still heading east, towards Olous. Cato nodded with satisfaction. By now the rebel army would have reached the sea, and walked into a trap of its own making. It was hard to believe that Ajax could make such mistake, and for a moment Cato felt a sudden anxious doubt. There had to be something he had missed. Some reason to explain the gladiator's apparent foolishness.

Once he had finished, Cato was about to bid good night to Fulvius when there was a clatter of hooves in the forum outside the temple. One of the headquarters guards shouted a challenge as Cato looked round. A moment later a scout came running in through the entrance. He glanced round until he saw Cato in his red cloak, then hurried over and saluted.

'Beg to report, sir, I have an urgent message from my decurion.'

'He's already reported today.'

'Yes, sir. That was before we moved on a little further to camp where we could overlook the rebel army at Olous.'

'Well?'

'Sir, the bay's full of cargo ships. Big ships, sir. Most of 'em are damaged. Broken masts and suchlike. Some of them were beached, being repaired it looked like.'

Cato frowned. Where on earth could the rebels have secured so many ships? A fleet of cargo ships from the sound of things. It suddenly struck him that there was only one such fleet on the seas of the eastern Mediterranean at the moment, and he chewed his lip briefly before he asked, 'Did you see any kind of identification on the ships?'

'Yes, sir. We did. There was a purple pennant flying from the top of each mast.'

Cato took a sharp breath and glanced at Fulvius. 'You heard?'

'Yes, sir.'

'Then you know what it means.' Cato felt a sudden chill of apprehension. 'Ajax has captured the grain fleet.'

'If it's true, then what in Hades is it doing in that bay?' asked Fulvius. 'They should be well on the way to Ostia by now.'

'It was that storm,' Cato explained. 'It struck a few days after the grain fleet left. Must have blown them far off their normal route, probably wrecking some and damaging the rest. They must have put into the bay for repairs.'

Fulvius clicked his fingers. 'That's why they abandoned the siege! Ajax must have got news that the grain fleet had been forced to make for the bay.'

Cato nodded. 'And now he's got his hands on the food supply of Rome. You can be sure that if we don't do what he says, he'll destroy the fleet and all the grain. If that happens, a month from now the mob are going to be tearing Rome to pieces.'

THE BAY AT OLOUS

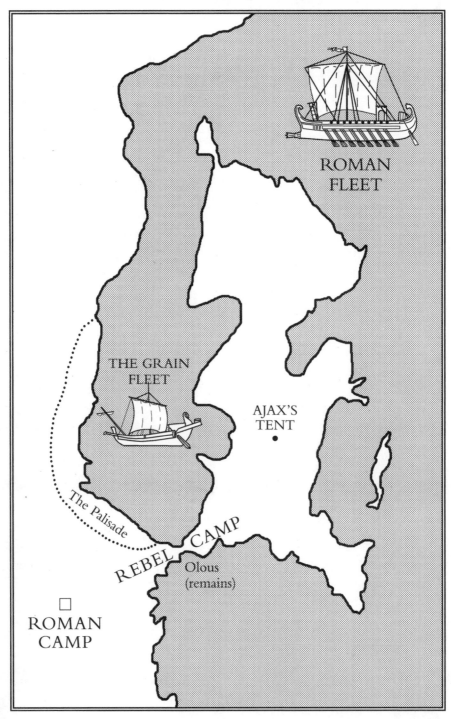

ROMAN
FLEET

THE GRAIN
FLEET

AJAX'S
TENT

The Palisade

REBEL CAMP

Olous
(remains)

ROMAN
CAMP

CHAPTER TWENTY-SEVEN

Macro stared out through the bars, down the slope of the hill into the bay. It was late in the morning and sunlight streamed through the bars of the cage, casting stark shadows across the grim interior. Around them the slaves settled into their new camp, which sprawled across the slopes of the hills. Ajax had chosen to have his tents erected on the narrow rocky peninsula that shielded the bay from the open sea. The men of his war band, together with their women and children, were camped around him in a rough circle, and Macro could see no way to escape from the camp, even if he and Julia could get out of the cage. Thanks to their filthy state they would instantly attract attention and would be quickly hunted down and recaptured the moment the alarm was raised.

Down in the bay, he could see the rebels hastily setting up defences around those ships that had been beached. A crude palisade was under construction a short distance inland, with towers at regular intervals. The crews of the grain ships, and the small marine contingents that had been put aboard to protect them from pirates, were being held in a stockade in the heart of the main camp. The ships themselves were now under close guard by the rebels. The most heavily damaged by the storm were beached, while the rest were rafted together and lay at anchor out in the bay. Ajax was taking no chances with his precious prizes, with good reason. Turning his head, Macro could glimpse the sea between two of the tents that comprised the rebel leader's headquarters. The unmistakable lines of three Roman warships lay hove to a mile from shore. That was something at least, he mused. Ajax might have captured the grain fleet, but he would not be able to use the ships to escape the island.

Macro's gaze flickered to Julia as she leaned into the opposite corner of the cage. Her head hung forward and was shrouded by the matted hair that hung down across her shoulders.

'You awake?' Macro asked softly. 'Julia?'

She looked up slowly, and he could see from the glistening streaks over the grime on her face that she had been crying again. She swallowed and licked her lips.

'I'm thirsty,' she croaked.

'Me too.'

They were given water at dawn, noon and dusk, along with a greasy thin gruel. It had been that way since they had been put into the cage, and each day of the march since the rebel army had suddenly quit the siege of Gortyna. Ajax had ordered that his prisoners be fed on the same diet that had been provided to slaves on the farming estates. At the appointed time the same old crone and a burly member of the rebel leader's bodyguard came to the cage to feed them. The routine was always the same. The man would order them to shuffle to the back of the cage before unlocking the door to admit the old woman. She quickly set down two battered copper pots with ladles, gruel in one, water in the other, and then retreated from the cage. On the first day even Macro's iron stomach revolted at the terrible smell of the stew of rancid gristle, fat and barley. But hunger had a way of making things palatable, and he soon grew to savour the small quantity of food that he was allowed. The water became increasingly precious as well, and the heat during the day was a torment of dry throat, leathery tongue and cracked lips.

The conditions of their imprisonment were made immeasurably worse by the lack of any arrangements for their sanitation and they had to live with the stench of their own filth. It had been bad enough for Macro to be stripped of all his clothes in front of Julia, and to have to live under such conditions, but Julia had never suffered any indignity like this, nor even imagined such an intolerable existence. Macro had tried to help her in any way that he could, by looking away when she needed to go, and by deliberately avoiding looking at her except straight in the eye. Fortunately she had been given a torn cloak by the old hag who brought them food. It had been thrust at her and Julia had seized it at once, wrapping herself in its rank, ripped folds. Even with this small comfort she had quickly become numbed by the grimness of it all and retreated into long periods of silence. Macro regarded her suffering with a growing burden of sorrow. She was young and beautiful, and in love with Cato. She did not deserve such a fate as this.

As he thought of his friend, Macro's sorrow increased. The girl was as dear to Cato as anything else in the world. Her loss would break the lad's heart. And, Macro was human enough to realise, his own death would be a hard blow for Cato. They were as close as brothers, though sometimes Macro felt they were more like father and son, and he dreaded Cato doing something rash once he discovered that they had been taken prisoner. Assuming that Cato was alive, he mused grimly.

Ajax had constructed their torment perfectly, Macro reflected. They were permitted to live, but stripped of every dignity, kept like animals – no, worse than animals. With little possibility of escape, and no seeming chance of being freed as a result of negotiations, a grim future awaited them, until the day that Ajax tired of their torment and had them butchered. Until then Macro watched for any opportunities and tried to keep his muscles exercised as far as possible in the confined space, so that his body wasn't stiff and hobbled if he needed to act swiftly.

He turned to Julia and forced himself to smile. 'Not long until noon.'

'Long enough,' she whispered, leaning her head back against the bars and squinting at the brilliant sunlight lancing through the slots overhead. She shut her eyes and was silent for a while before she spoke again. 'How many days have we been in here?'

Macro had to concentrate hard for a moment. Even though he had been keeping count, for some reason he doubted the number he had in his head. He counted back just to check. 'I make it sixteen. Yes, sixteen, I'm sure of it.'

'Sixteen days,' Julia sighed. 'Feels like sixteen years . . . I wish I was dead.'

'Don't say that,' Macro replied in a kindly tone. 'While we're alive, there's always hope.'

She uttered a cracked laugh. 'Alive? You call this being alive?'

'Yes, yes, I do.' Macro did his best to sit up straight and stare at Julia. 'We will get out of here, Julia. Don't let go of that thought. I swear it to you, in the name of all the gods. We will get out of here.'

She looked at him hopefully, then nodded with a sad smile. 'You're right, of course. They'll drag us out of this cage to kill us. Or maybe we'll be left to die in here and one day someone will pull our bodies out and throw us into a ditch for the rats and dogs and crows to feast on.'

'Stop that!' Macro snapped, then forced himself to smile gently. 'You're making me hungry.'

Julia stared at him intensely for an instant and then burst into laughter. Macro joined in, roaring with mirth and desperate relief that some spark of the old Julia still lived on. A handful of the nearest rebels turned to look curiously at the filthy figures in the cage, and then one of the gladiator's bodyguards came over and poked the butt of his spear through the bars and into Macro's back.

'Quiet, you!'

'Fuck off,' Macro growled back, and the man rammed the butt home again, much harder this time, sending a searing pain round Macro's ribs. He snatched a breath of air and gritted his teeth as he rode out the pain. The guard grunted, spat through the bars and then slowly strode back to the shade of a stunted olive tree.

'Macro, are you all right?' Julia was looking at him anxiously.

'I'll live,' he winced. 'But that bastard won't, the moment I get out of here.'

'Brave words.'

'I mean it. I'm going to take that spear and ram it so far up his arsehole I'll knock his fucking teeth out . . . Sorry, pardon my Gallic, miss.'

Julia shook her head. 'Don't worry. I think we've gone some way towards outgrowing social niceties in recent days.'

'Somewhat easier for me than you, I imagine.'

'Yes . . .' Julia shifted and then let out a low groan, trying to find a more comfortable position as she leaned her back against the bars.

Macro turned his head and examined the scene down in the bay again. The cargo ships were large, bulky affairs that would be completely at the mercy of any Roman warships that they might encounter. However, the rebels would have plenty of warning that the warships were coming. The peninsula stretched out for the best part of two miles before it reached the narrow straits leading out to the sea. Ajax's men would see immediately if the Roman warships approached the entrance to the bay. There would be enough time to burn or sink all the grain ships.

He was suddenly aware of a light snuffling sound and turned back to see that Julia was trying to hide her tears again.

He opened his mouth to offer some comfort, but found there was nothing he could say. There was no comfort to offer. None at all, he realised.

'Macro?'

'Yes, miss?'

'Sometimes I wish you had killed me, back when you had the chance.'

Macro felt a surge of guilt at her words. There were moments when he too wished he had not hesitated, that he had killed Julia with a quick sword thrust and then had time to turn his blade on himself. But he despised himself for even considering such an end when there was always a chance, however slim, to escape or get revenge. He cleared his throat. 'I would have done it, but I was knocked down before I could strike. Perhaps the gods spared us for a reason.'

'Really? And what reason would that be? To see how long we could endure this?' Julia let out a dry laugh, then coughed for a moment before she fell silent. At length she spoke again, in an anxious tone.

'Do you think Cato will still want me if we get through this?'

'Of course! Why would you ever doubt it?'

She bit her lip and glanced down at her body. 'Look at me. I'm disgusting. I am dirt. This . . . filth is so ground into me that I shall stink of it for ever.'

'It's nothing that a good scrub won't deal with,' Macro replied lightly. 'You'll see. When it's all over you can have a bath, a scrape-down and a hot meal and the world will be a completely different place. And there'll be Cato. You'll be a sight for his sore eyes, I can tell you.'

'There are some things, some kinds of dirt, that no amount of scrubbing can erase, Macro.' She looked quickly at him. 'I'm no fool, you know.'

'I never thought you were.'

'Then don't humour me. If – when – the time comes that Ajax tires of keeping us in here, he's going to torture us, isn't he?'

Macro's silence was eloquent enough for Julia, and she continued. 'I overheard some of his guards one night, soon after we were taken. They were talking about a woman who had been kept in this cage before us. The wife of Hirtius. When Ajax tired of keeping her, he turned her over to his men.' Julia shuddered. 'They used her all night, in whatever ways they could imagine. She was begging them to kill her before the end, but they ignored her and continued, until finally they left her to bleed to death. Macro, I can't face that. Even if I lived through it, I could never be with another man again. No one would have me. Not Cato anyway. I would be dishonoured and he would look at me with disgust in his eyes and turn away.' She gulped back her emotions and spoke so softly that Macro could barely hear her. 'I might survive the rest of it, but not that. Not losing Cato.'

'You underestimate him, miss. Cato is not some chinless wonder. He has a deeper sense of honour, and compassion. I tried to beat that out of him in the early days, but he was a stubborn bastard. Still is. He loves you, and that's all that will matter to him when he finds you again.'

'You really think so?' She looked at him with hope in her eyes.

'I know it. Now, that's enough crying.' Macro nodded his head towards the nearest rebels, clustered about a camp fire as they watched a suckling pig turn slowly over a pile of embers. 'We have to appear strong and fearless in front of those bastards. You can do it, miss. Just remember, you're a Roman aristocrat. You have a tradition to uphold.'

'But I'm afraid.'

'And so am I,' Macrao admitted. 'But you can choose not to let them use it against you. That is the only way we can defy Ajax at the moment. So, chin up and keep a brave face on for those bastards over there.'

'I'll try.'

Macro sensed a shadow at his shoulder and then a voice spoke close to his ear. 'Fine words, Centurion. We'll see how brave you can be when the time comes to do to you what you did to my father.'

Ajax moved round to the end of the cage and squatted down where they could both see him. He had a chicken leg in one hand and raised it to his mouth to take a bite. Then his nose wrinkled and he tossed the leg to one side. Almost at once, a pair of seagulls whirled down and began to fight over the meat, pecking away at each other savagely.

'You stink, the pair of you. More than enough to put me off my food.' He stared at his captives for a moment and sneered. 'Who would believe that two such disgusting examples of humanity could belong to the great Roman empire? You are like swine, rolling in your own filth. I wonder what your emperor would say if he could see you now? And you, woman, what would your father, the governor, think if he beheld you now as I do? I would not blame him if he disowned you. After all, you are not fit for decent company. And that's before I let my men loose on you.'

Macro saw Julia recoil at the thought, pressing herself into the far corner of the cage. Ajax laughed at her reaction and Macro felt a surge of rage sweep through his veins.

'You leave the girl alone, you bastard! If you want your fun, then take it out on me. She's just a girl. But me? I'm a centurion, a man of the legions. I'm your challenge, Ajax. Try and break me, if you dare.'

Ajax had an amused expression on his face during Macro's outburst, and he shook his head mockingly. 'It's as I thought. The best fun to be had is in letting you watch the governor's daughter die first, in front of your eyes. Something for you to dwell on before we come for you, Centurion. Then, while you are left to rot on the cross, you'll have plenty of time to remember what happened to her. And you'll know it's all your fault. If you had not killed my father and sold me into slavery, none of us would be here now.'

'If your father had not been a murdering pirate bastard then I would not have had to crucify him in the first place.' Macro smiled. 'Credit where credit is due, eh, sunshine?'

For a moment Ajax's features froze into a mask of bitter hatred, then he breathed in and took control of his feelings with a slow smile. 'I think I might just nail you to the crosspiece in person, Macro. Yes, I think I should like that a great deal.'

'Is that what you are keeping us for? I thought it was because we might be useful hostages.'

'Oh yes, that was the reason once. But then the girl's father decided that stubborn defiance was a greater virtue than paternal affection. And now I have hostages infinitely more valuable than you two.' Ajax edged to one side and gestured towards the captured ships. 'At one stroke I have the power to feed Rome, or let her starve. Once the emperor knows that I have his grain fleet, he will have to discuss terms with me.'

Now it was Macro's turn to sneer. 'And what makes you think he should bother with you? Those are Roman warships outside the bay. You cannot escape with those cargo ships, and you cannot defend them adequately if they remain in the bay. The navy will pick its own time, then sail in bold as brass and take those ships from you.'

'Really? You must think I was born yesterday,' Ajax mocked him. 'Those warships will not dare to enter the bay, because the moment they do, I shall give the order to burn the grain fleet. So, my dear friends, you can see the situation for yourselves. I have got your emperor by the balls. Sadly, that makes you two little more than a detail, an entertainment, and the time is fast approaching when I will have no further need of you.'

CHAPTER TWENTY-EIGHT

Cato gave orders for the camp to be constructed on the high ground overlooking Olous as the column completed the fourth day's march. The auxiliaries advanced a short way down the slope to form a protective screen while the legionaries set down their marching yokes, took up their pickaxes and shovels and began to dig into the stony ground. It was hot and the work was back-breaking after a hard day's march, but it was part of the daily routine while on campaign, and aside from the usual grumbling the men carried out their work efficiently. By the time the sun had set behind the hills to the west, a ditch surrounded the camp, within which a rampart and palisade provided adequate defence against any attempt at a surprise attack.

Once the camp was ready, the auxiliaries were called in and the column settled down for the night. There was no moon in the sky, and though the stars shone brilliantly, the landscape was wreathed in darkness. Mindful of the enemy's willingness to take the initiative, Cato doubled the watch and had a full cohort stand to along the palisade and keep watch over the approaches to the camp. Accompanied by Fulvius, he made an inspection of the defences before the two of them returned to the headquarters tents in the heart of the camp, occupying a small mound overlooking the ramparts and on towards the enemy. The fires of the rebels glittered in a huge arc around the dark waters of the bay, dwarfing the neat lines of the Roman camp. Out at sea, three lamps glimmered where the warships lay hove to, keeping watch on the entrance to the bay. The rest of the fleet was beached in a cove some miles to the north, and Cato had sent for the navarch in command of the ships to come and report to him the next day.

'The buggers aren't short of men,' Fulvius muttered as he surveyed the enemy.

Cato shrugged. 'Numbers aren't everything. We have better men and the better position. If they attack, they'll have to do it uphill, and they'll have to get over the ditch and the palisade. Our men can deal with any of them that get close enough to come to blows.'

'I hope you're right, sir,' Fulvius muttered. 'So what happens now? Looks like something of a stand-off. We can beat off their attacks, but we might not have sufficient men to take their camp.'

'The situation is to our advantage. We're camped across the only road out of Olous to the rest of the island. The navy blocks access to the sea, so we have them trapped. The main problem for us will be keeping supplied with food and water. We have enough for five more days before I have to send a detachment back to Gortyna with the wagons for more rations. Of course, that's not a problem for the rebels now that they have their hands on the grain fleet. They could live off that for months. With the streams that run off the hills, they won't be short of water either. However, the reality is that it is their turn to be under siege.'

Fulvius seemed doubtful, and gestured to the hills surrounding the bay. 'If they wanted to get away, they could slip over these hills easily enough.'

'If they wanted to get away. But they don't. They have their carts and wagons with them, weighed down by loot, and then there's the grain fleet. That is their one chance to cut a deal with Rome. And that's why Ajax won't abandon those ships.' Cato paused and looked over to where a line of torches marked the palisade that had been erected to protect the beached ships. 'The trick of it will be in finding a way of separating the rebels from the ships. We have to act soon. The grain fleet has already been delayed. Before long the stocks in the imperial warehouses are going to be exhausted, and Rome will starve. If we can't rescue those ships in time . . .'

Cato turned away and strode towards his tent. Fulvius scratched his cheek for a moment and then followed his superior. Inside the tent, Cato had unfastened the clasp of his cloak and flung it over towards his bedroll. There were few of the usual refinements of a senior officer in the tent, since there had been no time to arrange for any at Gortyna. Comfort had been the last thing on his mind when Cato set off in pursuit of the rebels, and so there was only a small campaign table and a handful of chests containing the column's pay records, strength returns and spare waxed slates. He yawned as he unfastened the buckles of his harness and drew it, and then the chainmail vest, over his head. He let them drop heavily by the bedroll. The march in the hot sun, and his exhaustion, had left him with a headache, and he declined the wine that Fulvius offered him from a jug that had been left out by one of the headquarters servants.

Fulvius shrugged, and filled a goblet almost to the brim before he eased himself down on to a chest with a sigh. 'So then, what do we do now?'

'Nothing we can do tonight. Tomorrow we'll scout the enemy camp and see if there are any weak points that we might attack.'

'You are thinking of an attack then?' Fulvius probed.

'I don't see what else I can do. Some of the grain ships will no doubt be lost during the fight, but we have to rescue what we can and hope that it is enough to keep Rome going until another fleet can be gathered to fetch more grain from Egypt. It'll be a bloody business if we have to attack, and if anything goes wrong, if the men break, then we'll be cut to pieces.'

'The lads of the Twenty-Second won't let you down, sir. They'll fight well, and if the attack fails then they'll keep formation when we fall back.'

'I hope you are right,' Cato replied wearily. 'Now then, that's all for tonight. I'm turning in.'

Fulvius drained his cup and stood up. 'I'll have one last turn round the camp, sir. So I can sleep easy.'

'Very well.' Cato nodded. Once the centurion had left the tent, he took off his boots, extinguished the oil lamp and lay down on the bedroll. Even though it was a hot night, there was a gentle breeze blowing, enough to cool Cato's brow and make it worth keeping his tunic on. His head felt thick with exhaustion, and it was a struggle to think clearly as he lay and stared up at the goatskin tent overhead. The moment he tried to settle into a comfortable position to sleep, his mind filled with images of Julia and Macro. If they were still alive, they were not more than a mile or two from where he lay. It had taken every fibre of his self-control to hide his feelings from Fulvius and the other men under his command. Inside, his heart felt like a lump of lead, weighing his body down. The worst moments came when his imagination thrust images of their torment to the front of his mind, making him feel sick with helplessness and despair until he forced such thoughts aside and concentrated his mind elsewhere.

He lay on his mattress, turning frequently, and ended up curled in a ball on his side before his weary body and exhausted mind finally succumbed to sleep.

Cato was woken by the blare of a buccina sounding the change of watch. He blinked his eyes open and winced at the stiffness in his back. Sunlight slanted through the open flaps of the tent and he instantly scrambled to his feet, furious that he had not been roused. He pulled on his boots and laced them up before hurrying out of the tent. Before him lay the camp, the men calmly going about their morning duties as they cleaned their mess tins and packed them away in their kit sacks before making ready their armour and weapons for morning inspection. Centurion Fulvius was sitting at a table in front of one of the other tents, writing notes on a wax tablet. He stood up and saluted as Cato came striding across to him with an icy expression.

'Why was I not woken at the end of the night watch?'

'There was no need, sir.' Fulvius affected a surprised look. 'The watch officers had nothing to report and there's been no sign of any movement down at the rebel camp. I was just about to complete the orders for the morning cavalry patrols before I came to wake you.'

Cato lowered his voice so that only Fulvius would hear. 'You know damn well that the senior officer should be woken at first light.'

'I had no orders to that effect, sir.'

'Damn orders, it's customary. Even when a unit is on garrison duties. On campaign there's never any question about it.'

Fulvius did not respond, thereby intimating his guilt. Cato glared at him for a moment, and then snorted with derision. 'Tell me, when was the last time you served on a campaign?'

'It's been a while, sir,' Fulvius admitted. 'In my previous legion, on the Danube.'

'How long ago?'

The centurion's gaze wavered. 'Twelve years, sir.'

'And since then you have served in Egypt: garrison duty. Little to keep you occupied but spit and polish and the odd field exercise, eh?'

'Keeps the lads on their toes, sir.'

'I don't doubt it.' Cato recalled the endless drills and route marches of his earliest months in the Second Legion. It was not the readiness of the men he questioned. 'So, having ducked out of the fighting for the last twelve years, you think you are better qualified to lead these men than I am. Is that it?'

'Something like that.' Fulvius was still for a moment and pursed his lips. 'Permission to speak freely, sir?'

'No. Centurion, I am the commander of this column and that fact ends any discussion on this matter. If you question my authority, or undermine established procedures again, I will have you removed from your position and sent back to Gortyna. Is that understood?'

'Yes, sir,' Fulvius replied sourly.

'I will not warn you again,' Cato growled through clenched teeth. 'Now get out of my sight. I want you to do a spot inspection of the first three legionary cohorts, and report back to me once you've done. Go.'

Cato saw a glimmer of anxiety in the veteran's eyes. Then he stood at attention, saluted and strode off to carry out his orders. Cato shook his head, then turned and marched back to his tent, barking at one of the orderlies to bring him some bread, meat and watered wine for breakfast. As he sat and stared down towards the rebel camp, he considered the stand-off once again. Ajax had the grain fleet, and therefore no need to attack the Romans, while Cato risked the loss of the grain fleet if he attacked, as well as having the added concern of commanding too few men to guarantee victory. Yet time was on the rebels' side, and there was no avoiding the conclusion that Cato would have to attack, whatever the odds.

As he was dipping the last hunk of bread into the bowl of wine, he noticed a movement down at the enemy camp. A small column of riders had emerged from the sprawl of tents and haze of smoke from the camp fires. They passed through their picket line and continued steadily up the slope towards the Roman camp. Cato soon lost sight of them behind the rampart and left the table to fetch his mail vest, helmet and sword belt from the tent, before making his way down to the rampart facing the rebel camp. By the time he reached the rampart the duty centurion had ordered his men to stand to. A cohort of legionaries were spreading out along the beaten earth of the walkway to face the approaching horsemen. Cato glanced at them as he climbed the ladder on to the platform constructed over the timber gates. Fulvius was already there and nodded a greeting to Cato as the latter joined him.

'Looks like the rebels want to talk,' said Fulvius.

Cato saw that there were ten of them, wearing good tunics, scale armour and Roman pattern swords – the spoils of Centurion Marcellus's column. One man carried a long standard with a bright blue pennant, which he waved steadily from side to side as he and his companions walked the mounts forward.

'Nice to see them observing the appropriate formalities,' Fulvius muttered. 'Just like a proper army, eh, sir?'

'Well, they certainly look the part, in our kit.'

'Our kit?' Fulvius's expression darkened. 'Oh, yes . . . Want me to order some of our boys to loose some slingshot in their direction?'

'No,' Cato replied firmly. 'I don't want them touched. The rebels have hostages.'

Fulvius shrugged. 'Assuming they're still alive, sir.'

'They're alive.'

The riders stopped fifty paces from the gate, and then one edged his horse a little closer. Cato saw that he had the dark features of the east, and he wore a curved sword at his side.

Fulvius cupped a hand to his mouth and bellowed, 'Stop there!'

The rider reined in obediently.

'What do you want?'

'My general wishes to talk with your commander. Here, in the open.'

'Why? Tell us what he wants and go!'

The rider shook his head. 'That is for my general to say.'

'Bollocks to him,' Fulvius muttered and drew a deep breath to shout his answer.

'Wait!' said Cato. He turned to Fulvius. 'Keep the men on the rampart, but have a cavalry squadron brought up to the gate, mounted and ready to charge. If I raise my left hand, send them out at once. But only if I give the signal. Is that clear?'

'You're not going out there?' Fulvius arched an eyebrow. 'For fuck's sake, sir. It's a trap. They'll get you out there and cut you down before turning tail and running.'

'Why would they do that?'

'To undermine the column, sir. Take out the commander and it's bound to hit morale, and disrupt the campaign.'

'If it is a trap and they kill me, that makes you the new commander.' Cato looked at him steadily. 'Are you saying you're not up to the job? I thought you wanted it. Maybe this is your chance.'

Centurion Fulvius had the good grace to let a look of shame flit across his features before he composed himself and shook his head. 'Not this way, sir. You watch yourself out there, understand?'

Cato smiled to himself as he turned away and climbed down from the tower. At the bottom he turned to the section of legionaries manning the gate. 'Open it up, but be ready to close it quickly if you get the order.'

As the men removed the locking bar and hauled the gate inwards, Fulvius called to one of his officers and gave them orders to have one of the mounted squadrons called to the gate as swiftly as possible. Cato puffed his cheeks and marched out of the camp, between the two ditches on either side, and on to the clear ground. Ahead of him the horsemen watched in silence. When he reached a point halfway between the gate and the waiting rebels, Cato stopped and called out to the man who had spoken for them.

'I am Tribune Cato, commander of the Roman column and the Roman fleet. Where is your general?'

There was a sudden movement from the rear of the group of horsemen as a rider spurred his horse forward and galloped it up the gentle slope. Cato sucked in a deep breath and his muscles tensed, ready for action. He let his hand drop towards the handle of his sword, where it hovered for an instant before he willed it to settle by his thigh. Straightening his back, he stood his ground and stared defiantly at the approaching horseman. At the last moment the rider reined in, less than ten feet from Cato, showering him with grit. The sun was behind the rebel and Cato had to squint and then raise a hand to shield his eyes. For a moment not a word was spoken, then the rebel gave a soft, menacing chuckle.

'The gods are kind to me, Roman. So kind.'

'Ajax?' Cato felt his heartbeat quicken.

'Of course. You remember me then?'

'Yes.'

'And you remember what you did to my father, before you had me sold into slavery?'

'I recall that we executed the leader of a gang of pirates.'

'We?'

Cato froze as he realised his mistake. Macro was in enough danger already, if he was still alive. He cleared his throat. 'The Ravenna fleet was charged with destroying the pirate threat.'

'It's funny, I seem to recall things being a little bit more personal than that. You see, I recall – very, very clearly – the names and faces of the two officers in charge of my father's execution, and they were there again when I was led away into slavery with survivors of my father's fleet. You were one of those men. The other I have already had the great pleasure to encounter once again.'

Cato felt his throat tighten and he concentrated on the man in front of him, fighting to control his expression. 'I take it your hostages are still alive.'

'They are. For the present.'

'Get down off your horse,' Cato ordered. 'I do not care to speak to you with the sun in my eyes.'

'Very well, Roman.' Ajax swung his leg over the horse's back and dropped to the ground close to Cato, but Cato did not flinch. Out of the glare of the sun, he could now see the man clearly. Ajax wore a simple tunic, plain boots and a sword belt slung across his shoulder. Tall, broad-shouldered and powerfully built, he was young, but his features were more lined and scarred than the face Cato dimly recalled from years earlier. There was something about the eyes, too. They were watchful and far-seeing, and Cato guessed that his time in the arena meant that Ajax was a man who missed nothing and was capable of reacting to any threat in an instant.

'More comfortable?' Ajax sneered.

'You wanted to talk to me,' Cato responded flatly. 'So talk.'

'I'll get to the point when I am good and ready. Before then, I am curious to know what you think of our little situation. It is not without dramatic interest, wouldn't you agree?'

'I am not interested in your games, slave. Just speak your piece and go.'

'Slave?' Ajax frowned briefly. 'Not any more. Not when your emperor concedes to my demands.'

'State your demands then, before you bore me any further.' Cato slowly folded his arms, loosely, with his left hand on top in case he needed to signal his men.

'I will, but first, tell me how it feels to be responsible for all of this.' Ajax gestured at the two armies. 'All the bloodshed during this rebellion. Surely you cannot sleep easily with all this on your conscience.'

Cato did not reply at once, then spoke with deliberate emphasis. 'This is your doing, Ajax. The retribution that Rome will visit on your followers will be your responsibility, not mine. If you surrender now, and give up your hostages, I give you my word that I will plead the case for leniency to be shown to your followers.'

'While I go the same way as my father?'

'Of course. How could it be otherwise? After all that you have done.'

'You are too generous.' Ajax laughed drily. 'You should take some of the credit.'

'Really?'

'Oh yes. You see, every day since you and your friend made me a slave, I have vowed to have my revenge. If I am honest, I never really expected to have the chance, but it kept me alive and kept my wits keen when so many others might have died in the arena. So, I have you to thank for that. You . . .' He pointed his finger at Cato's chest. 'It was you who made this rebellion possible, and you who will be the cause of Rome's humiliation. And,' Ajax's eyes flashed with inspiration and he smiled, 'and yes! It is you who will be the cause of your own greatest torment. But I am getting ahead of myself.' He paused and then pulled a red strip of cloth from inside his tunic. 'I have decided to give you a demonstration, Roman. To prove that I am serious, and to discourage you from any rash course of action.' He turned and pointed to the beached ships. 'You see that one on the end, apart from the others?'

Cato looked, and nodded.

'Good. Then watch.' Ajax extended his arm and waved the strip of red cloth slowly from side to side as it rippled gently in the light breeze. There was an answering signal from the deck of the grain ship, and moments later Cato saw a tiny glitter and a thin trail of smoke. The spark quickly spread as a handful of men scrambled from the bows on to the sand. A tongue of flame shot up from the main cargo hatch and within moments the ship was ablaze and a cloud of smoke billowed over the decks. Ajax turned back towards Cato.

'There. Every one of the remaining ships is ready to be fired the moment I give the signal. You had better bear that in mind in case you are thinking of making a surprise attack to seize the grain fleet. Now then, on to my demands.' Ajax raised his hands and counted them off. 'One, you send word to your governor that he is to issue a proclamation, in the name of Emperor Claudius and the senate, declaring that all slaves on the island of Crete are to be set free at once. Before you protest, I know that he has the authority to do this. Whether Rome ratifies it or not is not my concern. By then, my followers and I will be long gone. If the governor is not here with the proclamation in his hands five days from now, I will start destroying all of the ships. Two, after we have the proclamation, signed, sealed and delivered by the governor in person, you will allow my followers and me to board the ships and sail unhindered from this bay. Once we have decided on a safe place to land we will hand the ships over to you.'

'What's to stop you burning the ships after you have reached wherever it is that you intend to sail to?'

'Nothing.' Ajax smiled. 'You'll have to trust me.'

'Trust you?'

'You have no choice. And there's one other thing.' Ajax looked straight into Cato's eyes, and his lips parted in an icy grin. 'I imagine that you are wondering about the fate of the hostages . . . your friends?'

'Why should I?' Cato replied evenly. 'They are as good as dead already.'

'Your face betrays you. I think they mean far more to you than you would ever admit. If not, then the last demand I shall give you will be the easiest to comply with. Three, I will send a man back here tomorrow, at dawn. You will give him your response to this question.' Ajax paused, savouring the moment. 'I want you to choose who I will let live, Centurion Macro, or Julia Sempronia. It is your choice, Tribune Cato. You will tell my man who is to live and who is to die when he comes. If you fail to give him an answer, then I will have them both put to death, in full view of your camp, and I give you my word that their deaths will be long and painful.'

An icy dread filled Cato's body. He could not think, could not utter a response. So he stood and stared.

Ajax read his reaction well and nodded with satisfaction. 'Until tomorrow then, Tribune.'

He remounted his horse and spurred it back towards his followers, and then led them back down the hill at a gallop. Cato stood still and watched them, tracking the small band as it wound through the rebel camp, around the end of the bay towards a small hillock on the peninsula stretching into the sea. Only then did he turn and walk slowly back towards the gates of the Roman camp.

CHAPTER TWENTY-NINE

'We have to attack tonight,' Cato decided, after he related the demands made by Ajax.

The other officers in the tent stirred uneasily. Outside, the noon sun beat down on the Roman camp. The wind had died away during the morning, so that the air inside the tent was stifling. Cato had summoned his senior officers the moment Decius Balbus, the navarch, had reached the camp, after his gruelling ride from the bay where his squadron lay at anchor. Cato had made up his mind to attack the rebel camp as he had made his way back to his headquarters after confronting Ajax.

Centurion Casca, the prefect of the cavalry cohort, responded first. 'Sir, you said that the enemy would set fire to all the ships at the first sign of an attack.'

Cato nodded. 'That was what Ajax said, and I believe him.'

'Then why attack? The fleet will be burned and the people in Rome will starve. Surely the priority is to save the grain ships and send them on to Rome as soon as possible.'

'Even if that means agreeing to his demands?'

Balbus scratched his chin and thought a moment before speaking. 'If you attack, and he destroys the fleet, then we will have a political disaster on our hands. If you agree to his demands, then Rome will avoid starvation. You will, of course, be condemned for bowing to the will of this rebel and his army of slaves. I imagine that the emperor and the senate will show you no mercy.' He paused and looked directly at Cato. 'It seems to me that the choice is between the lives of many in Rome, or your shame and exile or execution, sir.'

Cato smiled slightly. 'You are right, and the choice is mine. However, I think there is something else you have to consider. What if we go along with Ajax, and he still destroys the grain ships?'

'Is that likely?' asked Fulvius. 'Why would he do that?'

'It's simple,' Cato replied. 'He hates Rome with every fibre of his being. And he hates me almost as much.'

'You? Why, sir?'

'It's a long story, but the key to it is that Ajax holds me, and Prefect Macro, responsible for the crucifixion of his father, and for his own enslavement. This is as much about having revenge on us as it is about winning his freedom.'

'Forgive me, sir, but are you certain of this?' Fulvius continued in a cautious tone. 'Is there a danger that you are exaggerating your influence over this man's actions?'

'I have thought about it carefully. I've been over every detail of the man and his words that I can recall from our encounter earlier this morning. I am certain that he means to do me, and Rome, as much harm as possible. Ajax lives for revenge. When he spoke to me, every word was calculated to increase my fear for my friends. He wants to see me tormented for as long as possible before delivering the final crushing blow. I could see it in his eyes.' Cato winced at the memory of the glint of madness in the gladiator's gaze. 'I am sure of it. He will burn those ships the moment he is confident that he and his followers are beyond our reach. If I am right, then we have nothing to lose in risking an attack. Those ships are doomed if we do anything else. That is why we must try to save them as soon as possible. I'm hoping that if we make the attempt tonight, we may catch the rebels by surprise.' Cato let the words of his argument sink in for a moment.

Balbus still seemed unconvinced. 'If the attack fails to take them by surprise and they set fire to the ships, then the emperor is not going to be persuaded that the rebels were planning on doing it anyway. Claudius will want the heads of those responsible for the destruction of the grain ships, sir.'

Fulvius rounded on the navarch. 'Then we'll bloody well have to make sure the attack is a success, right? You and the navy do your bit, and we'll do ours.'

Cato briefly felt his heart warm to his subordinate, before he responded, 'Balbus, if it puts your mind at rest, I will assume full responsibility for ordering the attack. I'll have that in writing for any officer here that requests it.'

The navarch nodded and replied flatly, 'Thank you, sir. I would appreciate it. On the off chance that the attack goes tits up and the ships are burned.'

Cato sighed wearily. 'Well, there's no point in having more of us paying the price of failure than necessary, is there?'

'No, sir,' Balbus agreed easily. Then he tilted his head slightly to one side with a questioning expression. 'There is one thing though.'

'Oh?'

'Why is there a need to attack tonight? It seems a bit rushed to me.'

Cato stood still and stared back at the navarch. This was the point of the meeting that he had feared. The question was fair, and although the answer he had prepared was well reasoned from a tactical point of view, he knew that his personal feelings had played the most important part in reaching his decision. If these men were to risk their lives in an attack, it was only right that Cato took them into his confidence and told them the full truth. He cleared his throat to address them in a voice unclouded by emotion.

'Most of you know that the rebels took the governor's daughter and Prefect Macro prisoner some time ago. Ajax let me know that they are still alive, and being held in his camp.'

'Then they will surely be killed the moment we attack,' said Balbus. 'All the more reason to delay any action. At least until you can try to negotiate their release.'

Cato shook his head. 'We can't wait. Ajax has promised to put one of them to death at dawn tomorrow. He said that I must choose which one. If I refuse, then he will have both of them killed. That is why the attack has to go in tonight.'

'Shit,' Fulvius muttered, looking at Cato in horror as the full implication of the threat struck him. 'I'm so sorry, sir.'

Cato rubbed his jaw. 'Ajax is playing games with us. All part of his plan to torment me as far as he can. In fact, this is an opportunity for us. If Ajax thinks that I am so paralysed with concern and indecision for my friends, then he will not be expecting me to act decisively. He will also assume that I dare not attack for fear of putting their lives at risk. That is why we must go in tonight, while there is still a chance of achieving an element of surprise.'

'What if this is a ploy to provoke you into an attack?' asked Balbus. 'To get you to act tonight?'

'Why would he do that? If I attack and the ships are set on fire, then the rebels have nothing to negotiate with.'

'Assuming that he has given orders to set fire to the ships.'

'Then why tell me that he has given such orders if he wants to provoke me into an attack?' Cato sighed wearily. 'Look, Balbus, you can't have it both ways.'

Cato was tired of discussion. He had known that there was bound to be some dissent over his orders. Balbus was clearly one of those officers for whom caution was a religion and indecision was dignified by claiming to consider every possible contingency, while acting upon none of them. It was a classic case of paralysis through prevarication. He could understand why Macro became so frustrated on such occasions and opted for the most direct solution to a problem. He had made his decision, Cato resolved to himself. He glanced round at his officers.

'The attack will go ahead tonight, gentlemen. Now, we must turn our attention to the plan.'

He picked up a roll of parchment on which he had sketched out a plan of the bay earlier in the morning. He laid it out across the table and called for his officers to gather round the other three sides of the table while he briefed them.

'The rebel camp is spread round the end of the bay, with the shore-based side protected by the palisade. There is a small redoubt at the end of the palisade to guard that flank since it is the most vulnerable. On the other side of the bay, on this peninsula, is where Ajax is camped. I believe that is the most likely place for him to be keeping his hostages. He is protected from any landward attack by the bulk of his army, and from the sea by the cliffs and rocks on the far side. There is a small bay with a sandy beach towards the end of the peninsula, but it's well guarded and too small to attempt any landing in force.' Cato paused as the officers examined the map. 'Our objective is simple. We must find some way of preventing the rebels, from setting fire to the ships before we capture them.'

'Nigh on impossible, sir,' Fulvius said at length. 'We have three choices. We either attack by land, or by sea, or both. The trouble is, the rebels will see us coming. Any attack from the land is going to have to fight its way over the palisade first. If we come in from the sea, then the rebel sentries will be able to see the ships before they enter the bay, even though it will be moonless tonight. Either way they will be alerted and have plenty of time to set fire to the ships.'

Cato nodded. 'You're right. Any conventional attack, from the land or the sea, is doomed to failure. Which leaves us only one alternative.'

He leaned forward and tapped his finger on the map, indicating the end of the bay, close to where it approached the open sea.

Balbus frowned. 'There? What good is that to us? It must be well over a mile from the end of the palisade.'

Centurion Fulvius pursed his lips. 'What exactly did you have in mind, sir?'

'If we can't start our attack from the land, or from the open sea, then we have to launch it from within the bay itself. It's the one direction that the rebels won't be expecting any trouble from.'

Cato had thought his idea through earlier. It was very risky, and relied on good timing. If things went badly for the men leading this attack, then few of them would escape alive. Worst of all, Cato knew he would have to lead them, and face one of the few things he feared in life: swimming. He stood erect and looked at Fulvius as he replied. 'I will lead two parties of men down the bay. We will take light weapons and swim towards the heart of the rebel camp, until we are opposite the beached ships. Then we will divide into two parties, one making for the ships on the beach, the other, under my command, for those rafted together at the end of the bay. It'll be about the same distance, so we should be able to attack at the same time. We'll take the ships, get rid of the incendiary materials and then I'll give the signal for the main attack to begin. The legionary detachment will take the redoubt and roll up the flank. The auxiliary units will defend the camp and block any attempt to escape. Meanwhile,' Cato turned to Balbus, 'your squadron will round the point outside the bay and enter as swiftly as possible, making for the end of the bay, where you will land your marines and support the legionaries.'

'Sir, this is madness,' Balbus protested. 'You're proposing that your men swim nearly two miles, while carrying arms, and then board

318

these ships and overwhelm the crews. What if the rebels have numbers aboard each vessel? If Ajax is depending on the grain fleet to make a deal with Rome, then he's sure to have them well defended.'

'I've been watching the ships this morning,' said Cato. 'I only saw a handful of men on each one. If Ajax has prepared them with incendiary materials, then he'll only need a small party aboard each one to light the fire and wait until it takes hold before abandoning ship. If we can get ten good men aboard each ship at anchor and twice as many aboard those on the beach, then we can take them. There're twenty vessels at anchor and twelve on the beach. So, one cohort should suffice for what I have in mind. They'll have to be good swimmers, and we'll use inflated waterskins as floats to help with the weight of the weapons. If we take our time and approach cautiously, we should be able to get close to the ships without being spotted, as there is no moon tonight. There will be two men with buccinas in each party. Once the anchored ships are taken, they will give the signal for the main attack to begin.' Cato looked round. 'Centurion Fulvius, you will command the land element of the attack. You will have to crush that redoubt and get down the beach before the rebels can get enough men out of the main camp to attempt to retake and destroy the grain ships.'

Fulvius nodded, and Cato glanced at the other officers. 'Any more questions?'

There were none, and he took a deep breath. 'Well then, gentlemen, I will have your orders sent to you this afternoon. Make sure your men are ready, and give them an early supper. It's going to be a long night. Centurion Fulvius, stay behind. The rest of you can leave. Balbus, you remain as well. That's it, dismissed.'

Once the officers had filed out of the tent, Cato rounded on Balbus. 'You have an important part to play tonight, Balbus. If the navy screws up, then we may well lose the battle. If that happens, then you can be sure that the emperor will show you as little mercy as he shows me when he receives the news. Do you understand?'

'Yes, sir. I will do my duty.'

'Good.' Cato reached for a waxed tablet and handed it to the navarch. 'Your orders. Including the signal to be given for your attack. Just make sure your ships are in position in good time. Now, you have a tough ride to get back to your ships, and I suggest you get going. That is, as soon as I have my clerk prepare a document noting your objection to my plan and confirming that I ordered you to take your part in the attack. You can wait outside.'

Balbus frowned, and thought a moment, his face eloquent testimony to the struggle that was going on in his mind. Then he sighed and shook his head. 'That won't be necessary, sir. As you pointed out, it's a long ride and I'd better waste no time in returning to my ships.'

'Then you should go. Good luck.'

The navarch smiled. 'It is you will need the luck tonight, sir. The gods protect you.'

He bowed his head, then turned stiffly and marched out of the tent.

'Sailors.' Centurion Fulvius nodded. 'Who needs 'em?'

'You won't be saying that when he comes to your support tonight.'

Fulvius looked offended. 'I aim to be through the rebel camp and nailing Ajax up by his balls before the first marine sets foot ashore.'

'Would that it were so easy.' Cato laughed for a moment. 'There is one last element of the plan still to arrange. Once I have secured the ships at anchor, I am going to need three of your best men. They must be volunteers, mark you. I'll not order any man to come with me.'

Fulvius stared at him. 'You're going after the hostages, aren't you, sir?'

'Yes. I have no choice. I will not leave my friends to the mercy of that gladiator.'

'I understand, but you must know that you have very little chance of rescuing them.'

'Long odds,' Cato agreed. 'But I've faced long odds before and seen the dawn of another day.'

'No man's luck lasts for ever, sir.'

'Really? I shall have to put that proposition to the test, Centurion. Or die in the attempt. Come now, we have plenty of work to do before night comes.'

'Good news, Centurion!' Ajax smiled as he squatted down at the end of the cage nearest Macro. It was late in the afternoon and the heat had finally gone from the sun. It had been some hours since Macro and Julia had been given their midday ration of food and water and their lips were parched. The gladiator had brought a water bottle with him and took a long swig before lowering it and smacking his lips with exaggerated satisfaction. 'Ah, I needed that! It's been a long, hot day, but I think we're ready for your friends if they try to spring an attack on our camp.'

'You mentioned news,' said Macro. 'Just tell us and go.'

'All right then. You'll never guess who I ran into when I went to discuss my demands up at the Roman camp?'

Macro turned his head to see Ajax. He knew it must be Cato, yet he would not give the gladiator the satisfaction of responding to his question. 'What do I care?'

'Oh!' Ajax feigned disappointment. 'No need to be such a grump, Macro. After all, I bring you news of your friend, Centurion Cato. Or Tribune Cato as he is now. Quite the coming man, it would seem.'

'Cato?' Julia raised her head.

'That's right,' said Ajax. 'I've set him something of a difficult problem to resolve before tomorrow morning.'

Julia frowned. 'What do you mean?'

'It's simple.' Ajax looked at them both before he continued. 'I've decided to have one of you killed at dawn, and I've tasked your friend Cato with choosing which of you it will be.'

Macro lashed out with one of his feet, kicking the bar in front of the gladiator's face. The cage rattled under the impact but Ajax did not flinch for an instant.

'You bastard!' Macro shouted in a cracked voice.

'Come now, Centurion, you knew that I would have you killed in the end. This way there is a chance you might live a little longer. If Cato chooses you. If not, then you'll know where his affections truly lie before you finally beg me to put an end to your life. Either way, I get to increase his suffering. I imagine that neither the good tribune, nor you or the lady here is going to have much sleep tonight, eh?'

Macro shut his eyes, fighting back the black rage that burned in every muscle of his body. He clenched his fists tightly. The urge to bellow at Ajax was almost irresistible, and yet he knew that it would only provoke laughter and fresh torment, so he kept his lips clamped together and tried to clear his mind of all thought.

'It will be a shame to lose one of you. Particularly you, Julia Sempronia. You were quite a beauty before I had you put in here.' He leered at her, and Julia clutched her covering more tightly about her body. 'Such beauty should not be wasted. I think I shall give you one last chance to enjoy the comfort of being clean, to have fresh clothes and to share the company of a man, before we find out what Cato has in store for you tomorrow morning.'

Julia stared at him, terrified as she spoke tremulously. 'What do you want with me?'

'Only to use you, as slave women are used by their Roman masters.' Ajax winked. 'It might be something of an education for you. We shall see.' He paused to sniff the air and made a disgusted face. 'However, it will take some hours to make you presentable. I'll have to give orders for you to be cleaned up at once, if there is going to be time to enjoy you tonight without having to pinch my nose.'

Ajax rose to his feet, clicked his tongue and pointed at Macro. 'You might want to try to get to sleep as soon as you can, Macro. Wouldn't want me and the lady here keeping you awake with the noise of our merrymaking tonight.'

This time Macro could not contain his anger. He let out an animal groan, then opened his eyes and stared at Ajax as he growled through clenched teeth, 'I swear to all the gods, if I get out of here, I will tear out your tongue and your eyes and rip you apart with my bare hands.'

'How charming!' Ajax laughed. He came round the cage and crouched opposite Macro before he rattled the bars. 'Don't count on it, eh?'

Then he rose and padded off towards his tent. Macro turned his attention to Julia. Her eyes were wide with terror.

'Macro! Don't let him take me. Please don't let him take me.'

Macro shook his head. 'I–I can't help you.'

'Macro, please!' Her lips trembled and she began to cry. 'Please don't let him! Please!'

He tried to shut the sound out, driven half mad by the knowledge that there was nothing, nothing at all that he could do to protect her. Julia's pleas suddenly stopped as their guard strode towards them. The guard unlocked and opened the end of the cage. He drew his sword and pointed it at Macro.

'Stay back there, you!'

With his spare hand he grasped Julia's arm and dragged her from the cage, before kicking the door shut and sheathing his sword. As he locked the door, Macro scrambled over to the bars nearest Julia and shouted, 'Julia! Look at me! Look at me!'

She winced as if he had struck her, and then turned fearfully as the guard reached down to grip her under the arms.

'Julia,' Macro continued with icy intensity, 'If you get the chance, kill him!'

'Yes.' She nodded. 'Yes.'

Then the guard pulled her to her feet and half dragged and half carried her across the ground towards Ajax's tent.

Macro leaned back against the bars, praying for the gods to release him from this torment, one way or another.

CHAPTER THIRTY

Cato and his men did not reach the small cove at the head of the bay until the second hour of the night. There was no moon, and even though a local shepherd had led the way, it was hard to follow the narrow track that wound along the side of the hills and then down a steep cliff to the shore. Like the others, Cato carried a haversack with a dagger and a sword bundled together and firmly tied to an empty waterskin. Although every man who served in the legions was trained to swim after a fashion, most never became proficient. Cato's officers had selected just over five hundred men capable of swimming the length of the bay, nearly two miles. The three men chosen by Fulvius marched directly behind Cato as he followed the shepherd. They had readily volunteered when asked, and Cato felt confident that they would serve him well. One of Fulvius's choices was an auxiliary optio from Gortyna who knew the area and had asked to join the column when it marched from the city.

When the man had been brought before him, Cato had looked up from his desk with raised eyebrows.

'Atticus.'

'Yes, sir.' Atticus nodded.

'I have to say, this is something of a surprise. I wouldn't have expected you to be at the head of the queue to save Macro.'

'Nothing would give me greater satisfaction than seeing his face when I rescue him, sir.'

Cato stared at the man for a moment before he responded. 'That's an unusual form of revenge to choose.'

'You know the man well enough, sir. It'll drive him mad.'

Cato laughed. 'You have the measure of him, Atticus. Very well, then. I'll see you later tonight. Dismissed.'

The other two men selected to join Cato were legionaries, Vulso and Musa, solid men with good records who were also chasing promotion. Musa had been issued with a buccina, which he carried in the same bundle as his sword belt.

The long, straggling line of legionaries picked their way down the cliff, and emerged on to the coarse sand of the beach. Cato paid off the shepherd, and as soon as he had the purse, with its fifty silver denarians – a small fortune for a night's work – he scuttled along the beach and disappeared up another track. As the men reached the beach, one of Cato's officers counted off each section and sent them to prepare for the attack. The force would swim in two columns, one closer to the shore as they made for the beached ships. Cato had been anxious to ensure that each force would remain close together, and the section leaders were tasked with keeping a regular count of their men. The soldiers heading for the beached ships would enter the water at close intervals to make sure that there was a small gap between each section. The first section would make for the furthest ship, and once the intervals were taken into account, it was Cato's hope that the teams would begin boarding the grain ships at roughly the same moment. With luck they would all be taken before the rebels on the shore had realised the danger and could react.

Cato would lead the other column directly towards the cluster of grain ships anchored in the middle of the bay. There was no need for his detachment to be staggered. They would have to keep together, so as not to tackle the ships in a piecemeal fashion.

Once the last of the men had descended from the cliff and had removed their boots and tunics, Cato quietly gave the word to enter the water. Each man inflated his waterskin and then, holding it in his arms, together with the bundle containing his weapons, waded into the sea with the rest of his section as the order was given. Wearing only a loincloth, Cato shivered in the cool night air. He had decided to swim close to the front of the column and allowed two sections to go ahead before he stepped forward with his three men. He had not mentioned to the other officers that he was a poor swimmer. He was ashamed of the fact, and though he had made some improvement since basic training, he was still far short of the standard of capable veterans like Macro.

There was a faint swell, and the waves crunched and hissed on the sand. Cato firmed up his resolve and strode down towards the surf. The water was cold and he gave a gasp as he waded out into the sea. A wave slapped up against his chest and he took the opportunity to launch himself forwards, submerging momentarily before shaking his head and kicking out into the bay as he held on to the waterskin bobbing on the surface in front of him.

'Atticus,' Cato called out as loudly as he dared. 'On me.'

'Yes, sir,' Atticus replied with a splutter, a short distance from Cato's shoulder. 'Come on, you two!'

Cato kicked out with his legs, hurriedly at first; then, as he got used to the water temperature, he realised that he must pace himself if he was not to reach the ships in too tired a condition to fight. It was hard going, and after a while he turned his head and was surprised to see that the cliff still seemed close by. Ahead, as he rose up on the swell, he could see the rebel camp fires glittering over two miles away. There was a faint glow on the hills to the right that marked the Roman camp. By now only the auxiliary infantry and half of the cavalry should still be there. The rest of the column was with Fulvius, making its way behind the hills before cutting across and forming up on the beach, a mile from the end of the rebels' palisade and the grain ships within. Out to sea, Balbus and his ships would be creeping cautiously round the headland, and would then heave to and wait for the series of three signal beacons to be lit on one of the hills above the bay. Cato took a deep breath and kicked out again, dimly aware of the hundreds of men in the sea all around him, struggling through the swell towards the grain ships and the desperate fight that awaited them.

Julia sat in numbed silence as the old crone dried her hair with a length of wool cloth, rubbing vigorously at the thick dark tresses that dropped down past her naked shoulders. She had long since given up resisting the wizened woman and the burly guard who seemed to be her inseparable companion. After being removed from the cage she had struggled, but the guard had slapped her and then punched her in the kidneys and told her to stop resisting or he would do it again. There was no chance of escape, and rather than suffer more pain,

Julia had given in to the pair of them, allowing her rags to be taken from her. She was sat down on a stool by a horse trough while the woman doused her with several buckets of water, before setting to work with a brush. The grime had worked its way into her flesh so far that it took repeated and painful efforts to shift it.

Julia's cries and muttered protests had no effect and she sat with gritted teeth. It was strange how the filth that had been caked to her body had seemed to hide her nakedness; now, and as it was cleaned away, she began to feel self-conscious under the constant gaze of the guard standing close by. Once the woman had completed cleaning her body and the skin was white and flushed red in places from hard scrubbing, she turned to her long dark hair, thrusting her head over the side of the trough as she ladled water over the back of her scalp and then worked her fingers in vigorously, pulling mercilessly at the tangles until they came free.

As the woman dried her hair, Julia forced herself to think through what Macro had said as she was pulled from the cage. There was a chance of finding something she could use as a weapon in Ajax's tent. Something she could surreptitiously get hold of. If there was a way to do it, she would attempt to kill him, and the thought of it filled her with a brief thrill of triumph. She felt her heart beat against her breast with excitement at the prospect. Then the woman threw the cloth aside and stuck a comb into Julia's hair. There was a sharp pain that made her cry out as the woman wrenched it through the remaining tangles. She turned instinctively and slapped the crone. 'Take care, slave!'

Julia regretted the outburst as soon as she had uttered the words. Rage glittered in the old woman's eyes and her hands clenched into claws as she bared her teeth.

'Fucking bitch! Call me a slave!' She lashed out, knocking Julia off the stool. At once she threw herself on the naked Roman, hammering blows at her face as Julia drew her arms up protectively. Fists rained down, battering her shoulders and arms as the old woman attacked her in a savage frenzy.

'Mother! That's enough,' the guard shouted, striding two paces towards them. He grabbed the old woman's wrists and lifted her bodily away. 'I said, that's enough!'

The old woman's lips were flecked with spittle as she snarled, 'Let me go! I'll kill her!'

'No you won't! Not unless you want to answer to the general.'

The woman was staring at Julia, and lashed out with her foot, kicking Julia in the stomach. The guard dragged her away and shook her. 'I said that's enough, Mother.'

Julia rolled on to her side with a groan, and felt the long, thin handle of the comb press into her side. She reached for it with one hand and held it against the inside of her forearm.

'You heard her!' the old woman wailed. 'Just like that bitch back in Gortyna. You've seen the scars on me back. You've seen 'em.' She began to sob and became limp so the guard had to hold her up, cradling her gently in his arms.

'It's all right, Mother. That's over. Shhh.' He brushed her wiry grey hair with his hand.

'What's all that noise?'

Julia looked up to see Ajax striding out of his tent towards them. His expression was dark and he glared at the three figures round the trough. 'What is going on? Get up!' he snarled at Julia before turning his attention to the old woman and the guard, who regarded him with a mixture of fear and awe. 'Well?'

'It was the lady, General,' the guard explained. 'She provoked my mother into attacking her. I had to separate them.'

Ajax stared at them briefly before looking at Julia, rising to her feet. Her skin was clean and his eyes feasted on her body. 'That is the nature of Romans, they bring out the worst in others. Don't worry.' Ajax turned back to the old woman. 'If she has caused offence then she will be paying for it tonight. When I have finished, you can do as you will with her. Only leave her alive, understand?'

The old woman nodded gleefully.

Ajax clicked his fingers. 'Then finish cleaning her up, and find her something to wear. Something fine and Roman. I want to enjoy soiling her.' He approached Julia, stood before her and raised his hand to tilt her chin. His arm brushed her breast and Ajax felt a flush of lust in his loins as he raised her face towards him. Julia met his gaze with a defiant expression.

Ajax laughed cruelly. 'Oh, you won't be so haughty before this night is out. I promise you. You'll beg for my mercy.'

'I'd rather die.'

'I'm sure you would, but you don't escape your punishment that easily.'

'Punishment?' Julia frowned. 'What have I ever done to deserve this?'

Ajax took his hand away and retreated a step. 'You were born a Roman.' He turned to the others. 'Prepare her for me as swiftly as possible. When she is dressed and scented, bring her straight to me.'

'Yes, General.' The guard bowed his head.

As Ajax strode back towards his tent, the old woman chuckled as she advanced on Julia with a chilling grin. 'Them stripes on my back will be nothing to the scars he's going to leave on you.'

After two hours in the water, Cato was beginning to shiver. As far as he could estimate, he had covered a mile and a half along the bay. He was doubting the wisdom of his plan. Around him he could just see the darker shapes of heads and the inflated waterskins bobbing on the surface. Every so often one of the section leaders would call out to his men and make sure that they were still with him. Optio Atticus and the others swam close by their commander. There was no telling how the group heading for the beached ships was progressing, and Cato could only hope that they reached their targets at roughly the same time that he and his men began to board the anchored ships. That moment was less than an hour away. Cato kicked out and continued forward, trying to ignore the numbing chill that was creeping into his body.

Ahead, the fires of the rebel camp gradually became more distinct, and he could see individual figures by the light of the flames. A dark mass directly ahead blotted out the fires beyond, and Cato realised that he was nearing the grain ships. He stopped and raised an arm. 'On me! On me!'

The water churned around him as the words were passed on and the men began to gather on the steady swell. Once the sounds of splashing had ceased and Cato was happy that as many men as possible were with him, he called out again, as loudly as he dared: 'Let's go!'

The men kicked out, spreading out a little as they approached the ships. They silently swam towards their targets with grim determination. Cato made directly for the centre of the rafted ships, and gradually they blotted out all sight of the camp beyond. He could hear the lap of the waves against their hulls, and even an occasional voice above the slap and hiss of the sea. He slowed his pace, kicking steadily but carefully so that he did not break the surface of the water. Ahead of him he saw a dark line against the background and realised he had come across an anchor cable. He made for it and grasped the coarse rope, finding it reassuringly steady. Slipping the shoulder strap of the waterskin and the bundled weapons securely over his head and shoulder, he eased himself on to the anchor cable and began to work up towards the bows of the ship.

Emerging from the water his skin tingled in the breeze, but the concentration and effort needed to edge forwards made him ignore the discomfort. He wormed his way up the cable, dripping as he edged towards the hawse, where it passed through the stout timbers of the grain ship. The further up he crawled, the more it began to sway, and his muscles tensed as he struggled to stay astride it. Then the timbers of the hull were within reach, and Cato held on with one hand while the other scrabbled up the weathered surface, over the side and gripped on. He pulled himself up, then grabbed at the side rail with his other hand. His shoulder muscles protested painfully as he drew his body up and peered over the side. There was no one visible in the bows. Beyond the foredeck there was a short drop to the main deck, where a sturdy hatch coaming led down into the hold. Aft, the deck rose up again to the steering platform. Several men lay or sat on the main deck, while one stood by the handle of the steering paddle, spear in hand. The stench of pitch filled the air and Cato saw a dull glow at the stern where a lamp burned inside a small leather screen. Ajax's threat to burn the ships was quite real.

Cato eased his feet up on to the cable and pressed down as he heaved himself over the side, controlling the movement as best he could so that he did not land on the deck with a thud. Instead, he landed on top of a man sleeping in the shelter of the ship's side. There was a grunt as Cato's knees winded the rebel, who gasped as he stirred to find a wet, near-naked figure sprawled over him. Cato bunched his fist and drove it into the rebel's face, snapping his head back against the deck with a dull bump. He hit him again, and again, until he was certain the man was insensible.

Cato sat on his haunches, his limbs shaking terribly from the cold and his exertions. He took a moment to rub himself vigorously to restore some warmth. Then he unfastened the length of cloth that bound his weapons, cursing under his breath as his fingers fumbled with the ties. As they came undone, he felt the reassuring touch of his sword blade. He crouched on the deck as he fastened the belt around his middle, and then cautiously rose up to help the next man over the side. It was Atticus, and a moment later he too was on the foredeck, armed and ready. More men swarmed up the anchor cable and joined them, while Atticus drew his dagger and cut the rebel's throat.

Once Atticus, Vulso, Musa and three other men were aboard and had their weapons to hand, Cato squatted down in front of them. 'All ready? When I give the word, we head across the main deck. Go in fast, and show no mercy. I want the ship taken without the alarm being raised. Atticus, you take Vulso and Musa and make your way down the port side. I'll lead the rest.' He glanced round at the shadowy features of his men, most of whom were shivering, like himself, from the cold and the terrifying exhilaration of the instant before battle began. Cato grasped his sword firmly and turned aft. 'Let's go.'

He kept low, crouching as he moved along the ship's side, where he hoped the shadows might conceal him long enough to surprise the rebels. At the end of the foredeck, three steps led down to the long, broad expanse of the main deck. Three of the rebels were sitting on the edge of the hatch coaming, talking in muted tones as they shared a wineskin. Cato saw one of them lift it up and swallow several mouthfuls. As he approached them, he increased his pace to a trot, then a sprint, drawing back his sword. He slashed at the first man, cutting into his head with a soft crack before the rebel had even begun to turn towards the sound of the sudden rush of padding feet. The second man just had time to glance round before Cato punched him hard on the jaw and thrust him over the side of the hatch and into the hold. The third man lowered the wineskin and let out a choked gasp as Cato caught him with the backswing of his sword, cutting through the hand holding the wineskin and into the man's neck. He crumpled on to the deck as the dark forms of the Roman legionaries swept on, hacking into the rest of the rebels.

The sentry with the spear had been looking over the after rail, but he turned at the sound of the commotion on the main deck. Cato leaped up on to the aft deck before the man could react and ran straight at him. There was no time for the rebel to lower his spear, and Cato thrust his sword out an instant before he crashed into the man, slamming him back against the sternpost. Winded by the impact, the man could only gasp as Cato thrust his sword up into vital organs. There was a brief struggle before his enemy sagged and released his spear, which clattered on to the deck. Breathing heavily, Cato withdrew his blade and turned to see that the rest of the crew had been disposed of. He crossed to the oil lamp and hurriedly blew it out.

'Next ship,' he ordered softly, pointing to where another grain ship loomed in the darkness. He led the way across the main deck and peered cautiously over the side. There were two ropes securing the vessels to each other, and Cato indicated them. 'Haul us in.'

His men took up the strain and braced their feet against the ship's side. Slowly the gap closed and the grain ships collided with a gentle bump. At once Cato scrambled on to the next deck, followed by Atticus and the others. He heard cries from some of the other ships and the clash of weapons. A voice called out, sounding the alarm, and Cato realised the element of surprise had gone. He filled his lungs and cupped a hand to his mouth. 'Up the Twenty-Second!'

Musa echoed the war cry and it was quickly taken up by other voices in the darkness. Cato turned to Atticus. 'Clear this ship.'

'Yes, sir!'

'Musa? Where are you?'

A figure came towards him. 'Sir?'

'You have the buccina?'

'Yes, sir.' The legionary held up the curved brass horn.

'Then sound it. As loud as you can.'

Musa fumbled for the mouthpiece, filled his lungs and blew for all he was worth. The first note was flat and clumsy, and while Cato swore, Musa spat and tried again. This time there was a sharp, shrill blare that cut through the darkness. Musa blew three short notes, rested and then repeated the signal.

'Keep it going!' Cato slapped him on the back and went to join Atticus and the others. As he made his way across the main deck, he stepped over a body and saw several figures struggling on the far side of the hatch. He hurried round, straining his eyes to make out friend from foe. Fortunately the legionaries were all stripped down to their loincloths while the slaves wore tunics and cloaks. Cato sensed a movement to his side, and turned to see a man emerge from a small cabin under the aft deck, falcata in hand. He ducked low, and lashed out with his sword, striking the man on the shin. With a cry of agony he toppled back into the cabin and out of sight. Cato stayed in a crouch, looking round for another enemy. His heart was pounding in his chest and the cold and the tension made his body tremble. Musa was still blowing the buccina, and in the rests between the repeated notes Cato caught the strain of another faint blast of notes in the distance. The other group had begun seizing the beached ships then. Moments later, up on one of the hills overlooking the bay, a series of sparks flickered into life, quickly flaring up as the signal was passed on to the warships waiting out at sea.

Cato backed into the side of the ship and took stock. All around him in the darkness he could hear the sounds of the vicious struggle being waged across the decks of the grain ships lying at anchor and bound together. The legionaries were giving full vent to their voices, partly to encourage each other, but mostly to add to the terror of their enemies. From the shore came the sound of more horns and the faint roar of Fulvius and his men charging the flank of the rebel palisade. Cato puffed out his cheeks. So far it was going to plan. Now it all depended on keeping the momentum going, before Ajax and his men could mount any organised resistance to the surprise attack.

CHAPTER THIRTY-ONE

'What was that?' Ajax eased himself up from his couch, ears straining to catch the sound he had heard briefly a moment before.

One of his bodyguards stood before him, holding Julia's arm firmly as she waited for Ajax's inspection. A long linen stola had been found for her, dyed a vivid blue, and he had paused to admire the spectacle of the Roman woman from his couch. She was quite a beauty, he had mused to himself as he sipped a cup of watered wine. He had felt his lust stirring as he ran his eyes over her figure, and had begun to fantasise about the kinds of pleasure he might exact from her, while inflicting as much pain as possible, when the faint notes of a brass horn sounded in the distance. It came again. Three sharp notes, and a rest.

Ajax was instantly on his feet and running across the tent. He swept the tent flaps aside and ran out into the night, where he stopped and stared across the bay. In the light of torches and camp fires along the palisade, he saw men fighting on and around the redoubt, with tiny flickers of red light as sword blades flashed reflections of flames. The notes sounded again, nearer than they should, and Ajax was puzzled for a moment, until he realised with a shock that the notes came from down in the bay, from the direction of the anchored grain ships. He ducked back into the tent and stabbed his finger at the woman.

'Keep her here! Don't take your eyes off her. If she escapes or is harmed, you'll answer for it with your life!'

Snatching up his sword belt, he buckled it on as he ran towards the horse lines. Around him the men of his bodyguard were tumbling out of their tents and shelters to investigate the commotion on the far side of the bay.

'Don't just stand there!' Ajax shouted at them. 'We're under attack! Get your weapons and ride to the palisade! Move!'

He took the nearest of the horses kept saddled and ready for use at any time of day or night, and threw himself on to the animal's back. Snatching at the reins, he kicked his heels in and urged the horse down the path towards the main body of the rebel camp. As he passed the cage where Centurion Macro sat behind bars, he heard the Roman cheering madly, but there was no time to stop and silence his tongue. Ajax resolved to do that the first moment that could be spared. It would be a pity to kill Centurion Macro quickly, but die he must, to honour the memory of his father. All around, figures were rising up in the glow of the camp fires and staring in confusion towards the distant fighting. Ajax bellowed at them to take up their weapons and make for the battle, before the Romans took the grain ships.

As he galloped through the camp, swerving here and there to avoid those who were too slow to react to the approaching rider, Ajax felt sick in the pit of his stomach. He had underestimated his enemy. He had been certain that the threat to destroy the grain ships, vital to the survival of Rome, would forestall any attempt to attack his camp. The ships had been carefully prepared by his men, flammable materials placed in the holds and doused with oil and pitch, ready to set on fire at the first sign of approaching Roman warships. So where were the fires? Ajax reined his horse in as he reached a small rise in the ground, and strained his eyes as he tried to make out what was happening across the bay. He could see one of the beached ships by the light of a brazier burning on the sand. Men were clustered about its bows, splashing in the shallows as they attempted to climb aboard and grapple with those defending the vessel. Then it hit him. The Romans had taken the ship. Taken all the ships . . . But then a sudden lick of flame from further down the beach lit up the deck and mast of one of the vessels. The fire caught and more flames gushed up into the night, accompanied by flickering tracery as the rigging started to burn. Out in the bay another fire started. Not all the ships had been taken then. There might still be a chance to beat off the attack and seize the ships back from the Romans, or at least burn them all to prevent them falling into the hands of his hated enemy.

Several of his bodyguards had caught up with him, and Ajax raised his arm and called out as he charged on towards the beach: 'Follow me!'

As they galloped on through the camp, he continued to call his followers to arms and order them to the beach. At the same time, part of his mind raged at himself. How had the Romans done this? How had they managed to get to the grain ships without being seen? He had taken every precaution. There were men watching all the approaches from land and out to sea. They could not have missed so many of the enemy. Surely? They must have used boats, but any boats would have been seen, even on this moonless night. It would only have been possible if they had swum the length of the bay, under the cover of darkness. That had to be it, he decided, furious with himself. He could not help a moment of grudging admiration for his enemy, and then the horses reached the beach.

A large group of his men stood clustered at the edge of the camp. Ajax halted and turned towards the riders following him. 'Kharim! Are you with me?'

'Yes, General!' Kharim edged his mount through the others. He was naked save for a loincloth and his sword belt.

'Stay here. Get these men formed. You are to hold this part of the camp. If I send for you, come at once, you hear?'

Kharim bowed his head. 'Yes, General.'

Ajax rode on, through the gates at the end of the palisade. They were inside the perimeter of the main camp and had been left open. Ahead of him there was utter confusion. Only one ship along the beach had been fired and it was now well ablaze, filling the air with the roar of its flames and the crackle of bursting timber as sparks swirled into the heavens. The intensity of the glare lit up the surrounding sand and water for some distance. The din of battle came from the far end of the beach, and yet all along its length his men were visible clustered about the bows of the beached ships, trying to clamber aboard and get at the Romans, who were stripped to the waist and desperately holding them off with swords, spears and even oars.

The enemy on the ships were not the real danger, Ajax realised. It was the force rolling up his flank. If they could be thrown back, then the ships could be retaken later. He drew his sword and rode on, bellowing to the rebels along the beach, 'Follow me! Follow me!'

He gathered more and more men as he hurriedly made his way towards the battle raging at the far end. The fight was not going well. The Romans had already overrun the redoubt and were surging forward over the sand, oblong shields smashing down their more lightly armed opponents, and then the legionaries finished off the rebels with thrusts from their short swords. Ajax knew that the vast majority of his men were no match for legionaries, but if they could amass a sufficient force to stall the attack, there was a chance the weight of numbers might yet force them back over the palisade. But first they had to be rallied.

'Bodyguard! To me!' Ajax bellowed above the clash of weapons, the thud of blows on shields and the cries of the wounded. Those horsemen who had followed him from the other side of the bay steadied their snorting mounts and held their weapons ready. Ajax saw that he had thirty or forty of them with him now. Enough to make a difference. He turned back towards the enemy, fifty paces along the beach, cutting their way through the dissolving ranks of the rebels as they began to fall back.

'Charge!' Ajax stabbed his sword out and dug his heels in. The horse whinnied, reared up for a moment and then plunged forward, head down and hooves thudding into the coarse sand as it galloped madly towards the enemy.

The rebels ahead of him heard the approaching horsemen and did their best to escape from their path, but several were mown down and trampled underfoot. Ahead of him, Ajax could see that the Romans were not in formation, but had scattered as they began their pursuit. At the head of his band of bodyguards, he crashed in amongst them. The legionaries were as well armoured as any man he had faced in the arena, and Ajax held his sword poised to strike at any unprotected arms, faces and throats. Two Romans stood ahead of him and were knocked aside as his mount slammed into their shields. Leaning to his right, the gladiator thrust down into the neck exposed as a legionary stumbled. It was a shallow thrust, no more than a few inches, but it would mortally wound his enemy, and Ajax rode on, keeping his head low. He saw a crested helmet to one side, and steered towards the centurion attempting to rally his unit. At the last moment the man turned, and in the glow of the ship blazing behind the gladiator his eyes widened. He was too late to react, and the tip of Ajax's blade smashed through his eye, shattering his skull as it plunged on into his brain. Ripping the blade free, Ajax turned his horse again.

Glancing round, Ajax saw that his charge had broken the Roman attack. Several legionaries were down, some had grouped back to back in small clusters, while others were retreating along the beach. He had bought his men only a brief respite. Less than a hundred paces away, the second Roman formation was advancing towards the rebels, a solid wall of shields with standards raised behind the leading ranks. An order was barked and the legionaries clattered their swords against the sides of their shields, producing a deafening metallic din that unnerved Ajax's horse.

'Easy, easy there.' He patted its flank and realised that his bodyguard was the only rebel group standing firm on the beach. The rest were falling back. With a hiss of frustration, Ajax knew that the fight on the beach was lost. It might still be possible to deploy Kharim's men, many of whom had weapons and armour looted from the Roman soldiers they had killed. They might hold the legionaries back long enough for the rest of the army to be rallied, ready to hurl themselves on the hated Romans.

'Fall back!' Ajax ordered. 'To the camp!'

The horsemen turned and rode back along the beach, covering the retreat of those on foot retreating before them. As they passed the ships, the Romans on board watched them silently, too exhausted to cheer as their enemy gave ground. But once they caught sight of their comrades advancing along the beach, below their standards, a cheer rose up, passed on from ship to ship, and as he heard it, Ajax's lips twisted into a bitter snarl of frustration.

When he returned through the gateway of the palisade, he saw Kharim on his horse, watching intently. Catching sight of him, Kharim waved an arm and spurred his horse forward.

'General! The sentries report another Roman force moving down from their camp.' He thrust his arm up towards the slope. 'Over a thousand of them, with cavalry on the wings.'

Ajax stared at him, then looked back at the enemy marching along the beach. Around him the rebels were milling about, directionless and afraid. He took a deep breath and roared, 'Form ranks! Form up and hold your ground! We can win this! We can beat them! We've done it before and we can do it again! Stand firm!'

His shouts were interrupted by fresh notes from the Roman horns along the beach, answered by more blasts from the direction of the hills, and the clatter of swords on shields began again, rising to deafening intensity. The rebels began to shuffle back, and those on the fringes of the crowd beyond the gate began to disperse, hurrying away from the converging Roman forces.

'Stand your ground!' Ajax yelled again, but it was too late. Fear passed through the rebels like a wind, and a tide of men flowed into the night, back through the camp, as they ran to save their lives. Ajax watched them go, and his heart set like lead in his breast. He suddenly felt a terrible burden of weariness settle on his shoulders and he turned to face the oncoming Romans.

'General!' Kharim shouted. 'What shall we do?'

'Do?' Ajax shook his head. 'All is lost. There is nothing we can do but die with a sword in our hands.'

'No!' Kharim edged his horse alongside Ajax and grabbed his arm. 'General, you still live, and while you live you can keep the fight against Rome alive. If you die now, then it has been for nothing. While you live, the rebellion is not finished.'

Ajax turned and looked at him with a bleak expression. 'What can I hope to achieve now, my friend?'

Kharim thought quickly. 'We have hostages. We can still make a deal if we escape with them. There are some fishing boats in a small cove not far from your tent.'

For a moment Ajax wanted nothing more than a quick death. But then the sense of Kharim's words penetrated his mind. The Parthian was right: the rebellion would never be over while some men kept the spirit of it alive in the hearts of the empire's slaves. He must escape, and take the hostages with him.

'Very well.' He nodded to his comrade. 'We will go. Come!'

He turned his horse and beckoned to his bodyguards, and then began to ride back through the camp around the end of the bay, towards his tents on the peninsula beyond. On all sides the rebels gathered up their families and loot and fled from the approaching Romans. Ajax spared them a moment's pity. The trap was closed. There would be no escape for them, only death or a return to slavery.

Three of the ships were on fire by the time Cato and his men had cleared the decks of the anchored vessels. Only two of the rebel fire parties had managed to set their ships ablaze before taking to their tenders and escaping towards the shore. The fire had spread to the third ship and all three now threatened the rest of the vessels anchored in the bay.

'Atticus!' Cato called the optio over. 'Gather up twenty men. We have to cut those ships out before the fire spreads any further.'

Cato turned and, with Vulso and Musa, made his way across the intervening vessels to the one next to the nearest burning ship. The heat from the flames roaring up from the vessel's hold struck him a stinging blow, and he raised an arm to protect his face as he looked around. Two lines joined this ship to the one ablaze.

Cato crouched down in the shelter of the ship's side to give his orders. 'You two take the aft line. I'll go forward.'

Crouching low, he scrambled to the hawse hole near the bows and drew his dagger. The cable was made from coarse hemp and was thick as a man's wrist. He began to saw at it furiously. The deck around him was brightly lit by the burning ships and the hot air was filled with the roar of flames and the crack of timber bursting from the intense temperature generated by the blaze. Sparks and glowing shreds of sails swirled through the air, and Cato winced as one landed on his back. He shook it off and continued cutting at the rope, hoping that they could complete the job before the fire spread to any more of the grain ships. One of the strands of the cable parted and the tension instantly increased on the remaining strands, making them easier to cut. Gritting his teeth, Cato worked at them with every ounce of his strength, the edge of the dagger biting through the dense material. Another strand parted and one remained, thin and hard as bone.

'Come on, you bastard,' Cato muttered. 'Break.'

With a dull crack the dagger severed the last strand and the end of the cable vanished through the hole. Cato rose up and squinted into the heated air as he waited for the burning ship to drift away. Glancing aft, he saw Vulso and Musa running towards him.

'Cable's cut, sir,' Vulso called out. 'But she's not moving off.'

Cato nodded. 'I saw. We'll have to fend her away.' He pointed to one of the sweeps lashed to the ship's side. 'We can use that. Come on!'

They hurriedly untied the simple fastenings holding the long oar in place and then manhandled the broad-bladed end over the rail, against the side of the other vessel.

Cato took a firm grip on the shaft and braced his feet. 'All right then, heave!'

The three of them leaned into the long oar with all their might. Slowly, slowly, Cato sensed the other ship begin to give, and he shuffled forward a pace and called out, 'She's moving! Keep at it!'

Burning debris was falling across the bows of the deck around them, but they could do nothing until the blazing wreck of the other ship was pushed to a safe distance. They continued to thrust the sweep against its side, chests heaving as their muscles strained, stiff and glistening from their efforts. Cato glanced up and saw that the gap between the ships had widened to ten feet. All the time the resistance decreased as he and the others steadily approached the side rail. There they fed the shaft along and continued until the other ship eased away from the oar blade. They hauled the sweep back and dropped it on the deck. The current had begun to draw the ship away from the rest of the anchored vessels and it drifted slowly towards the shore. Cato nodded with satisfaction before turning to inspect the deck. Burning debris lay scattered about the foredeck, but mercifully there was none around the hold, where the rebels had prepared their combustible materials, ready to set fire to the ship.

'Get these fires out!' Cato ordered, grabbing a length of sacking from a locker in front of the main mast. There was a water bucket there for the crew, and he hurriedly doused the sacking before running to a blackened length of rope, still alight in places. He beat out the flames and moved on, as the others followed suit. Soon the last of the small fires was out and they stood gasping as they watched the burning wreck drift away. Cato grabbed a shroud and climbed up on to the side rail. From his vantage point he could see that Atticus and the others had succeeded in cutting the other two ships free and were also fending them off. He could still feel the stinging heat even where he stood, and he briefly stared at the spectacle in awe as the brilliant flames transformed the surrounding sea into a glittering chaos of fiery reflections.

Glancing back towards the beach, Cato could make out the details of the legionaries as they advanced past the ship that burned there. He was relieved to see that they had already taken the whole of the area enclosed by the palisade. Beyond that he could see thousands of figures running in every direction in the glow of the rebels' camp fires. It seemed that the attack had succeeded as he had hoped. Taken by surprise, the rebels had broken and were fleeing for their lives. It was true that four of the grain ships had been lost, but that was acceptable given that the whole fleet had been at risk.

'Sir!' Vulso called to him, pointing back towards the mouth of the bay. Cato turned and his gaze followed the direction Vulso was indicating. Back through the rigging of the grain ships he could see the dark forms of other vessels approaching, and the faint sheen of a rhythmic disturbance on the sides of each, which he realised must be the banks of oars. He felt a release of tension in his body at the sight of the Roman warships and called back to Vulso.

'They're ours! It's Navarch Balbus and his squadron.'

Vulso let out a cheer, then passed on word of the navy's arrival. More men joined in the cheering as Cato gathered Atticus, Vulso and Musa and hurried back across the decks of the grain ships to meet the first, and largest, of the warships to reach them. A bronze-capped ram protruding from the bows was aimed straight at the side of the ship that Cato stood on, and for a moment he feared that the warship might crash into the hull. Then he heard a shouted order, and the oars on the port side dropped down into the water and stayed there while the starboard oars continued rowing and the warship began to swing round, beam on to the grain ship.

'Tribune Cato?' a voice called out. 'Is Tribune Cato there?'

'Here!' Cato waved his arms. 'Over here!'

'Thank the gods!' He recognised Balbus's voice, then the navarch continued, 'Have the ships been taken?'

'All but the three on fire. There may still be some rebels hiding aboard some of the ships. Send your marines over.'

'Aye, sir. Have your men ready to take mooring lines.'

One by one the warships came alongside the grain ships and the sailors cast lines to the legionaries to fasten to cleats, then the ships were hauled side to side. As soon as the boarding ramps were lowered, the marines boarded the grain ships and took charge of the prisoners and began to hunt down the remaining rebels. Balbus was one of the first men to cross over from his flagship, and he hurried up to Cato.

'Good to see you again, sir.' He saluted.

Cato could not help grinning. 'Sounds like you doubted that you would.'

Balbus shrugged. 'I'm delighted to be wrong. However, when we saw the fires I feared the worst. How many of the grain ships did we lose?'

'Four – three here and one on the beach.'

'Only four?' Balbus was relieved. 'Splendid. We only had a little bit of trouble ourselves. One of the liburnians ran aground near the peninsula. Not bad for a night operation so close to shore.' He puffed himself up with pride in his achievement.

Cato glanced towards the shore. Fulvius and his men had already broken into the rebel camp and were cutting the enemy down in swathes. He turned back. 'You take command here. Secure the grain ships and send some of your marines to reinforce the men ashore.'

'Yes, sir. Where are you going?'

'I still have one job left to do,' Cato said quietly. 'Try and save the hostages. If anything happens, I've left orders for Centurion Fulvius to take command.'

Balbus nodded. 'Good luck, sir.'

Cato laughed at the navarch's dour tone. 'You seem to make a habit of doubting me. I'll be back, Balbus. I give you my word.'

'Good luck anyway, sir.'

'Thanks.' Cato clapped him on the shoulder, turned to Atticus and the others and led them off to find one of the tenders moored to the remaining grain ships.

CHAPTER THIRTY-TWO

The tender grounded on the small strip of sand with a slight jar that sent Atticus sprawling on to his knees.

'Shit,' he muttered as he struggled up and then climbed over the side with the others.

'Better all speak in Greek from now on,' said Cato. 'If we're going to be taken for rebels.'

They had helped themselves to some tunics from the rebel bodies on the grain ships and fastened their sword belts over the top. If anyone took the time to look hard at them, the Roman swords might look suspicious, but they could pass them off as captured kit if stopped. From the sounds of confusion and panic coming from the camp, Cato hoped that the rebels would be too busy trying to save themselves to be worried about Roman intruders in their midst.

He indicated a rock a short distance away. 'We'll put the boat behind that.'

Once he was satisfied that it was hidden from view and would still be there if they needed to make a quick escape, he led the others up towards the large tents in that part of the camp he had seen Ajax and his escort make for the previous day. The slope was rocky and dotted with shrubs and clumps of gorse that snagged their tunics as they crept forwards. At length the gradient eased and they could hear voices more clearly. There were hurried exchanges of shouts, but none of the panic and pandemonium that was evident in the main part of the camp. The ground here was sparsely covered where the rebels had ripped up the dry plants and bushes for kindling. There was a sudden rustling to their right, and Cato waved his men down and dropped to the ground himself. Ahead of them a small group of figures ran by: a man, woman and two children, all of them clutching bundles. The man looked nervously towards the top of the slope and urged the others on. They passed a short distance in front of the Romans without seeing them, and ran off into the darkness. As the sound of their footsteps faded, Cato let his breath out.

'Come on,' he whispered.

They continued, and now the glow of camp fires illuminated the crest above them. Keeping low and glancing from side to side, they proceeded warily. The ridges of tents were visible over the crest, and Cato made towards a small outcrop of boulders that would conceal them as they took in the situation. There turned out to be a natural gap between the boulders wide enough for two men to lie down, and Cato ordered the legionaries to stay back while he crawled forward with Atticus. The rocks stood on a slight rise and the position gave them a good view over the flat area of ground that the enemy commander had chosen for his tent and those of his bodyguards. The largest tents were surrounded by an open area, then smaller shelters, and off to one side a small shack and pens that seemed to have been abandoned many years ago. A number of camp fires were burning down, having been abandoned in the rush to counter the Roman attack. As Cato surveyed the scene, he could see several figures close to the largest tent; some were armed with spears, and an old woman squatted to one side hurriedly loading possessions on to a blanket that lay open on the ground. Other rebels were visible flitting through the shelters as they ran from the Roman forces advancing round the bay. Cato could not help wondering what these fugitives might hope to achieve. When they reached the end of the peninsula they would be trapped.

'What now?' muttered Atticus. 'Where do you think Macro and the senator's daughter are being kept?'

'It has to be somewhere close to his tent.' Cato recalled the savage glee in the gladiator's eyes as he contemplated the suffering of Macro and Julia. 'He'd want them nearby, near enough to sense their torment. Somewhere he could keep an eye on them. In one of the tents perhaps, or in those pens. We have to get closer.'

Atticus nodded. 'Best circle round then, sir. Come up behind the pens from where there's not so much light from the fires.'

Cato examined the ground. 'Yes. You're right. Let's go.'

They shuffled back, rejoined Vulso and Musa, and then the four of them moved through the scrub on the fringes of the tents, in a long arc round to the far side of the peninsula. There were many more fugitives streaming up the hill from the direction of the main camp, and by some unspoken mutual consent the small party of Romans and the fleeing rebels warily shifted some distance round each other in the shadows, then hurried on. At last Cato saw that the pens were in line with the largest tents, and gestured to the men following him. 'Let's get in closer.'

They padded through the outermost shelters: makeshift tents spread over crudely cut frames, nearly all empty after the initial rush down towards the battle being fought on the other side of the bay. Some were not empty, however, and Cato felt his flesh freeze at the sound of a shrill shriek, before he realised it was an infant crying. A woman murmured gently and the crying quickly died away. There were others amongst the shelters, fleeing from the camp, who had taken the chance to pause long enough to ransack some of the empty tents they were passing through. Cato nearly tripped over one of them, a man bent down in the shadows as he dragged a large silver bowl through some tent flaps. Cato stopped in his tracks. The man jumped to his feet, where the glow from the fires lit up his features. A wrinkled face, half hidden by shaggy hair, and an unkempt beard. He snarled, revealing a handful of jagged teeth.

'Look out, sir!' Atticus pushed Cato aside as the rebel lashed out with a knife. Cato heard it swish close to his ear, and then there was a dull crunch as Atticus floored the man with a punch. As the rebel collapsed unconscious to the ground, the optio snatched the knife from his fingers and drew it back, ready to cut the man's throat.

'No.' Cato held his arm. 'Leave him. Let's go on.'

The pens were only a short distance ahead of them, and Cato weaved cautiously through the remaining shelters until they reached the rear of the structures. Beyond them the ground was open all the way to where the group of men were gathered in front of what Cato assumed to be the gladiator's personal tent. They were watching the destruction of their comrades down in the camp, and talking in anxious tones, though Cato could not catch the sense of what they were saying. The walls of the pens stood as tall as his shoulders, and he knew that if he stood up to peer over the walls to look for Macro and Julia he was almost sure to be seen.

He rose up as high as he dared and called out softly, 'Julia? . . . Macro?'

There was no reply. He called again, a little louder this time. Still there was no reply.

'They're not in there,' Atticus muttered.

'No.'

'So what do we do?'

'Keep looking,' Cato said firmly, and edged along behind the pens until he reached a gap where he could crawl forwards and look round from the safety of the shadows. He saw it almost at once – a cage a short distance from the largest tent and away from the other shelters. It was on the highest point of the camp, exposed to the elements. Cato edged back as yet more rebels fled past. The Romans flattened themselves to the ground and lay still. Once the rebels had gone, Cato turned to the others.

'I know where they are: Macro and Julia.' He told Atticus and the others about the cage.

'Did you actually see them?' the optio asked.

Cato shook his head. 'Too dark. But where else could they be?'

'I'm beginning to think they could be anywhere. Pretty soon this place is going to be overrun with slaves fleeing up from the main camp. We'd best find the hostages as soon as we can, sir.'

'Then let's move.' Cato gestured with his hand and rose into a crouch, making his way back a short distance from the pens and in amongst a cluster of the shelters. He paused to let the others catch up, then the small party continued through the last of the huts and along the slope, out of sight of the tents. To their right the sea was a dark mass, and the sound of the waves breaking on the rocks below came clearly to their ears. When Cato judged that they were parallel to the cage, he led them back up the slope, cautiously picking his way through the stunted bushes and rocks. Someone shouted a warning, then there were more raised voices, and Cato paused for a moment until he realised they could not have been seen. A few more steps and then the ground evened out and they could see the cage, twenty paces away. Beyond that there was a patch of open ground and the side of the tent with the men forming a screen before it as they fended off a stream of rebels rushing past. For the moment none of them were watching the cage. Cato squinted and saw the dark shape of a bulky figure within, slumped against the bars. Hope made his heart beat faster, then he felt a chill of fear as he realised that there was only one person in the cage, unquestionably male.

'Macro?' he called out.

The figure stirred, then replied gruffly, 'Who's that?'

Cato released a sharp breath of relief. 'It's Cato.'

'Cato?' Macro's voice was strained. 'By all the gods, let it be true.'

'Just a moment.' Cato turned to Atticus. 'You come with me. Musa, Vulso, you keep watch. Let me know if anyone comes.'

Cato kept low as he scuttled across the open ground, closely followed by Atticus. They kept a watchful eye on the rebels, but no one looked in their direction. As he reached the cage, Cato's nose wrinkled at the stench of human waste. He dropped down beside the bars, opposite Macro.

'It really is you.' Macro's voice rasped. 'Thought I was going mad. Get me out of here.'

'Where's Julia?'

'In the tent. Ajax sent for her. Had her cleaned up first.'

Cato felt the blood go cold in his veins. 'Did he . . .?'

'How the hell do I know?' Macro shook his head. 'Get me out of here and we'll go and rescue her.'

Cato examined the door to the cage. 'Damn, it's locked.'

'Of course it's fucking locked,' Macro hissed. 'Why else would I still be in here?'

Atticus chuckled. 'Nice change to see *you* locked up.'

'Who's that with you?' asked Macro. 'Not that twat Atticus?'

'The same.' Atticus grinned.

'Bloody great,' Macro muttered. He fixed his gaze on his friend. 'Cato . . . thanks.'

'You didn't think I'd leave you to die?'

Macro was silent for a moment before he replied. 'There were times when I gave up hope.'

'Thanks for the vote of confidence.'

Macro chuckled drily.

Cato grasped the bars of the cage door and gritted his teeth as he strained to prise them open. He gave up with a bitter grunt. 'We need the key. Who has it?'

'One of the guards, over there.' Macro pointed him out. 'If I can get him to come over here, can you two handle him?'

'We'll have to.' Cato crouched down behind Macro, and indicated to Atticus to lie flat.

Macro grasped the bars of the cage, drew a deep breath and bellowed, 'Guard! Guard! Over here!' He paused a moment and repeated his cry, shaking the bars more violently. One of the men by the tent turned in his direction and then spoke to the rebel who had been tasked with watching Macro and Julia since their capture. He picked up his spear and wearily approached the cage.

'Keep it down, Roman!'

'Fuck you!' Macro shouted back and shook the bars again. 'Fuck that old hag of a mother of yours!'

The guard paused and then growled with anger as he ran towards the cage and lowered the tip of his spear.

'Shit . . .' Macro just had time to mutter, before the spearhead rattled through the bars, and he dodged to one side to avoid it. Instantly he snatched at the spear shaft and thrust it to one side. The other end swivelled sharply, and caught the guard off balance so he tumbled over and crashed into the side of the cage. Macro released the shaft and thrust his arms through the cage, grasping the guard round the neck and hauling him up against the bars as he flailed at Macro's brawny forearms.

'Get him!' Macro grunted. 'Before he works loose.'

Atticus was up first, scrambling round the end of the cage and dropping heavily on the guard, driving the breath from his body as Macro tightened his grip, choking the rebel. He struggled violently for a moment and then went limp. There was a shout from the direction of Ajax's tent, and Cato saw that the other rebels were looking across the open ground. As soon as they realised what was happening, they snatched up their weapons and began to sprint towards the cage.

'Get the key!' Macro shouted at Atticus.

Cato glanced back towards Musa and Vulso and beckoned frantically. 'On me!'

Atticus snatched away the thong around the guard's neck, grasped the key and fitted it to the lock as the rebels ran towards them. As soon as the lock clicked, Macro burst the door open and grabbed the guard's spear. Rising up into a crouch, he swung the point round toward the rebels as Atticus and Cato drew their swords. With an animal roar Macro charged forward.

'Bloody hell, there he goes again,' Cato muttered under his breath as he hurried after his friend, moving to the right as Atticus went to the left. The fury on Macro's face must have been evident even in the wan glow of the fire burning in front of Ajax's tent, for the rebels hesitated and regarded him fearfully as they readied their weapons. There were seven of them, eight counting the old woman, who had picked up a hatchet and screamed in rage as she hurried after the others.

Cato glanced up and saw the rebels lowering their spears as the gap between the two groups of men closed. The rebels crouched, feet apart and balanced, spears held ready as Macro and his two companions charged in, Musa and Vulso sprinting hard to catch up.

'Five men against seven spears and a madwoman with an axe,' Atticus laughed. 'Not good odds!'

There was a sharp rap as Macro parried the thrust of the first man he encountered. Still running, he lowered his shoulder and slammed into the rebel, knocking the other man on to his back. Macro ran on, skewering the next man ahead of him before he stopped, wrenched the spear shaft free, presenting the point to the three men before him in turn. 'Come on!' he shouted. 'Who's up for it?'

Cato kept his eyes on the man who had singled him out and who now came on, spear lowered. He thrust at Cato's face but the point was easily deflected with a clatter. Cato lunged forward, forcing the man back, and kept with him, hammering at the shaft of the spear, knowing that it would numb the rebel's fingers. One more blow and the spear fell. The man turned and sprinted away. Cato let him go and turned to see Atticus locked in a duel with another man, more skilled with his spear than Cato's opponent had been. Musa was down, piked through the thigh and desperately warding off further blows from another rebel as blood gushed from the wound. Vulso charged into his man, knocking aside the spear, then smashing his fist into the

350

rebel's face a moment before his right arm swung, driving his sword through the man's stomach and up into his chest, carrying him off his feet. The rebel's knees collapsed and he sagged back on to the ground, a great tear across his front through which bloodied intestines bulged.

'Musa!' the legionary called as he turned to help his comrade. It was too late: the old woman had crept up behind the downed soldier and now smashed her axe down into the top of his skull. Musa's head snapped forward, eyes blinking. Then his body jerked furiously as he toppled over. The woman yanked her axe back with a shriek of triumph and turned towards Macro, snarling as she glanced at the body of her son stretched out by the cage. Cato started forward, but the man who had been fighting Musa blocked his path. Macro was in danger, so there was no time to stick to his training and take the man down by swordsmanship. Cato filled his lungs and let out a roar as he hurled himself forward. The spear point came up and the man braced his feet for the impact. At the last instant Cato went down low, rolled over and slashed at the rebel's leading leg as he came up. The blade shattered the bone and the man screamed as he collapsed. There was no time to finish him off as Cato ran on round the cage to catch up with the old woman. But she had a head start and threw herself towards Macro, the axe raised above her head.

'Macro!' Cato cried out. 'Behind you!'

Macro swung round, gritting his teeth, as he threw up the shaft of the spear to protect his head. The axe head splintered the spear shaft, but did not cut all the way through. Macro released the ruined weapon and clamped his fingers round her skinny wrist as the axe came down again. He managed to deflect the blow so that it hissed past his shoulder and into the dirt. She released her grip and clawed at his face with her spare hand as she swore and spat at him.

'That's enough!' Macro caught her by the hair and held her at arm's length. She spat and scratched at his hands as she tried to kick him. Macro took a sharp breath. 'I have had quite enough of you.' He punched her with his spare hand, and she collapsed on to the ground. He snatched up the axe and stood over her.

'Macro!' Cato caught his arm.

Macro stared at the old woman with hatred before his gaze turned to Cato. 'She had it coming, believe me.'

Standing up, Cato saw that Vulso had finished off his opponent, and there was a last clatter and thud as Atticus cut down his man. The surviving rebels threw down their weapons and ran off into the night. The Roman soldiers stood breathing heavily for a moment before Vulso knelt down at Musa's side. His eyes gazed blankly at the starry heavens.

'He's dead,' said Vulso.

Cato turned to Macro. 'I'm going for Julia.'

'Careful, lad, there may be more of them in the tent. I'll come with you.'

There was a sudden pounding of hooves, and Cato and the others froze.

'That'll be Ajax.' Macro turned to Cato. 'We'd better get to cover.'

'Not without Julia.'

'Don't be a bloody fool! They'll be on us before we could get her out.' Macro grabbed his arm and thrust him away from the tent, back towards the shelter of the pens. 'Go!'

The rumble of hooves was much louder, and then Cato could feel the tremor through the ground. He stared desperately at the tent for an instant, then turned and ran back with Macro and the others. A moment later Ajax and his bodyguards rode up through the camp and slewed to a halt in front of the tent. Ajax swung himself down from the back of his horse and barked an order.

'Stay in your saddles!'

He strode across to his tent and tore the flaps aside as he entered. From his position nearly fifty paces away, Cato watched intently, fearing for Julia's life, and at the same time hoping that the bodies near the cage would not be noticed in the darkness. He tensed, as if ready to spring forward, but Macro grabbed his arm.

'Keep still, lad. Or we're all dead.'

Cato turned and glared at his friend, then nodded slowly as reason returned. The strain in his muscles eased as he sank towards the ground. There was silence from the tent for a moment, and then the flaps opened again and Ajax emerged holding a small chest in one hand, while the other grasped Julia by the wrist. Cato stopped breathing as he saw her, beautiful as the dawn even at this distance. Ajax pulled hard, spinning Julia round so that she lost her balance and tumbled at the feet of the men standing in front of the tent.

'Get her on a horse. Kharim!'

'Yes, General.'

'You take charge of her. Guard her with your life, understand?'

Kharim reached down and with the help of the men on the ground pulled her up and across his thighs. Ajax climbed back on to his horse, clasping the chest to his side as he took the reins in his spare hand. 'Take her to the boats!'

As the bodyguards urged their mounts forward, along the track that led towards the tip of the peninsula, the gladiator glanced towards the cage, almost invisible in the dark, and pointed to two of his men.

'Kill the Roman, then get out of here.'

Then he wheeled his mount round and spurred it into a gallop along the track to catch up with the rest of his bodyguards. Cato stared after them, his heart heavy as lead as Julia was carried away from him. The two men detailed to kill Macro dismounted, tied their reins to the rail beside the tent and hurried across towards the cage.

'They're going to see the bodies any moment,' Macro whispered.

Cato nodded. 'We need those horses. They mustn't get away.'

He rose into a crouch and glanced round at the others. 'Ready?'

They nodded.

'Go!'

Cato launched himself forward, sprinting towards the two rebels as Macro, Atticus and Vulso scrambled after him. There was a sharp cry as one of the rebels saw the bodies sprawled on the ground. The sight momentarily distracted them, and it was only at the last instant that they turned towards the sounds of padding feet. Cato's sword swung out of the night, cutting into the shoulder of the nearest man and through to the bone. As he dropped like a side of beef, Macro took the second man with a thrust to the chest. He fell beside his comrade with a dull grunt and lay writhing at Macro's feet. Sheathing his blade, Cato turned to Atticus.

'Stay out of sight until Fulvius comes up.'

'No, sir,' Atticus protested. 'We can help.'

'There are only two horses. There's nothing more you can do. Macro, come on,' Cato ordered as he ran towards the tethered horses.

'Wait a moment.' Macro stopped to strip the tunic from one of the bodies and hurriedly pulled it on. 'That's better! What's the plan?' Macro panted as he chased after his friend.

'Plan?' Cato took the reins of the nearest horse and sheathed his sword. 'We go after them and free Julia. Or die trying.'

'Nice to know you've thought it through.'

They scrambled into the saddles, took up the reins and turned the horses down the track Ajax and his men had taken. With a shout, Cato dug his heels in and urged his horse into a gallop. He knew it was madness for the two of them to attempt this pursuit by themselves, but he would not be able to live with the knowledge that he had let Julia remain a captive of the gladiator. There was no way that he and Macro alone could take on over twenty of Ajax's bodyguard, but he did not care. All reason was spent and he was driven on by his heart, willing only to save her or die in the attempt. That last sight of her, terrified and vulnerable as she was carried off into the darkness, was branded on to his mind's eye as he leaned forward along the horse's neck and urged it on.

The path was broad and well trodden by generations of local people making the journey along the peninsula, perhaps to leave an offering at the shrine of a local deity, or to swim from one of the small coves along the coastline. Cato could only guess as he and Macro rode on, scanning the way ahead for sign of their prey. Ajax had spoken of boats. He must have some plan of escape. Cato had to find him before it could be put into effect.

To their left an expanse of the bay was lit up by the flames of the four ships, still ablaze. Beyond, the rebel camp was alive with tiny figures as the Roman soldiers cut a path through the shelters without mercy. Cato took one glance at the scene before he dismissed it and continued into the night. He knew the risk they were taking in galloping over unknown ground in the darkness. But already rosy-fingered dawn was lighting the horizon, and the route ahead was just discernible.

A mile after they had left the camp, Cato saw a shape ahead of him: another rider.

'We're catching them!' Macro called out.

Cato drew his sword, clasping the handle tightly, and slapped the flat of the blade on the horse's rump. The animal's flanks shivered between his thighs, and it put on an extra spurt as it closed on the rebel. More figures emerged from the darkness ahead of the man, and Cato felt a cold determination firm up his resolve.

He was no more than ten paces behind his quarry when the man glanced back over his shoulder. He stared at his pursuers a moment and then called ahead to the next man, who also looked back, as did another. They reined in and fell back as their horses slowed and then drew their swords. Meanwhile Cato closed on the rearmost man, watching him intently. As they began to draw level, the rebel slashed out with his sword. Cato clenched his thighs and threw his weight to one side, causing his horse to stagger, but it remained on its feet and the blade hissed through the air.

'My turn!' Cato snarled, stabbing out with his sword and catching the rebel in the side, just above his sword belt. The point pierced tunic, flesh and muscle before entering his guts, and then Cato ripped it free. The rider dropped his weapon and clasped his side as he bent forward over his saddle. Cato rode on. Macro had passed ahead of him. The two rebels had turned side on to block Macro and Cato. They held their blades ready. Macro dug his heels in, aiming straight at them. His horse did as it was bid until the very last moment, when it tried to draw up and turn and its flank smashed into the side of one of the horses, pinning the rider's leg. The man gasped, but before he could recover Macro hacked at his sword arm, cutting deeply into the flesh above the elbow. The blade dropped from the man's hand as his horse staggered back and trotted off the track into the bushes that grew on each side.

Macro glanced round as the other man swung at him. He managed to parry the blow but the blade glanced off and struck his horse on the neck just behind the ears. At once the animal let out a shrill whinny and reared up on its hind legs, kicking out with the front. Macro was thrown back. He toppled from his saddle and flew through the air before crashing down on his side. There was a brief flash of light as his head struck the stony path, and the air was driven from his body with a sharp gasp. He forced himself on to his hands and knees and shook his head to clear his vision.

He heard the rebel click his tongue as he steadied his shaken mount and edged it towards the fallen Roman. Macro saw the legs of the horse clopping towards him, and the dull gleam of his blade a few feet away. He lunged for it, snatching at the handle as he rolled under the horse. The animal's belly loomed above him and Macro thrust the sword up, wincing as it struck home and blood spattered down on to his face. The horse whinnied in agony and threw itself forward. A hoof crashed down beside Macro's head as the rider desperately tried to steady his mount. A dark shape appeared beside him, and Cato thrust his blade into the small of the rebel's back. Already half mad with pain, the stricken mount galloped off the path, down the slope, before stumbling. Rider and horse tumbled over and over amid the rocks and gorse for a moment, and then there was silence.

Macro staggered to his feet. He still felt dizzy and shook his head again to try and clear the sensation as he staggered towards the man he had wounded in the arm. The rebel was still in the saddle, moaning as he clutched at the wound. He did not see Macro until it was too late to escape. Macro took the reins and pointed his sword at the man.

'If you want to live, get off.'

The rebel nodded, and awkwardly eased his leg over the saddle and dropped to the ground on the far side of the horse. Then he rapidly backed away. Macro watched him carefully until the rebel was at a safe distance, then sheathed his sword and steadied the horse a moment before mounting it. The animal was skittish and Macro spoke to it calmly and clicked his tongue before walking it forward to join Cato.

'Are you all right?' Cato asked anxiously.

'Fine. Let's go.'

They urged their horses on and continued the pursuit. The brief fight had lost them some ground and Cato looked ahead keenly for any sight of the enemy as they rode along the narrow track. The route wound its way along the spine of the peninsula, and all the time he anticipated catching sight of the gladiator and his retinue again. But there was no sign of them, and a terrible doubt formed in Cato's mind. Then the track crested a small rise that afforded a view of the peninsula stretching out ahead for some distance. Empty.

'Shit!' Cato hissed between clenched teeth.

'Where in Hades are they?' Macro growled. 'How could we have missed them? How?'

'They must have gone off the main track,' Cato decided, cursing himself. 'We have to turn around.'

He yanked the reins round and trotted back along the track, glancing carefully from side to side. After a quarter of a mile he found what he was looking for; he had missed it as they had galloped past at speed a while earlier. A small path left the track, winding down the slope. They quickly turned aside from the main track and followed the path down as it wound between rocks and stunted trees. Below them they could hear the faint rush and hiss of waves on the shore, and then the track opened out on to the top of a small cliff before doubling back steeply as it carried on down towards a stretch of beach.

Cato heard voices shouting and the faint clatter of weapons. No more than a few hundred feet out to sea he saw the outline of a small Roman warship, and recognised it as one of the liburnians. A handful of smaller boats were clustered about the hull and Cato realised at once what was happening.

'Shit, that's the warship that ran aground. The rebels are taking it.'

They turned the horses down the path and urged them on. There was only a short distance to go, and then Cato and Macro emerged on to a thin strip of sand. The beach was a little over a hundred paces wide, and a handful of abandoned shacks lay clustered at the foot of the cliff. The rebels' horses had been left at the water's edge. A handful of small boats remained, and the two Roman swung themselves down from their saddles and ran across the sand towards them. Neither had sails, only oars. Cato grabbed the side of the nearest boat.

'Help me!'

He braced his feet in the surf and hauled the boat into the water as Macro grabbed the other side and pulled. It dragged stubbornly across the sand until a small wave lifted it up and they managed to heave it free of the shore. They pushed it out until the water was round their waists and then scrambled over the side. As Cato lifted the oars into the rowlock pegs and Macro sat heavily in the stern, the last sounds of fighting died away. The thin light of dawn filtered across the bay as Cato took his seat on the centre bench and desperately began to row out towards the liburnian. If the warship was still aground, then the rebels would not get away.

Cato knew that he and Macro were facing certain death once they reached the ship. He prayed that they might at least kill the gladiator before they were cut down, and that Julia could find some way to escape in the confusion. He looked over his shoulder and saw that he had closed the distance on the liburnian. Then he froze and looked more intently. The ship was moving up and down on the swell.

'I thought you said it had run aground,' said Macro.

'It was. The crew must have got her off just as the rebels came aboard.'

Cato realised that the marines must be dead, and the sailors and men at the oars were under the orders of Ajax and his followers. Cato started rowing again with all his strength, but his poor technique and frantic oar strokes were punished by the swell, which caused him to catch crabs on either side, one time lifting the oar right out of the pegs.

By the time they had closed to within fifty feet of the liburnian, Macro saw the long dark blades of the warship's oars bite down into the water. They made a stroke, rose, arced back and plunged into the sea again as the sleek vessel edged forwards.

'They're under way,' he said softly.

'No!' Cato groaned as he desperately redoubled his efforts. 'No. Please gods, no.'

The liburnian steadily gathered pace and began to swing out into the Bay of Olous, opening the gap between it and Cato. He kept rowing frantically, his limbs aching with the strain. The outline of the liburnian foreshortened as she presented her stern. With a sickening certainty he knew that there was no chance of catching her now. He dropped the oars, rose to his feet, turned and braced his legs apart as he cupped his hands to his mouth and cried out, 'Julia! . . . Julia!'

There was a pause before he heard her voice call back: 'Cato! Help me!'

Then she was cut off.

A pair of figures loomed up on the liburnian's stern rail: Ajax, holding Julia tightly by the arm. He called out, mockingly, 'You have lost her, Cato. Lost her for ever.'

'Julia!'

'She is mine now. Mine to do with as I will. Remember that. Remember the vengeance of Ajax every day for the rest of your life.'

'No!' The cry was torn from Cato's lips. 'No!'

Suddenly Julia's spare hand rose up. There was a glimmer of metal in her grip and she stabbed down into Ajax's shoulder. He recoiled with a bellow of surprise, pain and rage, glancing at the comb sticking out of his shoulder. Instinctively he reached for the wound with his other hand, releasing Julia. At once she threw herself over the stern rail, tumbling down into the sea with a splash. The liburnian was already gathering speed, and as Julia's head emerged above the water, gasping, the gap between her and the stern of the warship quickly grew. Cato had hurriedly taken up his oars again and was speeding the little craft across the water towards her as she struck out towards them with frantic splashing strokes.

Ajax had pulled the bloodied comb out and stood glaring down into the sea. There was nothing he could do to prevent her escape. By the time he could turn the warship round and head back towards the beach, the little boat would have reached the shore again and his enemies would have escaped on the horses still on the beach. Besides, one of the Roman triremes was already heading back down the bay to come to the assistance of the liburnian that had run aground.

As the boat approached Julia, Macro scrambled to the bows, leaning over to reach out for her. Julia grabbed his wrist, and he hauled her closer before stretching out his spare hand to lift her under the shoulder.

'Up you come, miss!' he grunted as he pulled her over the side. 'I've got her, Cato. Turn us round and get back to the shore, quick as you can.'

Cato worked the small craft round and started for the shore, expecting the warship to turn back towards them at any moment. But the liburnian headed steadily towards the mouth of the bay. The oars dipped and thrust through the sea at a regular pace as it drew swiftly away from the small boat. Ajax remained at the stern rail for a while, before he turned and disappeared from sight.

'We're safe,' Macro said in relief.

Cato lowered his oars and turned to embrace Julia as she stumbled towards the centre of the boat and fell into his arms. For a while all was still on the little craft. Cato held her tight, pressing his cheek to the top of her head as he breathed deeply. Macro turned away and stared after the liburnian as it disappeared around the small island at the end of the rocky peninsula and headed out to sea.

CHAPTER THIRTY-THREE

Three days later, Sempronius surveyed the remains of the rebel camp as he and his escort rode down to the beach where the remaining ships were undergoing repairs. The rest of the grain fleet had set sail the previous day, making directly for Rome, where the cargo should arrive in time to stave off any hunger and prevent the mob from having an excuse to riot. Despite his relief and joy that his daughter had been rescued, Sempronius's mood was soured by the inevitable aftermath of such a serious revolt on the island. The senator had little doubt that there would be small reward forthcoming from the emperor for saving the grain fleet, and consequently keeping the peace on the streets of Rome. Four of the ships had been lost in the attack, and the officials in charge of the imperial granary would inevitably lodge a complaint against those they held responsible for the recovery of the fleet. Some kind of official reprimand was inevitable. Sempronius sighed. Sometimes being in the service of Rome was a thankless task, and he had to draw satisfaction from the knowledge that he had served his Emperor as best he could, despite losing four of the ships.

The loss of the grain was least of it, he reflected. It would be years before the province of Crete recovered from the earthquake and the slave revolt that had followed it. Although the revolt was over, there were still some unsavoury matters to deal with. Centurion Fulvius and his men had shown no mercy to the rebels and the bodies were still being buried in great pits dug into the rocky soil around the bay. Thousands of them, men, women and children. The survivors had been sent back to Gortyna in long chain gangs under the guard of the hard-hearted men of the legions, who would show no pity to those who straggled or fell by the side of the road. Sempronius had passed them on his way to Olous: lines of captives with bleak expressions now that they had been returned to slavery after a brief taste of freedom. They were destined to be held in a special camp outside the city until their owners could be identified and informed. If the owners were dead then they would become the property of the emperor and auctioned off. The sums raised, minus the hefty commission due to the auctioneer, would be forwarded to the imperial treasury in Rome. Sempronius smiled bitterly at the thought that at least someone in Rome would profit as a consequence of the revolt.

An even graver fate awaited those slaves who had been identified as the ringleaders, or who had been captured under arms. They were being held at Olous pending shipment to Rome, where they would be put to death in the arena. It was rumoured that Claudius was contemplating a gladiatorial spectacle in an artificial lake being constructed outside Rome. A re-enactment of the battle of Actium, with scaled-down ships and thousands of condemned men to man the fleets. Sempronius was certain that the contribution from Crete would be welcomed and the rebels would be consigned to a role that left them little prospect of survival.

Sempronius felt bitter that Ajax had escaped. He should have been tortured and put to death, before the gaze of his followers. Every indignity that he had visited upon Sempronius's daughter would have been repaid with interest. As yet the details were mercifully vague, and Cato's report had been terse in its description of her and Macro's period of captivity. For that Sempronius was grateful. He tried not to let his imagination fill in the gaps in Cato's account. That was unbearably painful and caused him such grief as he had not known since the death of his wife, the only other person he had ever loved without qualification.

At least Julia was alive and safe, Sempronius comforted himself. She was with Cato in his camp at Olous. That made the orders he had sent back to Cato difficult to write. But he knew that he must authorise a pursuit of Ajax as swiftly as possible. The emperor would demand it. Therefore Centurions Macro and Cato were to pick up Ajax's trail and capture or kill him and his followers. Sempronius had revoked Cato's temporary promotion to tribune now that the crisis was over and he had returned to his normal rank. Their orders informed Macro and Cato that they were to act with the full authority of the governor of Crete in this matter, and all Roman officials they encountered were charged to extend them every possible aid. Ajax, and everything that he stood for, was to be eliminated as ruthlessly and completely as possible, so that every person in the empire knew the fate that awaited slaves who rose against their masters. Two of the liburnians from Balbus's squadron had been commandeered, as well as two centuries of legionaries. Centurion Fulvius had already complained and would no doubt try to stir things up between Sempronius and the legate back in Egypt. That was too bad, reflected the senator. He would always be grateful to Petronius for his support, and swore to Jupiter, Best and Greatest, that he would return the favour to his old friend one day.

Meanwhile, he made straight for the headquarters tent and the reunion with his daughter. After they had embraced, he held her at arm's length, looking for signs of injury, or a deeper hurt in her eyes. Julia smiled back.

'I'm all right, Father. Truly. You don't have to look at me like that.'

He held her close again, because he did not trust himself enough to contain the tearful joy that filled his heart. At length he eased himself away from her. 'Now then, where is this young man of yours?'

'He's down in the bay with Macro, provisioning their ships.' Julia paused and looked earnestly at her father. 'Must he go? So soon?'

'You know he must,' Sempronius replied firmly. 'It's his duty.'

'Duty.' Julia smiled sadly. 'Always duty. It's a curse, that's what it is.'

He nodded sadly. 'It is always the curse of those who serve the empire with distinction, my dear. Come now, let's go and find him.'

The two liburnians lay beyond the damaged grain ships, and as Sempronius and Julia rode up towards the warships they could see that the men were loading the last of their stores. Legionaries, stripped to their tunics, were carrying spare weapons, kit, rations and water aboard up the narrow gangways that stretched from the shallows to the decks. Macro and Cato were standing on the beach conferring as they checked the entries of supplies on a large waxed tablet. As they noticed the approach of the governor and his escort, they turned to salute him.

Sempronius dismounted and strode across to them.

'Good to see you again, Macro. I was afraid I'd be denied that pleasure.'

Macro was thinner and his face was still peeling from his prolonged exposure to the sun. He stepped forward to clasp the arm that Sempronius extended to him.

'I don't die easy, sir. Never have and never will.'

'Delighted to hear it!'

They shared a smile, and then Sempronius turned to Cato.

'Would you mind if I had a brief word with Macro before I speak with you?'

'No, sir,' Cato replied with a slight frown and turned towards Julia. 'You can come and sit with me.'

They walked beyond the final consignment of stores piled higher up the beach and sat down on the sand. Julia leaned her head against Cato's shoulder as he placed his arm around her. They did not talk for a moment, too aware of the imminence of their separation. At length Julia muttered, 'It's not fair.'

'No.'

'Have you any idea how long you will be gone?'

'That rather depends on Ajax. But I shall come and find you in Rome the moment he is taken or killed. I swear it.'

Julia nodded but kept her silence, and Cato knew that she was struggling not to show her feelings. Every so often he glanced back towards the senator and Macro, and saw that they were locked in earnest conversation. Sempronious held Macro's arm and seemed to be entreating him to share a point of view. At first Macro seemed reluctant, but then, as he looked briefly at Cato and thought a moment, he consented and they shook on it.

'Cato!' Sempronius waved him over.

He and Julia stood up and strode back down the beach to rejoin the others. Macro stood still with a serious expression as Sempronius regarded Cato gravely.

'I have had to make a difficult decision, Cato, and one that you might find hard to live with at first,' Sempronius began. 'But it is my judgement that this mission has the best chance of success with you in command.'

'Me?' Cato stared at him and then looked to Macro. 'Surely not?'

'That's what he says,' Macro replied. 'And he's right. I agree with the senator.'

'Why?' Cato felt pained by the situation. He had always assumed that he was destined to be Macro's subordinate in the years to come. It seemed the only natural way to be. Macro had taught him everything about soldiering. It was to Macro's experience and qualities as a soldier that Cato looked when he needed to set himself an example. He turned back to Sempronius. 'Sir, I am honoured, but I can't accept this. Macro is my superior.'

'He is that, in many things,' Sempronius conceded. 'But this task will require more skills, more circumspection than raw soldiering. That is why I have chosen you.' He reached into the small bag that hung from his belt and drew out a scroll. 'This is your letter of appointment to the rank of prefect.'

'Prefect?' Cato was astonished. The rank paved the way for appointment to the command of an auxiliary cohort.

'It is subject to the emperor's approval, of course,' Sempronius continued. 'But I hope that I can persuade Claudius to make the promotion permanent. If anyone deserves it, you do. Congratulations.'

They clasped arms briefly, then Macro stepped forward.

'I'd like to offer my congratulations too.' He gave a broken smile. 'Sir.'

The word cut through Cato like a knife. It did not seem right. Not natural. He forced a smile in return. 'Thank you . . . for everything.'

Macro nodded, then jerked his thumb at the furthest liburnian. 'My lads are done. I'll have the ship put into the water, if that's all right, sir?'

'Yes.' Cato nodded. 'Whatever you say.'

Macro sighed, wagged a finger, then turned and strode towards the gangway of his ship.

'He's a good man,' Sempronius said. 'You're lucky to have him as a friend.'

'I know that, sir.'

Sempronius turned to Cato and was silent for a moment. 'Do you have any idea where that gladiator is headed?'

Cato nodded. 'Once he put out to sea, the ship was seen to turn south, sir. Towards Africa.'

'I see.' Sempronius cleared his throat and stood back. 'You have your orders, Prefect. See they are carried out.'

'Yes, sir!' Cato stood to attention and saluted. He turned to see that the last of his stores had been carried aboard. There would be no privacy for his final parting with Julia. He took her hands, feeling the tremor of her flesh against his as she did her best not to let any tears show. He leaned forward and kissed her, letting his lips linger for an instant as they grazed hers. Then he released her hands and made his way up the gangway and gave the order to the trierarch to put to sea.

As he stood on the small aft deck, Cato watched the sailors, marines and legionaries crowd aft to raise the bows as the oarsmen unshipped their oars. Then, as the flute player began to give the time, the oars propelled the ship back from the beach into deeper water. Once they had sea room, the trierarch dismissed the marines and the sailors returned to their normal stations. The trierarch turned towards Cato. 'Your orders, sir?'

Cato looked down the deck, conscious that he was being watched closely by the men he was about to lead on as dangerous and difficult a mission as they would ever know. He cleared his throat.

'Pass the word to the other ship that we are heading out to sea. Once we leave the bay, we set course for Africa.'

'Aye, sir.'

As the trierarch cupped his hands to his mouth to relay the order across the sea between the two vessels, Cato turned towards the shore. The senator and his daughter were still standing where he had left them, and Sempronius raised his hand as he saw Cato look at him. Cato, mindful of his new rank and responsibility, simply saluted and then turned away. He swore a private oath at that moment to be worthy of the confidence of the senator, and more importantly of his friend Macro. He also swore that he would not rest until the gladiator was dead and he could return to Julia's side.

AUTHOR'S NOTE

This novel began life on a trip to Crete a few years back. Having exhausted the obvious list of ancient Greek sites, I took the opportunity to explore the remains of the Roman city of Gortyna, destroyed by a great earthquake in the middle of the first century. Only a small portion is contained within the official site at the foot of the acropolis. The rest is spread out across the fields on the other side of the main road, and it is only by wandering through the olive groves that one can get an impression of just how large and impressive a city the provincial capital was.

As I strolled through the ruins it occurred to me that the timing of the earthquake coincided rather nicely with Macro and Cato returning from their adventures in Judaea and Syria. What if they were to become embroiled in the chaos that followed from the earthquake? What effects would such an event have on a province like Crete? As I thought through the possibilities I realised that one of the main casualties of a natural disaster is social order. Besides the usual scrabbling for resources and breakdown of law and order there was the question of how the slave population of the island would respond to the opportunity to escape from their condition. So I conceived the idea of a slave rebellion. If the slaves were going to get anywhere they would need a charismatic leader – a warrior of some kind. Naturally, this suggested a gladiator. But I wanted a man who was driven to hate Rome in general, and Macro and Cato in particular. It took a few weeks before I found my villain. As ever when I get stuck on a plot point, I take the dog for a walk round the remains of the Roman town of Venta Icenorum, a mile or so from my home. Halfway round the walls, I remembered Ajax, and his anguish at the execution of his father, and the dreadful fate that awaited him as he was condemned to slavery at the end of *The Eagle's*

Prophecy. Now there was a man in whose breast the dark flames of revenge would be burning very fiercely indeed.

The institution of slavery played a major role in the society and economy of the Roman Empire, and the earlier republic. The massive expansion of Roman power across the Mediterranean that commenced in the third century BC led to the enslavement of vast numbers of men, women and children from the subjugated populations. By the end of the century up to a third of the population of Italy was made up of slaves. Many were herded on to the vast farming estates that were increasingly a feature of the rural landscape as the rich bought up the small farms that had fallen into neglect while their owners were away for years at a time on campaign.

Existence under slavery was often oppressive. The vast majority of slaves were condemned to a life of labour under harsh conditions and subjected to brutal discipline. This was especially the case for those who worked in mines, building sites or in the fields – often chained together. There were two categories of slaves: those owned privately and those owned by the state. The latter tended to be the more fortunate in that they were less likely to be sold on, and were permitted limited property-owning rights. Privately owned slaves were referred to as being part of the owner's 'familia'; if they served in the household they were part of the 'familia urbana', whereas if they worked in the fields they came under the label 'familia rustica'. For all slaves, living conditions could be hellish. One wealthy Roman, Publius Vedius Pollio, had a favourite party trick of throwing slaves into a pool filled with man-eating eels for the 'entertainment' of his guests. Clearly Pollio was something of a sadist. A more representative example of a slave owner is provided by the Roman historian Plutarch who describes a man who routinely flogged his slaves for every small failing and endeavoured to create an atmosphere of brooding jealousy and mistrust amongst his slaves.

It is hardly surprising then that from the earliest days slaves resisted their enslavement with petty acts of defiance, escape attempts (many of which were successful) and occasional uprisings, some posing the gravest of dangers to Rome, notably those that took place in Sicily and that led by Spartacus on the Italian peninsula. It would be wrong, however, to assume that there was any universal sense of resistance within the slave population. Any tendency towards a kind of class-consciousness was undermined by a number of factors. Firstly, the slaves were heterogeneous in terms of origins and language, a factor that their masters played on, ensuring that they were separated from their compatriots as far as possible. Secondly, those who were born into slavery had no memory of being deprived of liberty, and no homeland to which they could return. Thirdly, the institution itself was hierarchical and those slaves who did comparatively well for themselves sought to distance themselves from other slaves, rather than acting as any kind of leadership cadre for the disaffected.

As a consequence, most uprisings were isolated and amounted to little more than brigandage. If, however, an event occurred that affected the general population, then the conditions were ripe for a more ambitious form of rebellion. I reasoned that the earthquake in Crete would provide exactly the right circumstances in which such an uprising could occur. With a leader like Ajax, such a rebellion would pose a great threat to the empire by the example it gave to other slaves. The memory of the great gladiator general Spartacus would be rekindled in the hearts and minds of the slaves of Rome.

Gladiatorial combat was one of the traditions the Romans inherited from the Etruscans. Originally, gladiators fought as part of a blood sacrifice ritual at funerals, but in the frenzied political atmosphere of the last years of the republic, ambitious politicians began to put on displays of gladiatorial combat to win popular support. It was the first emperor, Augustus, who commenced the practice of holding gladiator fights for no other reason than as mass entertainment for the Roman mob. Subsequent emperors continued in the same vein, some offering spectacles in which thousands of fighters were killed at a time. Gladiators were recruited from the ranks of captured warriors, condemned criminals and even a handful of volunteers who aspired to win fame and fortune in the arena. Training was conducted in special gladiator schools where recruits underwent a harsh regime designed to build strength and agility before they were trained in one of the specialised roles – in the case of Ajax, as a heavily armed fighter. While some gladiators won a huge following amongst the fans of the arena, much like modern boxers or film stars, and might eventually win their freedom, most were fated to a crippling injury or death. Under such circumstances it is a gratifying irony that men like Spartacus were able to use their training against their former masters with such success.

Finally, some readers may wonder why no reference is made to the island now called Spinalonga. That's because the earliest historical mention of the island notes that it once formed the end of the peninsula of Kolokitha, and I have followed that description.

Simon Scarrow